SAVAGE

ROSEWOOD HIGH #3

TRACY LORRAINE

Andy and Amelia

1

ETHAN

The sound of his car pulling up in the driveway fills me with dread. I've avoided spending any time with my father since his secrets were exposed a few weeks ago, and, being the spineless prick that he is, he's allowed me the space. Any decent dad would force me to sit down to hear him out, but no... he ran. Ran back to *her*, no doubt.

My parents have been even more absent than usual recently—not that I'm complaining. It meant I had the place to myself and was able to do what the fuck I wanted whenever I wanted, just the way I liked it. But I had no idea that they weren't just on another one of Dad's work trips. The reality of it was that Mom had moved back in with her parents in Connecticut, and my dad was banging his assistant in Washington.

I shake my head, still refusing to fully accept what he's done. I'm not ashamed to admit that he is my idol, and the fact that he's just screwed my mom over in the worst possible way shakes me to my core. The man I've always looked up to, who I thought was a god, just pissed all over everything I ever believed. I thought he was honest, trustworthy, honorable. But it seems that all of that was an act, a lie. All it took was a woman in a short skirt with an easy smile, and he ruined everything we had.

My fists curl as the sound of the front door slamming shut echoes through the empty house.

"Ethan?" My name booms up to me. I want to pretend I'm out, but he's just parked next to my car. There's no chance I'm going to get away with this. "Ethan?" he shouts again, his feet pounding on the stairs as he makes his way to my room.

His knock on the door is strong and assertive, and it makes me want to slam my fist into his ribs just to show him how fucking strong he really is.

When he still doesn't get a response from me, he pushes the door open anyway and walks inside.

"There you are, son. Didn't you hear me calling?"

Keeping my head down for a beat, I then turn toward him. He's wearing his standard suit and tie duo, the one I thought always made him look so powerful and successful, but now, I just roll my eyes. He's a joke.

I don't respond. He knows full well I heard but that I have no intention of talking to him. He didn't just betray my mom when he stuck his dick in that whore; he betrayed our whole family. Our name. Everything we stand for.

Ignoring the fact that I clearly have no interest in what he's got to say to me, he continues nonetheless. "I've got tickets to today's game. Thought it would be good for us to spend some time together."

Although the thought of the game is appealing, especially knowing that he'll have fucking epic seats, if it means sitting next to him and pretending everything is perfectly fine, then no, thank you very much. "I'm good, thanks. I'm busy." I turn back to stare out the window. In reality, I'm doing fuck all, and the fact that I'm sitting on my bed with nothing turned on or even my cell in my hand should clue him in on that.

"Really?" he asks, the amusement in his tone pissing me the fuck off.

"Really."

"Ethan, come on. Don't be like that. I know you're pissed at me, but not everything is as it seems."

"Oh, really so you weren't dipping your pen in the office ink while being married to Mom, then?" He pales. "If I've got it so wrong, please, enlighten me, Father." I stand, stepping right in front of him. I'm taller and wider than him now, and I know how much he hates it. His neck ripples as he swallows. It's not with fear. This motherfucker's not scared of anything, especially not me.

"You wouldn't understand."

My teeth grind, and my chest swells with anger. "I'm not a fucking child," I seethe. Relationships are complicated, I get that. Things happen, I get that. But what I don't get is why he couldn't be a fucking adult and talk about it instead of fucking the first woman who crossed his path.

He stares me down, daring me to say exactly what's on my mind, but I refuse to acknowledge his behavior with that kind of attention.

"I had to pull some serious strings to get these. Are you coming, or what? It's supposed to be an outstanding game." He waves the tickets in front of my face.

I haven't been to an NFL game in forever with him out of town, and the temptation of the roar of the crowd, the shared excitement, the knowledge that I can forget about my own bullshit life for sixty minutes is enough to have me agreeing, although I'm not happy about it.

A smile of achievement curls at Dad's lip, and I regret it instantly.

"I'll meet you downstairs in twenty. We'll go for steak after, too." Damn him; he knows I can't refuse the offer of steak.

With a nod of his head, he ducks out of my room, leaving me to stew in my anger some more.

Pulling my shirt over my head, I drop my joggers and step into my en suite. It might have been different if I'd have seen it coming, but my parents have always seemed so happy, so solid. While I watched my friends at school fall apart over the years when their families were ripped in two, I always felt grateful knowing that that would never happen to me. I was that confident in the love my parents had. So the day I got a tearful phone call from my mom, it wrecked me in a way I could never imagine.

"I'm so sorry, baby, b-but I'm not coming home. T-Things are over between your father and me."

I've watched people break when their girlfriends have split up with them, when their teams have lost, when they've failed the test they spent weeks studying for, but I never thought it would feel quite like it did in that moment.

She begged me to leave and move to Connecticut with her, pleaded with me that she couldn't lose me as well, but my life is here. Everything I have—besides her—is here. I can't just up and leave everything I've worked so hard for, or my friends who I know have my back no matter what.

As much as it gutted me to do it, I had to tell her that I was staying put. I had plans for my future—none of which included moving in with my grandparents. Although, now thinking about it, following my dad's footsteps to study business at UFC isn't all that appealing. I always wanted to be just like him, but now, I'm thinking being the opposite might not be so bad.

The drive to the stadium is in silence. Only the sound of Dad's V8 engine could be heard as I kept my eyes on the world passing by outside the window. I might have agreed to this, but I don't want him under any illusion that there's been any kind of truce between us. There's a very good chance I might never forgive him.

The game is exactly as I hoped. The excitement and roar of the crowd seeped into me the second we stepped foot inside the colossal stadium. My buzz as the cheerleaders shook their pom poms filled my stomach with the kind of tingles I only get when a football is involved. I live for this. Shutting the world out and focusing on one goal. I love the cheer of the crowd, knowing, whether playing or spectating, that I'm part of something bigger than just my little life.

I'm sure everyone around me thinks it's the attention of being a Bears player that I love—and yes, that's part of it—but it's not all of it. Being beside my brothers, taking on the world together, means everything to me.

My focus is solely on the game and putting myself in the players' shoes. Playing in front of the Rosewood High crowd is a serious buzz; I can only imagine how those guys feel when they run out to this exuberant crowd.

It's a tight game, and it keeps us all on our toes throughout. My heart's racing when the whistle blows for the final play, not knowing which way it's going to go.

I fall down onto my seat, the high from the game making me want to celebrate. It might not be my win, but fuck if I don't have the same response. There's nothing like a good party and a fuck after a successful game.

I glance around to see if there are any options for the latter, but when I look to my left, I find my dad looking back at me with a smile on his face and my excitement immediately vanishes. My mom has told me stories from what he was like in high school. They didn't get together until years after, partly due to his reputation. Am I just as bad as him? Am I destined to make the same mistakes when it comes to women?

"Ready to eat?" he asks as everyone starts to leave.

I'm not. The last thing I want is food right now, but I doubt

I've got a chance of getting out of it. "Let's go." There's no enthusiasm in my voice, and the way my dad's eyes narrow, I know he doesn't miss it. It doesn't stop him from taking me to the most expensive steak house in the district, though.

The atmosphere is heavy, the tension between us becoming seriously uncomfortable as he orders us both a fillet steak and sits back with his beer, practically waving it in my face after refusing to order one for me, claiming that I'm underage—which of course is true, but it doesn't stop him filling the house every weekend for me, or leaving his credit card for me to stock up with more should we run out.

"I know you're angry, Ethan. I understand that this was a shock, but things haven't been right between your mother and me for a very long time. We—"

"I don't care, Dad. You didn't need to cheat. There are a million ways to deal with a failing relationship, and fucking your assistant isn't one of them."

He rears back slightly at my blunt tone.

"It's not like that with Ash." I raise a brow, not missing the fact he's talking about her in the present tense, like she's still very much a part of his life. "She was there for me as a friend long before anything happened."

"Spare me the details of your sordid little affair."

"Keep your voice down, Ethan. The whole town doesn't need to know our business."

A spiteful laugh falls from my lips. "And you don't think the gossip is going to be rife when they realize Mom's not coming back?"

He opens his mouth to respond but nothing comes out. "Listen, son," he says eventually, and my stomach drops. I should have known he had a hidden agenda with this spur-of-the-moment daddy/son bonding day. "I know you're not going to be happy about this but—"

I blow out a slow breath as I prepare for the next bit of information that's going to rock my world.

"Ash is going to be moving in with us."

"She's fucking what?"

"Look, I know this isn't ideal. I hadn't planned on asking her yet, but things are tough for her in Washington right now. She's lost her apartment and—"

"I don't give a fuck, Dad. We're not a fucking homeless shelter for women you randomly pick up."

His face turns beet red with anger. His eyes narrow and his lips twitch. I recognize it as the look he gets when he's trying to keep his shit together. "It's my house, Ethan. If I want her there, then she'll be there."

Well, isn't that just fucking great.

"It might be your house, but you're never there. Are you expecting me to play house with this woman, or is she going to disappear with you for weeks at a time?"

"She'll be with me, but—"

Fuck my life, there's another but. I stare at him, my expression blank as I wait for the next blow.

"Her daughter will be coming with her and enrolling at Rosewood. I'm going to need you to take care of her while she settles in." I wait for him to tell me that he's joking, but at no point do his lips twitch into a smile. "She's a lovely girl. I think you'll like her."

2

RAELYNN

"Hey, honey," Mom says, letting herself into our depressing apartment after working her second job of the day. "I hope you haven't eaten. I brought your favorite." The second she says the words, dread sits, heaving in my stomach. Mom only splurges on Chinese when she's got bad news to break. And more times than not, that news is that we're moving. Washington has been home now for almost eight months. It's the longest we've stayed anywhere that I can remember; I should have seen it coming.

Mom's been unusually settled, and I had hoped that I might get to complete school here, but as I round the corner into our living area to find her unpacking the takeout boxes, I know the reason we're about to up and move again. It's always for the same reason. A man.

Every time, she promises that it'll be different. That this time, he's the one and we're going to lay down some roots and make ourselves a real home. But every time, *the one* turns out to be a total douche and we end up leaving—or running, more like.

She's a serial fiancée. Almost every time things get serious enough that he buys a ring... and then he shows his true colors and it's all over. The one before last one was the worst. A shudder runs down my spine as I think of him.

Eric, though, seems like a good guy. He's the wealthiest of the men she's gone for in the past, and she does have a good nose for the ones with money. It's how she thinks she's going to make herself happy after years without anything to her name. I truly hope that one day she finds what she's looking for, but I fear it's all just one big fantasy.

"Smells good, Mom," I say, dropping onto our worn couch, breathing in the scent of real food. It's been a while since I ate something quite so substantial. "What's the occasion?" I ask, the words almost getting stuck in my throat.

She blows out a breath, stalling for time, and I realize that at no point does she attempt to look up at me.

"We're moving again, aren't we?"

"I'm so sorry, honey. But I think it's for the best."

I nod at her sadly, knowing the real reason she wants to move again right now but also knowing that she's not going to voice it. We never talk about that—about *him*. She just keeps trying to outrun the memories instead.

"Eric's got this amazing house by the sea. The local high school is incredible. You'll have so many more opportunities than you do here."

That is very true. The high school I'm currently at is the worst of all the ones I've experienced in the past five years. I certainly won't miss the place when she drags me across the country once again.

"When are we leaving?"

She swallows and pokes her chopsticks into her noodles. "He's coming to get us on Wednesday."

"Wednesday?" I almost snort rice out through my nose. "Wednesday? As in, the day after tomorrow?"

At least she has the decency to look guilty.

"He's not sure when he'll be back at the office again, and he doesn't want to leave us here longer than necessary."

Jesus, the way she says that makes me think we're kids' toys sitting on a shelf, waiting for a new owner.

"We're more than capable of moving on our own. It wouldn't be the first time," I mutter.

Guilt fills her features. I know this isn't how she wants us to live, but unfortunately, it's our life. Maybe one day she will get the stability she craves. I hope she does, I really do. Is Eric Savage it? Of the possible stepdads I've had over the years, he's got to be up there in the top three of real possibilities. But who knows what the future could bring? It's not ceased to amaze me this far.

"It's important to him to help."

"I'm assuming his wife's moved out?"

"Raelynn," she snaps, her eyes finding mine for the first time.

"What?" It's no secret that Mom and Eric's relationship started while he was still married. The whole thing just sounds a little too cliché for my liking. He was unhappy in his marriage, got friendly with his assistant, and the next thing we all know, he's taking her out to dinners to thank her for her dedication to the firm and I come home from school early to find them on the bed I'm forced to share with Mom in our tiny one-bed apartment. But it's all okay, because said wife found out and left, and now we get to move into his castle that overlooks the sea. I just about manage to stop my eyes rolling thinking about it.

"This is the last time, I promise."

"Sounds great, Mom." They're not the words I want to say. I want to demand to know how she can sit there and say that after all her past ruined promises that we'd settle down. I want to scream about how I'm once again uprooted from a school I've barely had time to get used to.

Silence descends around us. We don't even have a TV to break the tension.

After finishing my sesame chicken, which I struggled to force down after having my assumptions confirmed, I place the box back on the coffee table. "I have a test in the morning I need to study for. Not that it'll make any difference if I pass or not."

I'm almost in the bedroom when she calls for me.

"Rae?"

I pause, but I don't turn around or even speak.

"This is going to be the last one. I really feel it this time."

"I hope so, Mom. I really do."

I ignore the textbook sitting on the dresser as I walk into the room. I couldn't give a fuck about the test; I just needed a little space, not that I get much of that in this barely five-hundred square foot apartment. I might not be all that excited about packing up the few possessions we have once again, but the idea of living somewhere a little bigger is definitely appealing.

———

Exactly as promised, when I get home from school on Wednesday afternoon, our apartment is missing its possessions—not that there's a lot of them—and Mom and Eric are waiting for me with a couple of suitcases next to the couch.

"Did you have a good day?"

"Fine," I mumble. I spent all day wondering where the hell she was dragging me to this time. Eric does appear to be truthful, but really, until I see the evidence of this house overlooking the sea, I'm going to be skeptical. Mom's fallen for some very convincing liars in the past, so just because he wears a fancy suit and flashes his black Amex about whenever he buys anything, it doesn't really mean all that much to me.

"Did you say goodbye to your friends?"

My mom's not stupid—she's actually a very intelligent lady, despite her obvious flaws—so how has she not realized that we move so often that not only is it impossible for me to make any friends, but I'm at the point where I've actually given up trying? What's the point when in two, five, eight months I'm going to be dragged somewhere else in the country?

"Yeah," I lie. "They promised to stay in touch." I somehow manage to keep the bitter tone out of my voice. Getting into a fight with her now is only going to result in a tense journey to wherever it is we're going.

"Fantastic. Well, our flight leaves in two hours. Shall we go and get some food first? I'll have a driver waiting outside."

"Sounds perfect," Mom practically squeals in excitement.

"Do you want to change first?" Eric asks, running his eyes over my outfit.

"No, I'm good." I glance down at my ripped, paint-covered jeans and my slashed-across-the-midriff tee. I don't really give a shit if I don't fit into his fancy world. Mom's the one he wants, not me. He's only got to put up with me for a few months before I finally decide where I want to go to college and actually spend three whole years in the same place. I'm not one hundred percent on where I want to go, although I have a few definite no's after the places Mom's dragged me to.

"Okay then." He doesn't look happy about it ,but as I stand with my arms folded over my chest and my chin jutted out, he wisely shuts his mouth, clearly agreeing with me that an argument before boarding a plane is a bad idea.

With our suitcases and belongings in the back of his driver's car, we head toward the airport, stopping at a diner on the way. It's not the kind of place I expect Eric to choose, but he can hardly take us to a fancy restaurant with me dressed as I am. The thought fills me with joy. I might not get a say in where we live, but I do have control over some things.

"What did Ethan say about our arrival?" Mom asks, reminding me that it's not only Eric we're about to move in with.

"He can't wait to meet you."

The thing about having a million—or so it seems—men come in and out of your life is that you get really good at reading them. Mom's addiction to assholes has really helped me identify the bad ones way before she does, and right now, Eric is lying through his teeth.

"Really?"

"Of course. I've told him all about both of you."

I can't help rolling my eyes. He might know plenty about my mom—they've been seeing each other long enough to know the basics—but I would put money on him not having a fucking clue about the darker parts of our past that make us the way we are. Mom might be quick to fall in love and trust, despite having her heart shattered more times than I care to count. I, on the other hand, do not trust anyone, even my own mother to a point, with her terrible judgment. I will ensure no one knows enough about me to use it against me. I learned the hard way years ago that allowing someone in and trusting them only leads to pain, and it's not a lesson I'd like to repeat.

"I've enrolled you at Rosewood High. Ethan can show you around on Monday and help get you settled."

"Brilliant." I smile at him and he returns it, assuming mine's genuine. It's not. I've started over at schools so many times now that finding my feet is almost part of the fun. Plus, getting lost is always a good excuse for being late.

The rest of the journey is just about tolerable. We fly first class, obviously, and while Mom and Eric are otherwise engaged, I manage to snag myself a bottle of champagne. It's fancy as fuck—Christ knows how much it must cost him—but I don't care. I tip it back like it's sparkling water in the hope it helps me forget what's happening right now.

———

The second we're out of the airport, I know that Eric's words about where he lives and the money he has are true. There's a fucking limo waiting for us.

Mom squeals in excitement as he pulls her into his arms and kisses her sweetly. The champagne filling my belly threatens to make a reappearance at the sight.

It's so over the top and pretentious.

"I wanted you to arrive in style, sweetheart."

Jesus, I'm really going to hate this place.

Some poor member of the airport staff wheels out our cases on a trolley and proceeds to place them in the trunk. I follow his lead and grab the handle of the passenger door of the ridiculous car, much to the driver's horror. He's waiting patiently to greet his guests.

"What?" I bark. "Do *you* want to sit in the back with those two pawing each other?"

"Point taken, Miss. You are very welcome to join me."

"Thank you." I grace him with the first genuine smile I've given out all day and climb in.

I make quick work of changing his radio station to something a little more current and sit back and wait.

We've made it this far. All that's left is to see this house he's promised us.

The drive is longer than I was hoping for, and I find myself dropping off to the sound of the driver singing along with my music. If I cared, I'd ask how he knows the words when most of his passengers probably request classical or some other shit, but I don't.

I don't open my eyes until the ground under the tires starts to crunch. My chin drops as I stare at the house we're driving toward. It's fucking massive.

"Impressive, right?" the driver says, and I realize that I've moved forward in my seat to get a better look. The place is bigger than some of the apartment buildings we've lived in.

"It sure is something."

"I hope you're happy here, Miss. Rosewood is a great place to live."

Only time will tell. I don't respond with my reservations. Instead, I just smile and climb out of the car when he pulls it to a stop.

"It doesn't look like Ethan's here. I told him what time we were arriving," Eric grumbles. "Come on, I can't wait to show you around."

"Just point me in the direction of my room." I have no interest in a guided tour of his fucking mansion. If I have to live here, then I'm sure I'll figure out which room is which soon enough. Not that anyone could possibly need all these fucking rooms.

He pushes the doors open and a huge staircase is revealed. It's like those you see on wedding photos where the brides gracefully glide down toward her prince. The thought has the champagne sloshing around once again.

"Take the stairs, turn left. Your room is the last one on the right. It's got an incredible view and a balcony. You'll love it. I had Rachel make it all up for you, but if you need anything, please just ask."

I want to ask who the hell Rachel is, but assuming she's the maid or some shit, I just nod and follow his directions up the insane staircase.

3

ETHAN

"You know I love you, man, but are you planning on going home sometime tonight?" Mason says with a laugh. I turned up here under the guise of catching him up on the school gossip, seeing as he's been off since his accident last weekend.

"Dad's back," I say, hoping it'll be enough to stop him giving me grief for not wanting to go home. In truth, it barely scratches the surface of my reasons for not wanting to be there. No sooner had we got home after our father/son bonding day of horrors, he packed a bag and took off for Washington, promising to be back with my new ready-made family tonight. I'm even less willing to meet them right now than I was when he told me they were coming.

Anger burns within me that Mom's perfume has barely faded from the house, yet he's totally fine with moving in his mistress and her daughter. Asshole.

"Trust me when I tell you that letting all this fester inside isn't the best course of action. I know you're angry. I'm angry for you. But you need to talk to him. Get everything out in the open."

I mutter some kind of response before standing from the chair I'd taken over in Camila's room a few hours ago when I made myself at home here.

"We're here if you need anything," she says softly from her spot tucked into Mason's side. It's a harsh reminder that I'm now the gooseberry in our group. I used to live for times partying with my boys, but they spend almost all their time with their girls now. And where does that leave me? Apparently, at home with a replacement mother and a child to babysit.

I leave them to it, sadness and anxiety only growing stronger the farther I get away from them. My fingers curl around the steering wheel of my car with an unforgiving grip as I head toward home. Dad told me what time their flight got in—it was almost like he was expecting me to host a fucking welcome party. I shake my head. He's fucking delusional.

The lights are on when I pull up in the driveway and my stomach drops. This is really happening.

I sit out in my car with the engine off for longer than I'd planned. Dad and his new woman are in the kitchen, sitting at the table and enjoying a late dinner together. I watch as he reaches out and touches her arm, laughs at her jokes and smiles at her in a way I remember all too well.

Hatred that I've never experienced before begins to swell inside me until it's like an ugly monster wanting to escape. My hands tremble, my heart pounds, and my stomach turns over at the thought of having to go in there and accept them. It's not going to happen. It's never going to happen.

She and her daughter have ruined my family and my life, and I have every intention of ensuring they're aware that their presence isn't welcome.

After sucking in a few more ragged breaths, I push the car door open and make my way toward the house. The anger that's burning inside me fuels my movements until I'm opening the front door and marching inside the only home I've ever known that now feels like a stranger's.

Dad and his woman's laughter sound out from the kitchen. He'll expect me to come and introduce myself, so that's exactly what I do.

"Ethan, where have you been? I thought I told you what time we were arriving so you could be here."

I stare at him. The happiness on his face does nothing for my fury.

"I had better things to do," I spit, moving toward the cabinet that holds his precious scotch. The room is in silence as I pull the door open and grab a bottle from the back. One of his favorites.

Twisting the top, the sound of the thin metal breaking is almost deafening before I tip the neck to my lips and swallow down a generous mouthful.

Glancing at him over the end of the bottle, his eyes narrow in anger. I shake my head. What was he expecting? For me to welcome this woman into my life with open arms? She's the reason my mother has run back to her childhood home without so much as a glance backward in my direction. There's no way in hell he can really expect me to be okay with this.

His jaw twitches as he grinds his teeth before finally opening his mouth again. "Ethan, I'd like you to meet Ashlynn. Ash, this is my son, Ethan."

Her eyes sparkle with delight, and I just about manage to keep the scotch I'd just swallowed in my stomach.

"It's so nice to meet you at last. I've heard so much about you."

I wince. She could have the softest voice in the world and it would still be like nails on a chalkboard for me.

"I can't say the same." With the bottle in my hands, I storm from the kitchen with Dad's frustrated words sounding out behind me. I don't register any of them as my feet pound up the stairs.

I bolt straight to my bedroom. My fingers just grip my doorknob when a noise from behind me makes me still.

I think it's time to introduce myself to my new 'sister.' I roll my eyes at myself. I intend on getting rid of these two before anything crazy like that happens.

Turning on my heels, I push open her bedroom door instead of my own. I don't bother knocking. I have no intention of being polite or considerate.

My brows pull together when I realize the room is empty, but that's only for a moment, because the second water stops running I understand where she's hiding.

Dad told me that she was enrolling at Rosewood, but also that she's a lovely girl, so I'm expecting her to be a freshman, maybe a sophomore, if I'm lucky. Stalking farther into the room, I find a small suitcase sitting on the end of the bed.

Placing the bottle of scotch on the nightstand, I walk over, glancing at the contents. Some black lace catches my eye, and I hook my finger under it and pull. I reveal a tiny black thong and hold it up in front of me. Okay, so maybe not a freshman, then. Not content on just invading her privacy a little, I dive back into the case and discover a matching bra. While the thong had hardly any fabric to it, the bra is the opposite, making me really hope she's not a freshman. Finding the label, I flip it over. 32D. Now that's something I can definitely get on board with.

"What the hell do you think you're doing?" The atmosphere in the room becomes heavy as I'm caught red-handed with her lingerie hanging from my fingers.

A smirk curls at the corner of my lips, knowing that when I turn around, I'm going to discover who exactly is occupying this room and just how much fun I can really have with her.

With her underwear still laced through my fingers, I spin on the balls of my feet.

My smile widens at what I find.

She's covered only in a white towel that's wrapped around her body, and her dark hair is hanging in rat tails around her shoulders and sticking to her face. Her skin is still covered in water, but what really captures my attention is her eyes. They're dark, almost black, and they're staring pure hate into me.

The feeling is very much mutual, sweet cheeks.

There's no way this girl's an innocent freshman, and I don't just mean that because of what I know she's rocking under the towel she pulls tighter around her. There's a depth to her that only comes with age and experience.

Her eyes narrow as our contact holds, something crackling between us.

"Have you about finished snooping through my stuff?"

"I just wanted to know more about my new neighbor."

"Nothing to know. Now get the hell out."

"This is my house." I take a step toward her, but she doesn't move. Brave girl.

"Actually, I'm pretty sure it's your father's house."

"That's where you're mistaken. I'm very much in charge of what happens under this roof." I close some more of the distance between us, and I don't miss the hitch in her breathing.

She rolls her eyes and something explodes within me at her defiance. I step closer and right into her personal space. My blood races through my ears, the anger and hate mixing with her freshly showered scent and heading straight for my dick.

Dropping my eyes from hers, I take in her full lips, her slender neck, and her heaving chest. Her minty breath hits my nose and I bite down on the inside of my cheeks in an attempt to restrain the devil inside.

Unable to keep my hands away, I run one fingertip along the edge of the towel.

"Do I need to show you just how true those words are? Do I need to prove that I am the one in charge here?" It would only take one small movement from me to make the towel drop to the ground, she knows it as well as I do, yet she still doesn't cower down.

Her dark eyes flash with contempt, and it makes it really fucking tempting to expose her.

Dropping my face so our cheeks brush, I whisper in her ear.

"You're not welcome here."

She shudders as my breath hits her ear, and the wicked smile it causes is still on my face when I pull back and look at her.

"You know," I say, taking a step back and allowing my eyes to roam over her, "I think that getting rid of you is going to be so much fun." I wink as I back up to her door, grabbing my bottle as I go. "I think I'll keep these." I bring her tiny panties up to my nose and sniff. They're clean and mostly smell like laundry detergent, but there's still a hint of her. It makes my mouth water and excitement fill my veins.

We're going to have so much fun.

4

RAELYNN

I breathe a sigh of relief when he walks out of my room and slams his bedroom door closed. Racing over to my own, I gently push it to and fall back against it. I have no idea what I was expecting from him. Everything that Eric had told me about Ethan was all positive. But what I just got... that was anything but.

I understand this is a big change. I totally get that his mom only left recently, and his life has been thrown upside down. He's underestimating one thing, though. My life is in a constant state of upside down, and him threatening me does not scare me.

I've experienced, and handled, worse than jumped-up little rich boys who think they can throw their weight around just because they live in some fancy house and get to do whatever the fuck they like with Daddy's money.

Oh Ethan, you might think you're in charge here, but you're about to be bitterly disappointed when I don't bow down to your greatness.

I push away from the door and turn to look at it, hoping I might find a lock, but sadly it doesn't exist.

The sudden boom of loud music from across the hall makes me jump. My fists ball and my lips purse that he's got the power to make me flinch like that. I tell myself there and then that I'll never allow him to see my fear. I've locked it down before; I can do it again just to prove to him that I won't be beaten.

I dig into my suitcase for some underwear. Thankfully, I wasn't intending to put on the pair he just walked out with. *Fucking idiot.* I find a large t-shirt to pull over my head to sleep in. I brush out my hair and crawl into bed with it still wet. I'm not one of those girls who gives a shit how it ends up looking if by some small miracle I do actually manage to get to sleep tonight. I've been battling insomnia for a few years now, and if that wasn't bad enough, add the new bed, the different surroundings, and the asshole across the hall with his banging bass and I'm pretty confident that sleep is going to elude me. The one thing that I refuse to allow to mess with my sleep, though, is his threats. He can suck on those. He doesn't scare me.

I sit against the massive pillows with my back pressed against the ornate headboard of my bed and look around. The room itself is pink. *Do I look like a girl who likes fucking pink?* The fact that I can smell the slight hint of paint means this was done recently. Eric's known me for months; did he really think I'd want a pink fucking room? I thought he was supposed to be intelligent with this fancy-pants business empire.

Shaking my head, I look at all the furniture. There's more in this one room than Mom and I have had in any of our apartments put together. There's a hairdryer, straighteners, and products already lining the dressing table along with a fully stocked bathroom. Not a single thing has been overlooked. Probably modeled on the kind of hotel room he frequents—not that I'd have any clue what they would be like, since the best I've experienced is flea-ridden motels when we've run away from another of my mother's terrible life choices.

———

The pounding music from his room must have eventually lulled me to sleep, because when I wake the next morning, it's with the sun streaming in through the curtains that I apparently didn't shut last night.

The house is in blissful silence as I walk to my en suite to start the day, although I can't say that I do it with much enthusiasm. The ball of dread that formed while his haunted blue eyes stared into mine that I didn't want to acknowledge is still there, only I think it's bigger.

Still dressed in my oversized t-shirt, I open the doors leading out to the balcony and find a small outdoor loveseat tucked into the corner, and a coffee table. As I look out over the beach and the blue sparkling sea, a smile finds its way to my lips for the first time since I learned of this move. I think I've found my favorite place here. It's still early, but the nighttime chill in the air covers my skin in goosebumps and I welcome them.

I stand, leaning against the railing for the longest time—or at least it feels that way, seeing as I've yet to have my morning coffee. With the hope of caffeine giving me a little extra bounce in my step, I pull on a pair of jeans and a black shirt and go in search. With the amount of money Eric seems to have, I have every confidence that I'm not about to find a shitty discount store jar of coffee hiding in a cupboard but something that actually will hit the spot.

I'm proved right when I eventually find the kitchen and spot a scary-looking machine built into one of the cupboards.

I walk up to it, my head tilting to the side slightly as I try to figure out how the fucking thing works.

"It's not as complicated as it looks, dear," a soft voice says from behind me, and I practically hit the ceiling. I turn, my eyes as wide as saucers, my heart jack-hammering in my chest. "Oh, I'm so sorry. I thought you saw me sitting here." She lowers her own coffee and pushes the chair out behind her.

"I'm Rachel, the housekeeper. You must be Raelynn." She's probably early forties with light brown hair with flecks of gray. She's short, although not as short as me, and a little plump around the middle. But she has the softest eyes and the gentlest face I think I've ever seen. "The mugs are kept up here." She reaches up and pulls one down. I look at the size of it, and I don't realize my thoughts are written all over my face until she speaks again. "Bigger?"

"Much, much bigger."

"How big things are is certainly not something you need to worry about in this house." His voice makes my spine go ramrod straight.

Rachel shakes her head and sighs, clearly used to Ethan's brand of inappropriateness. "Good morning, Ethan."

"It sure is."

I don't turn to look at him, instead standing frozen to the spot in the hope that I might suddenly have the power to turn invisible.

When the heat of his chest seeps into my back, I start to wonder if I actually am and he's about to walk right through me. But sadly, it's not the case. He presses his front against me as he stretches up to the cupboard and pulls down a mug. It's red with a huge B on it, I assume for his dumb football team, but it's not what really catches my attention because it's his hands that my eyes focus on. They're rough. His knuckles look like he punched something in the recent past, but there's something about them that just captivates me.

"I hope you had a good night," he breathes into my ear, causing my entire body to shudder against his. "If I were you, I'd start sleeping with one eye open. You might be forced to leave at any moment."

My breath catches as his huge hand lands on my hip and squeezes until it starts to sting.

"Ethan, I hope you're playing nice."

He takes a huge step back, and it's almost as if I imagined the whole thing as he comes to stand in front of me and begins making his own coffee, totally ignoring the fact that I was quite obviously about to get a lesson on how to use it.

His wide shoulders and muscular back block my view, and I chastise myself for thinking about how damn sculpted his back is beneath his skin-tight shirt.

It's not until the machine stops that he turns. He takes a sip, not even flinching when the boiling liquid hits his lips.

"Oh, I'm sorry. Were you waiting?"

I roll my eyes at him, but I don't miss Rachel leaving the room as I do so. Sadly, Ethan glances up and catches it as well.

"You don't scare me, you know."

"Is that so? I'd rethink that if I were you, because I'm about to become your worst nightmare, sweet cheeks. Whatever it is that keeps you up at night, that's exactly what I'm going to be." I swallow nervously as one face pops into my mind. One that is most definitely not welcome.

He steps forward and I have no choice but to take one back to stop us colliding. My back hits the wall and I flinch.

His huge frame towers over me, a low chuckle falling from his lips. His eyes bounce between mine as I fight to keep my fear from them. His, however, are cold, and the sight has a tremble threatening to race through me, but I fight it. I will not show this, this... *bully* that he affects me in any way. I have a right to be here. I understand the circumstances of mine and my mother's arrival aren't all that desirable, but we're here nonetheless.

Leaning forward on his forearms, he continues to stare down at me while his freshly showered manly scent fills my nose and kickstarts a bunch of traitorous butterflies in my belly.

He opens his mouth, and my eyes drop to his lips. He leans forward and my heart skips a beat that he's going to kiss me. But at the last second, his face turns.

"Watch your back."

And then he's gone. He quickly pushes from the wall and disappears from the room and quickly out of the house.

I sag back, my breathing erratic and my hands trembling as I try to get my head in the game. He's trying his best to scare me, and although the emptiness in his eyes when he looks at me does instill a little of it in me, it's nothing compared to what I've experienced in the past. Nothing that Ethan can do will hurt me. He's all talk. He won't touch me.

"Good morning, honey," Mom says when she and Eric join me in the kitchen a while later. "Would you like a coffee?"

"Y-Yes." I've managed to move myself from the wall in favor of the chair that Rachel was occupying when I first walked in.

I watch as Mom practically bounces her way toward me. She's so fucking happy right now, it's sickening. I wonder what she'd think about the situation if I admitted to Ethan's less-than-welcoming treatment of me.

"We heard you chatting with Ethan. Did he already leave for school?"

"I-I guess so." All I know is that he's no longer in the house, and right now that's all I care about.

"That's a shame. Rachel's set us up a family breakfast. Sadly, they don't get to happen all that much with the traveling I do," Eric says, pressing the button that brings the coffee machine back to life. "What's your preference, Rae?"

It's only when he asks that I remember the reason I came down here in the first place was to get my morning caffeine fix.

"Black, please. No sugar."

"Sweet enough, huh?"

"Something like that," I mutter.

I follow both of them through to a different room, and my chin drops when I take in the fancy looking dining room, but what really blows my mind is the amount of food covering the fourteen-seat table. He's never here, Eric just admitted that, so why the hell they need a table for fourteen God only knows.

I hesitate in the doorway, feeling totally uncomfortable in this situation. I was much more at home in the tiny apartments that Mom and I have shared with half a loaf of moldy bread to eat between us.

"Come on, honey. Come and eat," Mom encourages, looking more at home than I think I've ever seen her. I'm glad this kind of wealth looks good on one of us.

I pick at a croissant while Mom and Eric chat away, but I have no clue as to what they're actually talking about. My brain is still trying to process how this is now my life.

"Rae, Rae, Raelynn..." Eric repeating my name eventually drags me from my inner turmoil, and I look up at him.

"Huh?"

"I was just explaining that Principal Hartmann is expecting you to start at Rosewood High on Monday, so you've got a few days to get a feel for the place before the hard work starts. Do you have any idea what you would like to do after graduating?"

"Um... no, not yet." That's not entirely true. I know I want to go to college, if I can afford it, and I know that I want to get out on my own. I'm aware that might mean me getting a job here and saving some money before I'm able to do so, but my dream is freedom, to find a home and to stay there.

"Well, that's fine. There's still time. Miss French, the guidance counselor at Rosewood, is fantastic. She's really helped Ethan try to figure out what he wants; I'm sure you'll find her just as helpful. Set up a meeting as soon as you can, yeah?"

"Sure thing. Are we done? Do you mind if I..." I trail off, hoping that my longing look toward the exit is clear enough.

"You've hardly eaten anything, honey. Are you okay?"

"I'm fine. I actually had something before you came down." It's a lie and one that I'm not proud of. The one solid thing that Mom and I have had over the years is our honesty. It's not always been pretty, but we've always told each other the truth, and I feel like I've just betrayed her. I walk out of that room with a heavy heart as well as a messed-up head.

I make myself another coffee before disappearing up to my room to try to figure out what the fuck I'm supposed to do with myself before I start school on Monday. I get what Eric was trying to do, but quite frankly, I think I'd rather be dropped in at the deep end and forced into my new life this morning. It's not like it would be the first time it's happened.

My coffee has long been drunk, and the sound of Eric's car has long since faded as it pulled out of the driveway. He'd promised to show Mom around town properly. I was invited, but aside from being forced to spend time with Ethan, quite honestly, I couldn't think of anything worse.

With the house all but empty, I eventually decide to go exploring. I poke my head into every single room I find. I swear they get bigger and grander with every door I open. I find countless bedrooms. A living room, a snug thing, a games room, even a fully kitted out home gym with indoor pool, along with all the other rooms I'd expect. After shrugging a jacket on and slipping my feet into my boots, I discover what outside has to offer. The infinity pool takes my breath away, but I can't deny that the glistening blue water doesn't beg for me to jump in. I don't even own a swimsuit. I guess that's something that's going to need resolving, seeing as this place has not one but two pools... and a jacuzzi, I find when I turn the corner. There's even a full-on pool house out here. If anyone had told me that this was going to be where I found myself at the end of this year, I would have laughed in their face.

Although it's obviously nice, I feel totally out of place and uncomfortable being here. I'm so far out of my comfort zone I can't even see it in the distance. I belong in a damp old apartment with barely-working appliances and constantly lukewarm water. Not here in what I can only describe as a mansion. Mom, on the other hand, doesn't seem to have had an issue settling into our new home, if her smile as she bid me farewell earlier was anything to go by.

I leave one room to last. Do I feel like a creep as I twist his doorknob and push it open? I sure do. But do I care? Not one little bit.

In my head, I had images of a dark, musty smelling, messy room, but what I walk into is very much not that. The walls are painted light grey, the bedding and the furniture are black, but the curtains are all open, allowing the sun to stream in. There aren't clothes all over the floor and the surfaces aren't covered in dirty dishes and moldy food. It's just... clean. My brows draw together as I look around. This perfectly organized room doesn't go with my image of Ethan at all.

Pulling the door shut once I start to feel awkward for intruding on his space, I get myself ready, grab my purse, and head out. I've explored the house; now it's time to find out what this little town is really like.

5

ETHAN

I don't bother to see if anyone else is here yet. Instead, I head straight for the gym before practice starts.

Every single muscle in my body is locked up tight after my interaction with *her* this morning.

I was expecting some young little kid to turn up, but it seems that what I've got instead is a defiant bitch who's brave enough to stand up to me. Stupid, stupid girl.

She might think that she's dealing with someone who's pissed off at the world, but she has no idea how deep the wound is that my dad's left me with.

I change into my sweats and a t-shirt and hit the weights. The pull of my muscles helps ease the ache in my chest that seems ever present these days. The easiest way to get rid of it is to drink, but I promised both Jake and Mason that I would ease up after turning up to school still drunk the week before last. I can't help it. It's the only thing that makes it all go away. To forget that Mom's left and Dad's moved his fancy woman, and her daughter, into our house. It's our house. My family's. Neither of them belong there.

My anger fuels me and keeps me pushing forward until a familiar face appears at my side.

"Well, I must admit that it's better finding you in this sweaty state than in any other you've been in recently."

Jake takes the weight from me and props it back up onto the bench. Sitting, I suck in a few deep breaths as the pain in my arms subsides.

"Come on, Coach is waiting."

I follow him out to the field, where Coach embarks on another inspirational speech after our division win. We're on a bye-week this week, so there's plenty of time to listen to him trying to fire us up and prepare for our first playoff game against Manor Crossing Bobcats next week.

We only get a few drills in before Coach calls time, telling us that he's going to grind our asses after class.

"If he talked less, we'd have time to do more," I mutter to Jake as we walk off the field.

"I heard that, Savage. Get your head in the game."

I glance over my shoulder at him, expecting to find his hard stare boring into me, but surprisingly I find a sympathetic look on his face. He dragged me into his office after he found Jake and Mason trying to sober me up that day and demanded to know the truth about what was going on. I understood his, and the guys', concern. I've always been the pretty level-headed one. My life's always been stable, aside from my parents mostly being in another state to me. While the others on the team have dealt with deaths and separations, I've just continued never expecting my life to explode before my eyes.

"You done that paper for English Lit?" Jake asks as we're getting dressed.

"No. What paper?"

"Mrs. Bailey is gonna have your balls if you don't hand something in."

"What was I supposed to do?" I complain, ready to pull something out of the bag at the last minute. English Lit isn't until this afternoon; I'm sure I've got time.

The two of us head of the locker room once Jake's given me a rundown on what's apparently been a two-week project that's completely passed me by. I haven't even read the book we're supposed to be writing about.

"Just tell her the truth and get an extension. It won't be a problem."

Thankfully, he shuts up the second we come to a stop by our tables. The rest of the team has already congregated, seeing as we were the last two out, and the cheer squad are already hanging off their every word. Don't get me wrong, I like the cheer squad, *a lot*, but Christ, they can be a bit much at times. I like a willing girl as much as the rest of them but sometimes, it's just too easy. Sometimes the challenge, the chase, is what it's all about, and all this group does is open their legs as soon as it's been suggested and do whatever we demand. I can understand why Jake and Mason haven't ended up with one of them.

"Hey, baby," Shelly sings, coming to sit on my lap the second my ass hits the wood of the bench.

"Not today." I push her off and she looks at me with her brows pulled together and a pout on her filled lips. She soon gets over it though, because she turns her attention to Zayn.

With everyone chatting away, it's easy to see the two giant holes in our group. Obviously, Mason's out of action after his car crash. This place and the team aren't the same without him, but according to him, he'll be back next week. But the other missing person isn't someone that a lot of people are acknowledging right now after her true colors were exposed. Chelsea. We all know that Chelsea's got a terrible reputation. She's a slut, she's easy, she's a bitch of epic proportions, but the thing with Chelsea is that she's the master at wearing a mask.

Everyone thought Jake was bad for hiding who he really is... well, they haven't met the real Chelsea. How do I know this? Because I have.

Chelsea isn't the mean bitch everyone knows her to be. I know she's done a load of bad stuff, and I won't forgive her easily for hurting some of the people I love, but I know that's not who she really is.

Dragging my cell from my pocket, I find our chat and send her a quick message. Everyone else might have happily forgotten she ever existed, but she needs to know she's got some friends, now more than ever.

> Ethan: Missing you here. I hope everything's going well x

I close it down before anyone else notices. They all think I use Chelsea for one thing, just like every other guy she probably comes into contact with, but it's not the case. The times we've disappeared off together, we haven't had sex. In fact, I've actually never slept with her, never done anything with her. She always had eyes for Jake, and I made the sensible decision to stay out of the middle of that situation just in case anything were to happen, although Jake made it very clear it never would. I'm all up for having fun, but not if there's even a chance the girl could end up with one of my guys.

As the bell rings and everyone makes a move for class, I head in the opposite direction to the library. No time like the present to get that paper written—after I've read the damn book, of course. It's probably going to leave me either further behind with the classes I'm missing, but fuck it. It needs to get done, and I really don't want to be on the wrong end of Mrs. Bailey. She's one scary woman.

I find myself a quiet corner to sit in and pull out the book that I find hiding at the bottom of my bag. It seems that I was in class for the day it was all set. No excuses there. Fantastic.

I read the first two chapters. It goes in, but by the time I get to the third, I lose all concentration and the only thing I can think about is *her*. The more I try to forget her dark eyes as she stared up at me earlier, the more insistent the image becomes. My grip on the book in my hands gets tighter and tighter until my need to rip it in two starts to get the better of me.

Shoving the book back where I found it, I throw my bag over my shoulder and march from the library and quickly out of the school.

I put my car in drive and crank up the volume on the music in an attempt to get out of my own head. It works for all of two seconds before the guy singing starts going on about a temptress with dark eyes that won't let anyone in. It touches too close to home. Turning it off, I continue the rest of the journey to the seafront in silence, with only my irritating thoughts for company.

I park in the almost deserted parking lot next to Aces and head inside.

I was in such a rush to get away from *her* this morning that I didn't grab anything to eat. I'm now starving after my stint in the gym and our, albeit short, training session.

There are a couple of people here having breakfast but, as expected, no one I recognize. I fall down into our usual booth and wait for Bill to notice me.

"It's not even ten am," he says, sliding into the other side of the booth less than two minutes later. "You having that good a day?"

"You have no idea," I mutter.

He's silent for a beat before he leans on his elbows, closing the space between us, and lowers his voice. "Have they moved in?"

I rear back in surprise. I wasn't sure anyone was aware of

our new house guests. I want to say they're temporary, but just seeing Dad and his new toy so happy last night, it makes me wonder if he really is serious about this.

"How'd you—"

"Not much that goes on in this town that I don't know about, son."

"Great." I slump back in my seat, staring out the glass at the front of the diner to the beach beyond.

"Just give it time. I know it doesn't seem like it now, but things will feel normal again. How's your mom doing?"

"Honestly, I have no idea. She makes out that she's fine, but I can hear the sadness in her voice. I haven't spoken to her since I found out about them moving in. I have no idea if she's aware or not, and I don't want to be the one to tell her that Dad's moved in her replacement."

"You need one of my burgers. It'll sort you out right now," he says, clearly out of helpful advice for me.

"Give me the works, Bill."

"Coming right up, kid." He walks off but stops halfway to the counter. "Don't let this affect your schoolwork. We need you out on that field, you hear me?"

I nod because it's the only thing I can do, but trying to focus on bullshit assignments right now is the last thing I want to do. My need to cause some pain is burning hotter than my need to graduate right now.

I pull the book back out and attempt another two chapters while Bill cooks my food, but although I read the words, I couldn't tell anyone what they were about. Feeling hopeless, I push the book across the table as if its mere presence offends me.

I've never been the best student, or the most gifted in the classroom. I much prefer doing things with my hands than sitting with a book. I'm a practical person, logical and methodical, but only on my terms, and most definitely not with a shitty English book I'm forced to read. Dad's paid for tutors for me in the past, but honestly, they've made fuck all difference. They just wound me up, having to spend more time on stuff that frustrated the hell out of me.

I'll achieve enough to get into college, especially with my football skills, but I'll never set the world on fire like Dad hoped I would. I don't know what his issue is; he was a terrible student in high school. He's even admitted on occasion that he almost never finished college, but look at him now. He's got a business empire most people in this town are jealous of and earns more than he could ever spend in a lifetime. Why can't I do that?

I finish my burger, and when the diner starts filling up and getting louder, I grab my stuff and head out, hoping to find some peace to attempt this fucking assignment somewhere else.

6

RAELYNN

I walk down the street for a few minutes before I come across a bus stop. After discovering that one is due any minute, I hang around with my hip against the pole and wait it out.

The street that the Savage house sits on is a stunning tree-lined road. The houses get bigger the higher up the small hill you get, and, surprise, surprise, Eric purchased the house right at the top. The ones around me now are quite obviously smaller, but they're still stunning and way more than I've ever had the privilege of living in before.

I'm just starting to think the bus isn't coming when it appears out of nowhere and comes to a stop beside me.

Digging in my purse, I manage to scrape together the fare and walk to the very back of the bus, past all the elderly passengers who look at me with shock on their faces. I guess I don't fit the ideal of the uber-wealthy around here. Oh well, sucks for them, because it seems I'm going to be here for a while.

I keep my eyes on the passing scenery, attempting to remember the trip back. I have no clue where this bus is headed, but when it turns onto a street that runs along the beachfront and then slows to a stop where there's a whole crowd ready to get on, I decide it's my time to get off.

I thank the driver and step out into the morning sun. It's warmed up significantly since I walked on to my balcony. *My balcony*. What the hell has my life become?

The blue sea glistens in the clear sky above, and I'm powerless but to walk toward it. It's been a lot of years since I've been to the coast. Too many to actually count. I don't even remember what the place was called that Mom moved us to when I was probably seven, maybe eight, and we ended up in a trailer not far from the sea. We didn't stay there long. The boyfriend she found was a druggie, and thankfully she found out sooner rather than later and off we went once again.

I shake my head at the memories. The best part about that place had been being able to sneak out when she was preoccupied and walking along the wet sand with the waves splashing at my feet. Everything seemed that little bit easier when the beach was involved. I wonder if it will feel that way here once I'm a little more settled.

I move along a little before finding steps down onto the beach. Dropping down, I place my boot-covered foot on the soft sand. I make quick work of pulling them and my socks off until I feel the grains seep between my toes. I sigh with contentment and allow myself to drift back to the peaceful times I had on that beach as a kid. I was naïve back then. I had no clue what my life was going to be or how I was going to be dragged around the country like a kid carrying their favorite rag doll as my mom attempted to find what it was she wanted out of life.

I begin walking. I pass young families making sandcastles and wonder what it must be like to grow up with two parents whose main focus is their child. Don't get me wrong, my mom cares, it's just a little misguided. She's done her utmost to ensure I have everything I could possibly need over the years. I think her wanting to give me the best is one of the main reasons she goes after these supposedly rich guys who promise her the world. She wants me to have the best opportunities in life, the kind she never had. But without her realizing, I think she's turned into her own parents, the ones she swore she'd never be like, always chasing the possibility of an incredible life but never quite getting hold of it.

When I get to some sand dunes, I slip between them and make myself a little seat in the sand. I fall down and drop my boots beside me as I stare out at the crashing waves.

The sun heats my face, and after a few minutes, I pull my jacket off and lie back. I wouldn't be able to do this in the height of summer. My porcelain skin wouldn't allow me. It burns at even the mention of summer sun, but this November sun is perfect for me.

With the sound of kids playing in the distance and the water crashing on the sand mere feet away, I find myself drifting off in a way I never do when I lie down in an actual bed.

I relax for the first time since I found out about this move and drift off.

———

When I start to come around again, my skin prickles. I have no idea how long I've fallen asleep for, but my thoughts about the sun being safe might have been wishful thinking as I feel it burning.

Lifting my arm, I use my hand to shield my eyes from the sun before attempting to drag them open.

I startle when I do and find a shadow before me, but that shock is nothing compared to what hits me when I realize who that shadow actually belongs to.

He takes a step forward, his body protecting my face from the sun, although I'm sure he's not doing that out of the kindness of his heart. His face is blank. There's literally no expression. The only thing that gives away how he's feeling is the haunting look in his eyes as he stares down at me.

My heart begins to race as he comes even closer. I'm used to being at a disadvantage height-wise, seeing as I'm a total short-ass, but being looked down upon while he looms over me is slightly terrifying—not that I'll allow him to know that.

"So, turning up unwanted in my house wasn't enough. You need to ruin my peace and quiet out here, too?" he fumes, his fists curling at his sides.

Pushing myself up so I'm sitting, I drag my eyes away from him. With the sun behind him, it makes him glow like he's some kind of fucking angel. What a joke. The guy standing before me is all devil. I think anyone would be hard pushed to find anything angelic.

I stand and close the space between us. I don't for a second think it's threatening at all, but I feel better for standing up to him and not cowering down like I think he's expecting me to.

"Shouldn't you be at school, little boy?" I tilt my head to the side in the hope that I look and sound patronizing as fuck.

His eyes run over every inch of my face, taking note of everything that's changed since he cornered me this morning.

"What's with the war paint? Don't want anyone to see your real face?"

As usual, my makeup is dark. My eyeshadow and liner are heavy and my lips a dark matte purple. My hair's the same though, pulled back from my face and out of the way. It might be long, but that's only because it's easier to tie up and forget about.

We stare at each other, neither of us saying anything as the air between us crackles with hate.

"You don't belong here. You need to go back to the trailer park you fell from."

A bitter laugh falls from my lips, an unamused smile curling at one side of my mouth.

"Wow, that the best you can come up with, posh boy? If you want to get rid of me, you're going to need to try harder than that."

Out of the corner of my eye, I spot his arm come out moments before the warmth of his fingers wraps around my wrist. I gasp in surprise when his touch burns.

He tugs and I have no choice but to step forward. My breasts press against his chest, my temperature increasing as his warmth surrounds me.

I have to tip my head back in order to keep eye contact, but as uncomfortable as it is, I refuse to break it.

"You want me to try harder? Are you sure about that, trailer trash?" I swallow and try to keep any fear or trepidation from my face.

I lift a brow at him, and his fingers tighten on my wrist. "And what exactly are you going to do?"

His eyes narrow, pure hatred pouring from their dark blue depths as his chest heaves and his increased breaths fan across my face.

He releases my wrist, but he only loses contact for a second because that same hand is suddenly wrapped around my throat.

"What am I going to do?" He laughs, and it's the sound of pure evil. His fingers squeeze but only lightly. He's not cutting off my air supply—not yet, anyway. "I'm going to make sure you leave this place with your tail between your legs and tears streaming down your cheeks."

"And where exactly am I going?" I quip.

"Anywhere. I'm sure your whore of a mother will open her legs for some other poor mug and you can move in with him."

My teeth grind. "She's not a whore." His grip tightens, and for the first time, my eyes water and I start to panic a little. There are people not so far away, but I have no idea if they'd hear me scream. If I even got the chance to.

"Oh no? So she didn't seduce my dad while he was a married man?"

"Whatever has happened between our parents, it's got nothing to do with me. I'm unfortunately along for the ride."

"I. Need. You. Gone."

"And I need you to let me go."

His eyes hold mine. His jaw pops and the muscle in his neck pulsates with anger.

"I'm going to fucking ruin you."

"Do your worst, posh boy. I've handled worse than you before, I'm sure it'll be a walk in the park."

"Fuck you," he spits, releasing me with a shove that's just about hard enough to force me to the ground. "Now get the fuck out of here."

A huge part of me wants to fight him. I was here first and this is a public beach, but as he stands with his arms crossed over his chest, the fabric straining against his muscular forearms and shoulders, I decide the best thing to do is what he says—for now, at least.

Grabbing my purse and boots, I start backing away from him. I can still feel the pressure of his hand around my neck as if it's still there, and it irritates the hell out of me seeing as there are now feet between us.

"Just because I'm walking away, that doesn't mean this is over."

"Not by a long shot, sweet cheeks. Already looking forward to the next time." He winks at me and I turn on my heel, not able to look at his pained face any longer.

I get that he's unhappy with how his life is right now, but seriously, I didn't ask for this either. Okay, so I may have got the better end of this deal with the fact that I now live in a mansion overlooking the sea, but I didn't want to be here any more than he wants me to be. I had no intention of starting my life over once again.

I walk past all the families playing and adults who've come to enjoy the warm sun, but unlike when I walked in the opposite direction, I don't really take any notice of them. My head's spinning thanks to Ethan's warning, and I quite honestly can't get away from him fast enough. A little trepidation fills my veins, but I'm not scared of him—at least, I don't think I am. He's a posh boy who's always got everything he ever wanted, I'd imagine. What's he really going to do to *ruin* me, as he keeps threatening?

After climbing the steps back up onto the sidewalk, I find a row of shops. I come to a stop outside a diner called Aces when the smell from its kitchen hits me. I pull my boots back on and push the door open. After not really eating anything at breakfast, I'm suddenly starving.

Trying to put my interaction with Ethan behind me, I walk inside, appreciating the decoration of the place.

Looking around, I find the sign for the bathrooms and head that way. Before I do anything else, I need a second to sort myself out.

Locking myself inside one of the stalls, I lower the lid, place my ass down and drop my head into my hands. My breaths are unsteady as I replay what just happened with Ethan down on the beach. He's angry, I get it. But I'm not the one he should be taking this out on. I'm as innocent as him.

My stomach feels as if there's a ball of lead sitting in it. How am I supposed to live with him if our encounters are going to continue like that—or worse. I'm supposed to be starting at his school on Monday. I can only imagine how that's going to go. He'll have had a two-day head start to ensure everyone hates me from the get-go. I shudder as I imagine everyone's eyes turning to me. Being the subject of everyone's attention as the new girl is easy, but being the new girl who ruined Ethan's life, their beloved football player... yeah, that could be interesting.

Once I feel able to face the world once again, I wash my hands before risking looking into the mirror. My face is even paler than usual and the black makeup around my eyes is all smeared from the tears that pooled in them. Quickly tidying myself up, I hold my head high and walk back out into the diner.

No one even looks up at me as I pass. It's a welcome relief.

I ignore the table and booths and head straight toward the bar stools at the counter.

"Good morning," a slightly graying man says with a warm and friendly smile.

"Morning. What's good here?"

"What isn't?" he says with a laugh that is infectious enough to have the beginnings of a smile pulling at my lips.

Reaching into my purse, I pull out my wallet. "What have you got for... five dollars?" I ask sadly, the reality of my situation hitting me full force. I'm in yet another place I never asked to be, I'm being forced to live with a guy who hates me, and I'm broke.

"I'll see what I can do for you, sweetheart. I'm Bill, by the way." The friendly smile he gives me as he walks away doesn't make me feel all that much better.

I spin on my stool and take in my surroundings, from the black and white checkerboard floor to the red walls and chrome fittings. This place screams 1960s diner, and I kind of love it.

I sit, staring out the windows at the sea beyond, lost in my own world when a voice behind me startles me.

"Here you go."

Spinning back around, the last thing I expect to find is a

huge plate with a giant burger and a massive stack of fries beside it and the biggest chocolate milkshake I think I've ever seen.

"Uh... I can't afford all this," I argue, knowing that it must cost way more than I have.

"It's on the house, Raelynn."

My eyes narrow. "How do you know my name?"

"I know everything in this town. And I know that things can't be all that easy for you right now. Just wanted to put a smile on that sad face of yours."

"I... uh..." I stutter, not knowing what to say. No one's ever this nice. "What do you want?" I snap, thinking that there must be a hidden agenda here.

Bill raises his hands in surrender. "Absolutely nothing. Just being welcoming."

"Are... are you sure?" I'm still skeptical, but now that it's in front of me, my mouth is watering for a bite.

"Of course."

I pick up a fry and throw it into my mouth, still waiting for him to tell me what the catch is, but he never does. Instead, he disappears to grab some plates when the chef calls.

That first fry turned into the whole pile, and before I know it, the plate in front of me is empty and I feel full and satisfied, and a little bit fat.

"That was so good," I all but groan when he comes back over to clear my plate. I still have the milkshake to start on, but I figure waiting a few minutes wouldn't hurt.

"So, how have your first few hours in Rosewood been then?"

I consider my answer for a few moments. "Interesting."

"That good?" He laughs.

"This is my tenth school in as many years. Moving and starting over is pretty much my life. I'm used to all this shit. Although..." I pause as I think about the guy in question.

"With all the guys my mom's picked out over the years, this is the first time I've had to worry about their child. Nothing like throwing me in at the deep end."

"Ethan giving you grief?"

"You could say that."

"Give him some time. He was kinda blindsided by all this."

"How do you know so much?"

"I'm the eyes and ears of this town. Nothing gets by me."

"Thanks for the heads up. Seeing as you know everything, do you know anywhere that's hiring? I need a job, and I need one soon."

"Sure do, kid. How about you start on Monday?"

"Huh?" I ask, crease lines forming in my brow as I stare at his amused face.

"You want a job? I need a waitress. My last one quit only yesterday. It's yours if you want it."

"You have no idea if I can bus tables or not."

"You seem like a pretty switched-on kid. I'll take my chances. What do you say?"

"I say that would be amazing, but I insist you take this out of my first pay check." I push the plate toward him and pull the milkshake closer.

"I'll see what I can do. Head over after school Monday and I'll get you up to speed in no time."

"Okay, sounds good." A little bit of happiness manages to poke its way into my otherwise miserable existence right now. At least if I have a job, I'll be able to afford to get away from Ethan when he runs me out of town. I shake my head at my thoughts. That asshole isn't going to see the back of me that easily. After the life I've lived, he's barely even a pussycat compared to the lions I've dealt with in the past.

He wants to fight? Bring it on, baby. Bring. It. On.

7

RAELYNN

After securing myself a job and walking along the rest of the promenade, I make my way home. *Home.* I'm not sure this place will ever truly feel like that to me. I know I've only been here a matter of hours, but I feel more like an outsider here than I have in any other place we've lived. I know that's Ethan's fault, and I hate that he has the power to make me feel that way.

Vowing to stand up to him and not allow him to ruin this new start, I begin making my way back to the mansion.

It takes longer than I expect to navigate my way back, but eventually I turn up the street I vaguely recognize as the one I left this morning.

When I get to the top of the hill, the Savage house comes into view and I breathe a sigh of relief. Although it's probably not hot to the locals, I'm melting in this late autumn heat.

The driveway is empty, hinting to the fact I have the house to myself. It's not until I have it confirmed that Ethan's not here that I truly relax. The last thing I need right now is to go up against him again so soon.

I briefly wonder what happened to him but soon chastise myself for even thinking about him. He could have been washed out to sea by the rising tide for all I care.

The house is blissfully silent. Even Rachel seems to have vanished. I have no idea if she lives here or just turns up from time to time or what. After pressing what feels like every single button on the coffee machine, I eventually manage to make myself a huge cup and take it up to my room.

The sun is still on my balcony, so I curl my feet up beneath me on the love seat and stare out into the distance.

My coffee's long gone when I glance down at the glistening pool water beneath me. The temptation to dip my body in that sun-warmed water eventually gets too much as I find myself depositing my dirty mug in the kitchen and heading out.

I don't have a suit, but seeing as I've got the house to myself, I pull my shirt over my head and drop my pants. I glance around, ensuring that I don't have an audience while I'm standing here in my underwear before diving in.

I sigh the second the water hits my skin. It's warm and relaxing, everything I hoped it would be.

I can't remember the last time I went swimming, but I soon find my rhythm as I paddle back and forth, my muscles starting to pull and ache and reminding me that I'm stronger than I think and that I can go up against Ethan asshole Savage.

I have no idea how many lengths I do or how long I'm in the water. All I do know is that my body aches to the point I'm unsure if I'll be able to walk back up to my room and my skin is all wrinkled.

With the sun starting to descend in the sky, I decide it's time to get out before anyone stumbles across me swimming in my underwear, and I slowly climb from the water. The sun kisses my wet skin as I emerge, and it feels incredible. Scooping up my dry clothes and boots, I hold them in front of me, trying not to get them wet, and I run back into the house. I'm just about to step through the door when some movement to my right catches my eye. I stop and stare, expecting someone to be standing there, but there's only a small tree blowing in the light wind. Assuming it must have been that, I head up to my room to shower.

Thankfully, the house is still as silent as it was when I first arrived back, and not wanting to have to deal with anyone, mostly Ethan, I spend the rest of the night locked in my room once I've grabbed a couple of bottles of water from the refrigerator.

Like I do most nights, I toss and turn listening to the sounds of the house around me. What I don't hear at any point is Ethan coming home. My mom and Eric do. She pokes her head in my room to make sure I'm okay but soon disappears to spend time with him after announcing that they're going out of town tomorrow.

That means I'm going to be alone in this house with *him*. Fan-fucking-tastic. I can't wait. That's probably the reason sleep eludes me most of the night.

I must drift off at some point, because I wake with the sun streaming in and the curtains blowing in the light wind.

After visiting my en suite, I grab a bottle of water I didn't drink last night and take it out onto the balcony with me. It's not the coffee I crave, but I need to wake up a little before potentially having to deal with Ethan.

I look out at the view I'm already becoming used to and sit on the edge of the love seat. A splash below catches my attention and I lean over so I can see the pool beneath.

The second I see his muscular body cutting through the water, I freeze. He's got a huge tattoo covering almost his entire back. I squint as he moves, trying to make out the details, but he's going too fast, so instead I focus on how his muscles ripple as he does length after length like a fucking pro. I'm fascinated watching him. I forget all about the person inside the body and lose myself in his repetitive movement as he continues.

I don't realize I've moved and am standing at the railing to get a better look until he comes to a stop at the edge. He must sense my attention, because no sooner has he found his feet is he looking up at me. His hand lifts to push his hair back from his face and I freeze, my breath getting stuck in my throat as our eyes connect. I want to back away, pretend this never happened, but I'm fucking frozen under his stare.

Still holding me captive, he puts his hands on the edge and pulls himself from the pool, revealing his toned and muscular body.

A bolt of lust hits my lower stomach. I can't help it. He's fucking gorgeous. His thick chestnut hair is soaked, and water droplets cover his tanned skin and run down to soak into the waistband of his navy swim shorts, which I now see are clinging to his body and showing me everything he has to offer beneath. Maybe his arrogance is warranted if he's packing in the downstairs department like he appears to be.

When I raise my eyes to his again, he's got a shit-eating grin on his smug-as-fuck face.

Okay, he's got me. He's hot. But the arrogance is such a huge fucking turn off.

He winks before blowing me a kiss. I just about come to my senses in time to flip him off before he disappears from my view.

I fall down onto the seat, my heart pounding and my panties damper than I'd ever want to admit from his little show. I need to remember that he's a massive asshole and not get blindsided by his body.

I'm still trying to rid the images of him from my mind

when my cell pings somewhere in my bedroom. Knowing it can only be Mom, seeing as no one else has my number, I go in search of it.

When I find it at the bottom of my purse surrounded by a few stray coins, hair ties, and a tissue, I pull it out and look at the screen.

Unknown number. I almost throw it back where I found it, thinking it'll be some kind of sales thing, but curiosity gets the better of me and I open it.

> Unknown: You can come and watch me in the shower if that's your thing.

My fingers tighten around my cell to the point of pain. How the fuck did he get my number? And why the fuck does he think I want to watch him shower? My mind runs away with me and I picture his ripped body with water and bubbles making their way south, only this time, there are no shorts.

Damn him.

> Rae: Fuck. You.

The little blue dots start bouncing immediately.

> Unknown: Not a chance, sweet cheeks. Not. A. Chance.

I growl, throwing my cell onto my bed. I shouldn't have responded, but it's too late now and he's found another way to torture me from afar.

He leaves his bedroom not long later, then the house. Eventually, my need for caffeine eventually gets the better of me and I'm forced out of hiding.

I find suitcases lining the hallway when I get down the stairs and I'm reminded that I'm being left here for Christ knows how long.

"Morning, honey," Mom sings when she sees me. "Coffee? Rachel's making pancakes. They are to die for."

"Sounds good." I look toward the stove when I enter the room and smile at Rachel, who's standing there with an apron around her waist and spatula in hand. I'm not sure how I feel about being served food in my own home, or Eric's home at least, but Mom sure doesn't seem to have an issue with it as she sits there and stuffs a chunk of maple syrup-covered pancake in her mouth.

"When are you leaving?" I ask, dropping down at the table opposite her.

"In about an hour. Eric's just popped to his office to take a call."

"And how long are you going for?"

"I'm not sure. Eric's got business in a couple of different states, so we thought we'd make a bit of a vacation out of it, seeing as I've got no work ties now."

"That's nice," I lie. Unfortunately, she sees straight through it.

"You'll be okay here, won't you? Eric's already spoken to Ethan about taking you to school on Monday and getting you settled. I'm sure he'll be around should you have any issues."

"Everything will be fine, Mom."

"I hear he's planning a party for tomorrow night. It'll give you a chance to meet some of his friends. That should make Monday easier, seeing some familiar faces."

"It'll be fine, really." I refrain from pointing out that starting a new school is almost as regular an occurrence as my morning coffee. Although, I must admit that the prospect of a house party fills me with dread. I can't imagine he'll want me attending.

"I've got something for you," she says, reaching for her purse that's sitting on the chair next to her. She rummages around before pulling something out for me and passing it over.

"What's this?"

"A bank card, silly." She shakes her head like I'm an idiot.

"I know what it is, I'm asking why you're giving it to me. I've already got a bank account."

"I know, but Eric wanted you to have this. It's to look after yourself while we're away."

"Mom, I don't want his money." I hold the card out for her to take back, but she just wraps her hand around mine and refuses.

"It's yours. The money in it is yours. Enjoy it, honey. Go and blow some of it on something you've always wanted."

I nod, but I already know that won't be happening.

Mom chats away while we both eat one too many of Rachel's pancakes, but before too long, Eric pokes his head into the room to say that they need to leave.

Mom's practically bouncing on the balls of her feet with the excitement of being able to go traveling with him. A small part of me is happy for her that she's no longer having to work a minimum of two jobs at a time to keep a roof over our heads. I can't help wondering what the cost of it all is, though. While she thinks she's got everything she ever wanted, I'm already drowning in her decision, and it's only been two days.

I spend the day lounging around the pool with my notebook and journal at my side. I found from a young age that if I write down my thoughts, I'm able to work through them better. I'm pretty sure learning that is one of the reasons that my past hasn't screwed me up more than I am. It was only a year or so ago that I got into lyric writing, but I'm becoming more and more obsessed with getting my thoughts down in song form, not just the jumble of words that spew out into my journal.

I get everything down about my move here and try to

make sense of Ethan's behavior, but even writing it all down doesn't help me try to figure him out.

I tap my pen against my notebook as I attempt to put the words I just poured into my journal to lyrics.

I don't get a chance to come up with anything, because the sound of a car pulling up in the driveway and then a door slamming has me sitting up straight in the lounger.

"Shit," I mutter. I had every intention of being locked in my room when he got home from school, but looking at my cell, it seems I lost track of time.

I quickly gather everything up and run toward the door, hoping that he might stop off at the kitchen on his way to his room. Sadly, I'm not so lucky. As I race down the hallway toward the stairs, he steps out of the home gym, staring at his cell, and I collide right into him. Both of the books in my hand go skidding across the tiled floor, along with my cell and two empty bottles with a half-full glass of water. It shatters at his feet after colliding with his chest, soaking his shirt.

"For fuck's sake," he barks. My eyes fly to his, and I retreat a little at the anger within them. He runs his palms over his stomach, trying to dry it off. Realizing it's a little too late for that, he reaches behind his head and pulls his shirt up and off in one swift move.

My eyes take on a mind of their own and drop from his to take in his sculpted body up close. If anything, it's even more defined than I thought it to be from a distance this morning.

He takes a step forward, and I don't have a choice but to take one back if I don't want him crashing into me. Sadly, instead of connecting with him, I do with the wall instead.

My eyes meet his as he continues to close the space between us.

His are full of hunger, but not the kind that excites me. The kind that terrifies me.

"You seem to like looking at my naked skin."

"I... I..." *Fuck*. I hate that he's turned me into a stuttering mess with his closeness.

"You want me?" He holds his arms out to the sides like he's offering himself up to me. But I already know him better than that.

"N-no."

"Really? Because that's not what your eyes are telling me. Or your nipples."

I look down despite the fact that I know that I put a padded bra on this morning and there's no way he'll be able to tell what kind of state my nipples are in right now.

His amused laugh has me looking back up at him. My lips are pressed into a thin line and my pulse thunders in frustration in my neck so hard I've no doubt that he can see it.

"Fuck you, Ethan. I wouldn't want you if you were the last man on Earth."

"Is that right?" He tilts his head to the side and lets his eyes drop from mine in favor of my body. Thank fuck for that padded bra, because the second his gaze lands on my breasts, they pebble beneath the fabric. Traitorous fucking body. "Because I wouldn't touch you with someone else's, sweet cheeks. Now." He leans forward once again, his scent filling my nose, and my mouth waters. He smells like weed, beach, and man. It's a heady mixture. "Pick up your shit and get out of my fucking way." His hand slams down on the wall next to my head and I gasp in surprise.

An evil smile curls at his lips. "You're too fucking easy, you know that? We're going to have so much fun, you and me."

"Is that another threat? Because I won't bow down to you."

"No, it's a promise, trailer trash. And don't worry about bowing, because you'll already be on your fucking knees with my cock in your mouth."

He steps back, accomplishment written all over his annoyingly handsome face while I stand with my mouth open in shock. Did he really just say that to me? I mean, I've heard plenty worse, but still, does he really think this is how it's going to go between us?

I'm too stunned by his words to notice him reach down and pick up my journal until he speaks.

"Aw how cute. The trailer trash writes a diary about how pathetic her life is." He flips through it, and I panic. There are things written on those pages that I wouldn't even want my best friend reading, let alone my worst enemy.

I launch myself at him, trying to snatch it out of his hands, but being the asshole he is, he holds it high above his head and well out of my reach.

I'm pretty sure there's nothing more irritating to deal with being short than someone forcing you to jump like an idiot to get something that belongs to you.

"You're a fucking asshole," I bark, jumping again and hoping like hell I make some kind of contact. When I'm still miles away, I decide on another tactic. One that will be much more fulfilling for me.

I stop jumping around and stand in front of him, holding his eye contact.

"You think you're so fucking clever, don't you?"

He shrugs. "I have my moments, sure."

"You're not going to beat me, Ethan. You picked the wrong girl to go to war with."

"Is that right?"

I spot the moment he forgets about what he was doing and focuses too much on what I'm going to say next. I use his distraction to my advantage and swiftly lift my knee until it connects with his balls.

He grunts, bending forward and dropping my journal to the floor. "Fucking bitch," he whines as all his breath leaves him and he bends over in pain, dropping to his knees.

"Now who's on their knees, *bitch*."

He growls, but he's unable to do anything other than breathe through the pain as I collect up my stuff, leaving the glass in shards on the floor for him to deal with.

"Clean up the mess you made, won't you?"

8

ETHAN

Tears burn my eyes as pain radiates from my groin.

Fucking bitch.

I should have seen it coming really, and I feel like an idiot for leaving myself open to her abuse. She might show signs of fear every now and then, but she could well be right when she says that I've chosen the wrong girl to mess with, because there's something dark in her eyes. Something haunts her, stops her being afraid when she really should be. I intend on finding out exactly what it is. If I find her vice then I can use it against her to get what I want: my family back, not that bullshit one my dad is trying to palm me off with.

When I eventually get back to my feet, I stumble my way up the stairs and to my room. I hesitate at her door, but, still feeling the effects of our last encounter, I decide against now being the time to get my revenge.

Instead, I head for the shower and to change, ready to head to Zayn's to hang out with the guys.

It's been a long fucking week and I'm ready to chill the fuck out with some booze, weed, and pussy. My body relaxes at the thought alone.

With my hair still wet from my shower. I slide my feet into my sneakers and pull my door open. I'm expecting to find the hallway empty and her hiding in her room, but the sight of her leaning against her door jamb startles me a little.

Her eyes stare at mine and then drop down my body once again. She can try and act the innocent with me all she likes, but her body screams that she wants me. A smirk curls at my lips.

"I'm fine, thanks for asking."

"I wasn't."

"Right, well. I'm out; you're not invited."

"Did I ask to be?"

"No, but even if you did, the answer would be no."

"Awesome."

I take two steps past her when she says my name.

"What?" I bark, already over this little... whatever the fuck it is.

"You got any weed?"

"Yeah, plenty. The fucking good stuff, too. Thanks for asking."

I look over my shoulder. Her next question is right on the tip of her tongue—I can practically see it. But the second she realizes I'm looking at her, she locks it down.

"Have a good night," she says instead, turning back into her room and slamming the door on me. My fists clench at how easily she thinks she can hide from me.

With a shake of my head, I leave both her and thoughts of her behind.

The guys are already at Zayn's, seeing as they all went straight from practice. I, on the other hand, thought it would be a good idea to go home first. What a fucking stupid idea that was. My balls are still aching now. Readjusting myself as I walk up toward his front door, my mouth waters in preparation for what I'm hoping to find inside.

Zayn's house is smaller than mine—but then that's not hard, seeing as my dad owns one of the largest in the town—but it's still a decent size. Ignoring most of the rooms, I head toward the back of the house where Zayn's den is. It consists of a giant flat screen, surround sound, and enough couches and beanbags for the entire team and a few chicks. Just perfect for tonight.

The guys are already lounging around with bottles of beer in their hands when I walk in. Someone almost immediately throws one to me that I just about catch at the last minute.

"Where the fuck's the pussy? We're division champs—I thought they'd already be sucking you all off," I say, falling down onto an empty couch.

"Probably gone home to shave, with a bit of luck," someone says from behind me.

I look around at the guys I consider my family, and it's immediately obvious that two people are missing. I never thought the presence of two people could make that much difference, but without Jake and Mason here, it's like two of our puzzle pieces are missing. We're no longer a whole unit, and I hate it more than I care to admit. It almost feels like being at home. There's a massive piece missing there too, although the two in its place most definitely don't fit the gaps.

I drain the first bottle of beer and have made a good start on the second when the sound of the door shutting and the clicking of heels filters down to us.

Thank fuck for that. I love the guys, but sadly they're unable to scratch the itch I've currently got.

Being the vice-captain of the squad, Shelly leads her girls in. I don't get a chance to see who follows her, because the second our eyes connect, she makes a beeline for me. Shelly's been my go-to girl for a while now. She's a nice girl, unlike some of the others. Although she'll still open her legs at the drop of a hat, she is a little more selective of who she gets with.

As far as I know, since she started hooking up with me, she's not been with any of the other guys. At least not that anyone's admitted to, anyway.

"Hey, gorgeous," she purrs, shedding her cropped leather jacket and leaving it in a pile on the floor as she hikes her dress up and climbs onto my lap with her knees on either side of my hips.

"It's nice to see you too."

She's wearing a black halterneck dress that's cut low on her chest, giving me one hell of a view. Her tits aren't all that big. Ideally, I'd probably like a little more to play with, but I'm not one to complain when they're thrust right in my face like they are now. Unfortunately, I can't help comparing them to another slightly larger pair I've seen recently, although covered in clothing. The thought pisses me off to the point I consider removing Shelly from my lap. But knowing I need this distraction if I'm ever going to get her out of my head, I leave her be, grinding down on my semi.

Her lips go to my neck as she continues. Everyone chats around us and like always, ignores what we're up to. This kind of activity is the norm around this group. None of us could be accused of being a prude, that's for sure.

It's not until someone clears their throat that I pay all that much attention to what's going on around me. When I look up to the entrance to the room, I find someone who is very much not used to our little get-togethers.

Noah.

He's got his arm wrapped around Tasha's shoulders as he looks around at all of us, the muscles in his shoulders pulled tight as he tries to figure out if coming here was the right thing to do, no doubt. Shane is standing behind him, looking a little more comfortable, but this isn't really his scene either. He's never come to hang with us before. Although he's part of the team, he's made it his mission to stay as far away as possible.

"You guys don't mind, right?" Tasha asks, walking into the room like she belongs. She does, I guess. She's one of us. Well, she was until she decided to steal Noah right from beneath Camila's feet.

"The more the merrier," Zayn says, slapping Justin on the shoulder to shift up a bit to allow Shane to sit.

The atmosphere in the room changes instantly. It goes from being easygoing and relaxed to everyone sitting a little straighter and watching what they say.

"You got any weed, baby?" Shelly whispers in my ear, dragging my eyes away from Noah, who looks a bit like he's about to shit his pants, being surrounded by us. I guess he should have thought about that before sticking his cock in a cheerleader instead of his girlfriend at the time. I guess I can't be all that mad at the guy—it meant that Mason got what he's wanted since he knew what a vagina was in the form of Camila.

"Does a bear shit in the woods?"

Shelly's eyebrows pull together. "Uh..."

"Yes, I've got some," I say, putting her out of her misery when her confusion at my question only gets worse.

Lifting her up a little, I slip my hand in my pocket and pull out everything I'm going to need to roll us a joint.

"Take that shit outside, Savage," Zayn barks, noticing what I'm up to. Rolling my eyes at him, I place Shelly down on her feet and we head for the door. That's the one issue with this house: the hard no smoking inside rule.

I pull out two of Zayn's garden chairs and fall down into one, watching Shelly do the same. Flicking my lighter, I light the joint and put it to my lips. The first hit is like fucking heaven as I feel some of the tension locking up my muscles drift away. I forget about Dad and his new hussy, I forget about school and the upcoming playoff game. I just focus on the here and now. Almost.

I pass it over to her and watch as she takes a long pull.

"It's nice out here, eh?" She makes a show of glancing around at the pool area that's covered in twinkling lights.

"I guess." To be honest, I don't really give a shit where I am right now. My only focus is to forget.

I rest my head back and look up at the clear sky. The stars twinkle above me and everything washes from my mind.

Needing another hit, I drag my head forward and look to the girl in front of me. I find Shelly has propped her foot up on my chair, her legs spread wide open, showing me exactly what she's not wearing beneath.

My eyes focus on her pussy, and I bite down on my bottom lip as I wait to see what she's going to do. Her chest heaves as she tries to read me. Her eyes bounce between mine, but she's going to be disappointed if she thinks simply opening her legs is going to get me moving tonight.

She must eventually realize that I'm not all that impressed, because she lifts the fingers of her free hand to her mouth, sucks on them for a second and drops them down between her legs.

I can't lie. The sight of her playing with herself before me does stir a little excitement within me, and my cock begins to swell. The more I stare at her, the more I start to imagine her pussy and her fingers belonging to someone else. Someone much more closed off, someone much less willing to put this kind of show on for me.

"Fuck," I bark, startling Shelly, her fingers pausing as her eyes narrow on mine, probably wondering what the fuck's wrong with me. On a usual night, I'd be all over what she's offering, but I just can't find it in me right now to want to.

"What's up, baby? Was practice that tiring?"

"No, I..." I have no idea what my excuse is. I should be on my knees with my head between her thighs, but right now, it just feels wrong.

When I make no move to touch her, she pulls her hand away and stands. She unties the knot behind her neck and allows the fabric covering her tits to fall to her waist.

"I know you're more of a boob man." She cups herself, standing only inches from me, and her head falls back as she pinches her nipples. "You know, Ethan, you've never fucked me outside before. I think maybe tonight is the night, under the twinkling stars. It's so romantic."

"I don't do romance," I bark, keeping my eyes on what she's doing to herself because she's not wrong. I'd do pretty much anything for a good pair of tits. *These aren't the ones you want,* a little voice says in my head. I shake it out, trying to focus on the here and now, because although my head's not in the game, I really could do with the release she's offering me.

She leans forward, her hands pushing my hair from my face and angling my head so she can kiss me. When her lips drop to mine, I don't push her away. I want to want this. I want her to distract me from my crazy thoughts and make me want to fuck her into next week. It's what I need. What my body craves. But still, I don't react the way I want.

She pulls away, kissing across my neck, her hand dropping down over my abs until she rubs at my cock over the fabric of my pants.

"Come on, Ethan. Where's my big boy, huh?" she purrs in my ear, and it's the final straw. I stand with such force that she stumbles back, landing on her ass with a thud.

"Shit, I'm sorry." When I glance up, I notice that we've got an audience. Or more, Shelly's tits do, as half the team are staring at her as she sits there, exposing herself. I hold my hand out for her and pull her from the ground. "Cover up. You look like a dirty slut." With that said, I storm around the side of Zayn's house and down his driveway.

9

RAELYNN

Assuming I'm going to have the house to myself seeing as Ethan went off to his little party, I run myself a bath in the hope that it'll do something about my tense muscles and spend the evening watching shit on TV.

It's heading toward midnight when I switch it off and attempt to get some sleep. I'm lying in the dark with only the silent house for company when there's a crash outside.

I sit up, straining to hear if there's someone out there. It goes silent again before the unmistakable sound of the front door slamming rings out.

Fuck.

As I sit with my heart trying to beat out of my chest, I debate whether a burglar or Ethan returning would be more preferable. It comes to something when you'd rather face a criminal than your possible future stepbrother.

There's a crash, and then another.

I swing my legs from my bed and search for a weapon in case I need it. My eyes land on the bunch of flowers in a vase that I assume Rachel thought I might like, and I walk over. I pull the flowers out and throw the water over the balcony before heading over to my door. As silently as I can, I slip out and make my way toward the noise.

I creep down the stairs, noting that none of the lights are on.

If this is a guy robbing the place, then I probably shouldn't be heading his way with only a vase as a weapon.

Shaking the voice from my head, I continue down until I get to a doorway where I think the noise is coming from. There's another almighty crash followed by an angry growl.

Pushing the door wider, I tiptoe inside, raising the vase above my head. The guy's dressed all in black with a hood up over his head.

I'm just about to launch it at him when he turns. A familiar pair of blue eyes find mine a milli-second before my arms follow through with their intent.

Thankfully, Ethan is quicker and manages to stop the vase from connecting with his face, sending it crashing to the floor.

"What the fuck do you think you're doing?" he roars, his voice slightly slurred, possibly explaining why he was down here fucking this room up in the dark.

His hands slam down on my shoulder and I stumble back, tripping over something in the process and finally colliding with the wall. My head slams back against it, making the room go a little hazy and my eyes pool with water.

When I eventually pull them open, he's right in front of me, breathing down on me with his teeth bared.

"This is all your fault," he seethes. His voice is so menacingly quiet it sends a shiver of terror through me. We're alone in this huge house, he's drunk, and I stupidly left my phone upstairs.

"Me?"

"Yes, you." We're toe to toe. Our faces only inches apart. I can smell the alcohol and weed on him. It makes my mouth water for a taste and a hit of my own instead of the water I've been drinking all night. "You are ruining everything. Everywhere I go, there you are. Everywhere I turn. There you fucking are. Even tonight. There you fucking were."

"I-I haven't been anywhere tonight," I say, confused by his comment.

"You're in fucking here," he spits, poking his finger into his temple. "Fucking tormenting me. Driving me fucking crazy."

I open my mouth to respond, but when I realize I've got no words I quickly close it again.

"You're going to fuck everything up for me. I. Need. You. Gone."

His hand lifts, his fingers taking my chin with a painful grip and forcing me to look up at him.

"You hear me, trash?" I swallow, not able to speak when he's holding me so tight. "But you're not going to fucking leave, are you?" His eyes are wild as he stares into mine. It's a look I've experienced before, and I know nothing good can come of it. "So what am I going to do about it?"

I don't know if he realizes he's having a conversation with himself, but I don't point it out. Instead, I just hope that the little voice in his head will have some reason in a minute and let me go.

Thankfully, after a few seconds, he does. But not so I can run. Instead, his hands find the top of my tank and in one swift move the worn, thin fabric practically melts under his touch.

My hands fly up to cover my breasts, but I don't get anywhere near before his fingers are around both of my wrists and they're lifted above my head. My back arches and the fabric that was still half covering my tits falls to the side.

His eyes hold mine for a beat before they drop. A smile pulls at the corner of his lips.

"At least there is something worthwhile about you, I guess."

"Ethan please, don't," I whimper, chastising myself for sounding weak and vulnerable when all I want to be is strong and in control of the situation. So what, he's looking at my rack? I'm sure he's seen plenty before.

My chest heaves as I try to get control of my racing heart and he eats it up. I'm playing right into the palm of his hands and giving him exactly what he wants. My fear.

"I wonder how you taste." He lowers down and looks from one nipple to the other, then up at me through his lashes.

Fuck, I hate to admit it, but with desire swimming in his eyes, I can't help but want him to lean forward and find out. My nipples harden as my core floods. I hate myself even more for the reaction, but I can't help it.

Here, in the dark with him almost hidden in the shadows and looking sexy and as dangerous as hell, I can't help my imagination running away with me, even though at the same time, I'm desperate for him to release me so I can go running back to my room.

He closes the space between us. His tongue sneaks out and flicks my tight bud. My entire body flinches with the contact and sparks shoot toward my clit, making it ache.

"Ethan." I intend for it to be a warning, but even I can admit that it comes out sounding needy as fuck.

I barely have time to blink and he's leaning forward once more, only this time he sucks me into his hot mouth, his tongue circling around me, making me crave more. My hands pull against my restraint, but he doesn't let up. He switches to the other side and I cry out despite fighting like hell to keep it in.

What the fuck is he playing at? Is this how he intends to ruin me? With pleasure?

His hands shift but only so he can free one of his own. He

continues pinning both of mine above my head, ensuring he has full access to my breasts, which he continues torturing.

My panties are soaked with my need for more, and the more he sucks, nips and licks, the worse the situation gets.

"Fuck. Ethan. Fuck, please?" I'm not aware of the words as they fall from my mouth, but the second I realize I'm begging for more, color stains my cheeks.

I shouldn't want anything from this asshole, yet here I am after one touch from him, sounding like a desperate whore.

"You want more, sweet cheeks?"

"Ethan," I cry when he bites down on my nipple.

"How close do you think I can get you to the edge? I'm going to watch you climb, make you think your release is in touching distance, and then I'm going to ruin it all, just like you have my fucking life. Is that what you want?" His words blur, the blood rushing past my ears and the desire coursing through me meaning I make no sense of them.

"Yes," I pant. "Yes."

His free hand brushes the sensitive skin of my stomach before it disappears inside my sleep shorts, his fingers parting me and finding my clit almost instantly.

"Fucking hell, I knew you wanted me," he groans as if he's in pain when he discovers just how wet I am.

"Oh god," I moan as he pinches my clit between his fingers before diving deeper and finding my entrance.

"Oh no, baby. I'm not God, I'm the motherfucking Devil."

Ain't that the truth. A bitter laugh falls from my lips as he pushes two fingers inside me.

"Jesus," he grunts, and I can only assume that's a good thing.

With his thumb pushed against my clit and his fingers bent inside me, I'm racing toward a mind-blowing release in seconds.

He pulls back from my breast and watches me. I want to

tell him to look away, but I don't have it in me as I fall headfirst into—nothing. Wait, what?

I drag my eyelids open, not knowing when they even shut, to find Ethan backing away from me. My arms drop to my sides, my muscles aching where they'd been pinned in position for so long.

Ethan's amused yet hungry eyes hold mine as he lifts his hand and sucks his fingers into his mouth. My imminent release makes itself known once again, my muscles pulling tight as I watch his eyes roll back in pleasure.

"I've tasted sweeter." His eyes drop from mine to take me in, only this time I'm able to cover myself.

"I fucking hate you," I spit, but his only response is a wicked smile that plays on his lips.

I watch as he steps over the mess of the shattered vase along with whatever it was that he sent crashing to the ground before I walked in on him.

"Clean up the mess you made, won't you?" he says, repeating our words from earlier before he disappears from my sight.

The sound of his footsteps pounding up the stairs fills my ears as I slide down the wall until my ass hits the floor.

My body shudders with the coldness he left behind now that all the adrenaline has left my body. My core throbs with my need for a release, and my body trembles with the knowledge of what I just let him do to me.

I shouldn't have allowed it to get that far. I shouldn't have allowed him to take that much from me.

I'm unable to keep in the tears that burn my eyes, and I sob on the floor of his den until my eyes sting and my ass goes beyond numb.

10

ETHAN

I slam my bedroom door with such force that I'm surprised it isn't falling from its hinges when I look back over my shoulder.

I pull my hoodie and t-shirt over my head in one fell swoop and quickly add my pants and boxers to the pile as I storm toward my shower. My rock-hard cock bobs in front of me, taunting me, reminding me what I just left behind downstairs. It's the exact reaction I should have had to Shelly, but the one that didn't appear until I turned around and found *her* wielding a fucking glass vase and about to smash it over my head. I guess I can't really blame her; I was walking around in the dark, smashing shit up.

After marching from Zayn's, I stopped in a store who believe my fake ID and always serve me whatever the fuck I want, and I got myself a bottle of whiskey. I spent the whole walk home drinking the fucking thing. By the time I got back here, my head was spinning and I was angry beyond belief with both myself and the way my life is right now. The last thing I needed was her, but there she was, and before I knew what the fuck I was doing, I had her backed up against the wall with her perfect fucking tits in my face.

I shouldn't have touched her, I know that. I *knew* that. Even with the whiskey racing through my system. But I couldn't help myself. The fear in her eyes called to me. Her rosebud fucking nipples called out to me. I should have walked away like I did from Shelly. But unlike with Shelly, my cock was fucking rock hard and the only thing I could think about was how fucking sweet she'd taste. And fuck if she wasn't even sweeter than I could have possibly imagined.

My mouth waters, the taste of her still on my tongue. I picture what it might be like to have my head between her thighs and get the sweetness straight from the source. My cock aches with the thought, but as I step under the shower, I refuse to do anything about it. I tell myself it's punishment for being so weak tonight. My only saving grace is that she's just about as blue balled as me right now, seeing as I left her right on the brink of orgasm like the total fucking asshole I am.

I stand with my face tipped up toward the showerhead and allow it to rain down over me. It does little to cool the fire raging in my body, even when I turn it to ice cold.

My cock's still rock hard when I step out and wrap a towel around my waist. As I walk through my bedroom, I kick my pants out of the way. The top of my foot connects with the corner of my cell, and I curse in pain. But it gives me an idea.

Pulling it from my pocket, I find our conversation.

> Ethan: Don't even think about finishing yourself off. You're mine now.

I expect her to reply, telling me where to go almost instantly, but the message doesn't even show as read. In the end, I get fed up waiting, and, with the amount of whiskey I'd consumed, I pass out naked on my bed.

———

When I wake the next morning, it's with a pounding head, my body soaked in sweat, and my heart racing from the dream I was in the middle of. A dream I need to forget about as soon as humanly possible. I don't need any more crazy ideas in my head about what could have happened last night had I not walked away when I did. I shouldn't have touched her. I knew before I even laid a finger on her that she was out of bounds, but I couldn't help myself.

"Motherfucker," I curse into my pillow, replaying the events of the previous night in my head. What was wrong with Shelly? She'd have scratched my itch perfectly fine. Why couldn't I have just used her like I usually do and stayed the night at Zayn's, passed out on his couch?

The doorbell ringing through the house eventually drags my ass out of bed. I wait long enough in case she decides to go and answer it, but when I hear no movement, I'm forced to go myself.

I stare at her door as I pass, wishing I could see inside to know if she's in there and hiding from me or if she's run. The sensible thing to do would most definitely be the latter.

Pulling the front door open, I find a guy standing there with my alcohol delivery for tonight's celebratory party. We won the fucking division. I should be pumped right now. Our first playoff game is next Friday night. That trophy we've all coveted for so long is almost in touching distance, yet I can't seem to rid myself of the anger, the hate that seems to have taken over every inch of my body.

I point the delivery guy in the direction of the kitchen and walk down the hallway to the doors that lead to the garden while he does his thing.

At first glance, it's empty, but after a few seconds, I realize that the ripples in the water aren't that of an empty pool.

Standing back behind the curtains so I'm out of sight, I watch as she makes her way across from one side to the other. It's not the first time I've watched her. I couldn't help myself when I got back on Thursday afternoon. Wanting to see what she was hiding under her clothes had me loitering in the bush like a fucking creep. It was fucking worth it, mind you.

With the guy unloading bottles behind me, I continue to stare, willing her to climb out so I can get another look at her banging little body. Not five minutes later do I get my wish, only it's better than I could have imagined. My lingering hangover immediately vanishes as other aches and desires erupt in my body. This time, she's not wearing her underwear, but a white tank that's gone totally see-through and a tiny pair of panties. My cock's instantly hard for her once again. The sight before me mixes with my memories from last night of her pleading with me to let her go.

Rubbing myself through the soft fabric of my sweatpants, an idea forms.

"See yourself out when you're done, man," I call to the guy in the kitchen before running up the stairs and pushing her bedroom door open.

I still the second I'm inside, because unlike last time, this room now smells of her. I jump onto her bed and look at the stack of books sitting on her nightstand. Each spine has a different year written on it. I go for one in the middle and pull it out. Resting back against her pillows, I flip it open to a random page and stare down at her writing. It's more feminine that I'd have imagined, and I can't help but smile when I turn the page again and find it written in pink. She really is a mysterious one, my new housemate.

Dear Diary,

Today's been great. Kurt took me out to buy some new clothes. I got the jeans I've wanted forever and the sneakers Mom said we couldn't afford.

I don't get a chance to read any more, because the sound of her footsteps out in the hall has me looking toward the door.

Seconds later, she's pushing it open. She doesn't spot me right away as she throws the towel in her hand into the corner of the room and peels her soaking wet tank up her body. She reveals her smooth skin and tiny waist. Her hair, as always, is tied up. She reaches up and pulls the band that's holding it hostage. It falls down her back like a wet curtain.

Unable to take the ache in my solid length as it presses against the fabric, I reach down in the hope of relieving it, but as I do, I must make more noise than I was expecting, because she turns.

Our eyes lock and she screams in fright before bringing her hands up to cover her chest.

"Get the fuck out of my room, Ethan." She glances down at what's in my hands, and more fear than I've witnessed from her before creeps into her eyes.

"That's not a very nice way to welcome a guest."

"You're not a fucking guest. You're not welcome in here."

"My house. I do what I like."

"Get. Out."

"Not until I get what I came in here for."

"And what's that exactly?"

I pause, because other than to torment her a little more, I didn't really come in here for anything specific. I run my eyes down her body that's now starting to shiver from the morning breeze coming from the window.

"Strip," I order.

"W-what?" An unamused laugh falls from her lips as her eyes widen in shock.

"What? It's not like you're really wearing much anyway. It won't make all that much difference."

Her teeth grind, her face going beet red with her anger as she tries to decide what to do. I can see that she wants to fight, but surely she must know it's only going to get worse for her if she does. The best thing she can do right now is exactly as I say.

"Come on, sweet cheeks. I already know what it tastes like. Might as well give me the whole experience."

Still, she stands there like a fucking deer in headlights. Dropping my gaze, I go back to her diary.

"I thought only silly little girls wrote diaries. I'm starting to wonder if I got you all wrong, trailer trash."

"Ethan, please."

"Please what? Please touch you again? Please finish you off from last night? I hope you took my warning seriously and didn't immediately finish yourself off after I left," I say, having a flashback to the text I sent her. The blush that's already staining her cheeks travels down to her chest. "Maybe I should get you to do it now. Give me a nice little show to start my day off with."

"Please, just leave." Her voice cracks, and it makes me realize just how hard she's going to be to break.

"Where was I? *Dear Diary,*" I mock. "*He took me for ice cream. Not the cheap kind Mom insists on, but the kind that comes in every flavor imaginable. I had toffee, he had chocolate. I regretted my decision when I saw the chocolate chips in his, but he let me try some.* I bet you had a good old lick, didn't you, you dirty bitch."

All the color's drained from her face when I glance up from her stupid diary.

"If it'll make you leave, fine." She shoves her thumbs into

the sides of her panties and shimmies out of them until they're around her ankles. She holds her hands out to the sides, trying like hell to appear confident while completely bared to me.

I take her in, every single curve, hair, and dimple. I can't deny that, although short as fuck, she's got all the right things in all the right places.

Placing her diary back on the stack beside me, I push myself to the end of her bed. My eyes stay locked on her body. On her full tits and rosebud nipples that are just begging for attention. I run my eyes down her smooth stomach as I focus on the small strip of hair that leads to what I know is a hot and tight little pussy.

Her body trembles before me, but I'm not sure if it's with the chill or terror.

I stand, dropping my head so I can stare down at her. A smirk pulls at one side of my lips. "Until next time, sweet cheeks."

I leave her standing stock still, but I don't close her door behind me. The thing irritates me. Not knowing what she's doing behind it drives me insane.

The second I'm in my room, I pull on a clean shirt and hoodie and drop my phone and wallet into my pocket before turning on my heels and marching straight out of the house. There's no way I can stay here knowing exactly what's right across the hall.

I could call an Uber, but I decide to walk the distance back to Zayn's to pick up my car. The time alone with only my thoughts might help clear my head. Now I'm away from her, my temples continue to pound with last night's alcohol, but still, I can't get her out of my head. The darkness of her eyes as she stared into mine, silently begging me not to hurt her. I must be doing a better job of scaring her than I thought if she's worried about me physically hurting her. I'd never hit a woman, and even she falls under that bracket. I may want to hurt her in other ways, but I'll never raise a hand to her.

I don't feel that much better by the time I walk up Zayn's drive. The only difference is that my cock's no longer trying to punch its way through my sweats. I don't bother going inside, knowing that it'll only invite questions about where I fucked off to last night when I had Shelly offering herself to me, quite literally. I have no intention of talking to any of those motherfuckers about what my issue is right now.

Jake, Mason, and their girls know the truth. Even telling them was hard enough. I'm happy to let everyone else think whatever the fuck they want as to my current state of mind and almost permanent pissed-off attitude.

Sliding into my car, I rest my head back and shut my eyes. My life is spinning out of control right now and I have no idea how I'm supposed to rein it back in. I need to stay away from her, that much is obvious, but I'm not sure I can. She's like that one thing in your house as a kid that you're warned never to touch, but no matter how wrong you know it is, you just can't resist.

Pulling my cell from my pocket, I find Jake and shoot him a message.

Ethan: Gym?

The little dots start bouncing, and in about thirty seconds I stare down at the response I was expecting.

Thorn: Can't. Doing house shit with Brit.

"Fuck," I bark, my hands slamming down on my steering wheel. It's always been the three of us. Jake, Mason, and me. But since things got serious with Amalie and Camila, it seems our party of three has almost immediately reduced to a lonely party of one. And exactly when I need them most.

Some movement from inside Zayn's catches my eye. I could go in there and invite one of whoever's left to join me, but it's not the same. Yes, they're my family, but they're not my brothers, not like Jake and Mason. I open up another conversation that I've been waiting for a reply on. When I look down at my last message I sent her, it shows as read. I blow out a breath, wondering if she's okay and getting the time out that she needs.

Deciding to send her another message, seeing as I could do with someone to talk to as much as I'm sure she could, I start typing.

> Ethan: I'm here if you need to talk x

I stare at it, but it doesn't even show as delivered.

"Fuck it." I pocket my cell, put my car in reverse, and drive toward the gym I try to hit up a couple of times a week. I've got a pretty kitted out gym at home, but the wider range of equipment, along with the steam room and sauna, drag me here. It's exactly what I need as I try to work through my issues. It also means I'm away from her, away from the temptation of doing something stupid again.

I work myself in the gym until I can't feel my limbs, then I drag my aching body to the sauna to sweat out the alcohol that's probably still in my system from the previous weeks' blowouts. Tonight should be fucking epic, and I need to be ready for it. I also need to figure out a way to keep her away. The last thing I need is her attempting to befriend mine, not that I think for a minute she'd fit in with them. I'm sure the cheer squad will take one look at her and turn the other cheek. She doesn't exactly scream joy and happiness, more dark, edgy, and will likely shank you in your sleep if you so much as look at her the wrong way.

I grab some food on my way home and then, despite the fact I only just showered at the gym, I have another and get ready for tonight.

Her door is shut, as usual, and the house is in silence. I have no idea if she's here or not, but I decide against finding out. I need to focus on tonight, on celebrating our epic win, getting drunk and having fun. The last thing I need is thoughts of her ruining it for me. We worked our asses off for that win, and we deserve to let our hair down before the craziness of the playoffs start next week.

I spray myself with my favorite cologne, run some gel through my hair, and pull on my lucky shirt. I tell myself that last night's disaster with Shelly was a one-off and that I'll be fully on board with any female who so much as looks my way tonight.

I've just done a lap of the house to make sure everything is as it should be before the crunch of car tires on the driveway sounds out.

Pulling the door open, I find cars everywhere and kids from school heading toward the house.

Almost all of them stop and greet me with a slap on the back or a slug to the shoulder. Some bring their own supplies, just to be polite, but everyone knows I'll have more than enough alcohol inside for everyone who arrives. They all walk in, assuming everything is the same. Little do they know that everything under this roof is very different from the last time they were here. Fuck, I'm different, thanks to our two new lodgers. The anger that's constantly burning away inside of me turns me into a person I don't like, but there doesn't seem to be much I can do about it, especially as *she* seems to be there, no matter which direction I turn.

The house fills up, someone turns the music on, and

everyone gets to it. I want to say their merriment is infectious, but it's not. I force a smile on my face and head to the kitchen for a drink.

Alcohol of every variety fills the counters. One good thing in all this bullshit is that Dad upped the spend on my credit card. I don't really want his guilt money, but I'd rather have my friends piss it down the toilet to fuck him off than not use it, I guess.

Most of the team are huddled together, some with girls clinging to their sides. The cheer team hasn't arrived yet, so it gives the others who are brave enough a chance.

"Hey, gorgeous," a girl purrs, coming up to me and running her hands up my chest until they lock around the back of my neck.

"Hey, I don't think I've had the pleasure of meeting you before." She's got bright red hair and wide hazel eyes.

"You're Ethan Savage, right?"

"The one and only, sweetheart."

A salacious smile curls up at her lips. "I've heard all about you and your... talents." She runs her tongue over her bottom lip, and I eagerly watch its movements before dropping down her body. She's wearing a small top that shows off both the swell of her tits and her stomach before a scrap of fabric wraps around her hips, barely covering her modesty. Something I can most definitely work with.

"Oh yeah?" I ask, stepping a little closer and wrapping my arm around her waist. Her sweet scent fills my nose. It's not unpleasant, but it's not exactly enticing, either. She smiles at me, pushing her tits into my chest. "Play your cards right and you might get to find out tonight."

She leans in, her lips brushing the shell of my ear. "I'll let you do whatever you like," she all but moans.

My cock stirs at the thought, but only a little, and I'm

pretty sure only because it's still after what was in touching distance last night.

I used to live for these shameless hussies who do anything on demand just because we're the kings of Rosewood High, but suddenly, I'm not finding the same appeal as I once did. A little voice in my head tells me I didn't have a problem until *she* turned up.

Anger races through me. She's ruining my fucking life, and she's not even here right now.

"How about we get a drink and talk more about that? I'd love to know what you can do for me."

11

RAELYNN

The second he walks through my bedroom door, I slam it shut behind him and pull the dresser in front of it to stop him from coming back.

My body is trembling from the memories he dragged up from just reading that small snippet of my diary. Why I thought leaving them on my nightstand was a good idea God only knows.

Racing over, I lift all but the one I'm currently writing in and spin. I don't exactly have anywhere I can hide them, but at least they'll be out of immediate sight if—when—he returns. I shove the whole stack into the ottoman at the end of my bed and close the lid, hoping it'll help to lock down the nightmares that are contained within those pages.

A cold shiver runs through me as a few flashbacks hit me. Ethan will never find out about the horrors that are written in there. If he were to find out—no, I'm not even going there.

Picking up my wet, discarded clothes, I throw them into the laundry and head for the shower to wash away not only the chlorine but also the shame of what Ethan just made me do. I try not to dwell on it, but it's there, tingling at my spine.

I turn the shower up as hot as I can bear and stand under it, hoping to wash away everything from both last night and this morning. It doesn't matter that this is my second shower, plus a dip in the pool, since he touched me last night; I can still smell him as if he's standing right next to me.

All I want to do is keep my head down and do what I need to do here before I can graduate and move on. I've got no intention of making his life harder than I'm sure it's already been, seeing as his dad just left his mom for mine. Both of us have been caught up in the crossfire of their drama, and as far as I'm concerned, neither of us deserves it, but it's exactly where we've found ourselves. Unfortunately for me, I'm the one Ethan seems to be firing all his arrows at.

The sight of all the bottles covering every surface in the kitchen when I eventually emerge from my bedroom has my stomach in knots. The last thing I want is an enforced house party. Seeing as it's already late afternoon, I decide to go out and stay out as late as possible in the hope of missing most of it. I might be happy with only myself for company, but that doesn't mean I want to lock myself in the fancy bedroom for the foreseeable future.

I make the same journey I did the other day, only I don't bother with the bus, thinking that I need to waste as much time as possible if I'm going to avoid the party. I walk along the beach before heading for the promenade and pushing through the door into Aces. If I'm going to be working here, then I may as well start getting a feel for the place.

It's much busier than it was the other day, but I manage to get a seat in the corner at a tiny table for two. I don't see Bill, but the waitress who comes over to take my order is really sweet, and thinking that she could be my colleague come Monday makes me feel better than I have since stepping foot on that damn airplane. Jesus, was that only days ago?

I eat, but seeing as the place is so busy, I feel bad about

hanging around when they could be serving a new customer at my table, so I pay and head out. The sun's starting to set over the ocean when I step out, so I head back down the beach once more.

I find myself a seat on the dry sand, staying away from the dunes I hid between yesterday, and pull my diary from my purse. I tap my pen against the page as I try to gather my thoughts about what's happened between Ethan and me in the past twenty-four hours. I recall last night, being totally honest with myself about how he made me feel. If someone would have told me that he'd have pinned me like that, and to a point pushed himself on me, I'd have thought I'd have freaked out, managed to somehow squirm out of his hold and hurt him as he deserved. But the reality of the situation was that I was powerless to resist. The fear I felt fused with a heady mix of desire and instead of fighting, I allowed it. My core throbs as I vividly remember how his fingers felt against my sensitive skin, the delicious stretch when he slid them inside me.

Fucking hell, Rae. Get your head out of the gutter.

None of that matters. What matters is that he's a fucking asshole who doesn't deserve my thoughts, let alone space in my diary.

Motherfucker.

I turn my thoughts to my new school and my new job. Aces is the one place that I've felt at home since being here, and it has a little excitement starting to tingle in my belly that at some point I might even fit in here.

That thought is soon wiped away when I get back to the house. Feeling like I'd exhausted my time aimlessly wandering around the seafront, I regretfully head back. There are cars littering the driveway, I discover kids everywhere, and music booming so loud that I'm sure the neighbors must be on the verge of calling the cops to shut it down.

I walk past two girls, one holding the other's hair back as she pukes into the flower bed. I turn my nose up at them as I pass, but they don't notice my attention. I have to shoulder barge a couple who insist on standing in the doorway, sucking each other's faces off as I attempt to get into my own fucking house.

Who am I kidding? This place is never going to me mine, or feel like home in any way.

The inside is packed with kids drinking, dancing, and getting high. My mouth waters for some alcohol and a joint between my lips. I look around, wondering how to go about getting both of those. Remembering the insane number of bottles littering the kitchen earlier today, I head that way. Ignoring the beer, I head straight for the spirits and pour myself one very generous shot of vodka and swallow the lot in one.

"Whoa, someone's ready to party," someone calls over to me. He takes a step in my direction, but one hard stare from me and he soon changes his mind. There's something to be said for the permanent scowl that seems to be on my face these days. It takes my usual resting bitch face to a whole new level.

A couple of the girls who are barely dressed on the other side of the kitchen run their eyes over my outfit of choice. I knew before walking in here that I wouldn't fit in in this world of rich kids. I have no idea if this whole town is full of 'Ethans,' but it's safe to assume it is instead of hoping for the best and being disappointed.

Dragging my eyes from their judgmental ones, I pour myself another giant drink and knock it back. It burns all the way down my throat, although not as bad as the first one did.

Heat from the vodka burns my belly and spurs me on. I

think maybe it's time I introduce myself to Ethan's nearest and dearest.

I almost do an entire lap of the house before I eventually find him sitting on the couches in the vast family room with his friends and some slut wiggling around on his lap. My fingers twitch at my sides as I watch her run her hands through his thick hair and whisper something in his ear that encourages his hands to run up her thighs until he's gripping onto her ass that's pretty much on display for everyone, seeing the fucking ridiculous skirt she's wearing.

My teeth grind as I watch them, and eventually I manage to drag my eyes to the others around him. I've seen enough photographs around this house to know that Ethan's on the football team, so it's a pretty easy assumption that the guys he's spending time with are also on the team.

Bored of watching from the sidelines, I take a step forward in the hope that I piss Ethan off by my mere presence.

As I get closer, one by one their attention lands on me. The dark-haired girl is the first to look my way before she nudges the guy she's sitting beside, and he brushes his long blond hair from his face to find me. The stunning blonde is next to look up. She's curled into the side of the guy talking to Ethan despite the whore on his lap.

Coming to a stop in front of the group of them, I turn to Ethan. "So, these must be your dumb jock friends. Jesus, you're so cliché it actually hurts to fucking look at you."

His eyes are murderous when they turn on me, the blue darkening before me as I stand with my hand on my jutted-out hip. His lips press into a thin line as a vein in his neck starts pulsing.

Did he really think I was going to cower away from him after last night and this morning? Just proves how little he knows me.

"And you are?" the dark-haired guy asks, looking from

Ethan to me with an almost equally furious expression on his face as he stands.

I laugh at his attempt to intimidate me by standing tall. Does he not think I'm used to that kind of shit by now? Why do I get the impression that he's probably the captain and leader of their little group?

Ethan shifts his chosen one to the side before bringing his hate-filled stare back to me. "This..." He points at me like I'm a fucking zoo animal. "This is Raelynn, my darling never-to-be fucking stepsister."

"Your what?" the blond guy gawks.

"Don't get too used to her being around. She's not staying. Not if I have anything to do with it," Ethan spits, his eyes holding mine to make sure I hear the warning.

"Do your worst, hotshot. I'm not as fragile as you'd like to believe."

"Oh, I don't know," he muses. "You crumbled beneath my hands pretty quickly last night."

I fume, fighting the heat that threatens to bloom on my cheeks.

"What?" I question, trying to sound as innocent as possible. "When you forced yourself on me?" There's a collective gasp from his friends, and the girl, now at his side, tenses.

"Oh fuck off. You were begging for a piece of this." He lifts his shirt, exposing his abs, and I scoff.

"Oh please, your dad's are better."

I'm not sure I've ever seen anyone go a brighter shade of purple before. It's almost amusing if it weren't for the murderous look in his eyes.

He stands, pushing the girl away. Thankfully, or maybe not, thinking about it, the guy on the other side of her manages to break her fall as she heads for the floor.

"You fucking what?" He takes a step toward me. Every

single muscle in his body tenses as he stares me down, hoping to get a reaction out of me. Sadly for him, I've had enough liquid courage now not to be affected by him in any way.

"Once a cheat, always a cheat," I taunt. "How many others do you think there have been?" Eric has never so much as looked at me the wrong way, unlike some of Mom's more questionable boyfriends, but Ethan doesn't need to know this. Nor that I'm pretty confident that my mom's been his only indiscretion.

"Shut. Up," he spits, getting right in my face, but I refuse to back down.

"He's probably been getting his dick wet on the side for years."

A menacing growl rumbles up his throat. He bares his teeth, closing the last bit of space between us, his nose almost brushing against mine.

"Your mom was probably—"

"Shut. The. Fuck. Up." He steps forward again, bumping into me and grabbing my arm to keep me pressed tightly against him.

"Ethan," someone calls from behind him, but his towering frame and wide shoulders are too big for me to see around. "Leave it, yeah?"

But he doesn't take the hint.

"Bro, she's not worth it." The guy I'm assuming to be their captain appears at his side, his hand landing on Ethan's shoulder.

"You've got that fucking right. You're not worth shit, trailer trash."

"Enough, Savage," he barks, successfully managing to pull him back from me, albeit only slightly.

A smile curls at my lips. "That's it, Savage. Be a good little boy and do as you're told. Fucking pussy."

He lunges for me, but his friend is quicker and manages to

hold him back. But when his eyes turn on me, they're almost as angry as Ethan's.

"Take a hint. Fuck off." He tips his chin to the door, as if he's got the fucking power to dismiss me.

"Who the fuck are you?" At no point am I going to cower down to these assholes like they want me to. Instead, I take a step closer, alternating my stare between the two of them.

"Me?" the guy asks incredulously.

"Yeah you, dickhead. Who. Are. You?" I ask slowly, as if he's an idiot who can't understand the English fucking language.

"I'm Jake. Jake Thorn."

"Well, Jake. Jake Thorn," I mimic, ensuring amusement dances in my eyes. "Keep your man here on a fucking leash. And maybe teach him a lesson in respecting women." I glance around him to his girlfriend, who's standing watching our interaction like she might need to jump in at any minute. "You seem to have a loyal girl over there. You could probably teach this asshole a thing or two."

Ethan spits out a laugh, but I don't hang around long enough to find out why. I do, however, hear Jake's voice as I head for the doorway.

"Oh man, you've got your fucking work cut out for you with that one." He chuckles, and when I glance back, I see him slap Ethan on the back and head over to his girl, who walks straight into his arms like she belongs there.

After pushing through groups of kids loitering in the hallway, I manage to get to the kitchen to find more to drink. The second I come to a stop by the bottles, silence settles around me. An unsettled feeling fills my stomach, knowing that when I turn around, all eyes are going to be on me.

I pour myself another vodka, stares burning into my back as I do. Sucking it down, I try to drag up the energy to deal with more assholes, and I turn around.

As I expected, every set of eyes in the room is trained on me. But it's the group right in front of me who seem most fascinated.

"I think you might have stumbled into the wrong party, princess," a deep, rumbling voice says.

I smile, because he couldn't be more correct. "Yeah, I can see why you might think that. Sadly, this is where I'm apparently supposed to be."

"I'm sorry," a sweet voice sings, "but Ethan never would have invited you here."

I shrug, not wanting to tell my life story to these judgmental assholes. "Anyone got any weed?"

The girl snorts as if it's the craziest question she's ever been asked.

They all stand there, no one offering anything, before I decide better of it and turn to leave.

I'm almost out of their sight when someone calls out to wait.

"Zayn, what the fuck are you doing?" the sweet voice snaps, but he doesn't reply. Instead, he steps up beside me.

"I think I've got exactly what you need." I breathe a sigh of relief and follow him outside.

The second he walks toward the sun loungers that sit around the pool, two other kids immediately jump to their feet and run off.

"Whoa, I need to learn that trick," I say with a laugh.

He doesn't comment, just falls back, pulls a joint from his pocket and lights it up. He takes a long drag. I focus on his pursed lips as he does so before running them over the rest of him. He's smaller than Ethan, although not by much, his hair is cut close to his head, and his skin is almost olive from the amount of sun he's clearly had this summer.

There's no denying that he's hot. The problem is that, just

like Ethan, he damn well knows it and probably uses it to his advantage.

He holds it out for me before allowing the smoke to plume from his lips. I think it's meant to be seductive, but he's going to need to work harder to get me interested.

"Thanks," I mutter, making quick work of lifting it to my lips.

I sigh in relief when I inhale and my muscles immediately start melting into the lounger cushion beneath me.

This is what I fucking needed.

I rest my head back and allow my eyes to close as I absorb the feeling, wishing it was enough to make me forget where I am right now.

"So," a deep voice says beside me. "Who are you? I don't recognize you from Rosewood."

"That would be because I don't start there until Monday," I say, keeping my eyes closed despite the fact that I can feel his burning into the side of my face.

"Oh, so we'll be seeing more of each other then?" His voice sounds a little too enthusiastic for my liking. "Have you moved far?"

"Washington."

"Where are you living?"

I open my mouth to respond, but I don't get a chance to say anything, which is good because I've no idea if I'm willing to admit the truth.

"What the fuck are you doing?" The joint that was happily pinched between my finger and thumb is ripped from me. My eyes fly open in time to watch it bounce along the tiles beside the pool before a large shoe lands on it and twists. My teeth grind. Such a fucking waste, I still had plenty left in that. *Asshole.*

Ethan grabs my wrist and pulls me from the lounger.

"Savage, what the fuck, man?" Zayn barks from behind

me. His own lounger squeaks as he gets up, covering Ethan's harsh breathing.

"Mind your own fucking business," Ethan barks, but at no point does he look up at the guy behind me.

"I would, but not while you're manhandling the girl I was getting to know."

"*She,*" he barks, his lip curling in disgust, "is no girl. And you won't be getting to know her because she's not staying. She's not welcome at this party. Trailer trash wasn't invited."

My entire body vibrates with anger as I attempt to put everything I hate about him into my hard stare. I have no interest in making a scene for the entire senior year of my new school to watch before I've even started.

"Ethan, seri—"

"Enough," he shouts. "*She's* leaving. Aren't you, trash?" Something crackles between us as both of us refuse to back down.

The longer we stand there, the more my temperature increases and the more my heart begins to race. I want to tell him to go fuck himself and spend the rest of the night at his pathetic party, but really, I want to be here about as much as he wants me here.

"I hope that skank gives you crabs." I step toward him, my shoulder slamming into his arm as he refuses to move out of my way. Pain warms the joint, but I refuse to show that he's had any effect on me.

I don't look back as I swing by the kitchen for a bottle of something to keep me company and then head up to my room. As I pass each door, I find some of them being utilized, so I don't know why I'm surprised when I get to mine and find a couple writhing about on my bed. At least they're clothed.

"Get the fuck out," I scream like a banshee. Both of them turn, wide-eyed, to me before scrambling off and disappearing out of sight.

"Fucking hell," I mutter, closing the door behind them and looking around the room, wondering what I can utilize to keep my door securely shut for the rest of the night. The last thing I need is more horny couples turning up for a quick fuck.

Not seeing anything other than furniture, I put the bottle in my hand on the nightstand and start the arduous task of pulling the dresser so it's in front of the door once again.

My arms burn as I attempt to move the solid wooden piece, but eventually I get it over enough to stop anyone trying to join me.

Happy that I'm safe, I undress, pull on a tank and sleep shorts and get into bed with my bottle and the sound of the party downstairs for company.

Over the years, I've been alone, a lot. But right now, with people enjoying themselves like they've got no care in the world right beneath my feet, I think it's the loneliest I've ever felt. Mom's always been by my side, but now she's got Eric, even she's fucked off for better things.

I hate that a lump crawls up my throat, but eventually with the alcohol only heightening my emotions, I allow myself to succumb to the emptiness inside me. *Maybe things will get better come Monday*, I try telling myself, but I know it's unlikely. I don't need to be told that I don't fit in here. I already feel it. Worse than anywhere I've been before.

12

ETHAN

"What the hell was that?" Zayn asks, rightfully intrigued by what he just witnessed.

"Nothing," I bark, hoping he'll drop it, which of course he doesn't.

"Oh yeah, that totally looked like nothing. I wasn't sure if you wanted to kill her or fuck her right there before my eyes."

"Kill. Definitely kill. I wouldn't fucking touch her with yours." I look over his shoulder as I say this, not wanting him to see the lie I've just told. Even as the words fall from my lips I can see her up against the wall last night with her tits on full display and my hand disappearing into her shorts.

"Whatever," he mutters, clearly not believing me.

"You're kidding, right? You just saw her. She's not exactly my type."

"She's got a pussy. I thought that was your type."

"Fuck off," I bark, walking away from him in search of more alcohol, not wanting to accept that what he's just said is totally true. I have not been all that selective about who I spend time with. It just so happens that I've not come across anyone quite like her before. I think that's most definitely a good thing, because despite the fact that she just did as she was told and fucked off out of my sight, she still won't leave my head.

Images of our short time together fill my mind, along with her banging little body she exposed to me this morning as she stood there, trying to look confident.

Finding a bottle of whiskey the second I walk into the kitchen, I tip the neck to my lips and swallow as much as I can until it burns too much.

The redhead who's been following me around all night appears in the doorway and saunters over. I let my eyes run over her curves, and although I appreciate her body, my cock doesn't stir like it usually would with a body like that stalking toward me with intent written all over it. Her hips swing, her tits bounce, and her eyes are begging me to fuck her.

"Hey, baby. Where'd you disappear off to? I missed you." Her voice is sweet and soft, and she gazes up at me like I've just hung the fucking moon but still, nothing happens. The only thing I desire for some fucked-up moment is for dark, angry eyes to be staring into mine, not these willing ones. It would be so easy to get this girl up to my room right now and take what I need. But that's just the problem. It would be too easy. Suddenly, the challenge that *she's* set is the only thing I can think about. The only thing that's getting my cock hard and my temperature increasing is the thought of breaking her down and proving to her that I can take whatever it is that I want.

Red's hand slips under my shirt, her long nails lightly scratching down my abs as her eyes alight with desire.

"Hmm..." she moans. "I can't wait to see these with my own eyes."

She turns her body into me, acting as a shield so her hand can drop to my crotch. She rubs my cock through the fabric of my jeans, and much to her delight, it reacts. Although it's partly due to the images in my mind about a girl who keeps defying me at every turn.

"Let's go upstairs," she practically growls in my ear. "I want to taste you, make you groan my name as you come in my mouth."

Fuck. Me. This one's not beating around the bush.

Part of me wants to deny her, to send her on her way with a big fat rejection. But in the end, my need for release wins out, and when she slips her small hand into mine, all it takes is a light tug from her and I follow her toward the stairs. I point her in the direction of my room and she eagerly makes her way down the hallway.

My footsteps falter when we pass *her* room. Part of me wants to burst in and insist she watches just so I can see her eyes darken with desire like they did last night, but something stops me. I have every intention of her being the one on the end of my cock when she's in the room while I've got it out, not some slut who's willing to give me what I need.

I push my door open and slam it shut behind us, just to be a dick. The second it's shut, I make quick work of undoing my waistband and pushing the fabric to my hips.

"What are you waiting for?" I don't mean to be such an asshole, but it seems I can't help it these days. He keeps appearing more and more.

Red looks from my eyes and down at my semi, which if I'm honest, is waning fast. If she doesn't hurry the fuck up and wrap her lips around it, then she's going to find herself on the other side of the door on her ass.

"But I—"

"But what? You said—"

"I know what I said," she barks, spinning away from me and taking a few steps. "I just thought—"

"Thought what? That I'd light a few candles and make love to you?" She stills at my words and I know I hit the nail on the head. "Un-fucking-likely, sweetheart. You offered to suck me dry. I only followed for that. I've no interest in anything else from you. So either kindly get on your knees or fuck off."

After tucking myself away, I move away from the door to allow her an escape. It only takes her twenty seconds to take it.

She leaves much quieter than we entered, and I can't help but smile thinking that *she'll* assume I've got some hussy in here doing fuck knows what.

Falling back on my bed, I twist the cap off the whiskey that's still in my hand and take another huge mouthful as my thoughts run away from me.

I have no idea how long I lie there drinking by myself as the party rages beneath me. I know we're supposed to be celebrating, but suddenly, being surrounded by people and pretending that everything is okay is the last thing I want to be doing.

I do have an idea for what might make this night worthwhile, though.

Pushing myself from the bed, I pull my door open and take the few steps so I'm standing in front of hers. I remember the words she said to me in front of Jake and Mason earlier, and my need to teach her a lesson for trying to embarrass me starts to burn through my veins.

I do her the courtesy of knocking this time, wondering if she'll willingly come to the door. Nothing happens beyond. There's not even any movement.

"Trash? You in there?"

Silence.

"Sweet cheeks," I sing, attempting to sound less threatening, but still it doesn't work. That or she's not there. Something stirs in my stomach that she might have gone somewhere.

Wrapping my fingers around the handle, I push down. A

rush of air passes my lips as I prepare to reveal the room beyond, but the second I push, nothing happens.

"What the fuck?"

The door barely moves enough for a slither of light to shine through the gap.

"What the fuck do you think you're doing? Do you really think this will keep me from getting to you?"

Silence.

"And to think, I brought you a new joint. I can hardly give it to you like this."

She's either playing a very good game, or she's fucked off over the balcony. Either way, it pisses me off that she's not at my beck and call. I'm also more pissed off than I want to admit that she's managed to put a barrier between us. Her door's pissed me off one too many times now. It's time to show her that I really mean fucking business about making her life her hell until she ups and leaves.

———

By the time I wake the next morning, the house is in silence, but the banging of my head more than makes up for it.

"Fuck," I grunt, rolling over and thinking on the reason for my current state. An empty whiskey bottle.

I lie on my side, facing away from the light that's creeping in through the curtains and curl myself into a ball, hoping it'll be enough to keep my stomach from turning over. I didn't eat anywhere near enough yesterday for the amount of alcohol I drank.

As I lie there wishing I could fall back into a blissful sleep, memories from the previous night start hitting me.

Finding *her* getting comfortable with Zayn in the garden. Just a hint of the anger I felt at seeing them together licks at my stomach. She shouldn't be here, let alone trying to befriend members of the team.

The redhead flicks through my mind and how she ran at the first sight of my cock despite trying to climb my body like a tree most of the night. Fucking pussy. If she couldn't handle me then I guess she did us both a favor in the end, even if I'm still craving a release I'm afraid only one girl will be able to provide.

I think about her door being locked, or what the fuck ever that was about last night, and my fingers fist the sheet as I consider what I might have done if that thing had flown right open and given me the access to her I craved.

My cock weeps, desperate for the kind of attention it usually receives on mostly a daily basis, or it had until *she* turned up.

She's fucking ruining my life in every sense of the word.

I spend what's left of the daylight curled up in my bed, hoping that at some point the hangover will vanish. I know that Rachel is downstairs putting the house back together. Before I turned into the asshole I am now, I used to go down and help, feeling guilty for the mess I'd made. But right now, I really don't give a fuck.

It's not until the sun's set that I emerge from my room. I make myself a protein shake in the kitchen before jumping in my car and heading for the gym. It's not unusual for me to do two good workout sessions two days running, but I don't usually head here for them when I've got a perfectly good gym at home. The need to get away is just too much, though. I had no idea if she was in her room, or even in the house, but I wasn't prepared to hang around and find out.

She'll be immersing herself in every part of my life come tomorrow when she turns up at Rosewood High for her first day. I need just a few hours of peace before every secret I've been trying to keep is exposed by her appearance. I might have kept her and her mother's arrival under the rug, but I have no doubt she'll sing just who she is from the rooftops if it'll piss me off.

I head home, still feeling the effects of last night's drinking and desperate to fall into my bed. The sight of the familiar little red sports car makes me groan. I should have known they'd turn up at some point to drag information out of me after my confession last night.

Needing to get this over with, I slam my car door and head inside. I stop by the kitchen to grab three bottles of beer before making my way down to my den, where I know they'll be waiting.

I find them, exactly as expected, laid out on my two couches staring at the sports channel that's illuminating the huge flat screen on the wall.

"Ah, nice of you to join us," Mason says, slowly pulling himself to a sitting position when I walk through the door.

"To what do I owe this pleasure?" They both look at me with arched brows. "Ugh, fine. Hit me with it."

I fall down onto the couch on the other side of Mason and lift a bottle to my lips.

They're silent for a few seconds, the three of us just looking at each other.

"Just spit it the fuck out."

"Stepsister?" Mason asks. "Were you ever planning on telling us?"

"I told you he was moving the whore in."

"No you didn't. You said you were expecting to have to meet her. You never said anything about them living here or that there was a stepsister situation."

"It's not a situation," I mutter into my bottle.

"Oh, so that electric hate that was zapping between the two of you last night as you stared each other down was... nothing?" Jake asks, amusement filling his voice.

I blow out a breath through pursed lips. "I fucking hate her, okay? She needs to fuck off and leave me to get on with my life."

"And what's she done exactly?"

"Except turn up and not cower down to your bullshit."

"And look hot," Jake adds. "Don't forget that."

Mason nods, knowing smiles forming on both of their faces.

"She's not fucking hot. She dresses like a fucking hobo."

"Really?" Jake asks, his eyebrows almost hitting his hairline. "Because from what I could see, she was a feisty little—"

"Unless there's an insult coming, then I suggest you shut the fuck up."

"You really hate this girl?" Mason asks as if this needs clarifying.

"She's ruining my fucking life. She needs to fuck off."

"Just as we thought," Jake says, looking at Mason with a smile playing on his lips.

"Did you two come for any reason other than to piss me off with this bullshit?"

"Just thought we could hang out." Jake lifts his beer to his lips, but amusement still fills his eyes.

"So, where is she now?"

"How should I fucking know? Back in the trailer park she crawled from, hopefully."

I can tell by the way they're both looking at me that they don't believe a word that's coming from my lips, but I don't give a fuck. I intend on proving to *her* just how much I hate her, then I can prove it to these motherfuckers at the same time.

Thankfully, they drop the subject in favor of the game highlights that start on the TV. All talk turns to football and our upcoming playoff match. Mason sulks the whole time that he's unable to play, but he gets little sympathy from me seeing as the fucking idiot ran a red light and almost killed himself. He came out of it pretty lightly, if you ask me.

It's long past a sensible time to call it a night when they head off, seeing as it's a school night and they've both got girls waiting for them when they get home.

As I head upstairs to finally hit my bed, I glance at her door, the girl who seems to always be in my head now. What I wouldn't give for it to be anyone else and to have them naked and waiting for me in bed right now like I'm sure Jake and Mason are about to find. As I push my door open, the image of her dark hair and curvy little body laid out in my bed fills my mind, and all my blood rushes south.

I look back over my shoulder at her door but decide to hold off for now. She's probably inside holding her breath, waiting for what I'm going to do. I want to build her anticipation; that way, she'll be even more ready for me when I make my move.

———

Dad told me before he left that I was to ensure she got to school this morning and to help her out getting her schedule and finding where she needed to be. He clearly couldn't see the darkness festering inside me as he delivered these orders, because he left believing that it might actually happen.

I sent her a message before I crashed sometime after midnight last night telling her to be ready by eight am. She read it immediately, but she never replied. I've no idea if she'd even willingly get into a car with me, but I thought I'd at least try.

At two minutes to eight, I'm sitting behind my wheel with the engine ticking over.

Thirty seconds before I told her to be here, the front door

opens and she emerges from behind. As usual, she's dressed in all black. Her skirt shows off her shapely albeit short legs, and her oversized shirt has been ripped almost in half, revealing her slim waist. Her hair is piled on top of her head, and as she emerges into the morning sun, she lowers a pair of sunglasses over her eyes, cutting me off from seeing how she's feeling about today—not that I really give a shit. I just hoped to see a little fear or at least some nerves in them for what today might hold.

She blows out a long breath before taking a step and heading toward me. I watch her every movement as she gets closer, and fuck if it's now that my cock decides it wants some action, because it starts to swell beneath my pants. Why's it her swaying hips that wakes it up? What was wrong with Shelly's the other day or Red's last night?

She reaches out and pulls the handle, and just as I'm expecting, she finds it locked.

Leaning down, she looks through the passenger window at me, her lips pursed in anger that I'd lock her out. When I don't do anything, she lets her arm fall back to her side as she waits for me to get my shit together. *You're going to be waiting a lot fucking longer than you think, sweet cheeks.*

A smile curls at my lips as pushed her sunglasses to the top of her head and stares at me. Something passes between us. A warning. A promise. Fuck knows, but it's there before I slam my foot down on the accelerator and speed from the driveway, leaving her behind in my dust. An evil laugh rumbles up my throat as I look back at her, standing totally helpless in the center of the large space.

Fucking idiot. Did she really think I was going to make it that easy?

13

RAELYNN

ucking asshole.

I don't know what I was expecting, and I feel stupid for ever thinking he might have taken me to school this morning like a normal fucking human being.

I was shocked when I saw the message, but I stupidly took it for what it was and made sure I was ready. I didn't have any other way of getting to school, so I took his olive branch. Only it wasn't one. I should have known better.

Dragging my cell from my purse, I pull up Uber and set about ordering a car, hoping I can still get there in time.

With the car only minutes away, I perch my ass on one of the steps leading to the house and wait.

Nerves rattle around in my stomach, but I swallow them down. This is just another Monday. Just another school.

Only this place isn't just another school; it's a school where I'm not wanted before I've even started.

I blow out a frustrated breath as a car pulls up into the drive.

The journey is in silence. I've no intention of making small talk with the driver.

At the first sign of the school, dread starts to weigh heavy in my stomach. The temptation to go running back to hide in my bedroom is high, but without graduating I've little chance of creating the life I crave. One where I'm in charge of my own destiny and where I live.

Sucking in a huge breath, I thank the driver and push the door open when he pulls to a stop at the edge of the parking lot. There are kids everywhere. It looks like just another high school. The buildings I can see look similar to all the others, and the kids loitering around fit the stereotypes I've found in every other school. Only this one includes Ethan.

Throwing my bag over my shoulder, I take off toward where the sign is pointing to the entrance to discover what this day is going to hold.

The second I start moving, heads turn my way. I'm sure after Friday night people are wondering who I am. I don't pay them any mind as I hold my head high and focus on the building I'm heading toward. That is, until I feel *his* stare burning into me. My skin prickles, and a hint of fear runs down my spine, but like fuck am I allowing any of these motherfuckers to see it. I don't care if I come across like a bitch; none of these kids will get to see the real me. The only thing they're going to experience is the hard outer shell I've learned to shield myself with.

I refuse to look his way, or for my steps to falter. I don't want him to think he has any power over me.

Relief floods me when I pull the door open to the entrance, and I shut off all the curious eyes.

I stand at a little glass window and wait for someone to help me. The women beyond all tap away on their keyboards, none of them bothering to look up even after I ring the bell.

Eventually, someone comes over. "Can I help you, love?"

"Yeah. It's my first day, I—"

"Ah... Raelynn, is it?" she asks after looking down at a piece of paper. "Principal Hartmann is waiting to meet you."

"Fantastic." The sarcasm in my voice is impossible to miss, but somehow it seems to go over her head as she directs me to his office before shutting the little window, halting anything else I might have had to say.

I'm standing at his door in seconds. I don't bother knocking—after all, he's expecting me.

He glances up from his desk at my intrusion, his brows creasing as he takes me in. I already know I stand out from his usual students like a sore thumb. I just saw most of them on my walk here, and none of them quite have the style or aura about them that I do.

He clears his throat, I guess hoping to cover the fact that he was gaping at my outfit of choice. "I guess you must be Raelynn."

I fall down into the chair in front of his desk.

"Correct. Do you have my schedule?" I've been in enough of these 'welcome to the school' meetings that I don't need to hear the bullshit he's about to spew at me.

"Is Ethan not with you?" he asks, looking back to the door.

"No."

"His father assured me that he'd escort you here and show you around today."

"That was nice of him. But there's no need. I'm capable of fending for myself. Just give me my schedule and a map and I'll get out of your hair." I barely contain a snort when I look to the top of his head to find he has none.

"Oh... um... if it's all the same to you, I'd be much happier if one of our students welcomed you properly."

"Oh don't worry, Principal..." I look down at his name badge, pretending that I've already forgotten what his name is. "Hardmann, I—"

"It's Hartmann, actually."

"Right. Well, I can assure you that I've had quite the welcome already. None of that will be necessary."

He waves me off, turning to press the button on his intercom. "Sandra, get a cheerleader here. I've got a job," he barks before releasing it and turning back to me.

"I'll hear nothing of it. No student of mine starts at Rosewood High without a proper welcome."

"Fantastic," I mutter under my breath.

Thankfully, he passes over my schedule and releases me without much further bullshit and allows me to start my first day.

"Jesus fucking Christ," I say, looking at the chirpy blonde waiting for me in her red and white cheer uniform outside the principal's office. "This day's just getting better and better."

"Hi, I'm Shelly. I'm going to show you around, welcome you to Rosewood." She's so fucking happy it makes me want to puke on her pristine fucking uniform.

I snort at her, pull my bag higher up my shoulder and take a step past her. "You're dismissed. I can figure this shit out myself."

"Um... but Principal Hartmann said—"

Looking over my shoulder at her, I laugh. "And of course, you always do what *Principal Hartmann says*," I say, mimicking her chirpy tone. "I bet he's got you sucking him off on a weekly basis."

She splutters in disbelief, her cheeks brightening in anger or embarrassment, I'm not sure. "I... um... fine. Do your own thing. See if I care."

I arch a brow at her minor tantrum over being dismissed and take off. I look down at my schedule to see I've got English Lit first. I come to a crossroads in the hallway and glance down each corridor. *I've totally got this.*

It must be at least thirty minutes later when I find a door that has the right number on it. I suck in a breath and knock before pushing it open. As expected, all eyes turn on me, but there's only one set I see. Ethan's.

Fuck my life. Of course, he's in my first class of the day.

His eyes hold mine and stop me from entering the room.

"Can I help you?" the teacher asks, turning from where she's writing something on the board.

It takes another full two seconds for me to rip my eyes from Ethan's.

"Sorry, I'm... uh... new here."

"You must be Raelynn. If you—"

"It's Rae," I interrupt.

"Okay, Rae. If you'd like to take a seat." She points into the room and I take a step in that direction. Karma once again bites me in the ass when I realize the only spare seat in the room is right in front of Ethan. Of fucking course it is.

Rolling my eyes, I make my way over as an evil smirk spreads across his face as I get closer.

"Nice of you to join us," he jokes, sitting back in his chair and crossing his arms over his chest. The guys around him join in with his amusement.

Huffing out a frustrated breath, I drop my bag to the floor with a bang and fall into the seat.

"You haven't missed too much. We've only just started this task, so I'm sure you'll catch up." I nod at the teacher as she drops a textbook and exercise book in front of me. "Page ninety-two."

I flip it open and try to listen to what she's saying, but most of it goes in one ear and straight out the other.

Being able to hear the low rumble of his voice as he says fuck knows what to his friend about me doesn't exactly help with my concentration, and when something hits the back of my head, I give up completely.

Clearly not happy with the fact that I let his ball of paper fall to the floor, he tries again. This time, it ricochets off my shoulder and drops down onto my desk.

I stare at it. He obviously wants me to open it. But as much as I might want to find out what vile message he's written inside it, I keep my hands in my lap and stare at it.

After a few minutes, my curiosity gets too much and I reach for it. I'm just about to reveal what's inside when the teacher stops beside me.

"That's not exactly the best way to introduce yourself, is it, Miss Pritchard." She snatches the note from my hand and pulls it open. She pales slightly at what's written before demanding to know who wrote it.

As expected, the entire class falls silent. I'm sure every single person behind me knows it came from Ethan, but equally no one is brave enough to go up against a member of the football team. It's the same in every school I've spent time in. It might not always be the football team that rules the school, sometimes it's the soccer or the basketball team, but ultimately it's a bunch of jacked-up, arrogant assholes who think they're fucking gods.

I roll my eyes and slump down in my seat.

"I think maybe you and I need a chat after class, Miss Pritchard."

"Great," I mutter. First class of my first day and he's already getting me in trouble.

After getting a ten-minute dressing down from my English Lit teacher about how passing notes isn't what is expected of Rosewood High students, I'm late for my biology class. She doesn't seem to care that I clearly wasn't the one to write it. I mean, I'm hardly going to warn myself of what's coming to me. But then again, I guess no one ever pulls up the legends that are the football team for their appalling behavior. At least I can blame the fact that I'm new and lost for my tardiness. Could this day get any fucking worse?

Finding the cafeteria at lunch is much easier than any of my morning classes, seeing as almost every student in the school moves in that direction.

With a tray full of questionable looking food, I glance around for a table. Every one is taken, so I head to a half full one with two people sitting at it, purposefully ignoring the one full of football players and cheerleaders. Thankfully, Ethan's attention is on the same girl who was forced on me earlier, so he doesn't notice my arrival.

"I'm sorry, do you mind?" I point to the empty seats.

The guy nods. "Sure, go for it."

Dropping my tray to the table, I feel their attention on me, but I don't look up. I'm really not in the mood for people after my shitty morning.

"Hey, you're Raelynn, right? Ethan's..." The female voice trails off.

"I'm not Ethan's anything," I snap.

Glancing over out of the corner of my eye, I vaguely recognize the girl from Saturday night, but I've no clue who she is. The guy isn't familiar at all.

"Oh, sorry. Yeah. So how are you finding your first day?" When I just stare at her without offering an answer, she opens her mouth once again. "I'm Camila, by the way. This is Shane."

"Great." I give her a very quick and equally fake smile before looking down to my plate.

An awkward silence settles around us before we're joined by another guy.

"Hey, baby. Having a good day?" I glance up to see the blonde guy from the couch on Saturday night very slowly and carefully lower himself down beside Camila.

"Are you sure you should be here? The doctor said—"

"Screw the doctor. I'm not sitting at home anymore."

"Fine. But if you do more damage, you know Coach won't let you play in the final."

"We've gotta make it there first. Don't you think you're being a little presumptuous, Cam?" the other guy says.

"Glad to know you're feeling positive about it."

"We're not the same team without you, man."

I roll my eyes, realizing that the other guy is also on the team. I look over to where the rest of the team and cheer squad are huddled around a few joined-up tables, and I wonder why these two aren't over with them.

I know the second their eyes turn to me. "Mase, you remember Raelynn from Saturday night?" Camila asks, clearly pointing me out.

"Hmmm, yeah. That was quite an introduction."

"Thanks," I mutter, still refusing to look their way.

"I need to go and see the guys. You going to be okay?"

"Of course. I'll see you last period. Take it easy."

The sound of them kissing makes me cringe before he gets up as gently as he sat down and walks toward the team, closely followed by Shane, although he looks reluctant to join them all.

"So what's his story? Bad tackle?" I ask Camila when she turns back from watching her boyfriend's ass walk away.

"Car accident."

I feel a little bad for jumping to conclusions, but I don't show it because I don't give a shit what she thinks of me.

"Listen—" she starts, turning her dark, assessing eyes on me.

"No, I'm not sitting here listening to a lecture from Miss Goody Two Shoes. You don't know me, nor will you get the chance to. You're Ethan's friend. I get it. You don't want me making his life hard so he's distracted from the game. Whatever. I don't give a shit. You do you, and I'll do me, and if we're lucky, our paths won't cross all that often."

Her chin drops at my words. I take her moment of silence to grab my tray and walk away with a smirk on my face.

I'm not here to make any friends, and it's about time that nosey bitches like Camila realized that.

14

ETHAN

I'd have put money on her selling me out to Mrs. Harris, so I'm pleasantly surprised when I get through the day without being called in to explain myself for the note I wrote. It wasn't pretty, but I couldn't refrain from playing with her.

I'm just finishing a lap on the track when the girls come out onto the field for their gym class. I search through them. They're all wearing skin-tight gym uniforms in the hope of attracting one of us. All apart from one. *Her.*

A smirk pulls at my lips as I take in her oversized dirty shirt and the shorts that hang to her knees that have clearly been pulled from the spares cupboard. The ones we all dread wearing because they've been in there as long as the school's been here and smell as such. I couldn't have planned it better if I'd organized it myself.

"Savage, pull your head from your pants and focus," Coach calls.

"Sorry," I mutter, dragging my eyes away from the girls as they start warming up, most of them flaunting everything they have, trying to get us to look their way.

Coach sets us off again, and after a while the girls head off on their cross-country route. I watch as they run, staring as their asses sway and their tits bounce, but no one really catches my attention until she runs past. She's totally uncoordinated compared to the members of the cheer team who've sprinted off, trying to show up the rest of the class. She's right at the back and plodding along like it's the worst day of her life.

I chuckle as I turn the corner and up my speed, pushing myself to my limits as I try to outrun *her*.

"Good, Savage. Use that aggression and push harder."

I put everything I have into my next lap, but the second the final lot of the girls come into view, I find I can't help but look up. They all run past me but one, the one I want to see. When I look to where they all appeared from, I find her bent over with her hands on her knees and panting like she's run a fucking marathon, not just the school's cross-country track.

"What's wrong, trash? Weaker than you think?"

Her eyes lift to find mine. They're narrowed, her hate for me shining bright.

"Maybe it won't take as much for me to break you as I was expecting. At least put in a bit of a fight." Fury fills her eyes as she sucks in deep lungfuls of air.

"I'll outrun you if it kills me. You won't break me." She sounds so sure in herself, but I don't share her confidence. She might act like nothing can touch her, but I've seen the hint of fear that fills her eyes. I fucking crave it more than my next tackle. I will see it again, and I will see her break before me. I'll put everything I have on it.

With one final hard stare, she finds some energy from somewhere and heads back toward the rest of her class.

I watch her progress as she makes her way across the field. Heat fills my veins that despite having a shit first day, largely thanks to me, she's still going.

Coach runs us ragged before dismissing the rest of our class but keeping the members of the team out on the field ready for practice to start.

Mason comes out, albeit slowly, after class and eagerly listens to Coach's pep talk before slinking back to the bleachers looking seriously pissed off at watching us all sweat out the weekend's alcohol consumption to ensure we're focused and ready for Friday night's game. The first one of the playoffs. I should be fucking stoked—I guess I am, to a point, but it's not my main focus, thanks to my dad and his wayward fucking dick.

Zayn slams into me when I'm not paying attention.

"What the fuck, man?" he barks when I push back, slamming my hands down on his chest hard enough that he stumbles back. He's still on my shit list for giving her weed on Saturday night.

"Get out of my fucking face," I spit.

"That's enough, Savage. Leave the bitch fights to the cheer squad, eh?"

His warning is enough to stop me, but it doesn't put a halt to the death stare I have trained on Zayn. "Stay the fuck away from her, you hear me?"

"Loud and fucking clear. She's really not your type though, dude."

"Did I fucking say she was?" I step toward him again, but this time it's Jake that gets between us.

"Fuck off, Zayn." Jake stands in front of me, his hands on my shoulders. "I get it. I fucking get it." An understanding passes between us. "But don't let her fuck it up for you, for us. Keep her off the fucking field, yeah?"

I want to kick back. I want to ask him if that's what he did when Amalie was messing up his head, but I bite back the spiteful words because this thing with *her* is very different. Amalie was messing up Jake's head because he wanted her.

That is not the fucking issue I have right now. The only thing I want from the trash that's moved into my house is her fucking gone. *After you've got your hands on her*, a little voice says in my head, but I push it down. I only want to get my hands on her to break her. To show her that she doesn't belong here. My home is not where pieces of shit like her belong.

By the time Coach lets us head for the locker room, my legs are like jelly. I've no doubt we're going to kick ass on Friday night—he's working us harder than ever, knowing that it's now or never.

"We've fucking got this, boys. That fucking trophy is ours for the taking," Jake shouts excitedly into the showers where we're all washing off layers of sweat and mud.

A chorus of agreement sounds out around the team, and when I look over, I find even Shane getting caught up in the excitement.

"Who's up for Aces? I need a fucking burger the size of my head," Zayn calls.

I'm not sure why he asks; it's pretty much tradition at this point. Some of the guys make their excuses and fuck off once they're dressed, but the normal crowd, plus Shane, all head toward the parking lot together to get in their cars.

Mason is still with us, having watched the entire practice, although he's starting to look a little worse for wear. It's like he's forgotten he was almost fucking killed a little over two weeks ago. I know he's desperate to be part of our playoff games, but I'm worried he's pushing himself too much too fast.

"Um…" Shane starts looking totally uncomfortable. "My car's in the garage. Any chance of a lift?" He looks between the three of us, I think half expecting us to tell him where to go.

I glance at Jake, his lips pressed into a thin line as he stares at Shane. We might now all know the truth about who drugged Amalie at his party, but he still doesn't trust the guy. I get it; he was after Jake's girl long before Jake pulled his head out of his ass and realized he wanted her.

"Yeah, man. Ethan's driving," Mason says, gesturing to the back door.

Shane nods but still looks hesitant, and the three of us pull open doors and jump inside.

"Not like you to join us, Dunn," Jake states, clearly not happy about it.

"Thought maybe it was time I joined in," Shane mumbles as he stares at the passing scenery.

"Don't you think it might be a little too late?" Jake barks.

"Leave it, Thorn. Shane's part of the team. He's welcome wherever we are."

"Would never guess you're banging his friend."

"Just the fuck up, Jake," I add, helping both Mason and Shane out.

He rolls his eyes but shuts his mouth.

The rest of the journey is tense at best. I'm not sure what game Shane is playing, but Jake's right with what he's saying. This is weird as fuck.

We pull up to Aces as the other guys do and pile out of the car. Shane immediately walks ahead, making me wonder who he's really meeting here.

The three of us hang back and allow the others to go ahead of us.

"Well, that was fucking weird," Mason says, echoing my previous thoughts.

"Oh, I thought you were on Team Dunn all of a sudden."

"I just don't think you need to be such a dick to him. He's not actually a bad guy. Just odd that he's suddenly latched on to us."

"He just wanted a free fucking lift."

"Whatever. Come on, I'm starving."

I march toward the entrance, Jake and Mason flanking my

sides. I know they're just as eager to get inside because their girls are there. I roll my eyes to myself that I'm going to have to spend the next however long watching them suck each other's faces off and whisper sweet fucking nothings into their ears. Fucking pussies. I expected it from Mason. The way he and Camila fought like cat and fucking dog for years, I'm surprised it took so long. But Jake... I never thought he'd get pussy whipped, but he's like a soppy fucking puppy where Amalie's concerned.

My steps falter the second I step foot inside the diner, causing Mason to crash into me.

"Ow, fuck. Ouch," he complains as a flash of dark hair runs past me to his side.

I feel bad for causing him pain, but most of my mind is consumed with the fact that *she's* standing over our usual table, setting plates down.

What the utter fuck is she doing here?

15

RAELYNN

By the time I finish that damn gym class, I'm a sweaty, hot, aching mess. The last thing I want to do is go and start my first shift at Aces. But knowing I can't use Eric's credit card for an Uber every morning to get myself to school, I force myself into the showers, ignoring the stares from the other girls around me wanting to know who I am and probably why I have 'bitch' written all over my face. Obviously, not literally, but I don't need to be told I've got a fantastic resting bitch face. I see it in the mirror most days. Never more so than since moving here. I'm not here to make friends, and I need everyone to know it before they start trying.

It works, because no one so much as asks my name. Fucking fine by me.

I call another Uber and jump in out front of the school when it pulls up. Looking at how short the journey is, I could probably walk it, but my first day isn't the time to show up late because I got lost. I already look a hot mess after doing a rush job of my makeup in the dirty, cracked school mirror I was left with after the cheer team monopolized the decent ones the second they pushed through the door into the locker room.

I'm still wearing the same outfit I was earlier. The only change I've made is to pull on a shirt that covers my belly; I'm not sure anyone wants their burger delivered by a girl who can't cover herself up appropriately.

A wave of trepidation flows through me as I step into the diner and find almost the entire senior Rosewood class inside. If I knew this was the school hangout, I might have chosen another place to work. Acknowledging that it's too late to worry about it now, especially as Bill's just glanced up at me and smiled, I walk toward the register.

"Good afternoon, Rae," Bill sings. "You're looking like a little ray of sunshine. Good first day?"

I bark out a laugh at his description of me. We both know that I'm about as far away from sunshine as physically possible.

"As far as first days go... I've had better."

He winces but thankfully says no more about it as he waves someone over. "Rae, this is Cody. Cody will be mostly working the same shifts as you, so he's pulled the short straw to show you the ropes."

"Hey Rae, nice to meet you," Cody says politely. I give him a quick once over from his sun-kissed shaggy surfer hair and down his slim, tall body. He's hot.

"You too." He smiles at me and only gets better looking. If I had to guess, I'd say he was a little older, maybe at college.

"Right, I'll leave you both to it." Bill wanders off, leaving me to follow Cody around as he points things out and tells me about protocols. This isn't my first waitressing gig, so most of it sounds simple enough.

"Here's your apron," Cody says, holding it out for me. "Notepads for taking orders are here, if you need them. I'll just show you how to put them through to the kitchen and then you should be good to go."

I nod and follow him over to the register. The system is exactly the same as one I've used before, so I instantly know what he's going to show me—not that I tell him that. He seems to be enjoying himself playing boss, so I let him get his fill.

"This place usually gets a little crazy when the Rosewood kids finish for the day, so you'll need to get out of school pretty quick to beat them all."

"I'm sure I can cope." I glance around to make sure no one needs anything before asking the question that's been on the tip of my tongue since meeting Cody. "So, are you from around here?"

"Nah, I'm a student at Maddison U," he says, confirming my suspicions that he's in college. "What about you? Rosewood born and bred?"

"Nope. Moved here last week. Mom shacked up with some guy who lives here and dragged me halfway across the country."

"Rough."

"Meh, it's pretty standard for me."

"How are you finding it?"

I look around the diner once again right as a group of cheerleaders arrive, the one who was supposed to be my chaperone earlier front and center. Her eyes find mine and they narrow in disdain before she elbows a couple of the others.

"Oh, great. I've fitted right in." A bitter laugh falls from my lips.

"Oh yeah, so I see. I wouldn't worry about that lot. You're not missing out on much by not being part of their group."

"I'm sorry, you think I want to be a part of that?" I snap.

Regret covers his face almost instantly. "No, no. That's not what I—forget I said anything. Looks like they want to order."

I groan, following his gaze and finding the entire squad with their eyes on me.

"Feed me to the wolves, why don't you? I'm sure they'd much prefer you."

"Are you kidding? All they want is their football jocks."

"I think you and I might just get along fine after all."

Pulling the little notepad I shoved into my skirt back pocket earlier, I twist the pencil in my fingers and make my way over, much to their delight.

"Well, well, well... new girl seems to have got herself a little job," the ringleader sneers.

"What can I get for you?" I ask, ignoring her barb and plastering a smile on my face.

"Oh look, she does smile," another comments.

Everything in me wants to tell them where to go and refuse to serve them, but seeing as they're my first customers of the first day of my job, I can hardly do that, so instead, I force myself to keep my cool as they each rattle off their orders, looking pleased as fuck that I'm quite clearly beneath them being their waitress.

"Coming right up," I sing, walking away and ignoring their petty comments about what I'm wearing and the state of my hair.

"You okay?" Cody asks when I join him back at the register.

"Of course. I've handled much worse than those spoiled brats."

"I had a feeling you'd say as much. Things can only get better from here on out, right?"

I'd like to say I agree with him, but not twenty minutes later when I'm putting the cheer squad's plates down in front of them does it get a whole lot worse.

I'm expecting it, because where the cheer squad goes, the football team generally follows, so when the door bursts open and excited male chatter fills the relatively small diner, I know exactly who's arrived.

I don't want to look, but it's like my eyes have a mind of their own. Turning away from the table slightly, I watch as they all come barreling through the door—well, except for the one I'm dreading.

Breathing a sigh of relief that he's not shown his face, I spin back to drop the last plate down. That's the exact moment when my blood runs cold. The atmosphere in the entire diner changes and my spine stiffens.

Standing straight, I look around the table and plaster a smile on my face. "If you need anything else, please let me know." Glancing at one of the guys, I say, "I'll be back in a few moments to take your orders." Then, I spin on my heels and get the hell out of there.

I race past Cody and out to the kitchen. Once I know I'm out of sight, I fall back against the wall and suck in a few deep breaths.

"Is everything okay?"

"Yeah, perfect."

"Ooookay." His eyes study me for a few seconds before I swallow down my apprehension and push from the wall.

"Right. I've got a job to do." I refuse to allow myself to shy away from that asshole. He has no right to have any power over me or to make me regret taking a job that I so desperately need.

"If you need anything, you know where I am." I nod at him and walk back to the table.

All eyes turn on me as I approach, the girls judging, the guys trying to place me and work me out. Good fucking luck with that. I imagine only the best shrink in the country would be able to sort my head out right now. The only person's attention I don't hold is *his*. I'm shocked. I thought this would be the perfect opportunity for him to humiliate me.

"What can I get for you all?"

I start with the guys I don't recognize before my eyes land on Zayn's, followed by the two guys who were sitting with Ethan on Saturday night. None of them acknowledge me; they just place their orders like they would with any other waitress.

Knowing that I can't ignore him and walk off without taking his order like I'm desperate to do, I wait for a beat, but the asshole still keeps his eyes focused on the menu in front of him.

"Ethan?" I prompt, pissed off that he's wasting my time.

There are a couple of gasps from the girls as they look between the two of us. The ringleader stares at me.

"You know this girl, Ethan?" Her voice is the one that drags his eyes from the table. He looks to her before glancing over at me. The way he looks at me has my nails digging into the notepad. It's like the simple act of even looking at me is more than I deserve.

"*Her?*" he spits. His eyes run the length of my body, his lip curling in disgust. "Please, I don't spend time with skanks."

My brow arches as I glance at the kind of girls he does spend time with.

"Good to know. Now, can I get you any food?" I try to take the high road, but I don't think anyone around the table misses my voice crack.

He sits back, placing his arm over the back of the bench he's sitting on like he owns the fucking place, a smug smile firmly on his lips as he assesses me.

"Burger, fries, soda. You to leave us alone."

"Jesus, Ethan," his blonde friend mutters.

Rolling my eyes, I note it down, not that I'll forget, and turn my back on them.

"Was that really necessary?" a guy's voice says before one of the girls pipes up. "You sure you don't know her?"

Shaking my head, I walk to the register and put the order through to the kitchen.

"Friends of yours?" Cody asks with a laugh.

"Oh yeah. Can't you just feel the love?"

He laughs. "How have you done one day at school yet managed to piss off both the cheer squad and the football team already?"

"I have very special skills."

His eyes glance over my shoulder and his face drops a little. "Do you need me to take over that table? I don't mind."

"No chance. I'm not allowing them to think they've won."

He nods before leaving me to greet a few more familiar faces who sit in his booths. It's the two girls from Saturday night. There's some shuffling from behind me before the two guys walk over and sweep their girls into their arms.

I watch them for a few minutes before the bell from the kitchen rings out to tell me there's food ready.

Sadly, Ethan's is the first prepared, but that doesn't mean it's the first I deliver. I push it to the back of the counter and pick up every other one.

With it still getting cold in the kitchen, I head toward where the two of his friends are now sitting at the other side of the diner with their girls.

"You guys want this over here?" I ask, able to breathe a little easier being away from the main group.

"That's great, thanks. Listen—" the blonde guy starts.

"You don't need—"

He interrupts. "I do. Ethan's being an ass. This whole thing with his parents has rocked him more than he'll admit."

"I don't give a shit. You think all of this is what I wanted?"

"No, no, of course not but—"

"Do not ask me to go easy on him or give him the benefit of the doubt or some bullshit. Not happening."

He holds his hands up in defense. "Was going to do no

such thing. You seem like you can handle yourself around him."

"So, as stimulating as it is, is there actually a point to this whole conversation?"

The other three around the table stifle a laugh.

"You know," the dark-haired guy pipes up, "I think the two of you might actually get along just fine. I'm Jake, in case you forgot. This is Mason. My girl's Amalie and this is Camila."

If he expects me to remember that, then he's got to be even more delusional than I think he is.

"You need anything, give these two a shout," Blonde says, nodding to the girls.

"Thanks." It's totally insincere, but I'm not really the kind of girl that other girls make friends with.

I leave them to it and head back to the kitchen. Ethan's food should be suitably cold by now.

I fight the smile that wants to spread across my face the entire journey toward him with his plate.

He looks up as I approach while everyone around him eats.

I drop it down in front of him a little harder than necessary, a few fries bouncing off the plate and onto the table.

His eyes narrow at me, his lips press into a thin line. He's desperate to give me a dressing down, but something's holding him back. I'm assuming it's his audience.

I smile at him. "Enjoy."

More and more students pour in through the front doors as they make their way from the beach once the sun starts to set, and I'm so busy that I hardly have a chance to acknowledge the hate stare coming from *his* table every time I so much as walk past, but he never tries to say anything and I avoid taking any more orders from them as they sit chatting.

It must be half an hour later that the noise of them all

leaving fills the diner. I look back over my shoulder as I head toward the kitchen to see I'm right. Most of the girls have already walked out, leaving a few of the guys hanging back, sorting out the check

Breathing a sigh of relief, I continue forward. That is, until warm fingers wrap around my wrist and I'm pulled none too gently into the dark bathroom beside me.

"What the—" My words are cut off as his hand comes down on my mouth. My eyes widen in shock.

He stands close, his nose only an inch from mine, his increased breath covering my face. I can only just make out his features with the emergency light illuminating the space around us. The rest of my senses are on full alert—it's how I know he smells fucking mouthwatering right now. Asshole. Why can't he smell as rotten as his personality?

"You have no fucking right being here. You're quitting. Tonight."

My eyes narrow. Who the fuck does he think he is, trying to dictate my life?

My chest heaves and my hands tremble slightly with his closeness and the evil hint in his blue eyes as he stares down at me.

16

ETHAN

This is my fucking place. My fucking escape. Why the fuck does she have to have found a job here of all places?

I was desperate to say something, to do something as she stood at the end of our booth with her little pad of paper in hand, but I didn't want everyone around knowing there was anything between us. As far as I'm concerned, Dad will get bored and the two of them will fuck off out of our lives as fast as they entered and no one will need to be any the wiser.

Anger swirls within me as I watch her deliver everyone else's food bar mine. She thinks she's fucking clever. Well, she needs to think again, because she won't win these games she's trying to play. I'm the fucking master here, and she's merely the puppet.

I see my opportunity the second everyone starts to leave. I excuse myself to the bathroom and double back on myself, following her down the hall that leads to the kitchen.

I watch her ass sway in her short-as-fuck skirt. What was Bill thinking when he offered her a job? Like fuck does she fit in here.

Her little gasp of shock when I pull her into the dark bathroom makes my lips twitch in achievement. The dim light above reflects in her dark eyes. I swear I see a little fear in them. It makes my cock hard.

She flinches when I demand she quits, but I'm not stupid. She's not going to listen to anything I say. She's already proved that my words don't affect her like they should. This girl's all about actions, and I have plenty of things up my sleeve to prove to her that she doesn't belong here. That she doesn't belong in my life.

I take a step closer, my hand dropping from her mouth but only enough so I can take her chin in my fingers and pinch hard enough to make her fight to get away.

"I took it fucking easy on you tonight. But bringing me cold food... you're not going to get away with that, trash. I left my check on the side; I'm sure your wages tonight will easily cover it.

Her defiant eyes hold mine, but the small amount of water that's beginning to pool in them gives her away.

"You scared of me?"

"Never."

I close the space between us, my nose brushing hers. I don't miss her sharp intake of breath at our contact.

"You should be," I whisper. "And it's not just me you've got to worry about. All those guys out there, they do what I say, and they'll make your life a living hell if I so much as whisper the words."

She swallows, her slender neck rippling against my palm. "Bring it on," she taunts, her lips curling up into a smile. "I've dealt with worse than a rich prick like you. You can't fucking touch me."

"Oh, sweet cheeks. We both know that's not true. We both know I've already touched you, and we both know just how much you were enjoying it."

Reaching forward, I slip my hand under the tiny scrap of fabric that's wrapped around her hips. She's wearing fishnets beneath, and the second I push my fingers inside two of the holes they practically disintegrate. The rip sounds out and it's like music to my ears.

"Ethan, you can't—"

"When are you going to fucking learn? I can. I will. And I'll do it whenever the fuck I like."

I trail one finger over her center that's covered in soft cotton.

"What's this? Granny pants? I thought you were a lace kind of girl."

"What do you care?"

"You're right. None would be so much better."

"Ah, fuck," she cries when I tuck my finger beneath the fabric and immediately find her swollen clit.

"You've been waiting for this since I pulled back the other night, haven't you? And if how wet you are tells me anything, it's that you followed my orders. You didn't get yourself off, did you?"

"Y-you're not getting any of my pleasure."

Her eyes shine bright and her chest heaves as I continue teasing her nub.

"Is that right? Because right now you're dripping down my fucking fingers like you can't get enough of me."

If it were lighter, I'd love to see the color I know is staining her cheeks at my comment.

Slipping my fingers lower, I find her entrance and push two fingers inside her tight pussy. A groan climbs up my throat, but I catch it before it passes my lips. She doesn't need to know that I'm imagining just how tight she'd squeeze my cock.

I lean in, my rough cheek scratching her soft face until my lips brush her ear. She shudders, and I smile.

"Next time, I'll be the one taking all the pleasure."

I pull my fingers from her and step back. My cock's tenting my pants, but with the darkness in here, I doubt she can see the effect she's having on me.

Learning from my mistake when I lift my hand, I don't suck my own fingers like I'm desperate to do. Instead, I lift them to her lips.

"Open," I demand. And in true trailer trash style, she keeps them firmly shut.

"I don't take kindly to you defying me. Open your fucking lips, or I won't wait until next time to push my cock between then."

I don't think she means to open her mouth, because she looks as shocked as I feel when her lips part and I'm able to push my fingers inside.

I realize my mistake instantly, and it makes me regret this even more than tasting her the first time.

Her lips seal around my fingers before her tongue licks around each one as she sucks.

My breath catches and my cock weeps. That is until just before she releases me and her teeth sink down into my skin.

"Argh, you fucking bitch." I pull my hand back, wiping her saliva off my fingers and pulling them up to see if she broke the skin.

"Put any part of your body in my mouth and that's what's going to happen, posh boy. Just because you've got money and a highly inflated ego, it doesn't mean I'm going to drop to my knees at the click of your fingers. Now, get out of my fucking way. I've got a job to do." She steps around me and pushes the door open. The move floods the room with light and she stops and looks back at me over her shoulder.

Her eyes run down the length of my body before lingering on my obvious hard-on. "Hmmm... looks like someone didn't get the message. Might want to tell your cock that I bite before you end up in the ER."

Her laugh fills the room as she steps out and allows the door to slam closed behind her.

"Fuck," I bark, lifting my hands to my hair and pulling to the point I think it might start coming out.

What the fuck is wrong with me? Why can't I just stay away from her? Leave her to do her own thing while I do mine? Why can't I just leave her the fuck alone?

Rearranging myself in my pants, I quickly wash my hands, not being able to cope with the scent of her lingering on my fingers. The memory of her hot mouth sucking on them is torture enough.

"Where the fuck did you go?" Mason asks the second I join him, Jake, and the girls outside the diner.

"Just went to the bathroom."

All four of them eye me suspiciously, but wisely, none of them say anything.

"Back to mine? There's still some booze left from Saturday night."

"It's a Monday night," Camila points out, looking a little shocked by the suggestion.

"Right, which means we've got the whole week still to get through before the game Friday."

"Even more reason why you shouldn't be drinking. We need you all sharp and focused if we're going to make it past the first game."

Rolling my eyes at her, I catch Jake's. His hold the same seriousness that Camila's do, but I already know he's reading more into this than I want him to.

The truth is that I just don't want to go home to an empty house right now. I can't handle the fact that they'll all head off home together to enjoy their evenings while I'm going to end up getting off-my-ass drunk just to escape reality.

"Yeah, let's head to yours. Cam's right, though. No alcohol, and definitely no weed."

"Spoil sport."

17

RAELYNN

"**J**esus, Rae. You look like you've just seen a ghost," Bill helpfully points out when I stumble into the kitchen a few minutes later.

What I really needed to do was lock myself in the ladies' bathroom and take a breather, but I'd lost track of how long Ethan had me pinned in that dark room, and I didn't want anyone to think I was taking the piss on my first night.

"I'm good. I'm good."

"Okay," he says, but he doesn't look convinced as he keeps his eyes on me for a few more moments.

"It's starting to quiet down out there at least," Cody says, joining us in the kitchen. Thankfully, he's too busy dropping off plates to notice my appearance.

My heart is still trying to pound out of my chest, and my veins feel like they're filled with lava from the way he was touching me. I'm not even going to start on the state of my panties, because he was right. I didn't get myself off after he had me on the edge the other night, and now, after he's had another go, I'm fucking desperate for a release.

Thankfully, the rest of the night is much less eventful.

We've had a steady stream of customers—some I'm sure are Rosewood students, but they're all polite and most tip me really well, which helps toward Ethan's unpaid check.

"Honestly, it's fine," Bill argues when I'm forced to explain why the register doesn't add up at the end of the night.

"No, I always pay my way."

"It's not your *way* to pay though, is it? I'll get it out of Ethan one way or another, don't you worry about that."

"But—"

"No buts. You've been great tonight, Rae. I think it's the beginning of a beautiful thing. Now get the hell out of here and go and do some homework or something that'll ensure you don't spend the rest of your life waiting on others."

"It's done okay for you," I say, now having experienced just how much he loves his place and his job.

"Maybe so, but I've seen the fire in you tonight. You're destined for greatness, kid. Not a diner. Now scoot. Both of you." Bill flicks a cloth in both mine and Cody's direction, and together we head to get our stuff and leave for the night.

"See, I told you things would get better," he says as we walk toward the parking lot.

"I guess."

"Are you going to have an even bigger fan club by tomorrow evening?" he asks lightly.

"Probably. No one here really likes or wants me here."

"Hey, that's not true. I'm starting to think you might be pretty awesome."

"Oh yeah?"

He shrugs, a little color hitting his cheeks at his admission. "You need a ride home?"

"Uh... it's okay. I was going to walk, clear my head."

"It's dark."

"And?"

"Come on, I'll give you a ride." I go to argue, but he soon

cuts me off. "It's just a ride, Rae. I'm not offering up marriage."

"I know, I'm just not used to anyone offering me anything."

His mouth opens to respond, but he soon changes his mind and closes it again. Awkwardness crackles between us until he comes to a stop behind a red Ford and points toward the passenger side.

The journey home is nice enough. Cody chats about college and his life here while I try to avoid any conversation about how I came to find myself in Rosewood, aside from what he already knows.

"It's just up here," I say, wanting the seat to swallow me up when the houses that line this street start to turn into mansions.

"Up here?" he asks, skeptically.

"Sadly. This one." I point to the driveway, expecting him to pull up at the curb so he can make a quick escape, but instead he pulls right up in front of the house. The gravel beneath the tires crunches as we make our way up the ridiculously long track and come to a stop behind the cars here. My heart drops that he's home, but knowing he's got company makes it that little bit better.

Risking a glance at Cody, I see his eyes widen as the house appears before him. "And you need a job at Aces why?"

"Don't be fooled. None of this has anything to do with me. I'm just an unwanted guest right now."

The car slows to a stop and the intensity of his stare hits the left side of my face as he turns to me.

"So how have you ended up here exactly?"

"My mom." I let out a huge sigh. "She's been seeing the man who owns this place. She moved us here out of the blue."

Peering at Cody out of the corner of my eye, I'm pleased when I find no evidence that he already knows the story of what's happening under this roof. After the way Bill seemed to know everything, I was worried the whole town was aware of

Eric's affair which saw his wife run out of town and for us to be shipped in.

"That's tough. Nice digs, though. Could have been a hell of a lot worse."

"Oh, don't worry. She's dragged me to hell and back before." The words are out of my mouth before I have a chance to stop them.

I stare out the window at the giant brick build mansion and sigh. Movement in one of the downstairs windows catches my eye and my blood runs cold. Oh goodie, Ethan's waiting for me.

I have no idea how long we sit there in silence, but eventually, Cody breaks it. "If you need to sit out here all night then that's fine. It would have been good if you'd have warned me, though. Could have got some food." His voice is full of humor, but it doesn't really hit his target.

"I'm so sorry," I say sadly. "You must have better things to do tonight than sit here."

I release the seatbelt and reach for the handle, but his soft voice stops any further movement. "If you need a friend, Rae. I'm here."

"You don't even know me." I don't mean to sound defensive, but no one's ever offered to be my friend before. They usually run as fast as they can in the opposite direction.

"I get good vibes. And forgive me for saying it, but I get the impression that you're kind of lonely."

A lump of emotion crawls up my throat at his words. "I'm used to it."

He stares at me for a beat, his mouth opening to say something but obviously deciding better of it. "Can I give you my number? Just in case you ever need a friendly voice."

"Sure." I pull my shitty cell from my pocket, open my contacts and hand it over. Cody does a double take on it before tapping in his details and then ringing himself.

"Thanks," I mutter, taking it back. "I should probably go."

I push the door open and stand before leaning back in. "Thank you. I... uh... really appreciate it."

"Anytime. I'll see you tomorrow night, yeah?"

"Can't wait." An almost genuine smile twitches at my lips before I shut his door and wave him off.

I stand at the front door for a long few minutes, still putting off going inside, but I know I can't stay out here forever.

Eventually, I turn and push the heavy front door open. The sound of the TV and people chatting and laughing filters down to me as I make my way to the kitchen for a drink.

I'm standing behind the refrigerator door, about to pull out a bottle of water, when a shadow falls over the floor beside me. My stomach twists, but fuck if it's not fear laced with a hefty amount of desire after our encounter earlier.

Blowing out a slow breath, I pull a bottle out and prepare to face him. Shutting the door, I keep my eyes on the floor, hoping he'll allow me to escape unscathed. I know it's wishful thinking.

I take a step toward the door, but he's right there, blocking my exit. My skin prickles with his undivided attention on my body, but still I refuse to give him the satisfaction of looking at him. I've had my fill of him today. I just want to lock myself in a room and try to block out any memory of ever meeting him.

"Who is he?" His words shock me so much that my eyes fly up to his. I find his stare hard and piercing as he waits for his answer.

"Why the fuck do you care?"

He takes a step forward and I suck in a breath before he steals all the air from around me. It's a huge mistake, because his manly scent invades my senses as he gets in my personal space.

"Ethan, let the girl get a drink, will you? She's been

working all night," a soft English voice says from behind him, but with his wide shoulders blocking my view, I don't see her as she joins us.

Ethan's teeth grind as he continues to stare down at me.

"Ethan, for fuck's sake." A delicate hand curls around his upper arm before she forces herself between us.

"Would you like to join us?" she asks me, looking back over her shoulder.

"No," rumbles up Ethan's throat at her offer.

"We're just in Ethan's den. You're more than welcome."

"No. No, she's fucking not."

"Down, boy." She laughs at Ethan, but it does nothing for the raging inferno that's blazing in his eyes.

"Whatever," I mutter, taking a step back and finally able to breathe. "I've got better things to be doing than hanging out discussing high school gossip."

I leave the room, but it's not until I turn the corner to head up the stairs that I lose his attention.

"What the fuck is your problem?" she barks at him, and I can't help but smile at her attempt. My steps falter so I can hear his response.

"I fucking hate her. She needs to get out of my fucking house and my fucking life."

"Riiight. Ethan, I'm neither blind nor stupid, and you may recall that I've been in a very similar situation. I know exactly where your head is at right now, and I get it, I do. But—"

"But?" he barks. Most people would probably cower at his booming voice, but I get the feeling she doesn't even flinch.

"But stop being such a fucking wanker. She's new. It's hard. And it certainly wasn't her choice to be here, so give her a fucking break."

"Whatever." His footsteps get louder, and I run up the remaining stairs as fast as my legs will carry me. I don't need him knowing that I was listening.

Closing my door behind me, I hope that he's too busy with his friends for me to have to bother with dragging the dresser across—for now, at least. I throw my purse down on the bed and start stripping out of my clothes for a shower. Ethan and his little pathetic posse aside, I enjoyed my shift tonight. It was awesome to be able to forget about the bullshit and chat to Cody and the other members of staff like I'm just a normal person. It was a bit of a novelty after the past few days of being treated like the scum of the earth.

I hang my head and allow the jets of water to thunder against my shoulders in the hope it'll release some of the tension pulling them tight, but I get little relief.

I run a brush through my hair, remove my makeup, pull on a tank and shorts, and climb into bed surrounded by the homework I was given today, ready to make a start.

My future is the one thing I have control of right now, and I intend to do everything I can to ensure I can get the hell away from here at the first possible opportunity. If Mom wants to continue living this life, then she's welcome to it. Ethan's right about one thing: I don't belong here. I knew that from the moment I stepped foot inside this house.

I'm just reading through one of the chapters I've been given when a knock on my door halts my movements.

I glance over, wishing I'd pulled the bloody dresser over before I crawled in here. My heart starts to race as I wait for what he's going to do. The second he realizes he can walk straight in here, he's going to, and Christ only knows what might happen once we're alone again.

Memories of his fingers moving against me earlier slam into me and my core clenches. Fuck him for making it feel so good.

Another knock sounds out before a voice I wasn't expecting calls my name.

"Rae, are you in there? It's just us."

"Fuck," I mutter under my breath, wondering how I'm going to get rid of them as fast as they appeared.

Climbing out of bed, I walk over to the door.

"Well, if it isn't Barbie and Sindy. What a nice surprise."

The brunette bristles slightly, but the blonde doesn't seem affected in the least.

"Hey. We wanted to come and make sure you were okay. Introduce ourselves properly."

"No need." I push the door to close it on them, but the Brit shoves her foot in the way. I arch a brow at her, hating that she's so damn tall I almost have to break my neck to look at her.

"I know how hard it is starting over here. I was you only a few months ago. I know how it feels."

"Trust me when I say you have no idea what it's like to be me."

"I'm not talking about you, I'm talking about your current situation."

"Ha, yeah, the Barbie doll who hangs off the football captain's arm knows anything about what I'm dealing with right now."

Something I must say ticks her off, because she steps toward me, quickly followed by her friend. "By all means, judge away. Most people do. But I can assure you that what you're thinking is wrong, and you and I have more in common than you'd like to admit." She glances over my shoulder and her demeanor totally changes. It's so fast that I almost get whiplash. "So, what are you working on?" She sidesteps me and marches straight into the room, followed by her friend.

"Uh..." I stare at them both as they walk over to my bed and sit down.

"I've been assigned this too. Boring as hell, right?" I stare at her in disbelief. "I'm Camila, in case you forgot. I'm sure you've had so many names thrown at you today that your head's spinning."

"Um..." My eyes flick between the two of them as I try to figure out what the fuck is going on.

"And she's Amalie."

"Right. I don't know what it is you're trying to achieve here, but I don't do friends."

"That's good, because we've already got enough. Just thought you might want some company while the guys watch football replays downstairs. Come on, we can do this together, make it quicker."

And that's how I find myself sitting on my bed, surrounded by books and two girls that I'm fairly sure I'll never connect with on any level aside from being stuck in this house with someone they're friends with.

I can't deny that doing homework alongside someone else makes it a hell of a lot easier, and I hate to admit it, but slightly more enjoyable.

Both of them chat away while we work and give me some of the high school gossip that I really don't give a shit about but listen to anyway.

They tell me about Ethan and their guys, and the sappy looks that cover both of their faces when they do makes me want to puke on the carpet. They both see it but also refrain from stopping.

By the time they leave, my homework is done and I fear I've had my first ever girls' night in. It's a weird as fuck feeling, especially as I curl down into my bed with my diary and relive the entire experience.

I have no idea if they go back downstairs to hang out with the guys; I don't even hear Ethan come up, because by some fucking miracle I actually fall asleep before two AM and end up being woken by my alarm clock the next morning.

18

ETHAN

Getting a lecture from Amalie was the last thing I needed after the day I'd had. The only thing I needed was to relieve some of the tension that was pulling at my body, and there was only one way I wanted to do that. I wanted *her*. I wanted her so fucking bad I could hardly think straight. The image of thrusting balls fucking deep inside that tight little pussy I've had the pleasure of dipping my fingers into was so fucking tempting. Hearing the little noises she makes when she's getting close, hearing her demand that I stop, that I release her. Fuck. My balls were so fucking blue I was expecting them to shrivel up and fall off any moment.

I've no idea what the time is when the others leave. I'd lost focus a long time ago; even Jake's chat about strategies for Friday night didn't drag me back to the here and now. The only thing filling my mind was her. It fucking infuriated me.

Listening to Camila's advice from earlier, I forgo grabbing the bottle of whiskey that taunts me from the side in the kitchen when I take the dirty glasses through and settle for a bottle of water instead. She's right. I need a clear head for the game, even if it means my reality is clear as fucking day.

I hover outside her bedroom door when I get there. It's so tempting to see if she's locked me out again, but the aching of my muscles from our grueling practice session earlier and the stinging of my tired eyes after nights of lack of sleep get the better of me. I don't even bother stripping down, I just fall on to my bed and almost immediately pass out.

When I wake the next morning, the sun has long risen, and school has long started.

"Fuck," I groan, dragging my sore body from the bed and toward the shower. I'm as quick as I can, but I feel like I'm moving in slow motion as I try to wake my ass up enough to function.

As I pull open my bedroom door, I find hers ajar. I want to go inside and dig around, but I've already missed morning practice. If Coach finds out I've also missed class because I was incapable of getting my ass out of bed, then there's a solid chance he could bench me Friday night, despite the fact we all know he needs me.

I force my feet to keep moving, I grab a black coffee as I pass the kitchen and make it out to my car to head to school.

She consumed my mind the entire day as memories from the fucking bathroom play out on repeat in my head.

Practice is fucking killer, so much so no one suggests even going to Aces in favor of quietly dying at home before it all starts again in the morning. The way Coach eyed me as I walked into the locker room after school, I had a feeling it was my fault for bailing on this morning that he put the team thoroughly through their paces.

When I get home, I find dinner on the counter that Rachel has left for me and warm it up. I barely taste the chicken and veggies as I pack it away, desperate for the energy it will hopefully give me.

I dump the plate in the dishwasher and drag my pissed off, exhausted, and horny ass up to my bedroom.

Her door is ajar just like it was this morning, and I can no longer resist. She's been messing with my head all day, so it's about time I ensure the feeling is mutual, seeing as we've had no classes together today and I've only seen a glimpse of her in the hallway.

Pushing the door open, I glance around the tidy space. I'm shocked she's not had the place redecorated black yet. The pink that adorns the walls sure doesn't suit her.

I pull open a couple of drawers and peer inside, finding nothing more exciting than a couple of her tiny skirts. It's when I open the first one on the opposite dresser that a smile curls up the corners of my mouth.

Her underwear.

I pick up the pair of panties on the top. They're exactly as I imagined what she was wearing last night at the diner. White, cotton and boring as fuck. A million miles from the sexy black ones I stole on her first night here that still sit on my shelf like a trophy in my room.

Moving them aside, I find the much more appealing lace that's hiding beneath. I pull a few out, imagining just how they'll look on her small yet curvy body. My mouth waters and my cock swells as I think of the body I've both seen and felt under my palms.

In a spur-of-the-moment decision, I scoop the whole pile up, along with her bras that are in the next drawer. I kick the door open that's swung back almost shut when another idea hits me. That thing's been pissing me off since the moment she moved into this bedroom.

With a newfound energy, I dump her underwear on my bed and go in search of my dad's tools.

By the time I hear a car pull up in the driveway hours later than I was expecting, I'm lying on my bed watching TV after showering the remaining sweat from my body from my evening exertions.

I tell myself not to, but I'm powerless to resist going to the window to see if that motherfucker from Aces has dropped her off again. I can't see her, so I can only assume that she's standing at the doorway and waving because he lifts his hand and nods at her.

The cheer squad are all about us and getting their teeth into any member of the team possible, but I've heard them fawning over surfer boy waiter before now. Any of them are welcome to him as long as he keeps his paws off *her*.

The front door slams shut and after a few minutes, the sound of her footsteps on the stairs fills my room.

"What the fuck?" she barks when she finds her empty doorway. I picture her standing with her hands on her hips, her lips pursed in anger and her eyes darkening with her need to hurt me.

I smile as I wait for what's to come next.

Her footsteps storm my way before my door flies open and her small, angry body appears.

"Evening, sweet cheeks," I drawl, running my eyes from the top of her head all the way down to her toes and back again.

She's wearing a white shirt that's tied around her waist, exposing her stomach and a ripped denim skirt with her standard fishnets. The whole look is finished off with a pair of heavy biker boots. I shouldn't like the look, let alone find it anywhere near sexy.

"What the fuck have you done?" she seethes, her hands on her hips as her chest heaves in anger.

I shrug and rest back against my headboard. My indifference fires her up. Her eyes alight with fury and her teeth grind.

"Where is my fucking door?"

"Gone. Easier access."

I rest my hands behind my head and watch as she tries to stop herself looking down at my bare torso. Credit where credit's due, she lasts longer than I was expecting her to before her eyes drop.

"G-give it back," she stutters, finding my eyes once again.

"So you can hide from me? I don't think so."

I glance around her and find exactly what I was hoping. Her bed. She follows my stare, her body practically swelling with anger. She storms my way, but not before I swing my legs from the bed and stand. Her arms lift, her fists clenched ready to fight as I stare down at her. The scent of alcohol surrounds her and now she's close enough, I see the glassiness in her eyes.

"You've been drinking," I state.

"And?"

She shrugs.

"Have you been with *him*?"

"Why the fuck do you care who I've been with? I haven't been here, that's all you should be concerned with."

"Where. Have. You. Been?" I demand.

The tension between us crackles, but she still doesn't drop her fists. I take a step toward her until her hands brush my chest. I fight to keep the growl in that wants to rumble up my chest from the contact.

"What do I need to do to get the answer out of you?"

She quirks her head to the side. My fingers grasp her chin and hold her in place. Her breath catches, and a little of the fear I crave mixes with the defiance in her eyes.

"I went to the beach," she admits eventually with a roll of her eyes.

"With whom?"

"With *him,* and a few of his friends," she taunts. "We had a great time. A little booze, a little sand, a little—"

"Don't," I warn, my fingers tightening to the point her lips open. It would be so easy to slam mine down on them right now, to plunge my tongue between them and take what I need.

"Why? You don't own me. I can do what I please—*who* I please."

In one swift move, I have her backed up against the wall beside the door.

"What are you going to do? *Touch me?* Bring me to the edge and leave me hanging once again? Does that make you feel like a man? Does it give you the sense of power you crave?" My jaw pops and the muscles in my neck twitch in frustration. "Does it make you feel special?"

Wrapping my hands around her wrists, I pin them to the wall at her sides as I close the space between us. Her face only comes to my mid chest, so she has to tilt it back in order to look at me. Her soft curves press into my hard places.

"Seeing as your mom walked away from you without so much as a second glance, I'm sure you enjoy feeling special."

"Shut up," I bark, having had enough of her spiteful words.

"Or what? What are you actually going to do? Finger fuck me into oblivion?" Her brows rise in challenge. "Maybe you'll just go the whole hog and bend me over your bed and fuck me until I'm raw. Would that make all of this better, eh?"

"Shut. Your. Fucking. Mouth."

"And what if I don't? Are you going to shut it for m—"

My restraint snaps and I slam my lips down on hers just to make her stop talking. A growl breaks free from my lips and I hate that I'm showing any sign of enjoying this. But fuck, if she doesn't feel fucking incredible.

My tongue delves past her lips, finding hers. She resists for about ten seconds, but when I press my body against hers and squash her against the wall, she soon caves. There's no denying my enjoyment then, because my length's pressed against her stomach.

I release her wrists, my need to feel her body beneath my hands too much to bear as her taste and scent render me useless for anything other than finding pleasure.

I find her bare waist and slip my hands inside until I find her bra-covered tits. She moans, her head hitting the wall, but her kiss doesn't falter.

She sucks on my tongue and my cock jumps at the possibility it could be next. It's about time I got something out of this war we have going on.

Her nipples pebble beneath my touch, and I desperately pull at the fabric containing them, needing to feel her skin against mine.

Pulling back from her lips to drag in a few deep breaths, I trail my lips to her ear.

"Did he make you feel like this?" I whisper.

"Ethan." I'm not sure if it's a warning or a demand for more. I take it as the latter.

Dropping to my knees, I push her skirt up around her waist, exposing the tiny pair of panties she's wearing.

"Did you wear these for him? Hoping he'd notice when you bent over in the kitchen and take you from behind?"

"No," she whispers so quietly that I almost miss it.

"Or did you save showing it off until you had an audience on the beach? Give him and his friends a little show?"

"No," she says louder.

"The things they could have done to you on an empty beach after you'd had a few drinks." I shudder at the thought. No one touches her besides me. My words might be affecting her right now, but fuck if they're not driving me crazy too.

Reaching up, I thread my fingers into her fishnets and pull until they practically disintegrate in my hands, leaving her just in her tiny red panties. They're almost too pretty to ruin. Almost.

"Ethan," she gasps as the sound of the lace ripping fills the silent space around us.

Pulling them from her body, I abandon them on the floor before dipping my finger into her heat.

"Oh god," she whimpers above me.

"You get so wet for me, sweet cheeks."

"How do you know it wasn't for him? For him and his friends?" she grates out between heaving breaths.

I don't give her an answer. Instead, I lift her leg over my shoulder, part her, and press my tongue to her clit.

"Fuck, fuck, fuck," she chants, her fingers threading into my hair and pulling so tight it starts to sting.

Her addictive taste fills my mouth, and I breathe a sigh of relief like a junkie getting his next hit. I lick at her feverishly as she chants incoherent things above me. Needing more from her, I lift my other hand and find her tight entrance. I circle around it, making her cry out my name. Every muscle in my body locks up as I fight my need to throw her down on my bed and fuck her into next week.

This woman drives me to insanity. I shouldn't want to touch her, let alone crave her this fucking badly.

Pushing up inside of her, I bite down on my cheeks as her walls ripple around my finger and I imagine just how that might feel on my cock.

"Come, sweet cheeks," I growl, her hands gripping impossibly tight as I find the spot inside her which makes her tremble with her impending pleasure.

I want to punish her, make her pay for turning up here like she did, but as she climbs to the point of no return, I'm powerless but to allow her to fall this time. My name is barely a plea on her lips, and fuck if it doesn't make me want to know how it'll sound as she reaches climax.

My teeth graze her clit and she stills, her pussy flooding my fingers before she cries my name, her head slamming back against the wall as she rides out her orgasm.

Unable to fight my need to look at her, I pull back so I can take in the look on her face as she loses control. It's fucking breathtaking.

I continue fucking her with my fingers until she stops pulsating around me. I pull them out, suck them into my mouth and stand.

Her eyes are glassy with lust, her lips parted as she tries to catch her breath.

Allowing her eyes to drop from mine, she takes her time running them over the ridges of my abs and following my v lines down into my very tented shorts.

"Off," she demands, nodding toward my only bit of clothing.

I'm solely thinking with my cock, and I foolishly do as she asks, dropping the fabric to my ankles and letting my hard length spring free.

19

RAELYNN

I try not to focus on just how mind-blowing that release was as I struggle to get my brain to fire. That motherfucker has taken my bedroom door off—the only thing I've got that allows me to hide in this goddamn house.

He's going to fucking pay for this. And if he thinks the orgasm he just delivered goes anywhere toward making it better, then he needs to think again.

He has no idea, but he's just upped the stakes on this little game of hate we're playing.

I stare down at his cock as I try to get my breathing under control. I must admit that it was easier than I thought it would be to get him to expose himself. But then, guys do think with their cocks, so I'm not sure why I'm surprised.

It twitches under my stare as he waits for me to do something.

Tilting my head to the side, I make a show of biting down on my fingernail. "You know, I thought for all your arrogance that you'd be rocking something much more impressive." He snorts a laugh, assuming that I'm joking. Looking up to his eyes, I see a little vulnerability sneak into them. No better way to offend a hot-blooded male than to insult his manhood. "I've got dildos bigger than that. Come back when you've hit puberty and I'll consider it."

Spinning on my heels, I race back to my room, leaving my ruined panties on his floor as a reminder of my visit.

His growl sounds out behind me, quickly followed by his footsteps. I stop in my doorway and turn to him.

"Stop," I demand, putting both my palms up to him.

He's still gloriously naked, having shaken off the fabric around his ankles, but I'm unable to appreciate it due to the fact that I just lied and told him he wasn't all that. Our eyes hold, something sparking between us. My core aches for more of what he just gave me, but I'm not giving him any more than I already have. Even that was more than he deserves, but the second he put his hands on me, I was powerless to resist.

"You might have removed the door, but this is my space. If you know what's good for you, you'll allow me it. Fuck the privacy; you've already seen everything anyway. But you do not take a step past this door frame. Understood?"

His eyes narrow. He wants to defy me, as I was expecting. Really, I don't have a leg to stand on. If he insists on invading my room then he will, he's already proved that, but I want to see if there's anything redeemable about my asshole housemate.

I take a step back to see what he'll do, mostly expecting him to follow me, but he doesn't. He and his still-hard cock stay on his side of the threshold. He lifts his arms and his fingers grip the frame above his head. The move makes his muscles ripple deliciously. It's almost painful to keep my eyes on his face.

"I suggest you go to bed, Ethan. It's late, and it's a school night."

"Didn't stop you drinking, did it?" he sneers, watching as my hand lifts to the bottom of my shirt.

"I'm a big girl, Ethan. I can do what the fuck I like."

His eyes widen in delight when I pull the fabric up over my head before undoing my bra and allowing it to drop to the floor at his feet.

A low groan rumbles up his throat and I just about manage to contain the smile that wants to make its way to my lips, knowing this is affecting him.

"Regretting it yet?"

"What?" he barks, his eyes locked on my bare tits. If the situation were anything else, I'd be cowering away, but something about Ethan makes me so brazen. It's probably my need to prove to him that all these little tricks he's playing, making me vulnerable by stripping me bare, aren't going to intimidate me.

"I could be hiding behind a door right now. You'd have no idea I was standing here almost naked."

His eyes darken. "I've got a fucking imagination, sweet cheeks."

"Good thing, really," I mutter, pulling open a drawer and dragging out an over-sized shirt.

"And why's that?"

"You're going to need it. You're getting no more from me."

"Is that right?" He lifts his foot to take a step forward, and my brow arches in warning. "Fine. But this isn't over."

"You're damn fucking right it's not."

His teeth grind and his jaw tics. After sweeping up my discarded bra, muttering something about having the set, he turns on his heels and storms to his room. My eyes feast on his muscular back covered in that stunning tattoo until he slams his door behind him so hard that the house rocks.

A bitter laugh falls from my lips. There's nothing amusing in the slightest about tonight, but I think the lingering alcohol from the beach along with the dying aftershocks from my orgasm make me slightly crazy.

I had no intention of going out drinking after work. I had homework to do, so as far as I was concerned, I was going to come straight back here and hope that I'd be allowed to get on with it. A small part of me even hoped Ethan's friends might be here. It was a weird feeling, because I've never done homework with anyone in my life, but even I can't deny how good last night was as we worked together.

Cody had invited me to join him down to the beach earlier in the evening, but I'd declined. I thought he'd accepted it, but as our shift came to a close, he started rattling off reasons why I needed to kick back and enjoy myself. I couldn't really argue with any of his points, but after a day at school, I'd had my fill of judgmental assholes.

He assured me that his friends were nothing like that, and after promising me a lift home, I relented, his promise of beer and a joint if I was really lucky getting the better of me.

It was a good night. At no point did the team or the cheer squad appear like I expected them to. There were other kids I vaguely recognized from school, but without their leaders here to influence them, they were shockingly polite as I took their orders and delivered their food. I know they recognized me, it was right there in their eyes, but no one said a word.

Cody promised that his friends were different, and seeing as he'd only been kind to me during our very short friendship, I had no reason not to believe him.

The second we stepped down onto the beach, I realized he was right. His friends all glanced up at me, smiled, and said hello before continuing as if I weren't some crazy person with three heads, which pretty much sums up the looks I get within the walls of Rosewood High.

Someone passed me a beer, and just like that I was accepted into their group. They didn't care that I didn't belong here. They didn't care I was a high school student. They just accepted me for who I was, and it felt so fucking wonderful.

While Cody sat there with a bottle of water, I accepted bottle after bottle until the world around me started to spin a little. It was only a few moments after I realized that that Cody suggested getting me home. I told him that I was capable of looking after myself if he wanted to drink with his friends, but he was adamant he make sure I was home safe. I refrained from pointing out that I felt safer down on the beach with him than I did being in that house. And I was only proved right when I walked down the hallway to find my fucking door missing.

Despite having zero privacy, I fall asleep miraculously early for the second night in a row. When I wake the next morning, the sun is streaming in through my open curtains and the door opposite mine is open, but the room is seemingly vacant.

Rolling over, I stretch out my limbs and glance over at the clock.

"Fuck." I sit upright, my heart pounding. I'm late. Really fucking late. Why didn't my alarm... "Motherfucker."

Jumping from the bed, I pull some clothes from the closet before turning to my underwear drawers.

My heart drops and my breath catches when I find them both empty. The only thing inside the drawer where my panties were is a folded piece of paper. Unfolding it, I stare down at his rough handwriting.

For easier access.

They're the same words he used to explain my missing door. Anger burns in my belly before it explodes to a raging inferno through my veins and pushes me forward.

I storm into his room and start pulling drawers open. If I don't have any, then I'll have to make do with his. I find a brand new pack of boxer briefs at the back of one of the drawers, and finding something else I can make use of on the top of the dresser, I swipe it off and take it all back to my room.

They're going to be huge on me, I already know that, so I throw my shorts back into my closet and pull out a baggy pair of jeans and a sports bra that I had in a different drawer, thank fuck.

I totally miss the first two classes of the day, so when I eventually walk down the hallway toward my locker, there are students in all directions, switching up books and having a quick chat with friends before the bell rings once again.

I make quick work of shoving the books I need in my bag before slamming the door closed and taking a step toward my next class.

The second I look up, I spot a familiar set of eyes staring at me, accomplishment filling his light blues and a smirk playing on his lips. Anger from finding my empty drawers explodes within me, and I storm over.

"What the fuck is your problem? Not content on driving me fucking crazy, now you've got to start stealing as well?"

"Like I said, sweet cheeks. Easy access."

"Like I'm letting you anywhere near me again."

He smiles, reaching out for my wrist and pulling me up against him before I get a chance to jump away. His head lowers so he can whisper in my ear.

"The sound of you moaning my name last night is still loud and clear."

My core clenches as I remember his fingers stretching me open.

"And now you're remembering it. Your breaths are increasing..." He reaches out and pushes the hoodie I'm wearing open to reveal my sports bra covered tits. "And I know your nipples are hard for me."

Desperate to wrap the fabric tighter around my body, I lift my one free arm to do just so, but before I get a chance, we're moving.

"Ethan, what are you doing?" His grip on my wrist is

painfully tight as he pulls me down the hallway toward a door I have no intention of going in.

"Ethan, no." I try fighting, but he well overpowers me. Slamming my free fist into his arm that's dragging me along does little to stop his progress.

"Fucking pain in my ass," he mutters before turning and lifting me. I'm none too gently thrown over his shoulder. I just about manage to keep hold of my bag as his arm wraps tightly around the back of my thighs. I kick my feet in protest, but I'm no match for him.

"Put me the fuck down," I bark as he pushes the door open and the smell of sweaty boy hits me. Amazingly, when I lift my head from being forced to look at his ass, the room is empty.

"You might as well stop fighting. No one will come and rescue you, trailer trash."

"I don't need rescuing, asshole. I can look after myself."

"Is that right?" His voice is almost amused as he lowers me to my feet and pins both of my hands behind my back in one move. My bag drops to the floor with a crash, a few books sliding from it.

My chest heaves with the effort I put in trying to kick him when I was in the air.

"When are you going to learn, trash? I get what I want when I want."

"Oh yeah? Because from what I saw last night, you wanted something." I glance down at his crotch before crawling back up his jersey to his darkened eyes. "But you walked away when I told you to."

A laugh falls from his lips. If I were a weaker girl it might have me quivering, but all I do is angle my chin to him in defiance. "Don't mistake my actions last night for me walking away, sweet cheeks. I was merely..." He waves his free hand around as if he needs time to come up with the word, but I know it's all an act. He is totally in control right now, and he knows exactly what he's saying. "Building the anticipation," he drawls eventually.

"There's nothing to anticipate. Nothing will happen."

He smiles, his eyes dropping to my own lips before he sucks his bottom one into his mouth briefly. I know he's thinking about kissing me last night, and I'm about to taunt him with it when there's a noise behind us.

I'm moving before I have a chance to blink. Ethan drags me around a corner to the farthest part of the locker room, the showers. He backs me up against the tiled wall, pressing his hips into mine.

Footsteps get louder before someone shouts out, asking if there's anyone here. My lips part a second before Ethan's large palm presses down on my face to stop any words that might be about to crawl up my throat.

"Don't. Even. Think. About. It."

His eyes drill into mine as I fight to drag as much air as I need into my lungs. My breaths were already coming out in fast pants before he half cut off my airways.

"Where's the little skirt today, huh? I was looking forward to watching you bend over in class."

"Fuck. You," I spit the second he releases me.

An evil smirk curls at his lips. Standing back, he pops the button of my jeans open. The fabric falls away enough to reveal what's beneath.

"Fucking bitch," he whispers, his hand coming up so his fingers thread into his hair and pull.

"What?" I ask innocently. "Mine seemed to have vanished, so I had to improvise. They're a little big, I must admit, but they're pretty comfortable."

His eyes are full of pent-up anger when he lifts them from the floor to find mine. I swallow nervously and wait for what's about to hit me.

"First you steal my mother, then my home, my peace, my motherfucking sanity, and now this? My fucking underwear?"

"You know full well that I didn't—argh," I squeal when his hand slams down beside me and the shower above sprays me with ice-cold water.

He watches in delight as the water soaks me through. The loose strands of hair that were flying around my face immediately stick, and I don't need to look in the mirror to know my makeup is already starting to run down my cheeks.

"And you're the one who's worried about the fact his life's been ruined." I laugh, but any trace of amusement is long gone. "You're a fucking joke, you know that?" I take a step toward him, but not away from the water. "A fucking waste of—"

My words are cut off as he takes a huge step forward. His chest crashes into my sopping wet body until I hit the tiles behind me. His fingers grasp my chin and my head's tilted so I'm at the right angle for him to slam his lips down on mine. He immediately pushes his tongue into my mouth despite me refusing him entry. He strokes my tongue, but still I refuse. My tightly balled fists lift and rain down fury on his chest, but he doesn't so much as flinch. In fact, he's so unaffected by the attempts to fight him off that his hand skims the wet skin of my stomach and is inside his boxers while I'm still hitting him.

"Give in, sweet cheeks. You know as well as I do that you're desperate for this."

I gasp when he finds my clit, giving him the access he needs to my mouth to really take what he wants.

"Fuck," he groans into our kiss when he finds what he was expecting. Me wet and ready for him. "You really love hating me, huh?" he whispers in my ear before sucking on the sensitive skin beneath.

Still the shower rains down on us, although at least the water is a little warmer now.

He circles my clit for a few more seconds, driving me higher and higher before dropping lower to find my entrance.

"Fuck. One day soon it's not going to be my fingers stretching you open."

"No, no," I chant, but my argument is weak at best. We both know full well that no matter how much I might deny it, the thought alone has more moisture heading south.

"I'm going to fuck you like you've never been fucked before. I'm going to make you fucking raw. You'll regret the day you ever fucking walked into my life. I'm going to fuck you so fucking hard that you'll never forget exactly how I felt inside you. No one will ever compare. Ever."

"Oh god." His words are like fuel to the inferno ready to detonate inside me.

"You'll remember my cock for the rest of your days. Always wishing you had another chance." He changes the angle of his fingers as he says this, and I break. My muscles tense before the first wave of pleasure hits me. Ethan slams his lips back down on mine to swallow my loud cries, but, not wanting to appear like I've just allowed him to take exactly what he wants, I suck his bottom lip into my mouth and sink my teeth into the soft flesh.

"Fucking bitch." He releases me, his fingers coming up to his lips to check for blood while I rest back against the tiles, dripping wet and fighting to catch my breath.

His eyes hold mine, the promise he just made me adding an extra spark, and fuck if it doesn't make my core clench for what he was describing.

Thankfully the water's stopped, but every inch of me is soaking wet. There's no way I can go to class right now.

"Get out."

"Or what?" I sass. "You going to follow through on your promise? Right here, right now?"

"Don't fucking tempt me, trash."

Holding the sides of my wet hoodie out, I show him the skin I've got on display. "But I'm already wet."

"Shut up," he barks.

"What? You going weak on me now? You ain't all that, you know. You're all talk. I doubt you could fuck me into the next hour, let alone next week."

"I said, shut the fuck up." His hand wraps around my neck, and I'm forced back against the tiles with a loud bang.

When he speaks, his voice is menacingly quiet. "You will get what I promised you. But on my terms. When I want it. Not when you're offering it up right in front of me like a whore."

He pushes away from me, reaches behind his head and pulls his wet jersey from his body. His back ripples as he moves, and I find myself motionless as I watch the ink covering his shoulder blades twist and flex.

"Why are you still here?" He doesn't look back at me. Instead, he continues the job he started. His hands lift to undo the waist of the jeans, and when he comes to a stop beside a certain locker, he pushes them and his boxers down, exposing his peachy ass.

He bends slightly to attempt to get the wet fabric from his ankles, and it's then that I see the black ink on the underside of his butt cheek.

"What the fuck is that?" I don't mean for the words to come out loud, but before either of us register, I'm close enough behind him to see it in all its glory.

A laugh bubbles up from somewhere within me. I feel fucking schizophrenic with the way my moods swing around this asshole, but seeing the tattoo on his butt, there's nothing I can do but laugh.

"Is that a fucking teddy bear?"

He spins, his angry eyes finding mine, but unlike last night I'm unable to resist the ripped body before me. He looks powerful when he's dressed, but like this, he's a fucking god. Not that those words will ever pass my lips, of course.

"And fucking what?"

"N-nothing," I stutter, staring down at his solid length. The head is purple and angry, proving just how badly he needs to do those things he whispered in my ear not so long ago.

"Either put it in your fucking mouth or get the fuck out."

I bite down on my bottom lips as if I'm even considering it and I take a hesitant step toward him.

"As tempting as that is, *Teddy,* I'm afraid it's a hard pass for me."

"Then why. Are. You. Still. Fucking. Here?" He's right on the edge of his control. I can see it in his eyes, and I've no doubt that if I hang around for even a minute longer, then I'm going to find myself in a position I've no intention of being in.

"I'm sure there's a cheer slut hanging around somewhere just desperate to gag themselves silly on that."

"GET OUT." His shout echoes off the walls around us, and it successfully gets me moving. I run over to where my bag and books are on the floor, gather them up, and head for the door. All the while, his eyes burn into my back.

Pushing the door open, I look back at him. He doesn't so much as flinch, knowing anyone could walk down the hallway and see him stark naked, but then I guess when you're as big a whore as Ethan Savage, most of the school's already seen your junk, so it really doesn't matter.

I nod once before disappearing from his sight and dragging in the first real breath of air I have since I locked eyes on him not so long ago.

20

ETHAN

"Fuck," I bellow as the door bounces shut. Turning, I bury my fist into the locker beside mine.

What the fuck was I thinking, dragging her ass in here? *You knew she wasn't wearing any panties,* a little voice says, breaking through the haze of anger and desire that's clouding my head.

"Fuck. Fuck. Fuck." The skin covering my knuckles splits, but I welcome the pain. It's a needed relief from the lead weight that seems to fill my entire body these days.

My banging must disturb Coach, because seconds later I sense him appear behind me.

"Get dressed, son. I think we need to have a chat, don't you?"

My head hangs between my shoulders. Disappointment comes off him in waves that I'm in here fucking up his lockers instead of being in class.

"Just give me a minute, yeah?" My voice is rough and barely sounds like my own, even to my own ears.

"Two. You can have two."

Yanking my locker open, I drag out a dry set of clothes and

tug them on. I run my fingers through my wet hair, pushing it back from my face, and with one loud slam of my locker door, I head toward Coach's office.

He's staring down at a clipboard with some plays drawn out on them, but despite my arrival, he doesn't look up. He just continues tapping his pencil against the plastic, seemingly deep in thought.

Coach is scary. He's intimidating, larger than life, and now, the only man I look up to. He's terrifying when he rips you a new one, but his silence is a million times worse than that. My stomach twists as I wait for him to acknowledge me.

"I'm ready when you are, son." Still, he doesn't look up.

I blow out a long breath, trying to figure out where to even start. Coach already knows the basics of what's happened, he knows I'm struggling, but fuck, putting this into words is harder than I thought it would be.

"I'm sorry, Coach. *He's* just fucked with my head. I'm so fucking angry all the fucking time."

"I get that, Ethan. I really do. But there's more to this than just your father. Tell me what's really going on." He sits back in his chair and finally looks up at me.

"He's moved her in. Her daughter too."

Coach lets out a breath. "Raelynn?"

My eyes narrow. "You knew?"

"Of course. Not much happens under this roof that involves my boys that I don't know."

I nod. It's all I can do. It's not the first time something like this has happened.

"She giving you grief?"

"No," I answer honestly. "The issue is all mine."

"As I assumed, seeing as she's started here and kept her head down. All the while you are spiraling out of control. Where is your father?"

I shrug. I thought they were supposed to be back by now,

but as usual, he just does what he likes. It was always Mom who'd call or text to let me know what they were doing and when they'd likely be home, but now, I guess it'll all just be a guessing game.

"Okay, so let me tell you what needs to happen." He leans forward and places his elbows on his desk as he stares daggers into me. "You need to focus, get your head in the game. Forget her, forget him. This is about you and your future. We win these playoffs and any college who knows their shit will want you. Three games, Ethan. You've got to keep your head for three more games. Hell knows I already lost Thorn to a skirt, Paine too if he manages to get back on the field. I need my best safety fully on board. You got that?"

"Yes, Coach."

"I'm sorry. I didn't catch that."

I lift my chin. "Yes, Coach," I shout, my deep voice echoing off his walls.

"Good, now get your ass to class. And if I so much as find you in here when you should be elsewhere, alone or not," his eyes narrow, telling me that he knows more than he's letting on right now, "then so help me God."

Rising from the chair, I walk toward his door.

"Ethan."

"Yeah, Coach?"

"Make your mamma proud, son."

Emotion clogs my throat. Unable to swallow it down so that I can respond, I nod my head and leave his office.

The temptation to march right out of school and attempt to forget this day ever happened is high, but I've already fucked up twice now this week. I don't need any more reasons for Coach to ride my ass before our first game on Friday night. So instead of walking out, I stop at my locker, grab my shit, and head to class.

The second I step into the room, all eyes turn on me. I

ignore the teacher, who barks something at me about my timekeeping, before walking toward the back and my seat that's waiting for me beside Jake. I pass another empty desk, but it doesn't register. I'm too distracted by the look on Jake's face.

"Where the fuck have you been, and why is your fucking hair wet?"

"Don't ask," I mutter, pulling my books out and none too quietly dropping them to the desk.

"Don't tell me—it has something to do with that other empty desk."

I shrug. "How should I know?"

"Don't bullshit me, Savage. I can see exactly what is going on. You hate her. I get that, more than most. But don't pull the same shit I did to try to deal with it."

"This isn't the same." His comparison of this situation with his and Amalie's pisses me off.

"Fine, okay. But let me just say this one thing..." He stares daggers into me until I've no choice but to turn to look at him. "Amalie is the best fucking thing that ever happened to me, and I could have very easily ruined it before it even started because of my stupidity and misplaced anger. She's innocent in all this, just like you are. Maybe you're not destined for anything together, maybe you're right. But she could be a friend, your sister. Don't fuck it up, whatever your relationship could turn out to be."

My breath catches as his words hit a little too close to home. "You know, I think I liked you better when you were an asshole."

His laughter floats around me before the teacher stops whatever it is she's talking about to ask if we're listening. I just about refrain from replying with 'does it fucking look like it?'

The rest of the day fucking drags. The only good thing about it is that I don't see her again. It almost means I can lock down the memory of her in the locker room as if it didn't exist.

I'm getting changed for practice when my cell rings. Dragging it from my pocket, I find my dad's name illuminating the screen.

My thumb hovers over the answer button.

"Just do it," Jake mutters over my shoulder.

Blowing out a breath, my lips press into a thin line and I swipe and put it to my ear.

"Yeah," I bark.

"I just received a call from the bank questioning a transaction made this afternoon in the mall. Victoria's Secret was one of the shops mentioned. They flagged it as unusual and wanted to know if something untoward was going on." The fact that he doesn't even say hello or ask how I am isn't lost on me.

"I'm in school. I haven't been shopping in—" My words falter. Trailer trash hasn't been seen since leaving the room I'm standing in right now. I rummage through my bag, find my wallet and flip it open. No credit card.

Bitch.

"Actually, no. It's fine. It was... Rae." Her name sounds weird falling from my lips. It's not lost on me that I've not yet used it, but there was something about her having an actual name that meant she was real and not just some part of my fucked-up imagination.

"Rae went shopping in the mall with your credit card when she should be in school? What the hell is going on, Ethan? And why wasn't she using her own card?"

"Nothing. It's fine. She just had a wardrobe issue, and I don't know. Maybe she thought mine was hers, I don't know," I ramble, just wishing he'd get off the phone. This is the reason she used mine, so I would get this phone call and have to explain myself.

"Did it burn down or something? She's spent a hell of a lot this afternoon."

"Yeah, something like that. It's fine, don't worry."

"Okay well… make sure she's back in school tomorrow," he demands, like it's my fucking job to parent the girl who's the same age as me.

"Whatever." Pulling the phone from my ear, I end the call and throw it into my bag.

"Everything okay?" Jake asks, but I barely register his question. My imagination is too busy running away with itself. *She spent all afternoon in Victoria's Secret.* My mouth waters and my cock begins to stir to life. I wonder what I'm going to find when she gets home from work tonight.

Easy access is one thing, but her curvy little body wrapped in lace… *Fuck.* My temperature soars at the thought alone. The image of her bent over with his ass on display, lingerie still in place as I slam into her fills my head and won't abate.

"Ethan?" It sounds like it's being shouted down a tunnel, but a quick slap to my head brings me back to reality.

"Get your fucking head together. Two days until this game, man. I need to be able to rely on you."

"We've got this, cap. Come on."

I make quick work of changing and head out onto the field for Coach to put us through our drills. He nods at me as I jog toward him, but I don't respond. I just get to work. I need the burn that only he can deliver if I'm ever going to successfully get that image out of my head.

My evening drags. I refuse the offer of heading to Aces, knowing that she'd be there working with fuck only knows what under her clothes. Instead, I head home, eat the food that Rachel's prepped for me and hang out in my den watching TV and attempting to do some homework. I'm not very successful at either and keep finding myself staring into space with only one thing on my mind. I know it's been a while since I got laid, but fuck. The permanent hard-on I seem to be walking around with isn't fucking necessary. I consider calling up Shelly or one of the other girls to come and relieve my situation, but the thought really doesn't appeal. The idea of someone else's mouth, on the other hand, I'm very interested in.

Pushing up from the couch ten minutes before I'm expecting his car to pull up on the drive to deliver her home—that's assuming she doesn't go out drinking with him again—I make my way up the stairs and into her room. I feel much less like I'm breaking and entering without there being an actual door to open.

The second I step inside, her scent assaults me and my mouth waters as I remember just how she tasted on my tongue last night.

Looking around, I find her diaries have vanished from the nightstand. Assuming they haven't gone far, I start opening the few pieces of furniture in here until I find them stacked neatly in the ottoman.

I pull out the same one I had the other day. I just lie back on her bed and flip it open when the front door slams.

Excitement fills my stomach as I wait for her to find me. She'll be pissed that I'm here again. Good. I want her fired up. She's more fun when she is.

21

RAELYNN

"Fucking hell, Ethan," I shriek, turning the corner to my room and finding him getting comfortable on my bed. "Get out," I mutter, my long-ass day getting the better of me. I've no idea why I'm so tired seeing as I've slept well the past two nights, which is something that hasn't happened in... forever.

"No fucking chance. I was just getting to a good part." Glancing up, I see what's in his hands that I missed when I first walked in and panic.

"How'd you find that?"

"You didn't exactly hide it, did you?"

"Where was I? Oh, here... *Mom's sick, so Kurt took me out for the day so she could rest. He promised me a fun day, but I didn't think in a million years that it would have been as fun as it was. He took me ice skating. Mom's always refused, telling me she's scared, but I've wanted to go forever and now I have. It was awesome. Then we went for pizza and ice cream. It was the best day. Kurt is by far the best boyfriend Mom has had. I hope things work out for them. I can imagine him being my stepdad one day. Aww, how cute.*"

I have to fight like hell to keep my body from visibly shaking as he takes me back to that time.

Mustering up the courage to speak in the hope that it'll stop him from reading further, I storm over, dumping my bags on the bed as I do. "Enough," I bark, leaning forward to snatch the diary from his hands. But he sees it coming and moves it away before I get a chance to get my fingers on it.

"Ohhh... someone's got their panties in a twist. You'd better be careful with them, seeing as you maxed out my credit card buying them."

My mouth drops open. I knew he'd find out. Hoped he would, actually. But I wasn't expecting it to happen quite that quickly.

"Wondering how I know?"

"Don't care," I mutter, turning my back on him and kicking my shoes off.

"My dad called," he starts, disregarding my comment. "The bank called him about unusual activity on my card. Wanted to know why I was buying women's underwear instead of being in school."

I'm glad I've got my back to him, because I know guilt is written all over my face. I didn't want to spend Eric's money, but the second I saw his card sitting on his dresser this morning after discovering my missing underwear, I couldn't resist. At the end of the day, it might be Eric's money, but it was Ethan's allowance I was splashing on the most insanely expensive underwear I've ever seen, let alone purchased.

After walking out of school, I continued with no destination in mind. When I came across a bus stop, I got on and just let it take me wherever while I stared at the passing scenery.

Everything was like a blur as I sat there, and that was fine by me. I needed to forget everything about this day that was entirely fucked up from the moment I woke up late and discovered my missing underwear. But the second I saw that we'd pulled up to a mall, the stolen card started burning in my pocket and I was powerless but to walk toward the shops. I didn't intend to spend much, just buy some cheap underwear to tide me over until the asshole gave mine back, or I found it. But when the first shop I came across was Victoria's Secret, a wicked smile spread across my lips and I couldn't help myself.

"Yeah, well. If his asshole son hadn't stolen everything I own, then it wouldn't have needed replacing, would it?"

Thankfully, when I turn around, he's closed and lowered my diary to the bed, his focus solely on me.

"So..." he says, flicking his eyes to the bags.

"So what?" My eyes roll in frustration. All I want to do is have a shower and get started on my homework, not have to deal with his bullshit.

"I want to see what *I* bought."

"You want to see my new underwear." *Of course he fucking does. Creep.* "Why? So you know what you're stealing next time?"

"No, because it's from Victoria's Secret and it's probably hot. I might even make you do a little fashion show for me."

"Make me?" I ask, my voice raising an octave in shock. "I hate to burst your little bubble there, hotshot. But you can't make me do anything."

"Now, that's where you're wrong, sweet cheeks." His voice drops as he says my one of many nicknames, and fuck if it doesn't make things flutter down south. "I can make you do a lot of things." He scoots to the end of the bed, his eyes roaming over my body. "One." He lifts his fingers to start counting, making me want to snap each one off. "I can make you want me. Two. I can make you scream my name when you come." My cheeks heat and I pray that he's too consumed with my curves to notice. "And three. I can make you beg for more."

"No fucking chance."

"You want to bet?"

I laugh. "No. I really don't want to make a fucking bet with you."

"Why? Are you afraid you'll lose?"

"No chance. I never lose."

"Well, then it looks like we might have an issue." He stands from the bed and stalks over. "Because I also never lose."

My heart picks up speed at his closeness, the heat from his chest seeping into mine and making my nipples pucker. His hand lifts to the zipper on my hoodie, and he slowly pulls it down.

"F-fine. W-what is it?" I stutter as he parts the fabric to reveal my sports bra clad torso beneath. Although the way he's looking at my chest, you'd think I was naked. I regret the question the second it falls from my lips, but the moment his dark, hungry and angry eyes meet mine, I know I've made a huge mistake.

"I make you beg for more, and you get on your knees and give *me* more."

"There's something fucking wrong with you." Somehow, I manage to sidestep him and escape to the other side of the room until I'm in front of the doors.

"Many, many things, sweet cheeks. But right now, my problem is simple." I keep my back to him, looking out over the view across the beach and to the ocean that's the other side of the balcony.

His heat presses to my back, the hard ridge of his erection pressing into my ass and making me bite down on my bottom lip as a wave of desire so strong washes through me. I hate him; he's an asshole. His closeness shouldn't affect me like this.

He pushes us both forward until we're on the balcony and looking out over the view.

"You think anyone down there can see us?"

I look to the people he's talking about on the beach who are only illuminated by the bright moonlight and gasp as his calloused fingers trail down the soft skin of my stomach.

"We can see them, can't we? So there's no reason why they can't see us." I would imagine the fact that we're backlit from the light in my bedroom only makes us more visible to them. A shudder runs through me at being watched, but I'm afraid to accept that it's excitement, not the fear I should feel.

"Hmm..." The vibrations from his low moan seep into my back. "That's what I was thinking. I was also wondering if they'd like a little show."

"Ethan." His name is meant to be a warning, but it sounds anything but.

"I can already taste this win. You're already moaning my name." His fingers tease across the waistband of my jeans before he pops the button and tucks them inside. "What happened to my boxers?" he asks when he finds the soft lace of my new panties.

"Burned them," I say between heaving breaths.

"Fuck," he groans before pushing deeper inside my panties until his fingers part me and find my sensitive nub.

I need to tell him to stop, to push his hand away. Anyone could look up here and find us in this position.

"Ethan, no." My argument is weak at best as he begins to circle my clit. My fingers wrap around his muscular forearm with the intention of pulling it from my body, but he presses a little harder, my body sagging against him as the pleasure races through me.

"You need to get out of my room." My voice is barely above a whisper and a far cry from the demand I was hoping.

"Is that right? So what I'm doing right now, with those people down there potentially watching, isn't turning you the fuck on?"

I shake my head against his chest, the only argument I have.

"That's weird, because what I'm feeling is very different. You're wet as fuck right now, sweet cheeks. And those down there," he threads his fingers into the back of my hair with his free hand and forces me to look down at the beach, "they're fucking loving it. Actually, I bet they're down there begging for more. You want to give it to them?"

"Ethan."

"Oh, baby. You've no idea what your begging voice does to me. You feel that?" he asks, thrusting his hips to ensure his solid cock presses into me. "It makes me hard as fuck just thinking about how hot that little mouth of yours is."

Oh fuck. My core clenches to feel something inside, his punishment on my clit not enough. But the second I start to think he's going to give me more, he removes his hand from me. My muscles go lax, and if it weren't for him at my back, I might fall to the floor.

"Nooo," I cry, immediately missing his attention.

His fingers grasp the shoulders of my hoodie, and in a blink, it's thrown back into the room somewhere.

"You think they want to see your tits?" he groans in my ear.

I shake my head, my panties impossibly damp at the thought, but it doesn't stop him. His fingers pinch the zip at the front of my top and slowly, so fucking slowly, he pulls it down until it releases my breasts. They were already swollen and desperate for his touch, but the second the cool breeze brushes over them, my nipples pebble and my back arches in the hope of more.

"You fucking love this, don't you, sweet cheeks? You like being put on display, being pushed to do something so sordid." His words dig up a memory that I spend months—no, years—trying to bury. The grip of the vivid flashback to someone else's words almost engulfs me, but as if he knows what I need, his warm palms cup my breasts and squeeze, bringing me back to the here and now.

I lean back harder into him and he palms them and pinches my nipples so tightly that a bolt of lust shoots straight to my core.

"You think all the guys down there are hard, watching me play with your tits?"

A low groan rumbles up my throat, my only answer to his question as my head rolls back on his shoulder, my eyes falling closed with the pleasure.

"Eyes open. I want you to watch them watch you."

In reality, everyone seems to be going about whatever it is they're doing down there, and although they can probably see our figures, I doubt they can see what we're doing or the fact that I'm topless.

"You want more, sweet cheeks?"

A "yes" falls from my lips before I even realize I've said it, my body so desperate for the release he can give me now he's started.

His hands leave my breasts in favor of my jeans. They're pushed from my hips, and in seconds they're pooled at my ankles. Ethan demands I step out of them before kicking them back into the room.

"Nice choice," he says, running his finger over the delicate lace of the G-string I'm wearing. "Did you know that red's my favorite color?"

I shake my head, although seeing as the school and his team play in red, it was a good guess that he'd like it. Not that that was why I bought it, of course. *Bullshit,* a little voice screams in my head.

His hands stop on my hips, and I'm spun and pushed up against the railing. The cold bites into my bare ass, but I don't have time to think about it because the darkness in Ethan's eyes captures my attention. He looks wild. I've no idea if he's been drinking tonight. I can't smell it on him, that's for sure, but he looks like a man possessed. I wonder if it's desire or just pure hate that's running through him.

For the first time tonight, a sliver of fear creeps in. Is he going to take this too far? Force me to do something that I'm not ready for? This game we've been playing, this push and pull is fun and all, but I'm very aware that it could turn into something very ugly very quickly, and if that happens then I'm afraid to consider the fact that he really could shatter me. He could drag me back to my past, and I'm not sure how I'd manage to get myself out of that dark hole I was once in. Especially while under the same roof as him.

His eyes bounce between mine, and for the briefest moment, I see something else in them. Something more than just the desire and anger. Something deeper. Something painful, and it's that I latch onto. He's acting out, trying to prove he has power over this house and the things that happen inside it, but deep down, his actions are coming from his pain over what's been forced on him. I get that. I understand that burning anger for something you have no control over. It's probably the reason I've allowed things to go as far as they have between us. The reason why I'm once again standing basically naked in front of him, giving him everything—or almost everything—he wants because I see more. I see deeper, and he fucking hates it.

No sooner has it appeared does it disappear, and his eyes harden once again before dropping to my heaving chest.

"Well, sweet cheeks. That's one sweet show you're giving those people down there."

I swallow my nerves as he takes a step toward me.

"You want to give them the finale?"

I swallow loudly and his eyes flick up to mine. They hold for a beat, and I swear he can see my fear for what comes next.

I'm out here, naked for all intents and purposes, and totally at his mercy. I could scream, but really, no one would hear it. He can do—take—whatever he wants right now, and as much as my body might be desperate for what he can give, I'm not sure it's worth it.

"Jump up," he demands. His eyes flick to where my palms are resting on the wide stone barrier that's stopping me from falling to the pool area below.

"Uh…"

"Do. It." He steps closer, looks at me from under his lashes, and helps me out by lifting my small frame from the floor.

I'm perched on the balcony. One wrong move and I'll end up a broken, probably dead, mess on the tiles below. My eyes hold his, too afraid to look around. Certainly too afraid to look down.

"I read something somewhere that fear only makes the pleasure better, more intense." A wicked smile curls at his lips and he leans around me to look at the ground below. "That's a long way down. Are you scared, sweet cheeks?"

I shake my head. In reality, I'm pretty terrified right now but have no idea if it's from possibly falling to my death or of him.

"Do you trust me?"

Again, the only thing I do is shake my head.

He laughs. It's deep and evil, and has a ripple of panic running through me.

"Wise. Very wise."

He pushes my thighs apart and stands between them. His own chest is heaving much like mine, although covered in fabric.

"So what happens next then, eh?" Our eyes hold but no

words form. "Are you going to give me what I want and beg? Or are you going to defy me, again?"

I tilt my head to the side slightly as if to say, try me. But I don't think he reads the move in the way I intend it, because he uses my angle to slam his lips to mine and force his tongue into my mouth. His hands slide down my bare back, goosebumps erupting in their wake as he drags my ass to the edge so he can press my core to his hard cock.

"Oh fuck," I moan, my head falling back. Pleasure takes over my fear as he rubs himself against me. His hardness and the roughness of the lace against my soft skin are too much to bear.

"Don't forget to hold on. I'd hate to have to clean up the mess when you hit the ground."

"Fuck you," I spit, suddenly finding my fire.

"Ah, so you're still in there then. I thought you were being too compliant." My teeth grind at his statement. Doesn't he realize how hard it is to keep my head on straight when his hands are on me? *Of course he does; it's why you keep ending up in this situation.*

I open my mouth to spit back some cutting remark about him being power mad, but he lowers his head and his lips wrap around my nipple. All thoughts leave my head in favor of feeling.

When he has his hands—or mouth—on me, all the voices in my head vanish. It's fucking addictive, which is why I'm here right now riding the very possibility of imminent death while desperately craving the lightness only Ethan can provide me with. My past vanishes, my present disappears, and I'm just a body craving release. We're just two people giving each other what we need to escape our reality. It's in that moment that I wonder if I should stop denying him more and allow him the same emptiness he must crave as much as me. If I can give him the same thing, would it make him easier to live with? Would he let up a little?

I don't get to dwell on those questions for too long, because he starts descending down my stomach. His fingers grip onto the lace of my panties and tug. I'm so lost to what he's about to do that I don't even chastise him for ruining them.

"I suggest you hold the fuck on if you want to see tomorrow," is his only warning before his fingers part me and he licks at my clit.

With the angle I'm at, I get to see everything. Every leisurely lick of his tongue against me, every time he grazes his teeth against my clit before he sucks it deep into his mouth and makes me cry out his name. I get to watch as he pushes one, and then two, fingers inside me. And I get a first look at my wetness covering his face when he pulls back to drag in some much-needed air.

When our eyes lock, I forget everything. Who we are, where we are, why I hate him so fucking much. The only thing I can think about is how much I need him to continue, how I need this and so much more from him. It's fucking dizzying how badly I need him right now, and although I hate to admit it, let alone accept it, words start tumbling from my lips.

"Ethan, please." I'm desperate to reach out, thread my fingers in his hair and drag him back to me, but I daren't move my hand from holding me up. "Ethan," I moan, flexing my hips a little in the hope that it'll entice him back.

"What is it you want, sweet cheeks?" He's sitting back on his haunches, his eyes following his fingers, teasing a trail over my heated skin.

"You," I moan.

"My what?"

"Y-your tongue. Your fingers. Please, Ethan. Please."

"Is that you begging for me, baby?" The achievement on

his face doesn't even register as he keeps me on the edge of earth-shattering pleasure with his slow movements and deep plunges of his fingers.

"It's whatever it is to get your face back between my legs. Argh, shit, fuck," I bark when he dives in.

I chant, scream, cry his name and many more things I'm sure as he pushes me toward the edge. I'm just about to crash when he stands, pulls me into his arms, wraps my legs around his waist, and carries me into my bedroom.

I'm dropped to the bed only a second before my legs are parted once again and he's continuing his previous actions. Only this time, he doesn't let up until I crash. And do I fucking crash. My entire body locks up as my release slams into me. I twitch and convulse on the bed, but Ethan doesn't stop. He doesn't pull back until I've ridden out every last second of pleasure.

He sits back, his finger still teasing me, sending aftershocks shooting around my body, his eyes locked on my pussy.

Once I regain the control of my limbs, I prop myself up on my elbows.

I expect him to immediately claim his prize for winning our stupid little bet. But instead, he's sitting there staring at me like he's lost in a daze.

"E-Ethan? A-are you—?"

Abruptly he stands, his hands lifting to his hair before he starts backing away from me.

My body fills with ice the second he moves away. Did I do something wrong? He seemed to be totally enjoying himself down there. Why's he freaking out?

He lifts his eyes. Our connection holds, desire crackling between us as I wait for him to come back and take what I now owe him. But he ever does.

He opens his mouth and closes it so many times to say

something that eventually I lose count. The silence drags out between us, the only thing that can be heard our increased breathing, before he eventually pulls his thoughts together and speaks.

"You're ruining my fucking life." And then he's gone. He leaves my room and, soon after, the house.

22

ETHAN

Unable to stay in the same house, I head straight for the stairs and climb into my car. I've got the engine on and I'm backing out of the driveway before my brain's caught up with my body.

It's late, I've got nowhere to go, but fuck, anywhere is better than being in that house with her.

My hands tremble as I drive. I squeeze the wheel in the hope it'll make it abate, but nothing helps. The image of her laid out before me totally naked and at my mercy is burned onto the back of my eyes, and no matter how fast I drive, no matter how recklessly I take the turns, it won't fucking leave.

Eventually, I pull up in the deserted parking lot beside Aces. I park so I can stare out over the beach and the calm sea beyond, hoping that the solitude will help clear my head, but it does fuck all.

I've no idea how long I sit there for. All I know is that it's too late to turn up on anyone's doorstep when I do leave. It doesn't stop me, though.

I forgo going to Mason. He's still living with the Lopezes,

and I doubt they'd be too pleased with a midnight visitor, so I go to the only other place I possibly can. Jake's.

As expected, the house where he lives is in darkness. I pull up on the street as I usually would and make my way around the house to his trailer at the bottom of the garden. I might think he's crazy to even consider moving in with Amalie, but one look at his dingy trailer and I realize why he's agreed. No one deserves to live in this shithole. We should all be grateful for Amalie for giving him a lifeline and being willing to help make his existence that much better. He's been screwed over from every angle all his life; it's about time he experienced some happiness.

His trailer is also in silence. I'm grateful it's not rocking—not that that would have stopped me letting myself in.

I flip the light on and I'm rummaging around his mostly empty fridge in the hope of finding a beer when footsteps make their way down to me.

"What do you—" Jake barks, probably assuming it's a burglar. Not that any burglar in their right mind would rob this place. "Ethan? What the fuck?"

I look over my shoulder to find him standing in only his boxers, his hair messed from sleep, although if Amalie's shoes by the door are anything to go by, I wonder if she had something to do with the state of him. I'm suddenly assaulted with the image I left behind. I could look like Jake right now, thoroughly fucked and sated, yet here I am, frustrated as fuck with the bluest balls known to man.

"Sorry, I needed somewhere to crash. You got any beer?" I ask, giving up on my hunt, shutting the fridge and turning to him.

"Your house not adequate enough? And no, it's game week. No beer. No weed. No—"

"Sex not on the banned list, I assume," I interrupt. The fucker doesn't even bother to hide his smugness.

"If you had a hot girl beside you every night, would you give it up?" His brow arches as if he really needs an answer.

"Fuck no. But you're our captain. We need you fully focused," I tease.

"I am. I'm fully focused on the game and fucking my girl into next week. Now, as nice as this little visit is, why the fuck are you here?"

"I needed to get out."

"Why? Your pare—dad back?" He catches himself at the last minute. The reminder of how much my life has changed in what feels like only a matter of days slams into me.

I stumble back with only a fucking bottle of water in my hand and fall down onto his sofa.

"No."

"So... oh," he sings as realization hits him. "What's happened?"

"Nothing."

"Okay," he drawls. "So really I should be asking what you've done." He sits on the other side of the couch, rests his elbows on his knees and looks at me, and I mean really looks at me.

"I..." I fall back and scrub my hands down my face. "Nothing. I've done nothing."

"Well that's bullshit, and you know it." The fucker has the audacity to actually fucking laugh. "You fucked her?"

"What? No. Of course I haven't fucked her." It's the truth, but fuck if it doesn't feel like I'm lying to one of my best friends.

"But you want to."

"No," I bark way too quickly and defensively. "I fucking hate her. Okay. That's it. She's in my house, in my life, in my face, and she needs to fuck off."

"Riiiight."

"She doesn't belong there. They both need to fuck off, and my mom needs to come back."

"It sucks, man. I get it. Family shit is, ugh... a fucking nightmare. Relationships are complicated, and although I'm in no way condoning what your dad did, clearly there had been issues with him and your mom for him to do that. You know better than I do that he's always been loyal, always respectful. It's out of character for him, so there's clearly shit you don't know about. But ultimately, what happened between them is exactly that: between them. What you need to focus on is them both finding happiness again, and if that needs to be apart and with other people, then so be it."

"Fucking hell, bro. When did you get so fucking deep with advice?"

"Having a family like mine puts things into perspective," he mutters. "You need to stop worrying about your parents. You'll be off at college soon, not giving two shits what they're up to or who they're fucking." I wince and he laughs. "Focus on you, not them. Focus on our final games, on your grades, on college. What the fuck ever. Just leave her the fuck alone. She's not worth fucking up your senior year over."

"Isn't she?" I mutter, and a shit-eating grin spreads across his face. Motherfucker.

"I don't know, Savage. I don't know her. But you do, and better than you're willing to admit, I'm thinking, if your being here in the middle of the night is anything to go by."

"Fuck you."

"Nah, save it for your girl."

"My wha—no. Fucking no. I hate her."

"I know. I get it, I really do. I hated Amalie, remember?" He looks to where I assume she is sleeping in his bed, and his eyes go all soft and glassy.

"You're so fucking whipped, man."

He shrugs. "Trust me, there are worse issues to have."

Silence falls around us. He continues staring at me as if I'm about to have some big epiphany while his words roll around in my head. I can't deny that some of his advice makes a lot of sense—not that I'm going to tell him that.

"So are you going to sleep here and let it spin around your head all night, or are you going home... *to her*?"

The image of her laid out before me hits me once again, along with the feeling that filled me in that moment. Since the day I learned of her existence and arrival in my life, I've needed to hurt her. Needed to prove to her just how badly she's fucking my life up. But in that moment, after she'd been begging for me to make her come, just like I told her she would, all I could think was that I needed her. I didn't need to hurt her, or teach her a lesson. I just needed her, and that was scary as fuck. She might have owed me a blowjob, but like fuck was I taking it from her when I needed her. I'm taking when I need to hurt her, prove to her who's in control of this thing between us. I can't let the lines blur. She's my plaything. My ragdoll to tempt and tease when I so desire. She has no control in this situation. None. Zero. *So why do you want to go and crawl into her bed to feel her against you again?*

"Motherfucker," I shout.

"Keep your fucking voice down. You think I'm good with advice? You wake Brit and she'll give it to you all fucking night."

"Oh yeah?" I ask, my eyebrows wiggling suggestively.

"You want me to fucking hit you?"

"I'd like to see you try."

It's in that moment when we're staring each other down that a figure appears in the doorway, clad in only one of Jake's jerseys and looking as happy as Jake was when I first arrived.

"You two need sleep. Your game is only hours away."

"Two days," I argue, and she narrows her eyes at me.

"Jake?" She holds her hand out, and the pussy-whipped motherfucker immediately gets up and walks over.

I'm still shaking my head at him when he looks back over his shoulder. "Listen to the master, Savage. There's no hotter sex than with someone you think you hate. Maybe you should give it a try."

My teeth grind, but any argument I might have dies on my tongue because I already know from the tastes I've had that it will be fucking mind-blowing. She's feisty, brave, unbreakable when she's clothed. But strip her bare and there's an innocence about her that I'm not sure she realizes comes off her in waves, and it's so fucking sexy.

Fuck.

————

I end up crashing on Jake's couch. Thank fuck they both go back to bed and seemingly go back to sleep; the last thing I needed was to lie there listening to them have a fuck fest and reminding me what I potentially walked away from.

Jake has me awake at the crack of dawn so he can get a quick workout in before our morning practice, crazy motherfucker.

Reluctantly, I head home to change and grab my stuff. My heart's in my fucking throat as I climb the stairs and prepare to look into her wide, dark eyes once again, but to my utter shock, when I get to her room, her bed is made and she's nowhere to be seen.

A mixture of relief and disappointment hits me, and I fight to keep the latter at bay. There's no way I should be disappointed about not seeing her. I should be glad.

I have a quick shower, drag on some clean clothes and head for school, ready for Coach to put us through our drills for the first time today.

Her bedroom taunts me as I make my way back downstairs, and I start to wonder if taking the fucking door off was the stupidest thing I've ever done. For easy access, I said. But fuck, easy access to her has only led to my head being even more fucked up.

Trying to push her to the back of my mind, I make my way to school via a protein shake from the kitchen and focus on the task in hand. Friday night's game. Coach deserves for me to be on the ball—hell, Jake and the rest of the team deserve it. We've worked fucking hard for his opportunity. I'm not going to let 'a bit of skirt,' as Coach would put it, distract me from my main goal: seeing Jake lift that motherfucking trophy.

I don't see her all day. By some miracle, she's not in any of my classes, and she must avoid the cafeteria at lunch because every time I casually look around I don't spot her. It's a relief, don't get me wrong, but there's this little nagging part of me that wants to know she's okay. That she's not as fucked up as me after last night.

It was fucking hot, though... my mind starts drifting over the events on her balcony the night before while I sit in last period. Watching her come undone and knowing we could have had an audience was a huge fucking turn-on.

I shift in my seat, rearranging myself.

"Get her out of your head, bro," Jake warns, leaning over and winking at me. Motherfucker.

"She doesn't exist."

"Right," he says with a laugh. "That's why you're squirming around like a bitch in heat."

"Shut the fuck up."

"Focus, remember. F-O-C-U-S," he says slowly, enunciating each letter.

I flip him off, but right at the same second our teacher turns around and stops what he's explaining to rip me a new one. Fucking great.

Practice is fucking painful but no less than I expected, and before I know it, I'm dragging my ass back up the stairs toward my bedroom. One look at her still empty and open bedroom and I know what I need to do.

After dumping my stuff, I eat the fish that Rachel left and then I go and find her door that I dumped in the garage. I make quick work of putting it back on. Fuck easy access; what I need is to stay away from temptation. Nothing good can come of things going any further between us, so I need to put a barrier up.

I'm aching like a motherfucker by the time I take the tool bag back to the garage. The sight of the water glistening in the garden catches my eye, and the relief of the jacuzzi becomes too much to resist.

I strip down to nothing, not having the energy or the care to head back upstairs for some swim shorts, and I lower myself into the soothing water. This is my fucking house and no one is home, so I tell myself that I can do as I fucking please.

I twist the top off the bottle of water I brought out with me and drink down half before resting my head back and allowing the bubbles to take away the ache in my muscles.

It's not until I hear a bang that I realize I must have fallen asleep. I sit up with a start, my heart racing as I try to figure out if I've managed to drown myself or not, but thankfully my head's still above water and aside from the moon and stars twinkling brightly above me, everything else is the same.

I rest my head back once again and stare at the stars.

Focus, Ethan. Focus on the game. Block everything else out.

Movement above me catches my eyes before she rests her arms on the railing of her balcony and looks out over the beach beyond. My cock immediately hardens as I think about what the view from down here might have been like this time last night.

Reaching down, I take my length in my hand. I've resisted this long, but my need for release is becoming too much and I've told myself time and time again today that she won't be the one relieving it.

I keep my eyes on her, wondering if she's reliving last night once more as well. What I wouldn't give to know her thoughts right about now. *I wonder if she'll write them in her diary.*

My hips thrust up as I remember just how she tasted last night, just how tightly she squeezed my fingers when she came. My grip tightens as I near the end, a low moan ripping from my throat. She turns as the noise hits her, and she finds me immediately. Her mouth parts as her eyes drop to the water. The bubbles finished long ago, and I have no clue if she can see exactly what I'm doing or not, but I'm so close to the end that I really don't give a fuck. With her eyes back on mine, my balls drag up and I groan out as my release hits me. My eyes are desperate to shut, but I fight it and keep them on her instead.

"Fuck," I pant, my heart racing as I come down from my high.

She doesn't say anything. She doesn't move. We're locked in our stare.

Something's different. I've no idea what it is. The tension that's always between us crackles like normal, but there's been a shift, and I worry it's me after my realization last night.

I desperately want to look away, to break whatever connection there is between us, but I'm powerless to do so. So instead, I push myself from the water and sit on the edge. I forget all about the fact I'm stark naked—not that I really care; she's already seen everything. Her eyes drop and release me from the daze I was in as she takes in my body. My temperature spikes and my cock twitches once again, knowing it's receiving attention from her.

Pushing myself to my feet, I turn my back on her. I know that if I continue looking at her dark come-fuck-me eyes as she stares at my body with desire oozing from them that I'll march straight up to her room and do just that. But I can't.

Instead, I scoop up my clothes, go straight to my own bedroom and lock myself in my en suite as I shower. The whole time thoughts of her rattle around my head, but at no point do I leave my room or see her, and that's the way it should be.

Between classes and practice, Friday seems to pass by in an exhausted blur. The excitement for our first playoff game has exploded to the point it's all any of us can think about. It's welcome relief from having her front and center of my mind, that's for fucking sure.

She hasn't paid me any attention since I was in the jacuzzi last night. Any crazy thoughts that she was going to appear in my room and do good on our bet were soon smashed when she didn't so much as knock on my door, let alone step inside. She just seems to be getting really good at avoiding me. It's something I'm allowing for my own sanity but equally something I'm intending on putting an end to very soon. She might think she's lost my attention, but it's very much the opposite. After lying in bed for hours after my late night nap, I managed to convince myself that I didn't really feel how I did when I had my head between her legs. My need is still there, still as strong.

I watch her in the couple of classes we share together, trying to figure her out, trying to figure out my game plan when it comes to getting her out of my life.

I know that Amalie and Camila tried reaching out to her the other night, despite the fact I told them not to, but other than the odd smile in their direction, it doesn't seem like she's making any effort to make any friends. It makes me wonder if she really has as much intention of hanging around in Rosewood as she claims.

I shake my head, focusing on what tonight is going to bring. The whole day has been a buzz of excitement. All anyone can talk about, including the teachers, is how we are going to smash the Beavers' asses tonight and move on to the next round.

I stand in the locker room, surrounded by the team with Jake beside me. He's fucking pumped, there's no other way to describe him. His eyes are firmly set on the end goal, and he's not letting anything slip until he has that trophy in his hands.

"This is it, boys," he says, taking over from Coach's pep talk. "This is what we've worked our whole lives for. We are so fucking close I can almost feel that cool metal in my hands as we take victory. This fucking season is ours, *motherfuckers*. Who's with me?"

A loud roar of agreement echoes around the locker room. We bump fists and slap each other's shoulders in excitement before Jake leads us out on the field.

The roar from the crowd is deafening as we run out to the cheer squad shaking their pom poms in delight.

This is the biggest crowd we've ever played for, I swear. The stadium is filled to the rafters. I can only imagine how epic it's going to sound in here when we pull off our win.

I glance over at the bench to find Mason watching from the sidelines, and my heart sinks a little. He keeps telling us that he'll be back for the final. I know that six weeks' rest should be okay after broken ribs, but shit, he almost died. The last thing I want is for him to push himself and do more damage than necessary after everything he's been through.

I nod at him, and he gives me a weak smile in return. I'm pretty sure he'd give anything to be standing with us right now.

I quickly glance around at the rest of the crowd. I spot some of the guys' parents cheering them on, but as expected, I don't find my own. Even *she's* not bothered to turn up, preferring to work instead of support her new school team.

I blow out a breath before Coach pulls us in for our final pep talk.

23

RAELYNN

"Shouldn't you be at school right now, getting into the spirit of things?" Cody asks as I lean my hip against the counter. Aces is dead tonight. We've had no more than three customers all night. Bill may as well have shut the place instead of paying both Cody and me to be here.

"Do I look like the kind of girl who'll wiggle her pom poms for the football team?"

Cody snorts with a mouthful of soda. "I wasn't suggesting you join the squad. Just thought you might want to—"

"Want to what?"

"Try to fit in."

"Meh, fitting in is overrated. I much prefer to be a social outcast. Makes things more interesting."

"I'll have to take your word on that."

"Oh god, you've always been the popular one, haven't you? Should we end our friendship now so I don't ruin your rep?"

"I wouldn't say I was in the popular crowd. That was reserved for the football and basketball players at my school. But I was never as disliked as..." He trails off. We both know what the end of that sentence is, but still, because I'm a bitch, I gesture for him to continue.

"As whom?"

"Err... you."

"It's really quite a skill, but by the time you've done ten schools in almost as many years, these things get easier." Cody pales slightly at my admission.

"Ten schools in ten years?"

"Not quite. More like eight, I think."

"You think?"

"Lost count after six." I shrug like it's no big deal, but really it is. A lot of my issues stem from my lack of a stable home. If I stayed anywhere for any decent time, maybe I'd have actually made some friends, have someone other than myself that I could rely on. But that's not how my life is, so I don't dwell on these kinds of thoughts. Well, I don't anymore.

Cody and I keep ourselves busy filling up the condiments and rearranging the cutlery tray—anything really to make the time pass. He offers time and time again for me to go and enjoy my evening, but each time I refuse. I'm more than happy there with him, and I feel much more at home than I'm sure I would at school with the others right now. I even feel more comfortable here than I do at home. Ever since Ethan walked out the other night, I can't settle. I've no idea where he went. All I do know is that he didn't come home. I can only imagine that he went to find a cheer slut after deciding I wasn't worth it. I still have no idea what went wrong, but I'm trying not to think about it. I shouldn't care. I should be glad that he seems to have given up on me, left me be to get on with things.

I blow out a long breath. Cody looks up, and I'm expecting him to tell me to leave once again, but as he opens his mouth, his eyes flick over my shoulder. "Looks like the game must be finished."

My stomach drops. The last thing I was expecting was for

them to all turn up here. I thought they'd go straight back to the house to start on the insane amount of alcohol that's been delivered. I've no idea how Eric allows Ethan to just do whatever he pleases with an open credit card.

Unable to resist looking, I glance over my shoulder. Only, I'm not met with either the exuberant or disappointed members of the football team like I was expecting. There's just one girl who pulls the door open and steps inside. She glances around, noting that it's basically empty before walking right up to me.

"Hey, Rae. Do you have five minutes?" I want to hate her, but her soft accent tugs at something deep within me.

"Um…" I hesitate, looking back at Cody for support, but the fucker doesn't help one bit.

"I think I can cope," he says, nodding toward one of the empty booths. "I'll bring you both a milkshake to give me something to do."

"Thank you." Barbie flashes him her megawatt smile and glides over to the seat. I'm not nearly so elegant as I follow behind.

"So, to what do I owe the pleasure? Shouldn't you be sitting on the sidelines screaming as we take the win?"

I stare at her. Her lips twitch as if she's trying to keep her excitement locked inside, but it doesn't seem to be a fight she's winning. "They've already done it. They fucking smashed them. It was incredible." Her excitement is palpable, and her eyes go all soft as she most probably thinks about the captain.

"Okay, so you should be celebrating then, right? I assume that's what the brewery's worth of beer is for at the house."

"Yeah, I'm heading there in a minute. I just thought that maybe we could have a chat first."

"Why?" I ask, surprised that she's taken time out of such a big night to talk to me.

"Ethan's…" She pauses as she tries to find the right words.

I have a few choice ones that I could fill in for her, but I keep my lips sealed, preferring to wait and see what she's got to say.

Cody appears at my side before she gets a chance and delivers two strawberry milkshakes that Barbie instantly reaches out for. I watch as she purses her pink lips around the straw and sit back to wait for her.

"You were saying?" I ask, ensuring it sounds as bored as I'm beginning to get.

"Ethan's a mess."

I snort. "You're telling me."

"No, I don't think we mean in the same way. Look, I've not been here all that much longer than you have, but those guys are already like my family. Yeah, they have their quirks, like everyone, but deep down, they're really good guys." I open my mouth to argue, but she cuts me off. "Ethan too. Ethan's this larger-than-life character who just wants everyone to be happy. He thought he had everything and then suddenly, his dad pulled the rug from under him and he's not stopped falling since."

"We all have shit in our lives. Why should he be given a pass because he can't handle it?"

"I'm not saying he should. I'm just saying that..."

I cross my arms over my chest and wait.

"Okay, look. When I first turned up here, Jake hated me. And I mean *hated* me."

"Please, that boy looks at you like you've just hung the moon."

A smug smile curls at her lips.

"Now, maybe. Then? He wanted me gone. He was hurting, badly, and he projected that onto the wrong person. Luckily— or maybe unluckily, I guess it depends on how you look at it— I gave him shit right back. I pushed harder when he tried to hurt me. I could see more. I could see the broken boy beneath who was desperate for love. Shit," she says, glancing away. "I probably shouldn't be telling you all of this."

"No, it's okay. Go on," I encourage.

"All I'm saying is that, in my opinion, Ethan is in a similar place to Jake back then. He's been hurt and he can't deal with it, so he's lashing out. He doesn't really hate you, Rae."

"I'm not really sure about—" My argument is cut off before it really gets started.

"Something's happened between the two of you, right?" My cheeks heat, and it must be enough to confirm her suspicions. "Thought so. I'm not telling you to give him a break, to go easy on him. I'm actually telling you the opposite. Fight back, push him. Show him what you're really made of, and maybe this thing between you will turn around."

"I don't want him."

"Never said you did. This might not turn out the same as things with Jake and me. But something's got to give at some point, and he needs someone, Rae. He's barely letting the guys in. The other night he turned up at Jake's place in the middle of the night. He was a mess. I probably shouldn't have been eavesdropping but..." She trails off with a shrug. "I should probably get back, Jake will be wondering where I am. I just wanted to reach out. He needs as many people in his corner as possible right now. I know it's not going to be easy, but one day, you'll get to see the real Ethan, and I promise you, it'll be worth it. Beneath that hard exterior is a soft and cuddly teddy bear." I snort a laugh as the image of the tattoo on his ass pops into my mind. "What?" she asks, a genuine smile forming on her lips.

"It's nothing. You'd better go before he sends out a search party."

"I wouldn't put it past him. Just think about what I said." She climbs from the booth and turns to leave but stops herself at the last minute. "You're coming to the party tonight, right?"

I shrug. "I'll probably just hide in my room."

"No way. Don't give him that power. Put on your sexiest... err..." She looks me up and down quickly, probably realizing that I'm not a dress kind of girl. "Fishnets," she finishes with a wink. "And show him what you've got. Drink, dance, make some friends. This is your home now, Rae. And believe it or not, some of us want to make you feel welcome."

Something burns at the back of my throat at her words, but I refuse to acknowledge what it is. "Thank you," I mouth.

She stops at the door and glances at me before watching Cody as he makes his way over. "Thanks for the milkshake. You're coming tonight as well, right?"

"What's tonight?" he asks, like he doesn't already know what's going on.

"Party at Rae's. If you're free, you're more than welcome. Any friend of Rae's is a friend of ours." With one more killer smile, she's out the door and gone as if she never appeared.

"What was all that about?"

"Ugh... high school bullshit. Whatever," I mutter, but I can't deny that her words haven't struck a chord with me. Especially her admitting that Ethan went to Jake's the other night and that he was a mess after we were together. What the hell is that supposed to mean? I tell myself he was just pissed off that he didn't stick around to get any and bury the little voice inside me that tells me it's more than that.

"So, party at yours?" Cody digs.

"Yeah, football party. They won, apparently. You up for it?"

"I've not got any other plans. Plus, if it means it'll stop you from hiding in your bedroom then I'm all in."

"You were listening?"

The fucker doesn't even have the audacity to look guilty. "You need to have some fun, Rae. Like *Barbie* said, put on your best fishnets and let's party."

And so that is exactly what I do.

The party is in full swing by the time we finish up for the night and make our way to the Savage mansion. There are cars everywhere, meaning that Cody has to practically park at the end of the street, and there are bodies everywhere celebrating tonight's win. The atmosphere is electric, and it almost makes me glad I'm going to get to experience it. Almost.

"You came," a soft voice sings the second we step foot into the house as Barbie comes around the corner with Camila not far behind. I'm surprised she didn't bring her to Aces; they seem to be joined at the hip.

"This one deserves a night off."

"A-fucking-men," Barbie calls, lifting her drink in the air. "Now, you need help choosing an outfit?" she asks, eyeing my current attire.

"I've been dressing myself for more than a decade, I'm pretty sure I'm capable."

"Nope, no way. Here, it's a fresh one," she says, handing her Solo cup to Cody. "Mason?" she calls behind her, and seconds later the blonde guy appears.

"You rang?"

"Yeah. This is Cody, guy from Aces, Rae's friend. Keep him company while we go and get Rae party ready."

"You really don't need to do anything," I mumble, but it falls on deaf ears because after passing her cup over, Barbie takes me by the shoulders and pushes me toward the stairs. When I look back, I find Sindy right behind her.

Fuck my life. This is why I don't have girlfriends.

The sight of my bedroom door hanging where it should is a welcome one. I wasn't expecting to come home last night to find it back, but I was seriously fucking relieved. Especially now, seeing how crazy this party is.

I'm pushed through it, neither of the girls behind me appreciating its significance. I wonder how I would have explained that to them if it was still missing.

"Sit," Barbie demands, going straight for my closet and pulling the doors open. "Okay, what have we got here?"

Sindy does something similar when she sits down at my dressing table. "You own any makeup that isn't black?" she asks.

"Yeah. There's purple lipstick there somewhere," I quip. It earns me an eye roll, but she doesn't say anything more.

Knowing I'm not getting out of this, I let the girls go to town, with one exception. My hair stays up.

24

ETHAN

I am fucking buzzing as I walk into my house with Jake beside me and the rest of the team hot on our heels. It was a fucking unbelievable game. We smashed the other team and proved that we deserve our place in the state playoffs. Rosewood fucking High is not a team to be messed with.

The crowd erupts when they realize we've arrived. The volume almost takes the fucking roof off the place, and my chest swells with pride. I love this. I love being someone to the rest of the school. I love belonging to something. I fucking love the guys who are standing around me. They are my family, and fuck if they've not proved they've got my back more than my actual family these days.

Drinks are handed to us and the cheer squad descends, mostly still in their uniforms.

"You were on fire tonight," Shelly breathes in my ear, pressing her body temptingly up against mine. I drop my arm around her waist and pull her tighter.

"Fucking right. And it was only the beginning. I've got plenty more fire for the rest of the night."

She smiles at me, a twinkle in her eye that holds promises for what's to come.

I slam my lips down on hers. It's what she—hell, it's what everyone—expects, so I may as well play my part. Only, everything about the kiss is wrong. It's nice, sure. But it doesn't have desire stirring in any part of my body.

"At least get through the door before you get her naked, Savage," someone shouts from behind as they push past us to get into the house.

"Let's go and get more drinks." Shelly slips her hand into mine, and I walk us through to the kitchen.

The music pounds and there are people covering every inch of the house. I couldn't think of a better way to drown everything out. It's almost like old times as I knock back shots with the team in the kitchen.

"Sooo," Zayn drawls. "Who's it going to be tonight?" He looks out over the crowd. "You tagging 'em?"

Jesus, we've not done this since the night at dash.

"Shelly," I announce, earning me a few groans.

"That's not even a challenge. One look from you and her legs are open, Savage."

I shrug, lifting my shot to my lips.

"No one said it had to be a challenge. Just that you had to name them."

"Dash night upped the ante, my friend. I'm calling your girl, and you've got until dawn."

Rolling my eyes, I pour myself another shot and knock it back. We just fucking won. No girl at this party is going to be a challenge for any of us tonight.

"I'm out," Shane pipes up from the other side of the group.

"Oh no, Dunn. You wanna hang with the big boys all of a sudden, then you've got to walk the walk. So... who shall we give Dunn?" Zayn looks over the crowd, assessing the girls in his eyeline.

Rich stands beside him, rubbing his palms together. "Victoria?" he asks.

"Nah, a cheerleader is too easy. Even for Dunn." Shane bristles, his lips pressing into a thin line. "That there, who's she?"

"No fucking way. Alyssa's my friend," Shane barks.

"That should be easy for you then; you already know her."

"Yeah, and I also know that she's after the basketball team. There's no fucking way any of you have got a chance with her."

"Zayn will give it a pop," I announce, pissed off that he started this game once again and wanting to give him a challenge.

"Fuck off, not if she's a hoop hooker."

"You called the game, but you don't get to call the shots. Shane can have Victoria— she'll have her sights set higher anyway—and you can have Alyssa."

"Fine. Whatever. I'll break her."

"But..." Shane argues, looking at the three of us.

"Sorry, but Zayn's right. You want to be one of us then you've got to act like it. Now, we've made it easy. So even a virgin like you should get the girl tonight." He pales, making me wonder how true that virgin title is, but I don't dwell on it. If he is, then it's high time he lost it.

"So if Savage is taking control, it's only fair he gets a challenge too."

Silence falls over our group as people start thinking about my target for the night. No single woman in this house is a threat right now. I so much as mention getting on their knees and they'll be down before they've even heard the words.

"Her," Zayn says, lifting his arm to point someone out.

As I look up, the world around me, along with the guys' excitement, fades into nothing, because descending the stairs and following Amalie and Camila is Rae. She's wearing the shortest fucking skirt I've ever seen with a simple black tank, but fuck if it doesn't make my cock swell on sight. Her tits are pushed up and are perfectly framed by the low cut of her top. Her hair, like usual, is piled on top of her head, but it's way more intricate than I've ever seen and her makeup, although still heavy and dark, is flawless.

As if she can feel my stare, she turns toward me. Our eyes connect and something crackles between us. The slightest of smiles curls at her lip before her normal scowl falls into place as she continues to descend and gets swallowed by the crowd.

I swallow harshly, knowing that after the shit I gave Shane and Zayn, I can hardly turn her down. Plus, like fuck am I allowing them to tag her for someone else. No other motherfucker touches what's mine.

Thankfully, I've had enough shots now that the fact I just claimed her doesn't really register in my head.

I turn to the excited stares of my teammates and take another shot when it's handed to me. "Fine. I'll have her on her knees in minutes."

"By that, I'm assuming you mean with a knife in her hand so she can cut it off," Rich adds, much to the others' delight.

"Ha ha. She's a pussycat, really. Stroke her right and she'll be putty in my hands." Zayn laughs before he turns his attention to the other guys, giving me the opportunity to slip away.

It takes me forever to get through the house. The place is packed, and with every turn I make someone wants to talk about some part of tonight's game. It's not that I don't want to relive our epic win, but I need her gone. Amalie and Camila might think that she's welcome, but she's really fucking not. I want to celebrate with my friends like old times, not have my reality rubbed in my face.

When I come to a stop in the doorway to the living room, I scan the dancing crowd in front of me.

I find Mason first, his blond hair standing out over the rest, and head over.

"Where is she?" I bark at Camila, interrupting their moment as they move together.

"Don't know what you're talking about."

"Right, like fuck you don't. Where is she?"

"Chill the fuck out, man." I glance at Mason and narrow my eyes. "If your girl tells me where she is, then I'll gladly fuck off."

I'm just looking back to Camila when I spot someone who really doesn't fucking belong here. Her little friend from Aces. He's a college kid. Why the fuck does he want to be at a high school party? Movement to the side of him catches my eye before I get my answer.

He reaches out and pulls *her* into his body. Their hips grind with the music, and he leans down to whisper something in her ear, or worse, to ki—no. Not fucking happening.

Anger swells in my belly and mixes with the one too many shots I've already had tonight. I push my way between Mason and Camila to get to them.

Mason's hand lands on my shoulder. "Think about this, man," he shouts over the music, but I barely register the words. I need to get his fucking hands off her hips. I need to get his eyes off her fucking body.

I barge through the people between us before lifting my hands and forcefully removing the motherfucker from what belongs to me. He stumbles back, the people surrounding us backing up a little to give us some space.

"Get your motherfucking hands off her."

"Or what?" the douchebag says, taking a huge step until he's standing before me.

"Or I'll fucking make you," I spit. I'm not aware that the music in the room has been turned down to almost nonexistent or that every single set of eyes has turned on me. All I can focus on is him. Him and the images in my head of his hands on her. His fingers running over her curves, dipping into places only I should be allowed to experience.

"Looks like you're going to have to, because as far as I see it, I'm doing nothing wrong." He holds out his hand, and I follow its movements to find Rae slip hers into it.

I see fucking red.

My arm rears back, my fist clenched, but just as I'm about to throw the punch, hands wrap around my upper arm.

"Don't even fucking think about it, Savage," Jake seethes in my ear, his voice low and menacing.

My chest heaves as he continues to hold me back. If I wanted to, I could break free, and he knows it. But I don't, I just stand there staring at him, warning him that he needs to back the fuck off and get out of my fucking house.

"What the fuck is your problem?" Rae stands between the two of us, her head tipped back so she can look me in the eye from her low position.

"You. You're my fucking problem; haven't you figured that out already?" Her teeth grind and her jaw pops in frustration. "Didn't you get the message last weekend? You're. Not. Invited. Now take this fucking pussy, and get out of my fucking house."

There's a collective gasp from the people behind me, but I don't pay it any attention, my eyes still drilling into hers.

"That's the thing though, Savage. This isn't your house. It's your dad's, and because of his wandering penis, you get the delight of having to live with me. So suck it up, asshole. This is my house too. You think you're king? Well, meet your motherfucking queen." She steps forward, closing the space between us. Her breasts brush my chest, and I don't miss the lowering of her eyelids at the connection. "So what are you going to do about it?" she taunts, her hand on her hips like the defiant trash she is.

Tension crackles between us as silence falls around the room. "Stay out of my fucking way."

I shake off Jake and storm from the room, needing some fucking fresh air.

This time, when I make my way through the house, everyone moves out of my way. Even those not in the room sense that now wouldn't be the time to step up to me. I'm unsure if that's because gossip really does spread that fast around here, or it's just the vibe I'm giving off as I make my way out to the pool area.

Even out here is packed, but as I make my way over to the loungers on the far corner of the pool, the kids who were sitting there scamper.

I fall down, rest my head back, and squeeze my eyes shut, but the only thing I see is them. I see them dancing, their bodies moving together, his lips pressing— "Argh," I shout into the night.

I don't bother to look up to see if I'm center of attention right now. I don't give a fuck. All I need is her out of my fucking head.

"Here," a familiar voice says. I crack an eye open to find Jake and Mason looming over me, holding beer and shots.

Sitting, I take a shot and a beer and down them in quick succession.

"You've got it bad, huh?" Jake asks, amusement filling his voice.

"Don't fucking start. I didn't get in the middle of shit with you and Amalie, so keep your nose out of mine."

He puts his hands up in surrender. "Maybe not. But he did" —he nods toward Mason— "and I'm fucking glad he did. I may not have wanted to hear a fucking word of it at the time, but fuck if I didn't need it. So, get comfortable. We're going to have a little chat."

"Sorry, but my dick is still firmly between my legs. You

want to have a little girly chat, then I suggest you go and find some girls."

"Suck it up, Savage. You're going fucking nowhere until I've said what I've come to say."

I cast my eyes away from him, not interested in a single word of it.

"You hate her. Fine. You think she's ruined your life. Fine, you think that. But know that the only one fucking up your life right now is you. So get your head out of your fucking ass and act like a normal human being. We're only seeing bits of how you're behaving when it comes to her, and I dread to fucking think how you're treating her behind closed doors. She didn't choose to be here, Ethan. She was dragged, probably kicking and screaming, if she had any idea of who she was going to live with. Now for the love of God, will you either go and apologize and make peace, ignore her, or fuck her." I blanch at his final option. "Oh, don't look so shocked. We all know you're hard for her. You've not touched anyone else since she arrived."

"I kissed Shelly earlier," I argue, weakly.

"Oh yeah, because one kiss in a few weeks is totally normal for Ethan Savage when his house is full of pussy." Jake waves his hand around my back yard. There are bikini-clad girls around the pool and others wearing not much more everywhere else. "The Ethan we know wouldn't be sitting here sulking; he'd be in that pool with his hand in some girl's panties and his tongue down her throat."

He's got a fucking point. It only makes all of this worse. The picture he's just painted is exactly what should be happening right now, but as I look at the girls before me, none of them spark even an ounce of interest. I glance up at the house just as a light comes on in her bedroom. Now that, that one small sign of life from her, and I'm drowning in fucking desire.

I bite down on my cheeks as I wait to see if she's going to appear. Unfortunately, the only girls who show their faces are Amalie and Camila as they join the boys. "Oh goodie, two more to join in the lecture."

"Nope, this is your funeral, Ethan. We're not getting involved," Camila says, cuddling into Mason's side and pressing her lips to his neck.

"Although you should probably know," Amalie adds, "she's just gone upstairs with him."

Something unpleasant stirs in my belly before it tracks its way through my veins. My temperature soars and my fists clench.

"So..." Jake taunts. "What are you going to do about it?"

"Fuck you," I bark, pushing from the lounger and storming inside to the sound of his laughter.

Once again, the crowds part as I make my way to the stairs. Taking two at a time, I run up until I'm standing on the other side of her door, praying for his fucking benefit that I'm not about to find him with his hands on her in any way, let alone anything worse.

I grasp the handle and push the door with such force it crashes back against the wall with a loud bang. A startled cry sounds out, but I'm so amped up that it takes me a few seconds to register that she's sitting on her bed. Alone.

Thank fuck for that. I really didn't want tonight to be the night I kill someone.

"Where is he?"

25

RAELYNN

"Why do you care? You didn't seem to like him all that much."

His chest swells at my response before he reaches out and slams the door so hard my bed actually rattles.

"I don't like him."

"Why? Because he's actually nice to me and that can't possibly be allowed?" I sass, scooting over until my legs are hanging off the bed.

"No. Because he wants you."

I laugh at the serious expression on his face. "Cody? Jesus, Ethan. You really are delusional. Fucking hell," I mutter, pushing to my feet and walking to the other side of the room, needing to put as much space between us as possible. He doesn't move, but I feel his eyes follow every one of my footsteps.

"From the way he was touching you, I'd say he was very much interested."

"We were dancing. Just like everyone else in the room. What's the big fucking deal? You hate me. Why do you care who I dance with? I thought you'd just be glad it wasn't a member of your team who took my interest."

"So you do like him?"

"What? No. Stop twisting my words."

He takes a step toward me, and I immediately take one back. It's clear in his eyes that he's been drinking, and so have I. That combined with the electricity that's crackling between us can't be a good thing.

"Y-you need to leave."

He takes another step, and another, but unless I want to have this exchange on the balcony for everyone to see, then I have nowhere else to escape to.

"Why? So when your little boyfriend comes back from wherever he's gone you can let him fuck you?"

My hand reaches out, and by some miracle, he doesn't see it coming. My palm connects with his cheek with a loud slap. His eyes widen in shock and he bares his teeth at me.

"You're going to fucking regret that, trash." His teeth grind, the muscle in his neck pulses, and he takes a final step toward me. I've no choice but to step back if I don't want to collide with him.

"What are you going to do?" I ask, holding my arms out from my sides. "You going to demand I strip naked again? Humiliate me in front of the kids I sit in class with? Maybe put on another little show out here? Only this time you really will have an audience." I glance over my shoulder at the students below all having a good time, totally oblivious to what's going on up here.

I lift my hands to the hem of my hoodie. "Shall I start with my top? Give them all a good eyeful of my tits. Would you like that? Them all knowing you have this kind of power over me?" I lift the fabric and pull it from my body.

"Sweet cheeks." I barely hear it, his voice is so low.

I hang my arm over the balcony and let it drop, knowing that it'll catch the attention of the people below.

"You think they're looking now?"

"Don't," he warns as I lift my arms to undo my bra.

"But this is what you want, isn't it? You want to show me up. Make me feel small. Worthless." I pop the clasp, feeling weirdly empowered in this moment as he's watching me like he's about to lose control at any moment.

The music is so loud from below that I've no idea if anyone is actually looking, and to be honest, I'd rather not know. I need to prove to Ethan for good that I'm not afraid of him or his little games. If he wants me stripped bare, then that's what he's going to get.

I allow the straps to fall down my arms and take the weight of my breast in my palms. "What is it you want tonight? Are you going to eat me out again with them watching? Or maybe you want to just fuck me while they all appreciate what a fucking king you are for breaking me down."

"No," he shouts at exactly the same time I let go of my bra and allow it to drop to the tiles at my feet. He darts forward, his hand wrapping tightly around my wrist, and I'm pulled into my bedroom before he turns back around and shuts the door behind us, cutting off the outside world from whatever is going to happen next.

His chest heaves as his eyes bounce between my eyes and my exposed chest.

"You're fucking right. I want you to strip, but I'll be fucked if anyone else gets to look at you."

My breath catches at his honesty. Something flashes in his eyes, something I've seen before but not been able to latch onto.

"Now. What the fuck are you waiting for?"

"I don't follow your orders, asshole."

He's on me in seconds. His fingers find their way into my hair and he pulls so I have no choice but to look up at him moments before his lips crash to mine. I stumble back with the force and hit the wall. His large body engulfs mine, but not in an intimidating way like I might imagine. His hard planes press against my soft curves, and I can't help the moan that rumbles up my throat when the length of his cock presses into my stomach.

"Jesus. Fuck," he mutters against the sensitive skin of my neck when he eventually releases my lips, allowing me to drag some air into my lungs.

My nipples tighten as his Bears jersey brushes against them, and a bolt of lust heads straight for my clit.

"You going to make me beg again?" I moan, breathlessly.

"No. This is happening with or without you begging. My restraint has its limits, sweet cheeks."

My breath catches at what he's implying. I should stop this now. This shouldn't be how it goes. But then he lifts his hand, cups my breast and pinches my nipple, and all my rational thoughts vanish as I turn into a ball of need.

"Ethan, fuck."

He lowers down, pulling one and then the other nipple into his mouth. My fingers thread into his hair in an attempt to hold him there, but I'm no match for his strength, and when he decides to move and continue his trail down my body, I have no choice but to let him.

He pulls the zipper of my skirt down, allowing it to drop to the floor before dragging my fishnets and panties down my legs.

"No one else ever gets to look at this," he says, staring right at my core. "You got that?" He glances up from under his lashes. His blue eyes are dark, darker than I've ever seen. I nod in agreement, because there's not much else I can do in that moment other than follow orders. I'm so lost to him it's embarrassing after the way he's treated me, but what he has to offer is too tempting. The escape from reality he can give me is too much to deny.

He reaches around me and lifts as he stands, as if I'm as light as a feather.

"Where shall I fuck you, sweet cheeks? Against the wall? Bed? Over the balcony?" We both know that final one isn't an option, seeing as he's already dragged me inside, but fuck if the idea doesn't turn me on a little.

"Bed," I breathe in his ear.

He does as I suggest and stops when his knees hit the mattress and lowers me down his body. The second his hands leave me, he pulls his jersey over his head, quickly followed by removing his pants and boxers until he's standing before me bare.

He takes his hard length in his hand and strokes slowly as he stares down at me.

Worrying that he's about to insist I come good on our bet, I scoot back on the bed. I'm not against doing it, but not in the mood he's in right now. He wants to punish me—that much is clear in his eyes, let alone his words—and I don't need him taking it out on my throat.

He doesn't seem to care that I back away, because he quickly lies on his front between my legs. He hooks his hands around my thighs and tugs until my center is right in front of his face. He blows a stream of air across my swollen skin, and I buck in his hold.

"I knew you were fucking desperate for me again."

Before I can even consider coming up with a response, his tongue is on me and I lose all ability to function. All I can do is feel.

His tongue teases as his fingers find my entrance. His movements are fast but measured, as if he's done this to me a million times and knows exactly what I like.

"Oh fuck. Ethan. Ethan," I chant.

"That's it. Let everyone know who's doing this to you, baby."

He ups the ante, licking, sucking, and biting until I scream out, my body thrashing about on the bed as I ride out my release.

My chest is still heaving, my breathing erratic, and I'm coming down from my high when the mattress compresses as he crawls over me much like a lion would its prey. If I hadn't just been eaten by the king, then I'd certainly think he was about to consume me.

His hand slips around the back of my neck and tilts my head so he can crash his lips to mine. The second his tongue parts my lips, my own taste immediately explodes in my mouth, and my core clenches for more.

His tongue sweeps in, teasing and dancing with mine. Our teeth clash as it gets more and more frantic with our need. My nails scratch down his back, eliciting a growl of approval from him and making me want to do it more, anything to make this man come undone and hand himself over when he craves being in control at all times.

I reach down between our bodies and wrap my fingers around his length, getting my first feel of him. He's hard as a rock but soft and velvety to touch. I run my fingertips over his head and he barks a curse as his arms threaten to give out.

Ripping his lips from mine, he sits up and pushes my knees toward my chest. He stares down at my heated skin as he runs the head of his cock over me.

I fight the fear that wants to take over, that makes my body want to tremble and scamper, but the second I look to where we're about to be connected, I forget all about that. All about the past, all about the nightmares that keep me awake at night.

He builds me high again just with the teasing of his cock. After a few minutes, he dips the tip inside me, and I will myself not to tense at his intrusion. The last thing I need right now is him knowing the truth. I'm sure that'll only feed his need to punish me, to claim something that's not his to have.

He looks up at me and licks his lips. His eyes take in every inch of my face before dropping down my body once again. What I wouldn't give to know what he's thinking right now.

"Birth control?" he asks after a long silence between us.

I shake my head.

He looks down at my pussy again for a few seconds, making me wonder if he's going to do it anyway, but eventually, he leans over the side of the bed and grabs a condom from his pocket.

I watch intently as he rolls it down his shaft and lines himself up again.

His eyes flick up again at the last minute, something dark playing in them, and I swallow down the lump that crawls up my throat.

Just let it happen, Raelynn. It's not a big fucking deal.

"Don't come. This is for me after all the fucking teasing you've been doing, for all the times you've defied me. You got that?" His eyes widen as he says it, making me wonder if he's already regretting it, but I'm not sure if this asshole ever regrets any of the shit that falls from his mouth.

He sucks in two breaths before his grip on my hips tightens and he pushes inside me. In one quick move, I'm so full of him that I can hardly breathe. It stings, burns, exactly like I was expecting, and I slam my eyes shut to hide the tears that are welling within them.

"Fuuuuuuck," he grates out. I expect him to move, to pull out and slam back in, but it's almost like it takes him a few seconds to remember what he's supposed to be doing.

"Ethan." My voice is no more than a whimper, but it's enough to bring him back from whatever daze he'd lost himself in.

"Christ, you're tight." His voice is so deep, so rough that it has desire pulling at my insides, making me desperate for him to move and show me what he's really got. He seems to think he's something special in the bedroom—well, now is the perfect time to prove his skills. To drag me out of my own head, away from my fears and to show me heaven. I could really use a fucking slice of that right now.

He pulls out slowly before pushing back inside. He groans as if it's physically painful, and my need to see the effect this is having on him is too much to bear. I open my eyes. They're still brimming with tears, but I can't not look.

My breath catches when I find him staring down at me. His eyes are dark, but gone is the anger. It's pure desire that's staring back at me.

His full lips are parted to allow his fast breaths to pass. The muscles of his neck are pulled tight, as are his abs. A fine sheen of sweat covers his body. I find where his fingers are digging into the skin of my hips, and the sight of him holding onto me so tightly unnerves me. No one's ever held on tight.

A ball of emotion crawls up my throat as his movements continue. His length strokes at places inside me that I didn't know existed, and in only the way that Ethan can, he starts to push away the pain and discomfort that I remember all too well and replace it with something else entirely. Pleasure.

I focus on that, needing it to be the thing I remember about this fucked-up situation. I might forever regret this, but at least I'll always have the lesson it taught me.

"Fuck, baby," he grunts, dragging my eyes back up to his. "So fucking good. You shouldn't feel this good."

He drops down over me, his lips finding mine in a wet and dirty kiss as his hips continue to piston in and out of me.

When both of us are desperate for air, he pulls away, drops his face into the crook of my neck and skirts his hand down my body. He squeezes my breast, pinching my nipple before descending to my core. His fingertips find my clit and he presses down. That, along with the things he's doing inside my body, has me racing toward an orgasm I was already told I wasn't allowed to have.

"Jesus, fuck," he moans as my muscles start to clamp down around him.

"Ethan." His name, a plea for more, falls from my lips without any instruction from my brain. My nails dig into his back with my need for more of him. I need everything he can give me to push the last remaining nightmare from my mind.

Twisting my head so my lips brush his ear, I whisper, "Fuck me, Ethan. Give me everything you have."

He roars into my neck, his body tensing at my demand before he sits, slides his hands under my ass and lifts me to just the right angle before slamming into me. I fly up the bed, my head hitting the wood, but his grip tightens even more, keeping me in place so he can keep up his punishing rhythm.

He pounds into me time and time again as I watch, enthralled, as he comes apart before me.

"Fuck, fuck," he chants, his cock swelling even more inside me, telling me that the end is in sight.

The second he reaches the point of no return, every single muscle in his body tenses before he lets out the most incredible groan and his cock pulsates, buried deep inside me.

I can't drag my eyes away despite the fact that my tears are about to drop at any moment. I refuse to allow this motherfucker to see me cry, but I'm not sure I have a choice right now.

The wave of emotions that engulfs my body in that moment is too strong to contend with. The hate I feel for him, and the relief I have that he's just given me that, even though I'm equally ashamed I allowed it to happen. Fuck, my head's a fucking mess.

When he's finished, he releases his hold on me, pulls out, and climbs off the bed. He doesn't look at me, not once. I keep my eyes on him as he turns away from me, drops the condom into the trash and bends to pull on his pants. His teddy bear tattoo catches my eye, but even the sight of such a ridiculous bit of ink on his body doesn't stir anything inside. Now he's released me, I feel numb.

I panic when he reaches for the door. "Ethan?" I hate how pathetic and weak my voice sounds, but I can't help it. I wasn't under the illusion that he'd lie down beside me and pull me into his arms. I didn't expect for this to heal everything that's so broken between us, but watching him just walk out without even acknowledging me? Well, it fucking hurts.

He halts, hearing his name, but he doesn't turn back.

A little strength bubbles up from somewhere, my need to have the last word getting the better of me. "We're done now, Ethan. You got what you wanted. You stripped me bare. Now leave me the fuck alone." My voice cracks on the final sentence, and I know he doesn't miss it. His shoulders tense as the words hit him, but still, they're not enough to pull on the decent part of him that I know is inside somewhere.

He doesn't say anything. He just walks out through my bedroom door with his head slightly hanging in defeat. My first sob erupts long before he's closed the door behind him, and once they start, they don't stop.

26

ETHAN

Forgetting the fact I've got half the school in my house, I run down the stairs in my need for a drink. I need to drown out what I just did.

I fly around the bottom of the stairs and collide with a body, sending her scattering back on the wooden floor.

"Fucking hell," I moan. Am I going to fuck everything up tonight?

I step up to the barely-dressed girl and hold my hand out to help her up. It's not until she's standing before me that I register who it is.

"Does your cousin know you're here?"

Poppy's lips press into a thin line. "I don't know. But this is a school party, and in case you hadn't noticed, I go to Rosewood." She places her hand on her hip, waiting for my response, but I don't really care.

"Don't say I didn't warn you."

Jake might have a fucked-up family, but he's protective as hell over Poppy. He'll flip his lid when he spots her dressed like a fucking whore.

I push past her and head for the kitchen. The bottles of whiskey that I know are there are too much to ignore.

I can see my prize, but fucking Zayn gets in my fucking way.

"How's it going with your dark horse?" he slurs, getting in my face.

"Back the fuck off," I bark, my palms connecting with his chest to push him away. I don't want to think about her right now, let alone talk about her.

"Or what, asshole?" Zayn's eyes are wild with the amount of alcohol he's consumed, and it seems to make him think he can take me. Fucking idiot.

Pulling my arm back, I land the punch I was desperate to plow into the dickhead's face earlier. I hit him square on the jaw, but it's not enough. It's nowhere near e-fucking-nough. Grabbing onto his shirt when he starts to stumble away in shock, I throw another and another. His nose explodes, blood pouring down onto his top, but even the sight of that isn't enough to stop me. Pain sears up my arm, but I welcome it. I need it. I deserve it.

"Ethan, what the fuck are you doing?" Jake hollers when the screams and cries for help around us alert him to the goings on in the kitchen. "Fucking hell."

His arms wrap around my upper body, pinning mine to my sides to stop me from throwing any more punches. The rest of the team descends. Some help Jake move me to the other side of the room while others tend to Zayn, who's now rolling around on the floor in pain.

Everything around me blurs. All I can focus on is the anger that's consuming me. I thought taking it out on her was going to get rid of it, but I realize it's not her I'm angry with. It's me. Everything I've done. All the shit I've pulled.

"What the fuck, Savage?"

"He was in my way."

"Then ask him to fucking move."

"What the hell?" Mason asks, coming to a stop in front of me.

"Whiskey," I groan, holding my arm up, hoping someone will place a bottle in my hand.

"Fine," Jake says seconds before the cold glass hits my fingers. Fucking heaven.

I twist the cap and down as much as my throat can handle.

"Can you and Camila get him the fuck out of here?" Jake asks, but I ignore him, happy to drown myself in whiskey. "Take him to mine. I'll finish things here. We'll meet you there after. This needs to end."

I've no idea if he directs that final statement at me or not, but I ignore him anyway.

I'm none too gently pushed to my feet, and Camila and Mason drag me from the house. It's not all that much of a feat for them, because being here, under the same roof as her, is the last place I want to be.

"Get the fuck in," Mason barks, pointing to Camila's Mini, and I do as I'm told.

He hops in the passenger seat while she drops into the driver's seat, and we almost immediately start moving.

I don't look out the window, my only focus the bottle in my hands and the relief it can give me from the memories that are rolling around in my head.

My legs barely work when we pull up outside Jake's aunt and uncle's house. Seeing as he's still suffering with his ribs, Camila ends up being the one trying to support me as I make our way to Jake's trailer.

"Fucking help, will you?" she fumes. "I'll happily just dump you here if that's what you want."

"Oh, Mase. Is she this feisty in the sack?"

"Shut the fuck up, asshole, or I'll let her dump you and not look back."

He doesn't mean that. Does he?

We eventually make it down to the trailer, and before I know it, I'm on Jake's couch, finishing off the bottle in my hands.

"Did you think to grab me another?" I ask the couple who are staring at me like I'm a green alien who's sprouted two extra heads.

"No, asshole, we didn't."

"Fucking bullshit. Jake must have—" I try to stand, but Mason, being sober, beats me to it and is in my face in seconds.

"Move," I demand, keeping my fists out of it this time.

"No fucking chance."

A growl sounds out around the trailer, but it doesn't register that it comes from my throat.

"I need—"

"No. You don't need whiskey. Or beer. Or fucking weed. What you need is to start talking. We can't fucking help if we don't know, motherfucker."

My fists curl, not knowing another way to deal with his demands. Like fuck am I talking.

"Go on then. Hit me, if it'll make you feel better."

"Mason, no," Camila says in a rush, coming to stand at his side protectively.

"It's fine, Cami. Sit down." She looks between the two of us locked in our stare-off but eventually does as she's told.

"Sit," Mason demands, his hands hitting my shoulders just enough to have me falling to the couch.

I watch as he walks into Jake's little kitchenette and grabs three bottles of water from the fridge.

"Drink." He shoves it under my nose and leaves it there until I have to take it if I want him to go the fuck away. "Great, now talk," he says, falling down beside Camila and pulling her into his side. The sight of them has my stomach turning over. So fucking happy and content with each other. It's sickening.

"Fuck you."

"Nah. You fucked her though, didn't you?"

Our eyes lock, a million words passing between us. We've been friends for too long for me to hide shit from either Mason or Jake.

"None of your business."

"It is when you're trying to drown yourself in a bottle of whiskey. You can do this now, or you can do it when Jake and Amalie get here, makes no difference to us. But get one thing straight. You are damn well fucking talking."

My teeth grind as I try to figure out a way to explain what I've done. How I've treated her.

"Fine. I fucked her. Happy?"

"I'm assuming I can safely say that she's now not out of your system." The fact he's almost amused by this situation pisses me off even more.

"No... I... Fuck." I sit forward and hang my head, running the events of the night through my mind.

I have no idea how long the three of us sit there in silence, but, eventually, there are footsteps outside and then the door's opening.

"Sorry. Took fucking ages to clear out," Jake says, walking straight up to me and slapping me around the head. "You sorted this waste of fucking space out yet?"

No one says anything, but I can imagine the looks that are passing between them.

"Amalie tried to see Rae, but she refused to speak, let alone answer the door. What the fuck did you do, Ethan?"

Things that I've said to her over her short time here run through my head. The things I've made her do, tonight included. My need to hurt her, to escape the constant anger that's always threatening to boil over was too much, and I took. I took what I wanted without any thought for her. That's not how I do things. That's not fucking cool.

"I fucked her," I repeat quietly.

"Right. And it was so bad she sent you running to a bottle?" Jake laughs.

"I..." Fuck. "I'm not sure she was totally up for it." I fall back and tip my face to the ceiling, squeezing my eyes shut so I don't have to look at their disapproving faces. The girls gasp, but otherwise no one says anything as the reality of the situation presses down so heavily on my chest that I struggle to suck in a fucking breath.

"I've been a fucking asshole since she arrived. Demanding she do shit. I just... I was so... fuck. I don't even know who I am right now. I fucking hate myself. But she... then her... FUCK," I shout, unable to even vocalize what it is I'm feeling, how fucking hurt and angry and fucked up I am.

"You need to sober the fuck up and talk to her," Amalie suggests after the longest fucking silence of my life. "You were drunk before you even went up there. You might not be seeing things clearly."

"Even if I'm not... All the other stuff. Fuck." I think about the day I made her strip. I watched her body tremble in fucking fear, yet I kept pushing. I remember the other night with her up on the fucking balcony. One wrong move and she'd have gone down. So what, she was wet as fuck and begging for me? I made that happen. She didn't. All she did was turn up. She doesn't deserve any of what I threw at her.

"She's stronger than you're giving her credit for, Ethan. If she didn't want something, I'm pretty sure she'd have just told you."

I think back to her biting my fingers in Aces' bathroom. Amalie is right, but she doesn't see what it's like when it's just the two of us together. It's like she hands me the control she always keeps a tight grip onto everywhere else. Why? What stops her kicking back more?

"Get some fucking sleep. Sober up. Then tomorrow, talk to her with a rational head. Maybe apologize for being an epic douchebag since the moment she arrived. The four of us sitting here are proof that asshole actions can be forgiven and things can turn around."

I lie back on the sofa. If the four of them say any more, then I don't hear it, because the numbness from the alcohol drags me under.

———

The trailer's still in silence when I wake with a raging hard-on from the dream I was having about being inside Rae yesterday. The tingling of desire lasts all of three seconds after I come to before reality slams into me right before the headache that's pounding at my temples hits as well.

Fuck. I'm a mess.

Regret. Shame. They both threaten to swallow me whole, and I can say with absolute certainty that the bright light of day has not brought me any clarity on the situation. If anything, without the whiskey fueling my thoughts, it's fucking worse.

The guys' advice from last night hits me.

Talk to her.

I drag my cell from my pocket, and my stomach drops when I see I've got a message. Only, it's not from her.

Needing a distraction, I swipe it and see what she's sent.

> Chelsea: Thank you for thinking of me. That means a lot. Hopefully I'll get to see you soon x

I sigh. If Chelsea of all people is attempting to get her shit together, then I guess I'd better make the effort too.

I almost change my mind and curl back up on the couch when I push the door open and am blinded by the almost midday autumn sun. My head swims, and last night's whiskey threatens to make a reappearance. I've no idea what time the guys left me last night, but seeing as it's almost lunchtime and Jake and Amalie are still in bed, they couldn't have called it a night too early.

I pull up my Uber app, ready to order a car to get me home, but at the last minute, I cancel the order in favor of walking. The headspace and fresh air might do me a bit of good. Give me some fucking clarity with regards to Rae and everything's that happened. And everything that might happen next.

I scrub my hand down my face as I allow the realization that I don't want what happened with Rae last night to be a one-off to settle. The bullshit that got us there aside, it was fucking mind-blowing, and I'm now craving to be inside her again, to feel her body against mine like I never have anyone else. Not that I deserve to feel any of that again after how I've treated her.

I grab some breakfast on the way when I'm confident my stomach can take it, and it's almost two hours later when I walk up the driveway toward the house. It looks exactly like it did before the party, almost as if last night never happened. There's just one difference. Dad's car is here.

Motherfucker. So not only do I have the grovel of my life ahead of me with Rae, but I've got to deal with him.

I don't see any sign of life as I walk into the house. I stop by the kitchen for a bottle of water before making my way toward the stairs. I figure that I'd rather deal with Rae than I would my father, which is really saying something. However, I don't make it to the stairs, because as I approach the family room, their voices ring out and I'm powerless but to stop when I hear Rae's name mentioned.

"I can't believe she just blanked you like that after not seeing you for over a week," Dad says softly to Ash.

"It's fine. I'm used to Rae's temper. She was always such a placid child. If I wasn't so stupid then maybe..." Ash's voice breaks, and I see through the crack in the door as Dad leans toward her.

"Maybe what?"

She blows out a breath. I know I shouldn't be listening in on their private conversation, but it's clear that Ash knows more about Rae than any of us, and hell knows I could use a little light shedding on her before we talk.

Her shoulders shake, the tension surrounding her obvious even from out in the hall. "It was all my fault. I thought he was God's gift. He was so sweet. The perfect boyfriend. Little did I know he—" She sniffles, and it cuts off her words.

Every muscle in my body is locked tight as I wait for what's to come.

"He what, Ash?" Dad asks, his own voice rough and full of emotion. He's clearly having the same thoughts—fears—as me right now.

She sobs, and I damn near march inside the room to demand she finishes that fucking sentence. But when she does say the words, all the fight leaves me.

"Only wanted her. She was only thirteen when he—"

I stumble back, unable to comprehend what she's saying. Refusing to accept it. Everything I've done to her. The way I've treated her. And she's been... no, no.

On shaky legs, I drag myself up the stairs. I need the truth. I need to know if I'm just one in a line of men who haven't treated her as she deserves.

I throw her bedroom door open the second I'm in front of

it, the weight of the regret I feel pressing down on me to the point I can't drag in the air I need.

I don't know what I was expecting, but the second I look up and find only an empty room, disappointment floods me. I need to talk to her. I need her to tell me what I just overheard isn't true, even though every fiber of my being knows that it is.

My eyes settle on her bed. It's covered in her diaries, the ones she'd hidden from me. No wonder she looked so terrified when she discovered me reading them.

Fuck. It was him. The asshole I was reading about. The one who was treating her to everything she wanted.

Racing over, I rummage through them until I find the one I was reading. I flick through for any sign for where I should look. All of a sudden, the pretty pink writing stops and a more rushed, scratchy handwriting starts. I stare down at the pages, flipping through and picking out important words. In places, the ink has run where she's spilled water on it, but it's not long before I realize that they were probably her tears.

27

RAELYNN

I didn't get a wink of sleep last night despite the party finishing not long after Ethan ran from my room. I can only assume he pulled the whole thing to an abrupt end after what happened between us. He wasn't in a good place when he first appeared in my room; I can't imagine he left any better.

Every time I drifted off, *he* appeared. I'd spent months thinking that he was the best thing that ever happened in my life. That for once, Mom had got it right. Oh, how wrong I was. He wasn't treating me like the daughter he never had. It took months for me to accept after the event, but all he was doing was grooming me. Putting in the legwork to ensure I'd trust him when he thought the time was right.

And fuck did I trust him.

I didn't bat an eyelid when he told me he'd run me a bath one night when Mom was working late. Yes, I thought it was odd when he suggested he join me, but he soon soothed my concerns when he reminded me how Mom couldn't afford for us to waste water.

A shudder runs down my spine as I revisit that night. I was

so young. So naïve. If I had any idea what he was capable of, I'd have run as fast as I could in the opposite direction that night, but I truly believed that he'd never hurt a fly.

I blow out a shaky, emotional breath as I stare ahead at the waves crashing up onto the beach.

I wanted to get out of the house before Ethan or our parents arrived home this morning. I needed time. Time to get my head together. Time to hopefully push *him* from my thoughts. I wasn't expecting Mom and Eric to be back already. They'd told me they'd be home tomorrow, but I guess things change. I couldn't cope with them, listening to all the wonderful things they'd done while they were away, so I ran. Ran right past Mom as she asked how I was. I felt awful as I did it, and I still feel terrible now.

Obviously, we moved after that horrific event—Mom's coping mechanism for life: running away— and she ensured I had counseling at my next couple of schools to help me with my insomnia and the nightmares that plagued me, but although I told her it helped, I'm not sure it ever really did. It helped me to accept what happened, but I don't ever think I'll understand it or be convinced that it wasn't my fault. He was the master manipulator, and I fell for it like the good little girl I was.

I both lost and found something that night. I lost my childhood, my innocence, but I gained an understanding of how strong I am, what I'm capable of. It was a hard way of learning that I need to be more aware of who I spend time with and look out for the signs I should have seen back then.

I learned that I have a choice, that I can stand up for myself. It taught me that just because it happened once, I don't have to be the victim again. Thankfully, I never came anywhere close to it happening again. Until I moved here and met the asshole across the hall.

But things with him were different. I had a choice. I could

see exactly what game he was playing and I either chose to play along or I didn't. I had power. The kind of power I never had back then.

If I truly didn't want him to lay a finger on me, then he wouldn't have.

From the very beginning, I knew that for the first time in my life, I was going to allow him to take what he wanted, what I craved from him. And last night was no exception.

I needed it to be him to show me what sex is, how it should be. I've never cared about anyone enough to hate them, to argue with them like I have Ethan. And, although scary as hell to admit, it's the truth.

It's the reason I cried most of the night. Not because I gave him something that he didn't deserve. But because after the event, he just walked out. He had no idea what a big moment of my life that was, how much I was trusting him with my body in those few moments. He had no reason to. But he walked away.

So either I was totally wrong about him and there being a redeemable human being hiding under all the hate and anger, or what I felt when we connected was totally one-sided. Maybe it was just sex for him. Maybe I was just another girl. Another notch in his bedpost. Rumor around school sure leads me to believe he's got a few.

I sit in that exact spot on the beach until the sun starts to set. My stomach grumbles, having not eaten anything all day, and eventually forces me to stand and move.

I grab a takeout burger from Aces and plaster a fake smile on my face as Bill chats away to me about last night's game, even though he knows I really don't care. If I were in a less somber mood, his excitement might be infectious. But as things stand, it's not.

I walk up toward the house with a ball of dread sitting in my stomach. Eric's car is still here, but Ethan's isn't. Even with it missing, my hands tremble slightly that he'll be home and want a repeat of last night... or worse, to talk about it.

I find Mom and Eric sitting at the table in the kitchen with dinner in front of them.

"Hey, honey. Would you like some dinner?" Mom asks hesitantly when I stop in the doorway.

"No, I've eaten, but thank you. Listen, I'm—"

"It's okay, Rae."

"No, it's not. I'm sorry for this morning. Things have just been... hard starting over here. I'm sorry."

"Oh honey, you should have called if you were having a hard time. You know I've always got time for you."

Have you? The question is on the tip of my tongue, but I don't allow it to slip out. What's the point? If it were true, she wouldn't have run the second we got here and forced me to find my own way.

"Has Ethan helped get you settled at school?" Eric asks, a hopeful look in his eye.

"Oh yeah. He's been great," I lie. More like a baptism of fire than a warm welcoming, but whatever. What's done is done. "Where is he?"

"I'm not sure. I hear last night's game was incredible," Eric says, like he's expecting me to have been there.

"So I hear."

"You didn't go?" I have no idea why Mom looks so shocked. I've never been one to go to school events.

"No, I got a job and worked." Unfortunately, admitting that means inviting a load of questions before I'm able to escape to the safety of my bedroom.

My bedroom door is closed—like I left it—when I get upstairs. I push it open, and the memories I tried to outrun when I left for the beach hit me full force. Why I didn't tidy up my diaries before I left, fuck only knows. I rush over and start sorting them out so I can hide them back in the ottoman where they belong when one catches my eye. It's the one I wanted. The one I wrote in after the events of that night. I don't remember how I left it exactly, but something tells me it wasn't open on this page or at this angle. I look at the page, but I refuse to read the words and look around my room.

Was he here?

That thought is only confirmed when I lift my most recent diary where I put my thoughts about last night. I'd left it on some possible song lyrics that seemed to sum up the situation nicely.

> You seem to want me gone.
> But I've done nothing wrong.
> I hate this stupid game.
> But I love it all the same.

Underneath those words is his handwriting, and my breath catches when I read the few words he's written.

> You should have told me.
> I'm sorry.

My heart pounds at having confirmation that he was actually here and that he read this. He knows.

"Fuck." My hands lift to my hair, and I spin on the spot, not knowing what to do. Depending on how he takes this, it could change everything, and as fucked up as stuff has been, it was becoming normal. I'm not sure I want another change in my life.

Deciding I need to pull up my big girl panties and be the bigger person about this, I drag my bedroom door open once more and march across the hall. I don't bother knocking, not wanting to know if he'd let me in or not if I gave him a warning, and like he's done to me so many times, I throw his door wide open.

Empty.

A huge rush of air passes my lips as I release the breath I didn't know I was holding. I feel totally deflated as I walk back to my room. What am I supposed to do now? Wait until he reappears and discover what he now thinks about this whole situation?

The rest of Saturday passes with radio silence from Ethan. I spend another fitful night's sleep between looking at the ceiling and waking up covered in a cold sweat with *his* eyes staring down on me.

I'm in a foul mood when I wake Sunday morning, but it doesn't stop Mom interrupting my silence and all but forcing me to have breakfast with her and Eric.

Neither of them have a clue where Ethan is, but Eric doesn't seem too bothered, assuming he'll have been at some party last night and still sleeping off the effects of the night before.

I try to be as nonchalant about it as he is, but I can't help something twisting inside me. Everything isn't okay. After Friday night and then him reading my diary, everything is far from being okay.

Digging in my purse for my cell the second I'm able to escape back to my room, I hope to see something from him. But as usual, no one wants me. I don't really know why I bother carrying the thing around with me; it's not like I have friends who want to chat.

I type a message out and delete it a million times. I don't want to look like I care, especially if Eric is right. Me appearing concerned will only be ammunition for him to hit me with later. I can already hear his words. *"Aw, it's so cute you care about me, sweet cheeks. Now how about you do something that really shows me you care?"* The image of his naked body and hard cock fill my mind, and every muscle south of my waist clenches in memory.

Damn him. Why do I want to do it all over again? I should be the one now wanting to push him over the fucking balcony, not craving that he fucks me over it instead.

I glance out of the doors to the small space and bite down on my bottom lip. I imagine looking out over the beach in the distance as Ethan fills me from behind.

Fuck. Get your head out of the gutter, Raelynn. The guy fucking hates you.

Without putting too much more thought into it, I hit send on the most recent message I typed out.

> Rae: Where are you? Your dad's home.

I sit and stare at the words, regretting them more and more as they taunt me from the screen. I thought by making it about his dad then it would look less like I'm worried, but I realize the fact I've sent it in the first place shows how I'm feeling. Eric's probably already been in contact to let him know they're home. He doesn't need to hear it from me.

Dropping my cell to the bed, I throw myself back onto the pillows with a groan of frustration. Even not here, he's fucking with my head... *and your body.* My thighs clench at that thought, my temperature increasing as I remember our time together. The look in his eyes. The way his muscles tensed as he was about to come. The fullness of his parted lips as he groaned in pleasure.

Fuck. Fuck. Fuck.

28

RAELYNN

"We need to talk." I look to my left and right where my arms have just been captured and find Barbie and Sindy attached to each one, looking like they're on a mission.

The three of us walk along as if we're best friends. I had a feeling something like this would happen, seeing as Ethan never reappeared yesterday or this morning. And if what the rumor mill is saying is correct, then he didn't turn up for morning practice earlier either.

Neither of them stops until the three of us are standing in the girls' locker room. Granted, it's a welcome relief from being dragged into the guys', but it's still not really a place I want to be. At least it smells better.

They both guide me over to the benches in the center of the lockers and the three of us sit, me one side, them opposite.

"I'm pretty sure this could be classed as abduction," I mutter.

Barbie cracks a smile, but Sindy keeps the hard expression on her face. "Cut the shit, Rae. We need to know what's going on with Ethan."

"Then you should probably go and find someone who cares."

"We have," Barbie states, her eyes drilling into mine as if she can read my mind.

I blow out and accept that I can either openly talk or be coerced into it, and I don't have the time or the energy for the latter.

"We know you slept with him."

"Right. And what's the issue? He worried I wasn't all that impressed and that I'll ruin his reputation?"

Both of them stare at me with blank expressions.

"No, he's worried you didn't want it. That he forced you."

My chin drops. "W-what? That's why he's vanished? Because he thinks he…"

"Yeah. We found him laying into Zayn, drunk off his face after the event, and we dragged him back to Jake's. He was a fucking mess."

"So did he…" Sindy adds.

When I don't respond, Barbie tries. "Did he force himself on you, Rae?"

"Do I look like the kind of girl who does things she doesn't want to?"

"No, but with things like this… that often doesn't matter." Barbie's voice gets quieter as she finishes her sentence.

"Ethan might be an asshole, but he's not a fucking rapist." The word is bitter on my tongue, but I refuse to beat around the bush about this, no matter what horrors lie in my past.

They both sag in relief, showing just how worried they both are for their friend.

Deciding I'm in this deep and that I may as well give them a little more, I open my mouth again. "I won't lie, things between the two of us haven't exactly been sunshine and roses since I turned up. He's not exactly been… *welcoming*, shall we say."

They fall silent, obviously sensing that I have more I want to get out. I don't want to tell these two anything, I don't want them thinking I want to be friends or any crazy shit like that, but having the opportunity to get all this off my chest after bottling it up for what feels like forever becomes too much. "I've pushed back against him just as much. I wouldn't say I'm innocent in all this. I also wouldn't say that I've not enjoyed some of it. I've never really had anyone..." I trail off, suddenly realizing I'm giving them too much. They don't need to know that I've been lonely since the one person I trusted ruined everything for me. I've refused to become attached to anyone else since for fear of the past repeating itself.

"Do you... do you know where he is?" Sindy asks, shocking the hell out of me, seeing as I thought he was with them.

"N-no. He's with the guys, isn't he?"

Barbie shakes her head. "None of us have seen him since going to bed Friday night. He was gone when we all got up the next morning. Not seen or heard from him since."

"Fuck," I mutter, the image of his writing in my diary filling my head. "He came back to the house. Our parents are back. He went into my room." I suck in a shaky breath as the feelings from finding out he'd read everything hit me once again. "I'd left something on the bed. It probably freaked him out more than he already was, if what you're saying is true."

"What?"

I shake my head, not willing to give these almost strangers any more information on my fucked-up life. "It doesn't matter. Just know that it wouldn't have helped."

"Okay, so..." Sindy starts before trailing off, hoping someone might have an idea.

"Have the guys spoken to the rest of the team? He's probably just crashed on one of their couches or something."

"Nope, no one's seen him. They need him, Rae. The next

playoff game is next Friday. He needs to be at training. Needs his head in the right place. Can you reach out to him?"

"I messaged him already. No response."

"Fuck. We need to find him."

"And in the meantime?" Sindy asks.

"We keep Rae here company."

"Oh, um... that's really not necessary."

"I think it is. We still hardly know you, yet you're already important to—"

"Don't say it," I groan, cutting Barbie off.

"You like him, don't you?" Both of their eyes bore into me as I try to come up with an answer.

"N-no, he's an asshole."

"Oh, hun. We know all about assholes and how they have this weird ability to steal your heart when you least expect it."

"No, he's not... I haven't..."

"We need to get to class, but we're hanging out after school."

"Can't. I have work." I'm sure I've never been more relieved that I have to work for my own money.

"Okay, well, how about we come over after? Hang out, do homework?"

"I don't have a choice, do I? If I say no, you're going to show up anyway, aren't you?"

"We sure are."

"Let's go, or Mr. Richards will have us all in detention for skipping," Sindy says, linking her arm through mine.

"Rae, please try reaching out again. We all need him."

I nod to Barbie, who takes off in the opposite direction to her own class.

We walk in silence for a few seconds before Sindy speaks. "You're allowed to have friends here, you know. Ethan might think he wants you to leave, but I have a feeling he'd miss you if he ran you out of town now."

"I'm not sure about that," I mutter as the door we're aiming for appears in front of us, and I sigh in relief.

"This is your home now, Rae. It's time you accepted it and realize that it comes with a side dish of friends, whether you like it or not."

Sindy lets me go as we enter the classroom only a few seconds behind everyone else. The chair at the back of the room beside Jake taunts me, but I keep my eyes down and focus on where I need to go as I walk through the room.

As the day progresses, the rumors get more and more unbelievable as to where he's gone, but equally the tension rises, because everyone in this school is relying on the Bears giving them a victory this year. More and more of the students' attention turns on me. Last week I was mostly invisible. But this week, word is starting to spread about who I am, or more so where I live.

By the time the final bell rings, I'm beyond ready to get the hell out of the place and the curious looks of everyone around me.

I walk straight out of school, foregoing a stop at my locker, and head straight for the bus stop that will take me to Aces.

If I thought it was going to give me a reprieve from the questions and stares, then I was very wrong, because by the time the bus has stopped a million times on its route, other members of my class have already driven here and got themselves comfortable at their designated tables.

At least the football slash cheer table is empty... for now. I've no doubt they'll all come tumbling through the door soon, looking for answers, just like everyone else.

"So..." Cody says, dragging me from my thoughts. "Friday night was... interesting. What's the deal with you and Savage then?"

"No deal. He hates me."

The fucker has the audacity to laugh at my comment.

"Rae, come on. I had you pegged as one of the smart ones. That boy doesn't hate you."

"Really? Are you sure we're talking about the same guy?"

"Yeah, the one who was about ready to take my head off just because I had my hands on your hips. He was so fucking jealous."

"No, he just wanted us gone. He doesn't think we belong in his world, and I've got to be honest, I can't really argue with that."

"Speak for yourself, sweetheart."

"You want to go back? Be my guest. He's fucked off, it seems, so the coast is clear."

"Where's he gone?"

"No idea. Not that anyone seems to believe me. It's like they all think I've locked him in a dungeon somewhere or something."

"You can be a little scary. I can see where they might get that idea from."

I swat him with my notepad before heading back over to check on my customers.

Bang on the time I'm expecting them, the Rosewood Bears come waltzing into the diner with the cheer team hot on their heels. Jake and Mason are noticeably missing, probably out on an Ethan search party with their girls. Groaning, I busy myself getting a couple of drink refills before reluctantly heading over.

"What can I get for you all?" I ask, forcing out a polite voice.

A couple of the guys give me their orders before a female interrupts them. "You know you were a bet, right?"

"I'm sorry, what?" I ask, getting a little whiplash from the random subject change.

"You. The guys dared Ethan to sleep with you Friday night."

I tell myself not to react. Not to show that her words have any effect on me. But from her reaction, I don't think I'm successful.

"Oh my god. You did sleep with him. What did he do, shove a bag over your head so he didn't have to look at you?"

My breath catches in my throat, a ball so fucking huge clogging it, stopping any smart-ass response I'd usually hit her back with.

"Enough, Shelly," one of the guys says. His deep voice is enough to bring me back to myself slightly.

"I don't know what you're talking about. The only girls stupid enough to open their legs for the likes of these douchebags are sluts like you."

She gasps, her hand coming up to cover her heart as if I've actually wounded her with my words.

"Oh come off it. You know as well as the rest of us that you've got no morals, just a desperate need to have your existence validated by having one of Rosewood's elite on your arm. It's pathetic."

Silence falls over the table as Shelly decides against going up against me and shrinks down in her seat.

"So, humble pie for Shelly," I quip. "What about the rest of you?"

I do the best I can writing down their orders with a trembling hand and run away the second I'm able to.

My head's fucking spinning as I put their orders through to the kitchen. The second I'm done, I turn on my heels, intending on slipping out the back for a little fresh air. I fucking need it after what I had to endure over the past five minutes.

I push through the fire exit and take what feels like my first breath since they all walked in. I'm just about to push a rock into the doorjamb to stop it locking me out when a figure appears. A figure in a Bears jersey. Fucking great.

"Fuck off," I say, not bothering to look up at his face. "I'm not interested in anything you have to say."

"I was just coming to make sure you were okay. Shelly was just being a bitch, trying to push your buttons." It's the genuine concern in his voice that has me looking up.

Kind green eyes stare down at me. His long, messy blonde hair is pulled back from his face in an annoying little top knot that has my fingers twitching to cut off. I recognize him as Sindy's friend. The one who is apparently part of the team even though he looks too... nice.

"I couldn't give a shit what she says."

"Okay, if you say so." It's clear he doesn't believe me, and I can't say I blame him.

Her words are on repeat in my head and only help to confuse me more when it comes to Ethan. *What, this whole thing just a bet?* No, it can't be. *Can it?* "Fuck."

I spin away from his probing eyes, worried that he can see too much. He seems much more perceptive than the others.

"Listen, I'm not here to pry or to tell you what to do. I just wanted to make sure you were okay."

"Was it a bet?" The words are out of my mouth before I have a chance to stop them.

"Err..." He looks away from me briefly, and it's all the answer I need.

"You're all a fucking joke, you know that?" I snap. "Do you have any idea how many girls' lives you ruin with your stupid, fucked-up games?"

"I couldn't agree more," he says, shocking the hell out of me.

"What?"

"I agree. Most of those guys are assholes."

"And you're hanging around with them why?"

"I have my reasons. But don't think they're my friends. They're not."

"But—"

"It doesn't matter. This isn't about me." *No, sadly it's about me and my fucked-up life.* "I just… it wasn't really a bet. There was no prize to win. Just a game the guys play where they pick each other a target for the night, giving them until dawn to… well, you know. I don't think Shelly or any of the girls really know about it. I think she was just trying to push your buttons."

"And I was Ethan's. Nice," I say, ignoring the bit about Shelly, because whether she knew or not, she's a fucking bitch.

"I'm sorry, Rae."

"It's fine. It's not like I'm stupid enough to fall for his charms."

He eyes me curiously, probably seeing right through my lie. "Well, that's… uh… good. I'm Shane, by the way. In case you'd forgotten."

"I'd like to say it was nice to see you again, but—"

"I know. I'd better get back."

I nod and watch him turn back toward the door. "Shane?" I ask before he disappears inside.

"Yeah."

"Maybe stop hanging around with them, eh?"

"I will, when I get what I want." My brows crease, wondering what on earth he could possibly need from assholes like them, but I allow him to go. I've got enough on my plate without worrying about his games.

Leaning back against the wall, I look out over the small courtyard space that mostly consists of old crap that Bill needs to get rid of and take in a deep breath.

He doesn't hold the power for me to care about this, I tell myself over and over before walking back inside with my head held high and ready to deliver food to my favorite table.

Cody eyes me suspiciously as I grab the plates, but thankfully, he doesn't say anything. I'm not sure what my answer would be if he did, because I'm sure as fuck not telling him the truth.

Their attention doesn't leave me until they finally pay their check and leave, and it's only then that I manage to breathe in a real breath.

Shane nods at me before he follows the others out like a sheep, and I wonder once again what he's playing at. He's either playing me by making out that he's a good guy, or something much more interesting is going on. I tell myself that I don't care before getting back to work.

———

When Cody drops me off at the house after our shift, Ethan's car is still missing and his bedroom is in darkness. I guess he hasn't appeared at some point then.

My eyes lock on the Mini sitting in the driveway beside it, and I groan. I guess they didn't get a better offer.

"Friends of yours?" Cody guesses when he looks over to find me staring at the car like I want to set it on fire.

"I don't have friends," I snap and immediately feel awful, because from the second he was thrust into my life by Bill, he's been nothing but a friend to me.

"Ah, yes. I forgot."

"I'm sorry. I didn't mean to snap. It's just been a long day."

"It's fine, I get it. Have a good night."

"You too, see you tomorrow." With that, I climb from his car, dreading what I'm going to have to endure once I get inside.

"Hey, honey. Did you have a good day?" Mom asks the second I step into the kitchen to grab a drink.

"Great," I lie, plastering on a smile as I pull the fridge open for a bottle of water.

"You've got two friends up in your bedroom waiting for

you." When I look over, she's got the biggest grin on her face. She's been desperate for me to connect with someone in all the different places we've been, never really understanding why I've not made any friends. What's the point when tomorrow, next week, next month I'm going to be calling a new place home and surrounded by a whole new load of students? "I've already sent up refreshments. They said you've all got a lot of work to do. They seem really wonderful."

She pulls me into her arms, her excitement at me being 'normal' causing a lump to form in my throat. I hate to disappoint her, but she must be aware that she's the reason I'm far from normal.

"I'd better get up there then."

"Rae," she calls when I'm at the door. "They're always welcome. If you want sleepovers or anything." Her eyes shine with emotion, and I can't help returning it as I nod, despite the fact I find her permission hilarious. Does she have any idea what goes on under this roof while Eric is away?

"Thanks, Mom."

There's music playing as I make my way to my room, grateful that I shoved all my diaries back in the ottoman where they belong and not left them out for more prying eyes.

I push the door open and they both look up from their books. I wasn't really expecting them to actually be working, but it seems they really did just want to come here to do homework.

"Hey, we were starting to wonder if you stood us up."

"You're in my bedroom."

"Wouldn't put it past you," Barbie says with a laugh.

Dropping my bag on the end of the bed, I snatch up one of the cookies Mom must have sent up for them.

"Your mom's nice," Sindy says. "She looked kinda shocked when we told her we were meeting you."

"I'm not surprised. Never had friends turn up at my front door before."

Both of their faces turn sad. I hate the pity in their eyes.

"Enough of that. What are we doing?" After kicking my boots off, I grab my books and find myself a spot on the bed for our late homework session.

29

ETHAN

"It's not that I don't like having you here, baby. But don't you think you should head back? You need to be in class. Coach needs you. Jake and Mason need you, not to mention the rest of the guys."

"I know, Mom." I twist the mug in my hands back and forth to give me something to focus on.

"It might help if you talk about it," she encourages for the millionth time since I arrived unexpectedly on my grandparents' porch at the beginning of the week.

The second I read those words in her diary, I knew there was no way I could hang around and look her in the eye. The way I'd treated her... it was inexcusable. Unforgivable. And that was before I knew the horrors of her past.

Slumping back in the chair, I rub my hand over my face and across my rough jaw. I look a mess—I don't need to look up into my mom's caring eyes to know that. I just don't know how to pull myself out of the pit I've fallen into.

Regret consumes me. Memories haunt me. And that's only the daytime. At night, it gets so, so much worse because my dreams are full of her. Of the way she smells, the way she sounds as my name falls from her lips, how soft her skin is, how hot and tight her pussy is.

Fuck.

Every morning I wake up, my cock's rock hard and begging for me to go back and beg for another chance. But then my brain kicks in and I know I can't. I can't look into those dark, haunted eyes that I now know are shadowed by what she was forced to endure, and I just can't do it. Every time she looks at me, she's going to remember. If I'm lucky, it'll just be the shit I pulled, or it could be worse. I could remind her of him. That monster. The cunt who took her childhood away from her. Who made her the closed-off person she is today. I've no doubt that she is the way she is because of him. Her inability to trust, her lack of friends.

"It's a girl." The words fall out of my mouth without instruction from my brain. My need to talk, to tell someone who won't—hopefully—judge me.

"I guessed that much, E."

I blow out a breath. Of course she fucking knows. She always knows. It's one of the reasons why she's left such a big hole in my life with her being gone. One look at me and she always knew what I wanted—what I needed. "And I miss you." I hate the guilt that fills her features.

"I'm so sorry, baby. I want to be there for you, but the thought of seeing them, seeing her..." She visibly shivers at the thought alone. "I still love him. I think I always will, and I'm not sure I'll ever forgive him for this."

"I understand, Mom, I really do. It just fucking sucks." She lifts a brow at my language but doesn't chastise me like she usually would.

"So, this girl..."

Placing my elbows on the table, I drop my head into my hands and suck in a breath. "I don't even know where to start."

"Try the beginning."

The truth about who she is is on the tip of my tongue, but I swallow it down, not ready to divulge that information yet. "I don't even like her."

"Yet she's got you so tied up that she's managed to get you to run here. There's a very fine line between love and hate, Ethan."

"It's hate. Definitely hate."

Her eyes drill into me until I'm unable to look into them anymore. "So what did you do?"

"Me? Why do you assume that I did something?"

"I'm sorry, baby. But you're the guy, you're genetically programmed to screw up more than the woman." My chin drops and she laughs. "I'm kidding, I'm kidding." I'm not sure I believe her.

"I've been a right ass to her."

"Because you hate her."

I nod. "Yep. Hate."

"And how does she feel about you?"

I shrug, although not because I don't know, more because there's no way she could feel anything but pure hatred for me. It's what I deserve. "Pretty sure she can't stand the sight of me."

"You kissed her?" Mom asks, leaning in like she's a little too invested in this conversation already.

"Mom," I snap, not wanting to go down this road with her.

"What? Would you prefer I ask if you've slept with her yet? Don't forget who you're talking to. I'm the one who bought you that first pack of condoms and a few more since. And I know for a fact that you're not collecting the things."

I blush, actually fucking blush, and she finds it hilarious.

"Okay fine. Yes to all the things, and you're not getting any more detail than that."

She sits back and thinks for a few seconds, and my stomach twists with what bit of advice could come from her next.

"Okay, I know many women claim to be able to sleep around like men and not allow feelings to get involved. And I'm sure there are women out there who can, but I've yet to meet one. In my experience, if she's let you kiss her, let alone anything else that we won't go into," she winks, and I want the ground to swallow me up. When I'm sitting in front of my mom, I'll always be a little boy, no matter how old I actually am, "then I can almost assure you that she doesn't actually hate you."

"No, I'm pretty sure she's one of those who can detach her emotions. I actually think she's a master at it."

"Huh. Well, I guess I'll have to pass judgment on that until I meet her."

I choke on my coffee. Yeah, that's not going to be happening anytime soon.

"No matter what I tell you, my original point still stands. You need to go home. For school, for the team, and to sort things out with your girl."

My girl. That should sound all kinds of wrong, but hearing the words fall from Mom's lips is anything but.

My mind takes me back to Friday night once again as I stared down at her on her bed. My cock swells, thankfully beneath the table, as I remember exactly how it felt as I sank inside her.

"Fucking hell."

"If you learn anything from this disaster with your father and me, let it be that matters of the heart are complicated things. You can be thinking that you're in the middle of one play while the other person is on a totally different pitch."

I smile at her. I love it when she tries to bring football analogies into day-to-day life thinking it'll help me understand, despite the fact that she almost always screws it up.

"Thanks, Mom." I refrain from telling her that I was fully

aware of how complicated love was before this mess. It's one of the reasons I've never had a girlfriend. I don't have time for that kind of drama in my life.

"Anytime." She falls silent again, and I risk a glance up. It's clear she's deep in thought, so I leave her to it. I'm just about to push from the chair when she speaks. "What's her name?"

"Nice try."

"Fine," she concedes. "I know you'll tell me when you're ready. Have you heard anything from Chelsea? Ohhh, it's not her, is it?"

"No, Mom. It's not Chelsea." I roll my eyes at her. Chelsea's mom and mine have been friends for years. Anything happening with her would be like getting with my sister. A shudder runs down my spine. Rae could be that one day. *Fuck.* I push the thought from my mind. I don't need that shit in my head. "I've messaged her a few times but only had one reply. I just hope she gets what she needs."

"I'm sure she will. Honey said that she's hopeful the time away was exactly what she needed."

I nod, hoping that she's right. Chelsea has always been a little wild, but recently it's like she's lost her grip on reality. "I'm going to have a shower."

"And then you're heading home?"

"Jeez, are you sure you're not trying to get rid of me?"

"Never. You're welcome here as long as you like. I just don't want you falling behind because of it."

"I know. I'll go back... soon." *Maybe.*

30

RAELYNN

When I walked into the kitchen on Tuesday morning, I soon learned of Ethan's whereabouts because Eric announced that he was with his mother. Eric was pissed—rightly so. He was missing classes that he needed and practice that he should be making the most of, but according to him, Ethan was refusing to come home for some unknown reason.

I kept my mouth shut, not wanting to get involved in what was obviously a tense relationship between father and son. Mom kept watching me, making me wonder if she suspected that I knew more than I was letting on, but she never said anything.

I thought my time was up this morning when she knocked on my bedroom door and slipped inside before I left for school.

"Are you glad it's nearly the weekend?"

"I guess," I mutter, dropping some books into my bag. It's been a long-ass week, what with the continuous questions about Ethan and the entire school's building tension over whether he's going to reappear for the all-important game next weekend.

Amalie and Camila have kept up their promise to me and followed me around while trying to strengthen our friendship. I won't be admitting it aloud any time soon, but, not only am I starting to get used to their presence in my life, I'm also actually looking forward to it. When they weren't here after I came home from Aces last night, I actually missed their company. It was a fucking weird feeling after being alone for so long, that's for fucking sure.

"Eric and I are heading out of town this afternoon." She drops this in as if it's our normal.

"Again? I feel like you only just got back."

"I know. There's been some emergency. I don't know. We'll be gone by the time you get home, but I've organized a surprise for you for tomorrow."

"Oh?"

"I can't tell you now, but I think you're going to really enjoy it."

"Okaaaay," I say curiously as she pulls me in for a quick hug.

"Rachel's been shopping. Everything you could want to eat and drink is in the kitchen, but if you need anything else then you've got your credit card."

I nod, already knowing that I won't be using it. I've got a little of my own money left before my first payday from Aces at the end of the month. Hopefully it'll see me through. "Any news on Ethan?" I ask, wondering if I should expect him to reappear the second his dad disappears.

"No idea. Eric hasn't spoken to him and only had a few messages from Kelly."

"Okay, well... I'd better head out if I don't want to miss the bus."

"I could take you, if you like." Guilt twists her features.

Whatever Eric's emergency is, I'm one hundred percent sure that she doesn't need to follow to help out, but it seems she's doing just that anyway.

"It's fine. I'm sure you need to pack or something. Have a good trip."

"Okay, I'll see you in a few days then. Be good."

"When aren't I?" I ask as I pull my door open and leave her standing in the middle of my room, looking lost.

My heart drops the second I step out of the front door. The last thing I want is to spend the weekend alone in the huge house. I might like my own company, but it's a little different being alone in the tiny apartments Mom and I shared compared to this mansion.

Shaking my head, I make my way down the long driveway on my way to the bus stop.

School is just deja vu of the rest of the week with everyone asking me if there's any news. So much for starting here and blending in; everyone now seems to know my name and my connection to the Savages.

By the time I climb out of Cody's car, I'm exhausted and the sight of both Amalie and Camila's cars sitting in the driveway doesn't fill me with any kind of excitement. All I want to do is crawl into bed in the hope that sleep claims me, unlike the rest of the week. My eyes sting and my muscles burn as I walk to the front door, reminding me of the few hours I've managed each night since this time last week.

It's all Ethan's fault. My lips purse as I think of him. If he didn't storm into my room last Friday night, then none of this would have happened. He'd still be here, and I might still have some control over my insomnia and the nightmares that are continuing to come thick and fast.

"What the hell is this?" I ask, walking into my bedroom and finding not only my bed like I was expecting, but two temporary ones on the floor.

"Your mom invited us to keep you company while she was gone." My chin drops as the cogs in my brain start working. I think back to her words Monday night after she discovered my 'friends.' Something about sleepovers and being normal.

"If you tell me we're having a pillow fight and playing truth or dare then I'm walking straight back out that door."

"No, you're safe," Amalie says.

"Although, we do still need gossip about you and Ethan."

"I told you we fucked."

"Yes, but there are a million and one ways that could have gone down—"

"Oh, he went down," I mutter much to their amusement—and excitement, if the seal clapping is anything to go by.

"Rumor has it he's got mad skills."

"Says who, the entire cheer squad?"

Amalie snorts a laugh, although her face looks anything but amused. "Sadly, those sluts have intimate knowledge of all our guys. Here's hoping they've sucked so many they don't remember which belongs to whom."

"Jesus, they've got some issues." I kick my shoes off and rummage in my drawer for something more comfortable to change into.

"You're telling us. And believe it or not, you haven't met the worst one."

"No?"

"No. Chelsea is the captain and she's—"

"A raging fucking bitch?" Amalie interrupts.

"That works," Camila agrees with a laugh.

"Where's she, then?"

"Fuck knows. With Ethan, for all we know. She vanished almost as quickly as he did."

Something stirs in my stomach, and when I turn to look at them both, it's clearly written all over my face.

"She didn't actually mean that they're together," Amalie says softly, making Camila wince.

"I don't care if they are."

"Really? So you can honestly say, hand on heart, that you're not missing the asshole from across the hall?"

"No, it's such a relief not to be constantly looking over my shoulder." *Liar.*

"Has anyone ever told you that you're a terrible liar, Rae?"

"No one's ever looked closely enough to notice." Fuck, why do I keep saying shit like this to these two and making myself look like a pathetic loser?

"Well lucky for you, you've got us now to point out all the things you don't want to know."

"Like just how badly you want Ethan back."

"I don't. I—"

"It's probably easier just to concede," Amalie says, elbowing Camila in the ribs. "This one is nothing if not persistent."

"Good to know. I'm just going to…" I hold up the clothes in my hand and move toward the en suite.

"Take your time."

"I hope you're hungry," Camila shouts just as I close the door behind me. "We've ordered enough Chinese to feed the entire football team."

Not needing another reminder of the one person I'm trying not to think about, I lean back against the door and press the heels of my hands into my eyes in an attempt to force him out.

My stomach's still twisting unpleasantly at Camila's suggestion that he might be with the bitchiest of the cheer bitches. I never thought of myself as a jealous person, but I hate to admit that I fear that's what I'm feeling right now. I don't want him, yet why can't I even consider the idea of anyone else having him?

Needing some time to get my head together before I go out and field more questions from my new besties, I turn the shower on and strip down. The water from the power shower above my head soothes my tense muscles, but it's not enough to keep it away, because the second I step from the water, I'm as uptight as I was before.

"Whoa, your hair is so long," Amalie says when I finally rejoin them and find them both surrounded by a million takeout containers. They weren't joking when they said they'd ordered enough to feed the five thousand.

I shrug before swiping a band from my sideboard and going to pull it back.

"No, don't do that. It's so beautiful."

"It gets in the way," I say. It's my go-to excuse. Has been ever since... no, not going there tonight.

"Trust me, I know." She whips her long blonde mane over her shoulder as evidence. "It just really softens your face. It suits you."

Telling myself it's just me and the girls—something I never thought I'd hear myself say—I put the band back down and continue toward the food.

Although totally out of my comfort zone, we have a good night. And I'm not sure if it's because of their company or not, but when we eventually turn the lights out long after midnight, I fall asleep a hell of a lot quicker than I have the rest of the week, and when I wake, I immediately realize I had a peaceful night and actually feel refreshed for the first time in days.

It's still early when I swing my legs from the bed and quietly make my way to the en suite. Both Amalie and Camila are passed out, so after grabbing a hoodie, I slip from my bedroom.

I make myself a coffee and head out into the morning sun. It's colder than I was expecting as I settle myself on one of the loungers looking out over the infinity pool and beach beyond. I tuck my knees up into my giant hoodie and wrap my palms around the steaming mug, allowing its warmth to seep into me.

I think back over last night and the girl chat. I've never had anyone to discuss things like that with before, and the first time they started talking sex, I'll be honest, I wasn't really sure I should stay in the room. I know their boyfriends; it was a little odd. But it soon became obvious that their conversation was a normal one for them, so I endured listening. It was a whole other ball game when they turned the questions on me and my time with Ethan. They wanted the ins and outs—quite literally—and my cheeks flamed red hot the second they turned their eyes on me.

I gave them the basics, enough that might get them off my back, but even just skimming the surface of what's gone down between us, I could see them both getting ideas in their heads that there might be more to us than I'm letting on. Plans for triple dates with their boys were literally playing out in their minds like a little movie.

I've no idea how long I sit out there, but my coffee has been long drunk and the sun's much higher in the sky when I hear the doorbell ring.

Regretfully untangling myself from my little cocoon, I walk through the house to the front door. I have no idea who it could be, but I can honestly say that I never would have guessed in a million years when I pull the front door open.

"Hi, are you Rae?" asks one of the ladies before me. They're all dressed in black tunics with flawless hair and makeup, and sitting beside them are silver pull-along trollies.

"Um..."

"We've been booked for the day."

Footsteps sound out behind me before they come to a stop on each side of me.

"Come in," Amalie says politely before wrapping her fingers around my upper arm and gently pulling me out of the way.

"Uh... what the hell is going on?"

"Think of it as a welcome to town present."

"This really isn't necessary," I whisper, watching as the three women grab the handles of their trolleys and march in.

"Where would you like us to set up?"

"I'll show you," Camila says, pointing down the hallway.

"Would any of you like a drink before we start?" Amalie asks. I watch it all play out like I'm not really here.

"Coffees would be great. Thank you so much."

I watch the four of them disappear around the corner, my stomach in knots. "What... um... is this really necessary?"

"Looking at how tense you are, yes. It's totally necessary."

"I've... um... never..." I trail off. I've never really thought about what was lacking in my life. I had Mom, I've always been healthy, things and money have never really bothered me, but suddenly I can't help thinking about how much I've missed out on. Something as simple as a girly sleepover like last night is one thing, but a full-on spa day with friends is well out of the norm for me. The closest I've come is a discount face mask I've picked up from the store on occasion.

"Lucky for you, I'm a pro. Come on. It's time to put your feet up, forget all about the world, and relax for a few hours." She links her arm through mine, and together we head for the kitchen for coffee before joining Camila in the family room while the therapists set up in the sun room.

"I'm assuming my mom had something to do with his," I whisper to Amalie and Camila when the three of us are laid out with gunk on our faces and cucumbers over our eyes.

"She might have mentioned a few things that sparked off

the idea."

"T-thank you," I whisper, not really wanting to acknowledge that I'm enjoying this but needing to let them know how much I appreciate it.

"Trust us, it's our pleasure. And bonus, you'll be looking extra hot for when Ethan reappears."

I immediately sit up. "Do you know something? Is he coming back?" The rush in which the questions fall from my mouth make it clear to everyone in the room just how desperate I am for him to be here.

"Whoa, calm down. No, still no news. But he's got to be back sooner rather than later. He can't miss too much more school or practice."

I lie back down, a knot tightening my stomach as I think about what our first meeting is going to be like.

I never thought I'd say it, but I actually really enjoy my day of pampering—not that I'm going to tell anyone that.

"So what now?" I ask when the therapists have left and the three of us are lounging around on the couches, thoroughly relaxed.

"Now? Now, we order food, find some drinks, and watch some shit on TV."

"You're both staying again? Don't you have anything better to be doing than babysitting me?"

"One, we're not babysitting you. We're getting to know you. And second, not really. The boys are spending the whole weekend working on plays and shit for Friday, and as hot as it is to watch them, a whole weekend of it is a bit much."

"Okay, but—"

"No buts. All you need to worry about is what food you want delivered."

And that's how the rest of our day goes. We order a mountain of food and drink way too much vodka before once again crashing out in my room.

31

ETHAN

I know the guys are spending the weekend putting in extra practice sessions ready for Friday. I see all the messages come through to the group chat that Jake set up, and I feel guilty as I think about all the work they're doing while I'm here wallowing in self-pity after my deplorable actions.

I know Mom's right. I need to go back and face the music, but more than that, I really need to get back for school and the team. They'll never forgive me if I miss any more practices before Friday night's game, and I'll never forgive myself if I get myself benched and miss the final games of my high school football career.

Blowing out a long breath, I push myself from the bed, knowing that if I'm not with them then I should still make some kind of effort to keep myself in shape for Friday. I drag on a pair of sweats, a hoodie, and my sneakers. I swipe my cell from the nightstand and push my earbuds into place.

Mom is in the kitchen with Gran when I pass. They both look up and smile as I head for the front door.

I take off without a destination in mind, just knowing that

I need to run until my lungs hurt and my muscles burn. Running away feels too damn good, but I know what I'm doing right now is taking the pussy's way out. I need to get a grip and head back. A feisty, short-ass brunette should not hold the power to make me second guess going home, but somewhere along the line, it seems I either handed her my balls or I grew my very own vagina, because just the thought of seeing her again has my heart rate increasing.

By the time I turn back down my grandparents' street, my hoodie is soaked with sweat and I can barely catch my breath. It's exactly what I need.

Mom and Gran are exactly where I left them, both hugging their mugs and shooting the shit.

"Would you like some breakfast?" Mom calls as I come to a stop in the doorway.

"Yeah. Let me shower first."

"Damn right," Gran says, fighting her smile. "I'm not having you dripping sweat in my kitchen. Scram."

I salute her and disappear to my room.

I just shut the door behind me when my cell starts ringing. Assuming it's going to be Mason again trying to find out when I'm coming back—the fucker's been relentless all week—I pull it out and almost answer without looking, but at the last minute my eyes land on the screen.

Shane?

What the fuck is he calling me for?

I almost ignore it and throw it onto my bed, but my need to know why he's reaching out gets the better of me.

"Yeah?" I ask, putting my phone to my ear.

"Uh... hey." Silence surrounds me, and just as I'm about to ask what the fuck he wants, he starts talking. "So... I was just wondering when you were planning on coming back."

"Why the fuck do you care?"

"I don't, but... fuck, she's going to fucking kill me for this," he says quietly, sounding like a crazy man.

"Spit it out or get off my cell," I bark. I'm hot, sweaty, exhausted, and hungry. I don't have the energy for this bullshit.

"Rae. You need to come back for Rae." His words make my breath catch.

"Why? What's wrong with her?" My question comes out in a rush, and any hope I had of sounding unaffected by her goes straight out the window.

"Nothing's wrong but..." He trails off, but it's obvious he has so much more to say.

"But?"

"Shelly's been giving her grief—"

"You've met Rae, right? I'm pretty sure she can handle herself around the likes of Shelly."

"Yeah, yeah. Of course she can. But... I think she's missing you."

"I highly fucking doubt that, man. She fucking hates me."

"Maybe so, but your parents are gone again and—"

She's alone. I have no idea if those are the words that fall from his lips, because his voice fades away as I picture her in the house with no one.

"And anyway," Shane says, my senses coming back to me once again, "we fucking need you on the field Friday night."

"I'll see what I can do," I mutter, thoughts of her alone still at the forefront of my mind.

"I gotta go, Jake's busting our fucking balls."

"Sure, yeah." I pull my cell from my ear before thinking better of it. "Shane?"

"Yeah?"

"Um... thanks for looking out for her, man."

"No worries. Just do the right thing, yeah?"

I hang up before my mouth runs away with me. I've not

exactly been focusing on doing the right thing when it comes to Rae since she arrived. I've just got to go home and find out if it's not too little too late.

I shower, pull on some fresh clothes, and pack the little I brought with me. It's time to face the music.

———

It's late Monday evening when I eventually drive through Rosewood. I'm fucking exhausted and wished I'd flown the long-ass journey to Connecticut when I first fled town. I'd put my seat back and crashed on the side of the road last night, not wanting to waste time getting a motel, but I'm fucking paying the price for it now.

It's dark when I pull up out front of Jake's aunt and uncle's house. I debated where to go. Home would have been the most sensible place, but call me a pussy, I'm still not ready to look her in the eyes.

Jake's trailer lights are on, and I breathe a sigh of relief even though I know I'm about to get ripped a new one for skipping out on the team.

I knock but don't bother waiting for a response, seeing as it's pouring down with rain. I pull the door open and step up inside.

"Well, he is alive," Jake says after doing a double take. Amalie lifts her head from his shoulder and also looks my way, but unlike Jake's angry eyes, hers are full of sympathy and concern.

"Yeah, look, I'm—"

My apology is cut off when he pushes from the couch and steps toward me. I wince when he lifts his arm, because from the anger rolling off him, I expect him to plant his fist in my face. It's the least of what I deserve for everything, but the pain never comes. Instead, he pulls me in for a quick man-hug and pounds me on the back a few times.

When he pulls back, he barks out a laugh when he looks at my face. "No need to look so freaked out, bro."

"I... uh... thought you were going to rip me a new one."

"Oh, don't worry. It's coming. Beer?"

"Yes." One thing about spending time at my grandparents' is that it's an alcohol-free house. Not exactly what I needed after these few weeks, but in hindsight, it was probably for the best.

He walks over to the fridge and pulls two bottles out. I leave him to it and walk over to where Amalie's still sitting on the couch, looking at me.

"Good to have you back," she says softly.

Every inch of my body fills with guilt for leaving, but I couldn't see any other way after what I discovered.

"I'm not sure everyone will think that," I mutter. I know she's been spending time with Rae. Mason let it slip in one of his messages that the girls had been over at my house doing homework with her.

"You need to talk to her, Ethan." Her slim hand lands on my knee and squeezes encouragingly. "I'm not getting in the middle, but I think you might be blowing things a little out of proportion."

"Am I?" I snap. "I doubt she's told you the whole story."

"You're probably right, but she's told me enough that I know that you need to pull your head out of your ass and talk to her."

"And here I was thinking that it would be Jake giving me a tongue lashing."

She quirks a brow at me, but she doesn't say anything else.

32

RAELYNN

The second I step into school on Tuesday morning, it's obvious something has happened. The buzz around the students is electric, but as I make my way to my locker and then to my first class of the day, I can't get a handle on what it is from the tiny snippets of conversation I hear.

All that changes once the students around me start filling the room.

"Apparently he just turned back up to practice this morning like everything was normal."

"I heard Coach really laid into him."

"Yeah. He threatened to bench him for Friday night's game."

"Lisa said that Jake had him pinned against the wall."

The gossip goes on and on, but after the first few I'm unable to listen as my pulse starts to race and nothing but white noise fills my ears.

He's back.

I glance around, noting that none of the team have yet arrived in class but knowing it doesn't really matter. He's not in any of my classes today.

Blowing out a slow breath and hoping my sudden bout of anxiety over seeing him again disappears with it, I sink back in my chair and try to ignore the gossip surrounding me. I have no doubt most of it is bullshit.

I look for him all day, but the closest I get is spotting Jake at the end of the hallway, presumably heading for the locker room for afternoon practice.

"Have you seen him?" Amalie asks, coming to stand next to where I'm gazing down the hallway.

"Um... no. You?"

"Yeah."

"And? How is he?"

"Honestly, I've no idea. But it's not really for me to discover. You need to talk to him."

"I know. But I have a suspicion that he's doing everything possible to avoid me."

"He's got a lot going on for the game." It's clear the second the words leave her lips that she believes them as much as I do.

"Whatever. I'm going to be late for work."

"You want me to drop you off?"

"No, it's okay. I'm sure it's well out of your way."

"Shut up. Come on. You can buy me a milkshake to say thank you."

I grab the books I need before following Amalie out toward the parking lot. I don't really have much of an argument as I'd much prefer a lift from her than getting on the bus. It's well worth the milkshake she's after.

I spend all night watching the door and waiting for the team to arrive, but they never do. I tell myself over and over that it's just because they're focused on the Friday night and not because Ethan's demanded they boycott the place.

I expect his car to be sitting outside the house when Cody

pulls up to drop me off, but his space is still vacant, like it has been for days.

"This is fucking bullshit," I mutter as I storm to my bedroom and dump my bag. If I thought he was driving me crazy by running off after discovering my secrets, it's nothing compared to knowing he's close yet avoiding me. He really must hate me after discovering the truth.

Pulling my clothes angrily from my body, I storm through to my en suite and stand under the shower before turning it on. When I flick the switch, I'm blasted with ice-cold water. It's a welcome relief from thinking about that motherfucker all day.

I toss and turn all night as I wonder what the next day is going to hold. Is he going to turn up to the classes I know we have together, or is he more serious about not seeing me than even I think he is?

I'm a nervous fucking wreck as I walk into class the next day, knowing that he should also be in it.

I'm the first in the room, so I find my seat and pull my books out, ready to get started.

Students soon begin to fill the room around me. The teacher arrives, and I just start to think that he's not going to show when the door pushes open. Every set of eyes in the room turns to see who it is seeing as we're all silent, ready for class to start. My breath catches as I get my first look at him in almost two weeks. He's just as annoyingly handsome as the first time I laid eyes on him. He's wearing a pair of dark jeans that are teasingly tight across his thighs—and, I'm sure, his ass, should I get a look at his back—and a skin-tight white V-neck t-shirt that shows every ripple of muscle beneath as he closes the door behind him and nods in apology to the teacher.

As he takes a step to the back of the room, I swear to god that I stop breathing. I stare at him, willing him to look at me so I can get a read on him. Is he ashamed of what happened between us, what he thinks he did? Is he just repulsed by me now he knows my past? Does he care more than he's ever let on? That last one is a long shot, but in the long hours I've had awake at night trying to figure this shit out, I've thought of every angle possible.

He steps up to my desk, his scent filling my nose and my mouth watering, but still, he refuses to look at me and instead keeps his eyes on the floor.

Fucking pussy.

I realize there and then that if I want to have this out with him, I'm going to have to be the one to confront him.

I don't get a chance for the rest of the day. He's out of class before I even pick up my book to leave, and he remains irritatingly invisible. Knowing it's too late to do anything seeing as I should be heading for work, I vow to find a way to intercept him tomorrow and head off to find the bus.

"Is there any chance I could get tomorrow night off?" I ask Bill, poking my head into his office.

"Is everything okay?" he asks, concern filling his eyes.

"Y-yes, of course. I'm just falling a little behind this week and—" Thankfully, my rambling is cut off when he agrees, although I can see in his eyes that he doesn't totally believe me. I get out of there before he feels the need to play the part of my dad and sit me down for a talk.

There's still no appearance from the team or the bitch squad. It's a relief as much as it is frustrating that Ethan has so much control over his idiot friends that he can stop them coming here.

"You fallen out with your friends or something?" Cody asks when we pull up to the Savage house later that evening.

Both Amalie and Camila have been busy this week so haven't been here. Amalie's buying a house for her and Jake. I think she's utterly insane, but I guess when you have that kind of money, what else is there to do? And Mason's had doctor appointments. I can't really complain at either of them, and I hate to admit it, but after their almost constant company last week, I miss them.

"They're busy."

"So... I'll see you Friday then?"

"Yeah. Thanks for the lift."

"Always." He turns and gives me a sad smile before I climb from the car. I've been trying to put a brave face on, but I fear that Cody can see right through it. I'm grateful, however, that he doesn't seem to want to dig into what's put it there.

The rest of the evening drags. I end up getting talked into a late night dinner with Mom and Eric and am forced to listen to their plans for leaving again tomorrow. They've only been back a matter of hours and they're already talking about leaving again. I bite my tongue to stop myself asking if he's ever been here to support Ethan, but it's not my place to get involved.

"Have you seen him?" Eric's voice drags me from my thoughts, making me wonder if I said Ethan's name aloud.

"I've seen him at school," I mutter.

"I keep calling, but it just goes to voicemail. I swear he's not been here yet this week."

I shrug, not wanting to confirm his suspicions.

"Just keep trying. I'm sure he's just busy," Mom adds, like this kind of behavior is normal. Although, we've only been here a few weeks, so maybe it is. Maybe Ethan often just fucks off without a word to his parents.

Pushing my dinner around my plate, I try not to focus on

the look on his face in class earlier. He was hurting, that much was clear, but why? And why did he even refuse to look at me? Is he that ashamed to even glance my way after learning the truth? That thought causes my heart to constrict. He might be an asshole, but I always thought there was someone redeemable beneath the hardened exterior.

"Can I be excused?" I ask once my dinner is cold and the two of them are reliving a memory from their last trip.

"Of course." I get to the door with my plate when Mom's voice calls me back. "Rae, it's Thanksgiving next week. We'll be back so we can all celebrate as a family." A lump forms in my throat. Are we a family? I almost laugh at the hopeful look on her face.

"Sure thing, Mom. Looking forward to it." They must be the least sincere words I've ever said, but she accepts them and thankfully allows me the escape I'm desperate for.

33

ETHAN

I thought avoiding her would be easy. She's just one person in a huge school full of students, but I swear to fucking god that every time I look up, there she is. Without her even realizing it, she's driving me fucking crazy. Those fucking short shirts she wears that show off the smooth lines of her stomach. Her ridiculous excuse for skirts that make my mouth water to rediscover what's hiding beneath. She's all I can fucking think about, and it's the reason I continue to stay away. I don't need her distracting me more than she already is. Coach, Jake, and the rest of the team deserve my undivided attention for tomorrow night. I can't allow her to take up any more of my headspace, and I know talking to her will do just that. There's so much that's been left unsaid between us, and after everything, she deserves my time to hear her out properly, and I know I can't give her that right now.

Thursday afternoon's practice session is grueling beyond belief. We thought Coach was upping the ante earlier in the week, but nothing could have prepared us for this afternoon.

My legs feel like jelly as I pull my bag up onto my shoulder and head for the locker room door.

What I really want to do is go home, relax in the jacuzzi and sleep in my own bed, but I fear that if I do that, sleep won't come for one reason or another. I want to say it'll be because I'll be inside her all night like I keep dreaming of, but realistically, it'll be because I'm in bed on the other side of the hallway, tossing and turning for being a pussy and hiding from her once again.

I need to man the fuck up and get it over with, I know this. But still, I keep telling myself to get the game out of the way and then I can do what needs to be done.

Sadly, those intentions come crashing down around my feet when I pull the locker room door open and find her leaning back against the opposite wall with one foot propped up and a can of soda halfway to her lips.

Our eyes lock. My heart damn near falls out of my chest as something crackles between us.

Someone crashes into my back where I've stopped so suddenly. "Savage, what the fuck, man?" But still, I stand there staring at her.

I'm jostled to the side as a few of the guys leave and head toward the exit.

"What do you want?" I grunt, dragging my eyes from her dark ones in favor of the floor.

"I think it's time we talked, don't you?"

Voices get louder behind me as she pushes from the wall and closes the space between us. As usual, her hair is pulled back from her face, her makeup is heavy, her eyes and lips dark in a stark contrast to her pale skin. She's anything but my type, but as she stands there demanding more from me than I'm willing to give right now, I'm hard-pressed to say I've ever wanted anyone more. Her ripped black shirt has *whatever* scrawled across the front of it in white, and her black skirt is almost pointless. When I make it down her pantyhose-covered legs and to her biker books, I take my time in heading back up once again. Only now, she's got her hand on her jutted-out hip and one brow raised in question.

"No."

"N-no?" she questions, her head pulling back in surprise.

"No. We're not doing this here."

"Why?" she asks, her chin lifting in defiance in a way I love. I'm not used to girls standing up to me—they're usually heading down to their knees instead. It's a refreshing change to the norm. As she opens her mouth, the voices behind me get louder still. "You ashamed of me now? Now you know the truth?"

The guys come barreling through the doorway and hesitate when they see us together in the empty hallway.

"Fucking hell, Savage. You slumming it tonight?"

The words and their assumptions about Rae piss me off—only, not enough to show her that. They give me the perfect distraction and moment to think to get me out of this situation.

Ignoring them, I turn my stare back on her. "Yeah, actually. I am." I put as much hatred into my voice as I can. "We're done here, *trash*." I narrow my eyes at her as she gasps in shock, a couple of the guys slapping my shoulder as I get to them. Thank fuck it's not Jake or Mason, because they'd call me out on this bullshit in a second.

With her standing there looking like I've just told her I've killed her puppy, I make my retreat. We find the rest of the guys still in the parking lot, and when Zayn suggests heading to his place to watch some old games, I eagerly agree. Anything to attempt to forget the look I just put on her face.

I end up sleeping on Zayn's couch. Thankfully, the girls

didn't turn up. Fighting them off was the last thing I needed, especially seeing as there was no alcohol. I offered to get some in, but all I got in return was some seriously pissed-off faces. Their only concern is the game. It should be mine too, but the second I left Rae standing there, I knew I'd made a mistake. I was avoiding talking about it, hoping that it would help clear my head, but in doing so, it's only made it worse. If I'd just taken her up on her offer, or even gone home last night, then all this could be sorted.

I don't spot her until she's carrying a tray toward a table in the cafeteria at lunch. Ignoring the guys around me, I push from my seat and head over.

"Rae." She stills at the sound of my voice but refuses to turn. Instead, she lowers her tray to the empty table in front of her and sits, never once even glancing over her shoulder at me.

Dropping down beside her, I wait to see if she'll even acknowledge she has company. "Rae, I'm sorry. I—"

"Not fucking interested," she barks, staring down at her plate and poking at a fry. "What the fuck are you even doing here? I'd thought you'd be too ashamed to be seen with me."

"I didn't mean it. I'm not—"

"Well, maybe you shouldn't have fucking said it, eh?" She finally turns her dark stare on me and my breath catches when I find tears pooling in her eyes.

Fuck. My chest aches and my hand twitches to reach out to touch her, to do anything to show her that I didn't mean what I said yesterday, that I didn't really mean any of the fucked-up things I've said and done to her since she arrived here. With that, she stands, snatches her uneaten food up and dumps it in the trash on the way out. She passes Camila and Amalie, who don't have a choice but to stand aside. They look to her before their eyes find me. Both sets narrow slightly before they turn on their heels and follow her.

"Fucking hell," I shout, causing a few others to look my way. "What?" I bark, getting up and storming from the cafeteria.

I head straight for the gym, ignoring anyone who calls out to me as I pass. The only person's voice I want to hear just ran away from me as fast as she could. Rightly so. I'm just surprised that her lunch made it to the trash and didn't end up on my head. It's what I deserve. I know that.

I go straight for the weight bench and lie down, ready to distract myself with the burning of my muscles. I wrap my fingers around the cool metal bar, but at the last second, I release it, knowing that I'll never forgive myself if I push too hard and fuck up tonight. There's too much riding on it.

"Fuck," I shout, my voice echoing around the empty room.

I pull my cell from my pocket and find her name. I want to call her, demand she tells me where she is so I can find her and ensure she listens to me, but I know it's pointless. Even if she agreed, I have a feeling that Amalie and Camila wouldn't let me within a mile of her right now. They want me to talk to her, sure. But not when we're both this angry.

Instead, I find someone else's number and hit call.

"Ethan?"

"Mom." My voice breaks, and her gasp of shock sounds out loud and clear. "I've fucked up." It's painful to admit, but I need to get it out.

"Go on, I'm listening."

"The girl I mentioned. She's *her* daughter." Mom's breath catches once again, telling me she knows who I mean. "I've... I've done some stuff that I'm really ashamed of. But I was so fucking mad. So fucking angry for how he treated you. Then he had the gall to move them in, and I made her the target of all my hate. It was wrong, and fucked-up, and... and... fuck." I drop my head into my hands as memories of all the despicable things I've done and said to her play out in my mind.

"Ethan," she says softly, dragging me from my turmoil. "It's going to be okay. The most important thing is that you know you were wrong. You can only right something if you truly accept you made a mistake in the first place."

"She's never going to forgive me... and..." I trail off, not knowing if I should, or even can, voice the next bit.

"And what, sweetheart?"

"I... I need her." My voice is barely a whisper, the honesty behind my words slamming me in the chest and making it hard to breathe.

"You've really fallen for her, huh?"

"I know it's wrong, but... fuck." The image of her laid out naked on her bed before me fills my mind. "She's never going to forgive me. And she shouldn't. I... I..." I can't even bring myself to say the words out loud for what I fear I did that night. "She's got a rough past, and the way I've acted toward her. How I've treated her. I... I think I've..." My chest heaves as I fight to drag in the air I need.

"Ethan. Ethan. Just breathe," Mom says softly. "Calm down. Take a moment and tell me as much as you like. I'm your mom. Judgment-free zone here, remember?" It's the same thing she's said to me time and time again over the years when I fuck up. And I know it's true. She's never judged me when I've made a mistake. She's only ever listened and supported me. And fuck if that's not exactly what I need right now.

I squeeze my eyes shut, blocking out everything around me, and force the words out. "I think I might have forced myself on her."

The halt in Mom's breathing shatters me. I hate that I've shocked her, that she's now going to think differently of me. That I could be *that* kind of man.

"Okay, start from the beginning. Tell me everything."

And so I do. Much to her horror, I'm sure. I explain about how I've treated her, what I've made her do. I hold nothing back, including what I know about her past.

"I wish you'd have told me this when you were here," Mom says when I've eventually finished.

"I-I just couldn't," I admit. The only reason I can now is because I'm on the phone. It makes it just that little bit easier to handle.

"I understand. You need to talk to her. Not in the middle of school, or before tonight's game. You need her to be somewhere she feels comfortable, safe, and you need to listen to her. I mean really listen to her. There's a very good chance that a lot of this isn't as bad as you're making it out to be."

"And what if it is?" I ask, terrified of what the reality could be.

"We'll deal with that when we get to it. But the facts remain that she's done nothing to show that she thinks you did anything wrong. She could have reported you. This could be a bigger issue than what it appears to be right now."

I blow out a long breath I didn't know I was holding, because she's right. If I really did force her that night, she would've have told someone. Reported it. I'd have been hauled off in the back of a cop car by now and questioned.

"I know it's hard, but focus on the game. It's only hours away. Do what you need to do. Take the win. Then go and find your girl and get everything out on the table."

"Okay." I nod, her words settling into me. I can do that.

"And Ethan?" she quickly adds. "Don't pussyfoot around how you feel. If you're falling for her, then damn well tell her."

"Okay. Okay." My heart pounds at the thought, but I know she's right. "Thanks, Mom."

"Always, sweetheart. I'm always here, no matter how many miles are between us right now."

"I miss you," I admit. I've already laid my heart and fears on the line; I may as well be totally honest.

"I know. I miss you too."

We say an emotional goodbye before I fall back onto the bench once again and allow my eyes to close as I think about everything she just said to me.

34

RAELYNN

"Jesus, it's even quieter than two weeks ago," I complain as we look around at the empty diner. "Guess I'll make the most of the time." I pull a couple of books from my bag and hop up onto one of the stools at the counter to get some work done. "Chocolate milkshake would be a real treat right now," I say, glancing at Cody.

"Guess I've got nothing else to do," he mutters before disappearing back to the kitchen.

I sigh and flip my book open. Half of the town has headed to Thunder Valley to watch the Bears thrash the Bobcats, and those who haven't gone apparently don't care for a night out.

Five minutes later, Cody places my drink in front of me. "Thank you," I mumble. Lifting my eyes from my chemistry book, I find a somber look on his face.

"What's wrong?" I ask, feeling guilty that I didn't notice his mood before.

"Nothing." He grabs a cloth and starts cleaning down the already spotless counters.

"Cody?"

He blows out a breath. "I've just got a date after work. I'm... uh..."

"Wait. Are you nervous?"

He stills and looks up at me. "I've been chasing her for a while. I didn't think she'd ever say yes."

My heart swells for the sweet guy before me.

"Why don't you get out of here and head home to get ready?"

"No, no. I can't leave—"

"Of course you can. We haven't had a customer for thirty minutes. We're hardly going to get a mad rush this time of night. Harry is in the kitchen. I'll be fine."

His eyes flick to the door and then back to me. He really wants to do as I suggest, but being the good guy he is, he doesn't want to leave me alone.

"I'll be fine. Go and make yourself sexy."

His chin drops. "You mean I'm not always sexy?"

Laughing at him, I shoo him toward where his stuff is and watch when he returns with it a few moments later.

"Call me if you have any issues," he says, stopping by where I'm still sitting.

"I will," I promise, but like fuck do I mean it. I'm more than capable of closing this empty diner up for the night.

"Thank you."

"Have a good night. Don't do anything I wouldn't do." He looks back over his shoulder and laughs before pushing through the door. I hope the woman he's meeting knows how lucky she is.

As expected, the rest of my shift is dead. Even Harry comes out from the kitchen to sit with me when he gets bored of sorting shit out back.

"This is bullshit," he complains.

"I think we call it a night. No one's going to turn up now; seems like a waste of both of our lives being here."

"I couldn't agree with you more. If we close now, I might get home in time to put my kids to bed."

Smiling at him, I jump up. "Let's do this, then. You get your stuff and go. I'll cash out and then head home."

"I can stay."

"No, no. I insist. Your kids will love it." His wide smile as he thinks about them only goes to prove that I'm right.

He helps me sort some closing duties out before I walk with him to the main door with the intention of locking up behind him, putting tonight's measly takings in the safe and heading home myself.

As I stand in the doorway, the moon sits high in the sky and the light reflects in the inky black ocean below. I blow out a breath as I stand there for a few moments, allowing the serenity to seep into me. It was raining earlier in the day, and the scent from that downpour mixes with the fresh sea air. There might be so many things about this place that haven't been all that welcoming since I stepped foot in town, but being down here by the sea, I feel more at home than I can remember feeling in any of our previous places.

I take a step back inside, reaching out to pull the door closed behind me, when it happens. A body, dressed head to toe in black, slams into me, sending me careening back into the diner. I slide across the tiles before crashing into one of the booths. My head hits the corner of the wooden benching and my vision blurs from the impact.

Squeezing my eyes shut, I will myself to focus, to try to figure out what the hell to do. Loud footsteps get closer, and I fight to keep my breathing steady. I don't want to show whoever this motherfucker is that I'm scared. I can only assume that he's been watching and now knows I'm alone. Fucking pussy.

Dragging my eyelids open, the bright lights above burn, making the place of impact on the back of my head pound.

He's right in front of me, crouched down by my side, but all I can see is his eyes. The rest of him is covered in black fabric, hiding his identity.

"Give me whatever cash is in this place and I'll have no reason to hurt you, princess." His voice is low and calculating.

I scramble to sit so I'm not in such a vulnerable position.

"Fuck you," I spit.

His eyes crinkle at the sides, making me assume that a smile is currently playing on his lips.

"Oh you're going to regret that."

He reaches behind him and my heart jumps in my chest before he reveals what I was dreading. The spotlights above reflect off the glistening metal of the gun as he moves it toward my head.

My mouth goes dry as he presses it to my temple. Leaning in, his eyes run over every inch of my face. He's looking for my fear, but like fuck am I going to give it to him. I jut my chin out.

"Now... where were we?" The cold metal presses harder into my skin, and I fight not to react. "Oh yes, you were going to direct me to the safe and open the motherfucker for me."

I allow him to lift me when he fists my shirt and drags me from the floor. Although he doesn't lift me enough to be able to find my footing. He pulls me to the back as I kick and fight behind him.

When we get to Bill's office, he throws me down on the floor, my shoulder smarting when it hits the tiles.

"Open it." The gun in his hand is still trained on my head, but his eyes flick to where the safe is.

"I can't."

"Don't fucking lie to me."

"I-I'm not." I hate that my voice wavers. It only serves to tell him one of two things. One, I'm scared. And two, I'm lying. Neither of which I want him to know.

"Liar," he bellows.

I don't get to argue my case any more. He steps up to me, his arm lifting before the gun connects with the side of my face. My head snaps to the side with the force, the entire right side instantly burning up. Something cool trickles down and drips from my chin, but I refuse to look to see the blood soaking into my white shirt.

"Now. Open it."

"No."

"You're a real fucking stupid bitch, you know that?"

His gun lifts once more, and, only two seconds later, pain like I've never known explodes in my skull and blackness claims me.

I tell myself to fight. I keep my eyes open, but I have no chance.

35

ETHAN

"Holy fucking shit, that was something fucking else," Jake practically squeals as we bound into the Bobcats visitors' locker room that we'd overtaken for the evening. I can only imagine that the atmosphere in their own is very different, seeing as we just carved them up and served them to their own home supporters.

"Fucking finals, baby," someone calls before Jake is pounced on by almost all of the team as chants and cheers echo in the room around us.

"Cheer the fuck up, dickhead. We've made it." Mason's arm wraps around my shoulder as we watch the scene playing out in front of us. It's basically just a pile of Bears rolling around on the floor.

"You're gonna be with us, aren't you?" I ask, turning to look at him.

Hope shines in his eyes. "I really fucking hope so, bro. The doctors aren't all that happy, but I'll do anything to be on that fucking field with you guys as we win this thing."

"Too fucking right," I shout, and his eyes light up that I'm getting in the spirit of things. "Right, you winning motherfuckers, get your asses up. We've got a party waiting for us," I holler and watch as players begin climbing off of Jake, who's trapped at the bottom of the pile.

"Cheers," he mutters when I reach a hand out to pull him up. The wide smile on his face is contagious, and I pull him straight into me and slam my fist down on his back.

"We're so fucking close, man. How're you feeling?"

"I can't even..." He shakes his head, a delighted laugh falling from his lips. "Fuck, I really fucking need Brit. Right the fuck now."

"Get your horny ass in the shower and you'll be inside her in no time." I push him in the direction of the showers and Mason trails behind us, not wanting to miss any of this.

I was half expecting Amalie and Camila to be waiting for us and to have to come up with some bullshit excuse as to why the five of us weren't getting the team bus back, but when we eventually emerge from the locker room, neither of them are in sight.

"Where are your girls?" I ask as we find seats on the bus, ready for the journey back.

"They're meeting us at your place. Insisted we celebrate as a team."

"Fair enough. Hey," I shout to the rest of the guys once they're on board. "Anyone manage to smuggle any beer on this piece of shit?"

A few call back that it was my job before Coach stands from his seat. "Savage, get control of yourself. You've all got one more game. One more game to focus on, and that's what I need. Keep your eyes on that motherfucking trophy and not a can of beer or some skirt. Can you lot do that for me for two fucking weeks?" A series of 'yes, Coach' sounds out despite the fact that the entire team is about to descend on my house for the party of all parties.

A pang hits me in the chest that this is going to be the last post-game party I'm going to hold. Shane's dad announced at the beginning of the season that, should we make it to the state finals, he was holding that party. And with his experience in the NFL and his reputation, no one could really argue with him.

Leaning forward, I hit Shane upside the head. "I hope you're ready for what's going to descend on your house in two weeks."

He turns to look at me, something haunting in his eyes. "It ain't my fucking house. These guys can do whatever, it was Dad's dumb shit idea."

"Okaaay," I mutter. Shane and I still haven't discussed *that* phone call. I was expecting him to accost me when I got home, but he just nodded, gave me the smallest hint of a smile and carried on with his life. It was fucking weird, but then that's Shane in a nutshell. I've never been able to figure that motherfucker out.

The drive back is long as fuck as all of us crave alcohol and girls. Jake is antsy as fuck to get his hands on Amalie, and I can't say I blame him. If I had someone as hot as her waiting to celebrate with me, then I'd be impatient as fuck too.

Thoughts of Rae have never been far from my mind. The idea that she could be with Amalie and Camila waiting for me hits me like a fucking truck. I know that Hell is more likely to freeze over than that actually happening, especially after she so easily dismissed me earlier, but a guy can dream, can't he?

Now this game is over, we need to talk. And I don't give a fuck if it's in the middle of tonight's party. I'll cancel the fucking thing if it means I get the chance to attempt to put things right. To tell her how I really feel.

"Thank fuck for that," Jake mutters the second the bus pulls into the school parking lot. The cheer squad's bus was in front of us, and they're all waiting impatiently for us to join them, just as ready to party as we are.

I glance out the window and find Shelly staring right back at me. She winks and bites down on her index finger. I assume she's going for sexy, but after what Shane told me she said to Rae, she can fuck right off. I've fucked up enough when it comes to Rae; I don't need her fucking assistance as well.

The guys at the front start moving before the bus has even stopped, and in only a few minutes the three of us are following Shane down the stairs.

"Ethan." Shelly's high-pitched voice goes straight through me. She comes over, her hand wrapping around my bicep as she presses her tits into me.

"Shelly, I'm not—fuck," I bark when my cell starts ringing in my pocket. I'd finally conceded and spoken to my dad, so I already know he's out of town for this party—not that I'd have cared if he were here. He doesn't seem to give me a second thought when he fucks off, allowing me to use his house however I see fit, so why should I care? Pulling it out, thinking there's an issue, I freeze when I see a name I never expected.

Rae.

Shrugging off Shelly's unwanted attention, I swipe the screen and turn away from the excitement so I can hear her.

"Rae?"

Her sobs fill the line, and my heart drops into my fucking shoes. "Rae, what's wrong? Where are you? Fuck," I ask in a panic. She doesn't cry. Something has to be wrong.

I don't look back. Instead, I pull my keys from my pocket and run toward my car.

"A-Aces. Ethan, please—"

"I'm coming, baby. I'm coming. Sit tight." Yanking my car door open, I start the engine and fly from the lot.

"D-don't h-hang up," she whispers through my car speakers once they connect.

"Fuck, no. I'm right here. I'm on my way right now." My heart races as I try to come up with the reason she's calling me in the state she's clearly in. "Are you okay? Are you hurt?"

"Yeah, he—I'm sorry, Miss. We need to assess you," a deep voice says.

"Wait, just wait. I'm coming," I shout into the phone as I pull into the parking lot.

I just about forget to turn the engine off before I jump out and run toward where she is.

There are police cars, an ambulance, flashing lights and officers everywhere. A crowd is starting to form, nosey fuckers.

"Get out of my fucking way," I bark as I shoulder through the bystanders until I come to a line of cops in front of the diner.

The place looks like it always does, police aside, and I relax ever so slightly. At least the place isn't up in flames with her inside.

I rush through them, my desperation to see her getting the better of me.

"Son, you can't go in there," one of the officers says, his hand wrapping around my forearm.

"Like fuck I can't. My girl's in there. She just called me. I need to get to her." Ripping my arm from him, I run before he can reach for me again.

The restaurant is empty aside from a couple of officers at the cash register, so I run toward the kitchen and Bill's office.

There's another small huddle of officers in the office doorway, telling me everything I need to know.

"Excuse me." I storm through them. None of them stop me; I think they're too shocked to react.

"Fucking hell." I come to a grinding halt at the scene before me.

Rae is sitting with her back resting on the back wall of the office, but that's not what stops me. It's the blood that's covering her face and shirt that has me on the verge of a fucking heart attack.

"Fuck, Rae." I drop to my knees beside her, forcing the paramedic to stop whatever it was she was doing as I pull her into my arms.

She trembles against my body, and for the first time since I met her, vulnerability oozes from her. She rests the non-bloody side of her face against my chest and cries. Each gut-wrenching sob is like a fucking spear to my heart.

I hold her tighter, hoping like fuck that I'm helping, that it's what she needs right now. "It's okay. I'm here. You're safe." It feels so fucking weird to comfort her yet at the same time, so natural.

"I'm really sorry, but I need to assess this head wound."

My eyes meet those of the kind-looking paramedic also sitting on the floor.

"You okay?" I whisper to Rae, and she nods slightly.

Reluctantly, I release her and rest her back against the wall. I move back slightly to give the paramedic some space, but a startled cry from Rae stops me. "No." When I look up, her eyes are wide and full of panic as she reaches her hand for me.

Slipping my own into her blood-covered one, I keep our connection while she's patched up. My eyes hold hers and I swear to God that as I look into those brown depths, I'm seeing her for the very first fucking time. Gone is the hard-ass bitch part that she plays so well, and staring back at me is just a girl who's as broken and fucked up as I am.

"I'm so fucking sorry," I whisper, guilt over everything that has gone before hitting me like a fucking sledgehammer. Emotion clogs my throat as even more tears mix with the blood on her face and drop down onto her shirt.

She nods, accepting my apology, but like fuck is that the

only one she's going to get from me. I owe her a fucking lifetime's worth before she even considers accepting them.

I sit with her hand in mine, feeling like my heart's going to pound out of my chest as I wait to get her back in my arms. The paramedics finish what they need to do before telling her that she needs to go with them to the hospital for stitches once the police have finished with her. I have to bite my tongue to stop me from refusing and demanding that I just take her home to look after her. She's fucking terrified and exhausted; the last thing she needs is to deal with all these people.

It can't be more than thirty minutes later when Rae's given her statement to the officers and they allow the paramedics to take her.

"Can you walk, sweetheart?" the paramedic asks as they tidy up to leave.

"Fuck that." Standing, I scoop Rae's tiny body up into my arms. "Okay?" I ask once she's wrapped her arms around my neck and lightly pressed her head to my shoulder.

"I will be."

"You're fucking killing me here, you know that, right?"

"I'm sure I can walk."

"I'm not talking about your weight, baby. I could bench press you all fucking day." I drop my nose to her hair as I wait for the ambulance doors to open and breathe her in. "If something fucking happened to you, I never would have—"

"Stop. It wasn't you who robbed the place. You were... fuck." She blows out a breath. "The game. Fuck. Did you win?"

A smile curls at my lips. With the stress of the last hour, it feels like the first one I've pulled in about a year.

"Of course we fucking won. Was there any doubt?"

"With the size of your ego, probably not."

I laugh as I stare down at her. "Good to know he didn't knock the quick wit out of you."

"Never."

I place her down on the gurney in the back, but she still refuses to release my hand.

Sitting in the chair beside her while the paramedic deals with some paperwork at the other end of her bed, I close my eyes and rest my head back for a second.

"Are you okay?" Her soft, concerned voice fills my ears, and I turn to look at her.

"I don't even know where to start to attempt to explain everything that I am."

Her eyes hold mine, and she swallows as she thinks. The smooth skin of her neck ripples, catching my eye, and my need to have my lips on her gets the better of me.

Leaning forward, she gasps as she must realize my intention, but she doesn't move to pull back.

"I'm so fucking sorry," I whisper so quietly that I doubt she even hears it as my lips gently brush hers.

"Enough of that, you two." The paramedic laughs.

I lift my lips from hers but rest my forehead against hers instead. Our eyes hold, her dark to my light as a million things pass between us.

"I could never be ashamed of you, Rae. None of this has been about you. It's all been about me and my fucked-up head."

Her warm palm rests on my cheek, and it makes me wonder how we went from me comforting her to her comforting me in a split second. "Let me get my head sewn back together and we'll talk, yeah?"

I nod, unable to speak around the lump that's formed in my throat. If she's willing to talk then maybe she will forgive me, or at least put up with me so I can continue to apologize.

———

Watching her be tended to and knowing that there's fuck all I can do to help is frustrating as fuck. But I do what is expected of me and sit in the chair beside her bed as everyone but me, it seems, gets to touch her.

A nurse stitches her up and gives her some pain relief, and a doctor checks her over before writing her a prescription for a load more painkillers. They want to keep her in but Rae refuses point blank, insisting that she's leaving.

"I'm not happy about this," the doctor says, signing off her paperwork. "If anything changes—any extra pain, dizziness, blacking out, anything—you get her back here immediately, you hear me?"

"I will. I've had a concussion a time or two, I know the drill."

"You better, because she's about to be in your care."

"I've got her. I promise."

With a hard stare, he leaves us to it.

"Are you sure about this?"

"Ethan," she sighs, sounding exasperated. "I'm fine. It looks worse than it is with all the blood."

"You'd better be fucking right. Come on."

With my arm around her waist and her clinging on to her bag of pills, we make our way to the exit.

Our Uber is idling in the taxi bay, and after making sure she's settled and comfortable, I run around to the other side and join her.

"What are you doing?" Rae asks when I pull my cell from my pocket.

"There's a raging party going on at home. I'm calling it off."

"No," she snaps, shocking the hell out of me. "You guys won; don't ruin the night for them as well."

"I'm not taking you back there. The music will be loud and—"

"So take me somewhere else."

"Whe—okay." Leaning forward, I give the driver our new destination before sliding into the middle seat and pulling Rae into me. She almost immediately rests her head on my shoulder and sighs in contentment when I wrap my arm around her waist.

"Thank you," she whispers. The sincerity in her voice makes my breath catch.

"Baby, you have nothing to thank me for."

"There wasn't anyone else I wanted to call," she admits, her body noticeably tensing beside me.

"I'm glad it was me."

"Really?"

"Yeah, really." I press my lips into the top of her head and hold them there until the car pulls up in front of a hotel. I've never stayed before, but it's got the best reputation in town, along with being the most exclusive and expensive.

"We're staying here?"

"As long as they've got a room."

I help her from the car before booking us a room for the night. Although I ensure it's not just any room.

"Holy shit, Ethan. This is insane," Rae gasps as I hold the door open for our suite. The far wall is floor-to-ceiling windows that showcase not only the huge balcony but the beach beyond.

"W-we can't stay here," she says, turning her concerned gaze back to me.

"Why not?"

"Because this place is for..."

"For?" I ask when she trails off.

"Adults." Her brow furrows, and I bark out a laugh.

"I'm not sure there's an age restriction as long as you can afford it."

"Yeah, that's the other issue. You shouldn't be spending this kind of money on me."

Stepping up to her, I press two fingers against her lips to keep her from saying any more.

"I thought you'd learned by now that I do what I like when I like." I wink, and her cheeks heat a little. "And what you've just said is utter bullshit. You deserve this and more. I know I've fucked up, but let me show you how it should be. How you deserve to be treated."

She swallows and bites down on the inside of her lips as she continues to stare at me.

"Tell me what you need, and it's yours."

"I don't—"

"If you say you don't need anything, then I'll just order everything I can think of to make you happy. So unless you want his place filled with everything, then I suggest you just be honest. Are you hungry? Thirsty?"

"I need..." I raise a brow as I wait for her to finish her sentence. "A wee."

Barking out a laugh, I drop my hand down to hers and squeeze her fingers. "I think that's the door." I lift my chin over her shoulder and she turns to look.

"I'll just be a few minutes." She takes a step back but doesn't get very far. "You're going to need to let go."

"Are you going to be okay?"

"Ethan, he only hit me on the head. It's nothing."

My eyes flick down to her shirt that's still covered in her blood, and I remember the panic that filled me the second I stepped into that room and saw her.

"It's not nothing. You should be in the hospital right now, not here with me."

"I'm fine. I promise." When I still don't release her, she sighs. "You wanna come?"

"Thought you'd never ask." Rolling her eyes, she walks toward the bathroom with me trailing behind.

"Whoa, it's huge."

"So I hear," I mutter, unable to stop myself.

Ignoring me, she continues. "Most of our apartments have been smaller than this."

I look around the bathroom and realize that it is a bit over the top. A huge walk-in shower with more jets than I've ever seen. A huge roll top bath in the center of the room and a his and hers basin with more worktop space than I'm sure any woman could fill.

"Look at that bath. I bet that's incredible."

"You want to try it out?"

"Um... yes."

"Your wish is my command."

"Aww, you my fairy godmother now?"

"I'll be whatever you want me to be, baby." She stills and stares at me. "What?"

"It's just weird, is all."

"What is?"

"You being nice. It's unnerving."

"Rae," I say on a sigh, stepping up to her and taking her face gently in my hands. "I was a fucking asshole. The things I said to you, the things I did." I cringe. "They're unforgivable. I don't even know how to start apologizing. Then that night, when we... when I... and then I found your diaries. Fuck," I bark, turning away from her. Placing my palms on the marble counter, I hang my head in shame.

"Ethan," she whispers, coming to stand behind me. I flinch when her hands land on my side and slip around to rest on my abs. "I never wanted you to find out like that. What happened in the past, that's... in the past. What happened between the two of us has nothing to do with that."

Her body heat burns as she holds onto me.

"But—"

She spins me until I'm facing her, my butt resting on the

counter, but still, I refuse to look at her, instead keeping my eyes on the shiny tiles on the floor.

"No buts," she says softly, her palm cupping my rough cheek. "Look at me," she demands, and I have no choice but to follow orders. My eyes meet hers, and, the same as earlier, everything she's feeling is right there. For some reason, she's dropped her walls and she's willing to let me see her, the real her. "You didn't do anything that I wasn't fully on board with. If I didn't want to, I can assure you that you'd still be trying to retract your balls from your chest now."

The corners of my lips twitch up in a smile. "I love your fucking mouth." My eyes widen as I realize the words that just fell from my lips. "I... uh... never know what's going to come out n—"

Copying my move from earlier, she places her fingers against my lips to stop my rambling. "Every time you touched me, I wanted it. Craved it. That night, I needed you inside me just as much as you wanted to be there. I promise. And if you'd just stuck around or answered your damn phone, then I'd have told you that."

"I'm so fucking so—"

Her lips press to mine and my words die as her heat seeps into me. My hands find her hips as her tongue teases my bottom lip. Knowing that she's stretching up, I lift her and spin so she can sit on the counter. Pushing her legs apart, I step between them, our lips still connected.

With one hand on her waist, I wrap the other around the back of her neck to cradle her head and slide my tongue between her lips. The kiss is like none we've shared in the past. It's not full of hate, anger, and a need to hurt. Instead, it's slow, passionate, and full of all the words we're holding back from saying to each other.

Her tongue slides against mine as her taste explodes in my mouth. My fingers tighten against her in my desperation for more, but I can't forget everything she's been through tonight. I need to hold back where I would usually go all in.

Her fingers find the bottom of my jersey and slip inside. My muscles twitch as she lightly scratches over my abs.

"Off," she mutters against my lips as she pushes the fabric up. I'm powerless to do anything but follow her demand, and I reluctantly reach behind my head and pull my jersey up and off. Our lips only part for the few seconds it takes for the fabric to pass.

I step back up to her and pull her to the edge of the counter so she has no choice but to feel just how turned on I am by her. She gasps as I press against her sensitive center, her legs wrapping around my hips and pulling me closer still.

36

RAELYNN

I run my hands over the expanse of his muscular back and lose myself in his touch and kiss. It's the exact distraction I need right now. I hand myself over to him willingly.

When I came to earlier, I found myself curled in a ball in Bill's office, lying in a puddle of my own blood. I thought I was going to pass straight back out as my heart began to race and I fought to drag in the air I needed. But thankfully, after a few minutes, my panic diminished as my fear took over that he was still there somewhere. I strained to hear any movement outside of the office, but everything was in silence.

Breathing a sigh of relief, I pulled my phone from my pocket and called 911. I have no idea what came over me, but the second I hung up the phone I felt so alone and only one person's face popped into my head. He was the only one I wanted in that moment to support me.

Before I had a chance to put any more thought into it, I found his number and dialed. I was so disorientated that I had no idea what the time was or where he might be. All I knew was that I needed him. Just like I do right now.

A low moan rumbles up from the back of his throat and my core clenches.

"Jesus, Rae." He moves his lips from mine and kisses across my jaw and down my neck. "Do you have any idea how fucking scary that was? Seeing you covered in blood?" He moves back from my skin slightly, looking at the red-stained shirt.

"Take it off me."

My words seem to bring him back to himself and he puts a little space between us. His eyes widen in panic as his chest continues to heave.

"Ethan?" I ask, wondering what the hell I just said wrong.

"I'm sorry. I'm supposed to be looking after you."

"And you call that *not* looking after me?"

"Oh, continuing that could certainly be classified as looking after you, but it's not what you need right now."

"I beg to di—"

"Don't," he says, stepping away even more. "I need to do the right thing, and taking you like an animal on the counter like I want isn't doing that."

"I'm not compl—"

"Rae," he moans, almost as if he's in pain. "Just... just let me look after you."

"Okay," I whisper, my need to experience this softer side of Ethan that I knew was always there almost bigger than my need for him.

Glancing around the room, his gaze locks on the bathtub. He stalks toward it, leans over, and runs the water before grabbing the little bottle that's sitting on the side and pouring it in. Bubbles appear almost instantly, but I pay more attention to his muscular, tattooed back as he moves.

Feeling my stare, he looks over his shoulder. A wicked smirk appears on his lips, but unlike all the times I've seen it before, I'm confident that nothing vicious is going to come out of his mouth. He turns and walks back over, his eyes trained on mine, but instead of dropping his lips back to mine like I want, he just slips his hands around my waist and lifts me from the counter.

"You do your thing while I go order us food for after. Anything you want?" I bite down on my bottom lip as my eyes drop to his torso and then the deep V lines that drop into his pants. *Fuck yeah, there's something I want.* "To eat, Rae. Is there anything you want to eat?"

"N-nothing too heavy," I say, not even bothering to lift my eyes from his body.

"I'll just be a few minutes. Call if you need me."

"I'll be fine."

Reluctantly, he leaves me standing in the middle of the ginormous room, feeling a little lost. After a second or two, I remember what I'm supposed to be doing and make use of the toilet before risking a look at myself in the mirror.

I gasp when I first see my reflection. Why the hell he felt the need to kiss me, fuck only knows. I look like a mess. The right side of my face is tinged pink with my blood, my hair is a mess, and I don't even need to mention the patch they had to shave to stitch me back together. I guess it could be seen as intentional, although it's certainly not a look I'd go for. I might hate my hair, but I've still refrained from cutting it all off after all these years, so clearly I'm more attached than I want to admit. My shirt is no longer white, although my skin is paler than I think I've ever seen it in comparison.

Lifting my fingers, I gently touch my new wound. I suck in a sharp breath when it hurts like a bitch.

"Don't," Ethan says, stepping inside the room. "Just leave it alone to heal."

"It's fucking ugly."

"Scars are cool, baby. I thought of anyone, you would understand that."

I shrug, allowing what he's really saying seep into me. "All of mine are on the inside. I'm not sure about this one."

"Your hair will cover it," he says, stepping up to me. His arms wrap around my waist and his chin rests on my left shoulder as he stares at me in the mirror. "You're still beautiful. It just makes you even edgier. Some might say scary."

I laugh, grateful he steered away from the awkward beautiful comment so quickly. "You think I'm scary?"

"Fucking terrifying, baby. You have no idea."

My chin drops as a million questions run around my head, but I don't get the chance to ask any of them.

"Your bath is ready." He releases my waist, and we both watch his hands as his fingers wrap around the bottom of my shirt and lift. He's very careful when it gets to my head and ensures he removes it without causing me any more pain.

His eyes hold mine for a beat before dropping to my bra-covered breasts.

"I never told you before." He drops his lips to the curve of my shoulder. "I was too busy being a dick, but you're so fucking sexy. Your curves. Fuck, Rae."

I gasp at the honesty in his words. I have to avert my eyes. I can't look into his intense stare as he says these things. They make me want to believe him, and that's dangerous.

"Look at me." Without instruction from my brain, my eyes fly back to meet his darkening blue ones. "I wanted you from the moment you arrived. I wanted my hands on you. To know just how soft your skin would be. How you'd taste." He licks up the column of my neck, and I shudder.

I bite down on my bottom lip to stop myself saying anything, and a moan rumbles up instead.

"Then I dared you to get naked. Fuck, baby. You brought me to my fucking knees with your confidence and your defiance. Like fucking kryptonite."

His hands tickle around my back before he releases my bra and lets the straps fall from my shoulders. But his eyes don't drop. They stay firmly on mine.

"Then I tasted you. And fuck if I didn't become addicted."

"But—"

"No buts. Not right now." His hands skim down my stomach and come to a stop on the button of my skirt. He pops it open and pushes the fabric from my hips. His lips tickle against the shell of my ear and goosebumps cover my entire body. "And then... then I slid inside you and that was it. You ruined me, Rae. Fucking ruined me."

His words have my heart thundering against my ribs. I'm waiting for the other shoe to drop. For him to tell me he's currently streaming this to the entire school or some other douchebag move that I'm sure he's capable of, but he never does. Instead, he rips his eyes from mine and kisses a line down my spine as he peels my pantyhose and panties from my body.

I'm left staring at my naked, broken body in the mirror as every touch of his lips sends a bolt of lust straight through my body until my core is aching. It should be the last thing I want after what I've been through tonight, but fuck, Ethan is a law unto himself, and right now I want him. I want him more than my next breath.

I lift each foot when I'm instructed to do so before a squeal leaves my lips when a pain radiates from my ass cheek. "You did not just bite me?" I ask in shock.

Turning, I find him sitting on his haunches, looking at me. His lips are parted and his chest heaves with his increased breathing, and when I drop lower, I find the unmistakable bulge of his erection beneath his jeans.

He swallows, making his neck ripple and his Adam's apple bob. "Th—" He clears his throat before continuing. "The food will be here in an hour. Let's get you cleaned up."

Standing, he holds out his hand for mine. I slip it in, loving the way he squeezes it tight. He continues holding while I climb into the bathtub and sink down into the bubbles.

He loiters awkwardly beside me, deep in thought.

"What are you doing?"

He takes a few seconds to answer. Trepidation fills me, because I can't get a read on him.

"I'm just... I'm just wondering why me? Why did you call me tonight when you could have called others?"

"I didn't want anyone else," I admit. If we're being honest, then I'm going all in.

"But why? I've been nothing but an asshole to you. Why?"

I shrug, because really, I don't have the answer he's after. "I don't know. All I do know is that I came to, terrified that he was going to come back, and the only person I wanted was you. It's fucked up, I know. But..." I blow out a breath. "Something told me that you'd protect me. That although you've hurt me, actually, you wouldn't accept anyone else doing it."

He hangs his head in shame. "No one will hurt you again. Me included." His voice is so broken it has a lump forming in my throat. "I know I don't deserve your forgiveness, but I swear to fucking god, I'll do anything to prove to you that I'm not that person. I was angry. I was hurt. I was lashing out because of things I had no control over, and then you appeared: the perfect target. I didn't expect you to fight back. I didn't expect you to push me, to dare me. To make me want you. But fuck, Rae. I want you so fucking bad. And I don't mean to prove a point or to take my hate out on you. I mean, I want to protect you. I want to make you smile, because when you do, it's fucking breathtaking. I want to be the kind of guy you deserve. I want to show you how you should be treated. I want you to be my motherfucking queen."

"Ethan," I whisper, tears streaming down my cheeks at his raw honesty.

When he eventually looks up, his own eyes are full of water threatening to tip over the edge. His breath catches at the look on my face, but I don't miss a little hope seeping into his eyes.

"What the fuck are you waiting for?" His brow quirks in confusion. "Get the fuck in."

Faster than I thought possible, Ethan has his jeans and boxers on the floor and is stepping into the soothing water with me. The bubbles swallow up most of his body, which is a damn fucking shame, but I soon find myself turned so that I can lean back into him, and it totally makes up for it.

His legs cage me in while his hands rest teasingly on my stomach. I gently settle my head on his shoulder and tip my chin so I can look up at him. His eyes are closed, his lips pressed into a thin line. He looks like he's in pain.

"Are you okay?"

"Couldn't be better." He opens his eyes, and his dark blue irises find mine. They're so full of need and hunger it makes my stomach clench.

He presses a sweet kiss to my forehead and rests his lips there. I relax, allowing his warmth to soothe me, and I close my eyes.

I've no idea how long I stay there, but sooner than I'd like, Ethan speaks behind me. "Baby, you can't fall asleep."

"I'm not," I whisper back.

He laughs. "I'm pretty sure you were just snoring."

"I really doubt that."

"Really?"

Leaning forward, he grabs a washcloth and a bar of soap. "Tell me if it hurts, okay?"

I nod, too busy watching his hands lather up the cloth to pay much attention to what he's saying. He starts on my face before dropping down to my neck and to my shoulder, washing away the evidence tonight has left on my skin. He's so gentle and I feel myself starting to drift off once again as he rubs the cloth over me. That is, until it brushes one of my nipples. My breath catches, and I tense.

"Fuck," he mutters behind me.

"Sorry."

"Never. Never be sorry for that."

"O-okay."

He does it again to the other side, but I'm pretty sure it's not by accident this time.

"Ethan," I moan, wiggling against him as need flows through me. With him wrapped around me like this, his hands on my body, his length quite obviously pressing into my back, all I can think about is him and the way he's able to play my body.

"What do you need?" he whispers in my ear, the deep rasp of his voice not making the situation any better.

"You."

He stills for a second. "Are you sure? Your head…"

"Is perfectly okay, like I keep saying. Please, Ethan. Make me forget."

"Fuck. I don't stand a fucking chance with you, do I?"

I smile but don't reply. I can't, because he abandons the cloth in favor of running his fingers down my stomach. I open my legs when he gets to the apex of my thighs and lean back into him a little more.

His fingers tease over my lips before zeroing in on my clit.

"Jesus, Rae."

"I told you," I moan as he starts pressing harder exactly where I need. "I need you."

"Christ. I don't deserve this."

"Stop thinking. Right here, right now. That's all that exists."

He nods against me before reaching lower to find my entrance.

"Fuck, you're so ready for me."

"Mmm..." I moan, pressing my lips to the thundering pulse in his neck as he works me to a frenzy.

His other hand cups one of my breasts, and he pinches my nipple hard at the same time he thrusts up into me and bends his fingers just so.

"Ethan, fuck, shit," I chant as he pushes me higher.

"I fucking love it when you moan my name," he groans, his entire body locked up tight behind me. "You're so close, I can feel it."

"Oh god," I whimper before crying out his name as I fall over the edge into mind-numbing pleasure. In those few seconds, nothing else exists. There're no gun-wielding robbers, no stitches, no dickhead I'm forced to live with, just the two of us. Me taking what I need and him willingly giving it.

"Fucking hell, Rae." He continues stroking me as I come down from my high.

I lie a limp, exhausted mess on top of him as I try to regain control of both my breathing and my limbs.

"We should probably get out. The water's getting cold and our food will be here soon." The thought of eating makes my stomach growl loudly. "Yeah, see. Your stomach agrees."

I've no idea how long ago it was since I last ate. I've no idea what the time is now, but he's right. Suddenly I'm starving.

After gently pouring some water over my hair in an attempt to get some of the blood out, he releases the plug.

"Sit forward."

I do as I'm told, and in seconds I'm alone in the huge tub as Ethan climbs out. With his back to me, I get a great shot at his ass and that damn teddy bear tattoo that I'm so intrigued about. He reaches for a towel and sadly wraps it around his waist before turning around, although when he does, I smirk, noticing that the fabric does nothing to hide what's happening below his waist.

"What?" he asks innocently when he spots where my eyes are focused. "I just had this hot-as-shit girl wet and laid out on top of me as she rode my fingers. What else do you expect?"

I hate that his words have color tinting my cheeks, but I can't help it. There's something about him and his dirty words that bring out the innocent little girl within me.

"Check you out, getting all shy. I've already seen it all, baby. It's a little late for that, don't you think?"

"It's different," I admit and then slam my lips shut.

"Oh, how's that?"

You're looking at me different. It's like you see me now, not just your anger. "I don't know. It just is." I lift my hand to his outstretched one so he can pull me from the bath.

"You're lying, but you're also buck naked at this very second, so I'm going to let you get away with it." He watches as some bubbles slide down my body before he reaches out to grab me a towel. He wraps it around my body and tucks it into place before passing me a second for my hair.

A knock sounding out from the main part of our suite stops him asking me the questions that are right on the tip of his tongue. He looks at me for a second longer before turning and leaving me alone.

I gently wring my hair out before drying my body off. Spotting his jersey on the floor where it fell earlier, I carefully pull it over my head and hang the towels back up.

I know we're alone once more because the door to the suite closed a few seconds ago, but Ethan must appreciate that I need a little space because he has not come back yet.

I stare at myself in the mirror, thankfully looking a little more normal now the blood's been washed away, but still nowhere near what I'm used to. But I think that's got more to do with Ethan than it does what happened tonight. My eyes are lighter, my walls are down. It's a weird feeling after being so closed off for so long. I've yet to figure out if it's a good or bad thing, mind you.

Deciding I need to go out before he comes back to find me, I pull the door open. I immediately find him sitting on the edge of the couch with the biggest display of fruit sitting on the coffee table behind him.

"Whoa, that's a little much, don't you think?"

He startles at my voice, obviously lost to his own thoughts. "Oh... um... yeah. I just asked for a selection of fruit. There's even chocolate dipping sauce." His eyebrows wiggle suggestively, and I can't help but laugh.

"Give me one orgasm and you think I'm a sure thing, eh?"

I lower myself down on the opposite couch to him. "No, that's no—"

"It was a joke, Ethan. Don't look so worried. I meant what I said in there." I nod to the bathroom. "I was fully on board, every single time. Amalie and Camila said that you—"

"Motherfuckers," he mutters, rubbing his hand over his face.

"They said you thought you forced yourself on me, that it was the reason you left."

"That was part of it..." He blows out a long breath, his eyes focused on the huge windows that look out at the beach beyond.

"And the rest of it was my diaries," I add, filling in the gaps that he seems to be skirting around.

Silence descends around us. The only thing I can hear is his heavy breathing as he tries to form the words he needs.

Sitting forward, he rests his elbows on his knees and drops his head into his hands. "I just... I read some of what you'd been through, and all I could see was me doing the exact same thing. I pushed you until you didn't have a choice but to give me what I wanted."

"Ethan, no—"

"I freaked out," he continues, cutting me off. "I was already ashamed of everything I'd done and knew that no matter what I told myself, I didn't hate you or blame you for how my life had turned upside down. I panicked because I realized that what I felt for you was something very different. That night when I…"

"When we had sex?"

"Yeah. It was different from any other time I have. It was… incredible, mind-blowing, and I knew it was never going to be enough for me. I knew I wanted more. That I wanted you. But I also knew that I didn't deserve you. And then I read all that and… fuck. I don't know, Rae. It was just so much all at once. I freaked."

"I understand. It's a lot to take on board."

"I don't mean what happened to you. I couldn't give a shit about that…" I gasp, and he must realize how what he just said sounded. "Wait… no. That came out wrong."

"Look at me," I demand, needing to see his eyes.

He looks up at me, although he doesn't move his head. His eyes are dark and haunted as he remembers. "Of course I care. I fucking hate that you went through that, and I hope that one day you might be willing to tell me all of it in detail so I can totally understand. But knowing about it… it doesn't change how I feel about you. I'm not ashamed like I made out the other day. That was bullshit to keep you at arm's length. All of it has just been fucking bullshit." He lifts from the couch before dropping down on his haunches before me. He takes my hands in his, his eyes laser-focused on mine. "Can we start again? From tonight. From right now?"

Memories of everything he's said and done to me since I arrived flash through my mind like a movie. "I… I don't know."

A huge part of me wants to say yes and jump into his arms, because this side of Ethan Savage is one I can get on board with. But there's that other part, one that I remember all too well still. The wounds are still too raw.

He nods, his eyes full of emotion as he stands and backs away from me. Every muscle in my body aches for me to reach out for him, to pull him into my arms and to tell him that I'd love to start over as of right now, but I know I'm not in the right place after the events of tonight to make that kind of decision. I need food, I need sleep, and I need a hell of a lot more painkillers.

"Okay, okay. I understand." He walks back into the bathroom, his shoulders sagged in defeat, and I hate myself for hurting him but know it's the right thing to do—and nowhere near what he deserves for how he's treated me.

When he returns only a few moments later, he's picked himself back up and replaced the towel that was still around his waist with his boxer briefs.

My eyes feast on his toned and tanned skin as he makes his way back over to me. But unlike I'm expecting, he doesn't stop at the closest couch to him. Instead, he falls down beside me. "Not hungry?" he asks as if our previous conversation never happened.

"Uh... yeah."

I sit back as he grabs a selection of fruit from the vast arrangement, some of which I've no clue what they are, but I'm not going to point that out. The vast differences between us are already stark; I don't need to remind him of why he spent our first few weeks calling me trailer trash.

"Thank you," I whisper when he hands me a plate.

"Are you feeling okay?"

"Yeah, my head's getting worse though. I think it's time for more pills."

Ethan grabs his cell from the coffee table. "Fuck," he barks, rushing to get up. When he returns, it's with the bag full of pills the doctor insisted I left the hospital with. "I'm already doing a shit job of looking after you," he mutters, pulling the boxes out and reading the instructions to find out which ones I should be taking.

He stills when I rest my hand on his forearm, stopping his movements. "You're doing a great job. Stop worrying."

He sighs and relaxes back. "Why were you even there alone tonight?" He already knows the answer to this—he was there when I answered the officer's questions.

"Because it was quiet and it seemed like a waste of time for us all being there," I repeat.

"I know, but it was fucking stupid."

"Hindsight and all that," I mutter, feeling pretty fucking stupid for allowing it to happen in the first place.

"He could have fucking killed you, Rae."

"I know. But he didn't. I'm here, and aside from an unexpected haircut and a headache, I'm fine."

He glances over at me. His question's written all over his face.

"Really. I'm fine. Stop worrying."

"Not possible."

I smile at him before holding my hands out for the tablets he's holding and accepting a bottle of water when he hands it over for me to take them with.

37

ETHAN

I awake with a start. My heart pounds as I turn to look at Rae beside me.

"It's okay, I'm still alive."

"Fuck," I bark—first because I was supposed to stay awake to wake her every so often because of the concussion, but also because the last thing I was expecting was to find her wide awake. "You scared the shit out of me."

"Well, if you hadn't have fallen asleep on me then you'd have known every so often that I was awake."

"Smart-ass."

She shrugs and goes back to staring at the ceiling like she was when I first looked over.

"How are you feeling?"

Dread sits heavy in my stomach, because from just looking at her tense body, I know she's shut back down. I guess I should have expected it. Last night she'd had the shock of her life. I wasn't her biggest concern. She's probably kicking herself for letting me in like she did last night. But it's too late now, because I remember all of it. Every word she said to me and the exact look in her eyes as she did.

She can tell me as much as she likes this morning that she hates me, but I know it's not true. Not really.

"Like shit," she mutters. "We should probably go home and see if the house is still standing."

I know she's right, but that doesn't mean I'm ready to walk out of this suite. I need to know where we stand.

"Rae," I say, turning onto my side so I can look at her.

From here, she looks totally normal, and as if last night never happened. Sadly, I know that's not the case. She's in pain, and that's only confirmed when she briefly glances at me. Her eyes are dark, proving that she didn't get much sleep last night, and the bruising is really starting to appear on the side of her face.

"Fuck." I reach for her, but the second she stills, I pull my hand back, not wanting to push her too much.

Sitting on the edge of her bed, she keeps her back to me. "I shouldn't have called you last night. It was a mistake. Clearly I wasn't thinking straight."

"What? No, baby. No. I'm so glad you did."

She pushes to her feet and walks to the end of the bed. "Why? So you could see me suffering? See me in pain? I bet you fucking loved that after everything, didn't you?"

"What? No. I fucking hated it. What the hell are you talking about?"

"You think I believed a word of what you said last night? The bullshit you spewed about how you *really* feel about me? Like fuck did I. We both know that you were just taking advantage of me when I was at my lowest. Well, congratulations. Last night savas probably the second worst in my life. But I doubt even you could beat my worst."

"Rae, stop. Just stop talking." I'm in front of her in seconds, my fingertips running down her arm to find her hand, but she pulls it away as if I've just burned her.

"I'm done with this bullshit. Where's my purse?" My

mouth opens to respond, but no words form. "Fuck it. I don't need your help."

She spins on her heels and races around the room until she finds her purse on the dresser. She pulls her cell out and taps on the screen for a few seconds before rushing into the bathroom and slamming the door behind her.

The loud bang is what I need to drag me from my daze. "Rae. You need to hear me out."

I stand on the other side of the door, knowing that she can't hide in there forever, and wait.

The toilet flushes, water runs and there's some rustling, but she's silent no matter how many times I knock on the door and beg for her to come out and listen to me.

I pace back and forth, knowing she's going to have to emerge soon. The second the lock clicks open, my heart jumps into my throat. I crowd her in the doorway, my eyes burning into hers, begging her to listen, to believe what I've been saying to her.

"Rae, please. I swear on my life I meant every word I said to you last night. This thing between us, the chemistry, the need, that pull you feel. It's real. Please."

"I'm done, Ethan. There's a car waiting for me outside. Don't follow me." It's only now I notice that she's no longer just wearing my jersey but also her skirt and boots.

She pushes past me. I'm so lost that I allow her to do so, I even stumble a little with the force she uses that's not necessary.

"Rae, please. I'm begging you. Come back and we'll talk. Just give me a chance."

"You had a chance when I first arrived and you were a cunt. You made your bed, Ethan. Now you need to lie in it. Alone." And with those parting words ringing in my ears, the suite door slams behind me and I drop to my knees.

"Rae."

I hang my head, trying to work out what the hell went wrong, allowing myself to wallow in self-pity for two seconds before I make my way back to my feet and rush toward where my pile of clothes still sits on the bathroom floor.

I tug on my jeans, pull my hoodie on—sans jersey, seeing as Rae's still wearing it—and shove my feet into my shoes, foregoing socks because they'll take too long. Emerging from the bathroom, I spot the white bag full of painkillers that Rae will need. I swipe them from the side table and run from the room.

I request an Uber as I race down the stairs, not bothering to wait for the elevator, but I regret it when I see I've got a ten-minute wait for the car to arrive.

Hoping I might find her outside the hotel also waiting, I run out, but she's not there.

"Fuck," I pant, my hands landing on my knees as I stare out over the hotel grounds.

The ten-minute wait for the car is the longest of my life. I've fucked up royally when it comes to Rae, time and time again, but as far as I'm aware, I did nothing but look after her last night. She told me everything was fine and I believed her. I thought I could read her. I thought the way her body responded to me last night was all the evidence I needed. Well, this morning just proves that I could be very, very wrong.

She was just freaked out over what happened to her. She was craving the feeling of safety. She wasn't of sound mind. You took advantage... again.

"Yes," I hiss when what I hope is my car pulls up to the entrance. I jump in the back and bark my address at him. I don't need her going back to the mess my house could be in.

The roads are deserted but still, the journey still takes forever. My knees bounce and I fidget my hands in my lap as nervous energy races through me.

"Thanks," I call to the driver, but I'm already flying up the driveway toward the front door, so I have no idea if he hears or not.

The front door is unlocked, and I basically fall through it in my need to find her. There are bodies littered everywhere as expected, but what I'm not prepared for is five people to emerge from the kitchen, each one looking stressed and harassed.

"Ethan, what the fucking hell?" Jake barks, his voice full of anger. "Where the fuck have you been?" He steps up to me, and his palms slam down on my chest, forcing me to take a step back.

Fuck. It's the first time I register that I just took off last night, no explanation, no reason, no destination. I just left them.

"Where's Rae?" Shane asks, standing shoulder to shoulder with Jake, a darkness to his eyes I've never seen before.

"She's... She's..." I stutter, but I don't get a chance to finish it before the front door opens.

"She's here."

"What the fuck?" The question is asked by all of them simultaneously as they turn toward her. The bruise on her face is unmistakable, but when she steps toward us and they get a look at her head, they all gasp in horror.

Everything after that is a blur as Jake's fist connects with my jaw, and I fall back into the wall. I don't make it to the floor before he grasps the front of my shirt and pulls me up to face him.

He cocks his arm back once more before it lands on my cheek and another to my mouth that successfully splits my lip before Amalie manages to pull him away. At no point do I fight back, because I might not have anything to do with Rae's current state, but I deserve a few good hits for what I have done.

The hate in his eyes rivals my own that I've felt over the past few weeks.

"What the fuck?" I ask, lifting my hand to wipe the blood. "That wasn't me. Fucking hell." I shake my head before locking my eyes on Rae, waiting for her to explain. Both Amalie and Camila are now at her sides, checking her over, but the concern's not left her face.

It takes too fucking long for her to say something, but eventually she breaks the silence. "Aces was broken into. The guy had a gun. Thankfully he only hit me with it."

"Jesus. Fuck, Rae. Are you okay?"

"I'll be fine."

"Where have you been?"

"Ethan took us to..." She hesitates, not wanting to admit that we've spent the night together, despite the fact nothing really happened.

"I took her to a hotel so she didn't have to deal with this lot." I gesture to the still passed out bodies surrounding us.

"You better have fucking looked after her," Jake seethes.

"Fucking hell, I know I've been an asshole, but shit, Thorn."

"He did," she whispers. "If you don't mind, I'm going upstairs."

Everyone takes a step back to allow her the space she needs, and we all watch as she climbs the stairs and turns the corner.

Every inch of me aches to follow her, to make sure she's okay, but she's made it more than clear this morning that she doesn't need or want me. The thought is like a baseball bat to the fucking chest.

"Get these motherfuckers out of here."

I push through my little crowd in favor of the kitchen. I might need to follow Rae to make sure she's okay, but I'm not a fucking idiot. She doesn't want me right now, and as hard as the rejection is to take, having it witnessed by half our fucking class is not necessary.

I power up the coffee machine before falling down in one of the chairs to the sound of the five of them waking bodies and pointing them toward the exits.

Dropping my arms to the table, I rest my head on them and try to block everything out. I need sleep.

"Everyone's gone," a voice says, dragging me from my uncomfortable slumber. My back aches and my neck pulls as I try to sit up.

"Yet you're all still here," I snap, looking at them all.

"You can be an asshole to everyone else, Savage. You can push them away until they never return, but you can't fucking get rid of us. We're in this for the long haul, so I suggest you pull up your motherfucking panties and get a grip."

"Fuck you," I spit at Mason as all sets of eyes bore into me. "I've done fuck all wrong. She called me. I went to her. I looked after her. I was fucking nice, did everything for her I can think of, and the second I woke this morning she ran as fast as she fucking could."

"And you blame her?" he bellows. "You've been a fucking cunt to her since the moment she arrived."

"She seemed pretty happy with me being there last night. After all, she called me and not any of you."

"You're a fucking idiot, Ethan."

"Why? What the fuck am I missing?"

Mason shakes his head. "I can't, I just fucking can't."

He spins away from me and shakes his arms out.

"You guys go and... hit the gym or something. We've got this," Camila says, taking a step toward me.

"No, I don't need a fucking girly intervention." I stand, and both Camila and Amalie have the balls to stand toe to toe with me.

"Yes. Yes, you fucking do," Camila states.

Our stare holds, my lips pursing in frustration, but I know I can't move them like I would if it were Jake and Mason staring at me like them.

"Fuck, that's hot," Mason mutters, looking his girl up and down, desire filling his eyes.

"Fuck off, you three," Amalie says, waving them off.

After a little hesitation, they leave.

"What the fuck is Shane even doing here?"

"He was helping us look for the two of you last night. He's not the dick you guys think he is, you know. I'd kinda hoped that now it's been proved he had nothing to do with all that shit before that you'd all give him the benefit of the doubt." The reference to Chelsea has me wondering once again how she is and when she's going to reappear.

Not being able to argue with them after he did call me with her concerns about Rae, I shut up, sit down, and take a sip of my cold coffee. "Ugh, that's shit."

The girls make me a fresh one before sitting down opposite me.

"So..." Amalie starts.

"So?" I snark back.

"You're an even bigger fucking idiot than I thought you were." I open my mouth to respond, but Amalie continues. "She likes you, Ethan. Fuck knows why, but she does."

"Oh yeah, that's why she freaked out this morning." I roll my eyes at both of them.

"It was probably exactly that. You're... you're a lot to take at the best of times. After what she'd just been through, I'm sure her head was all fucked up. Just give her some time. Be there for her like you were last night. Show her the real you, yeah?"

"We know you like her too, and we also know you're scared," Camila adds.

"Who are you, fucking Oprah or some shit?"

"No, I'm just someone who's been watching this all play out. Give. Her. Time."

"What if I don't want to?"

"Tough. If you think she's worth it, then you're going to have to wait. And no, contrary to your beliefs, I'm sure it won't fall off through lack of use." Camila flicks her eyes down to my crotch and lifts a brow. "So how about you try to act like the kind of guy she deserves while you wait, eh?"

"You two are a pain in the fucking ass, you know that, right?"

They both smile innocently. "Now, we're going to make her a coffee and go and make sure she's okay. You go hang with the guys. Soak up their advice. Although, you might want to ignore most of it. And like we said, give her time. If it's meant to be, it'll be."

I watch as they make Rae and themselves a coffee and leave me with their words spinning around in my head.

After a few minutes, I wander through the house to find the guys. I hear them before I see them in my home gym.

"The girls chewed you up and spat you out, huh?"

"Something like that," I mutter, sitting on the weight bench.

Jake brings the treadmill to a stop, Mason leans back against the bike while Shane looks totally out of place in the corner.

"You want her?"

I nod at the three of them. No point denying it now. They all know the truth anyway.

"Then you need to fucking show her, bro. Stake your claim."

"But the girls said—"

"Fuck the girls. We got them, didn't we? You want her to believe how you feel, fucking show her."

"How?"

"Fuck knows. You're Ethan Savage. I'm sure you'll figure it out."

38

RAELYNN

I'd been expecting the knock at my door since the moment I shut it. The only thing I wasn't sure of was who'd be on the other side. I'd hoped that Ethan got the message this morning that I needed some space, but he's never exactly been one to figure shit out that easily.

Last night was a mistake. I never should have allowed him to take me to that hotel. I never should have been alone with him. Because now? Now all I want is him. More of his touch, more of his kisses. Just more of him, full stop. I feel like a fucking junkie craving my next hit, and just as much as that shit is bad for you, I know sure as hell that Ethan fucking Savage is bad for me too. He sees me as a plaything. He's made that more than obvious in the past, and just because he whispered some sweet words to me last night and looked after me, it doesn't mean that it wasn't all one big fat lie just to make me trust him. If I trust him, if I let him in even more than he already is, then he will have the power to truly shatter me. And I already know I won't survive it. One man has already tried his best to ruin my life. I will never give another that kind of power, no matter how fucking good he looks with bubbles running down his naked skin or how skilled he is with his fingers. My thighs clench as I remember what he did to me in the bathtub last night. But I soon chastise myself for putting myself in the position in the first place. It's what he wants. He wants to play me.

The knock comes again, only this time it's followed up with a soft female voice and words I can't ignore.

"We've got coffee."

"Fuck's sake."

I pull the door open to find two smiling faces looking back at me, although I don't miss the concern in their eyes. I fucking hate it. It reminds me of the looks I got from the officers and the social workers after Mom came home early that night and discovered what was really going on under her roof.

I shudder at the thought and accept the steaming mug when they pass it over to me.

I stand back and they walk inside. "You don't have to talk if you don't want to. We just wanted to see if you wanted or needed anything, and then we'll get out of your hair."

"I really appreciate that," I say, taking a cautious sip of my coffee.

I turn my back on them and walk out to the balcony, assuming they'll follow. And they do.

We make ourselves comfortable before the low rumble of male voices sounds out below us as the guys make themselves at home on the loungers around the pool.

"I don't know what you did to him, girl. But he's a fucking mess right now."

"I didn't do anything."

"Yeah, you did. You showed him that for the first time in his life, he can't have exactly what he wants. And it's exactly what he needs."

"He doesn't want me. He just wants to hurt me. Prove that he's better, stronger, more powerful."

"You really believe that?"

I shrug, his sweet words from last night coming back to me. "I have no idea what I believe right now," I admit. "Last night was... fuck. It was fucking scary. But I shouldn't have called him to come and help. I don't know what I was thinking."

"You were thinking that he'd look after you in the way only he can. You knew he'd be there in a heartbeat, because beneath all his hard, outer shell is a huge teddy bear who just wants to care for someone and be cared about in return. You knew he'd be mortified if you turned to someone other than him. You knew—"

"I get it," I say, cutting her off, unable to hear any more. Her words are cutting too close to the truth, and it's freaking me out.

"He's been a wanker. We all know this," Amalie says. "But he really likes you, Rae. Now, all you've got to do is decide if you're willing to give him the benefit of the doubt and see if he's worth it."

"I think he is," I whisper so quietly I don't think they hear.

"I fucking knew it," Camila squeals, a huge smile curling at her lips. Amalie shakes her head and laughs at her friend.

"We've told him to back off, but—"

"Ethan doesn't do what he's told," I interrupt.

They both laugh. "Exactly. None of those three do things how they're meant to be done." They both look over the railing at their guys, soft, happy smiles appearing on their faces.

"Ugh, you guys are sickening."

"You can join us. It's not such a bad place to be."

"What's the story with Shane?" I ask after a few moments of silence.

"Honestly, he's a good guy. But as for what he's up to, suddenly hanging with the team and wanting to get involved in stuff he's always run a mile from... we've no idea."

"Probably a girl."

"Ha," Camila barks. "Maybe he's hoping to steal you from under Jake's feet."

"I think he's well aware that won't be happening."

"Yeah, could be fun to watch though."

"Nah, it's something else."

They chat away for a while longer before I start yawning. "We should leave you to rest. Call us if you need anything, even if it's just to put Ethan on a leash."

"I can handle Ethan."

"Oh, we know, girl. We know." Camila winks. "Just... make him work for it before you decide to give him a chance."

"Do you not know me at all?"

They both laugh before saying their goodbyes.

I stay where I am for a while and watch as they approach their guys, who both make space for them on their loungers and immediately wrap their arms around them.

Ethan's face, however, drops before he looks up toward my room. His body stills when he finds me staring back at him and his chin drops, his eyes lightening a little with hope.

I stand with his eyes burning into me and shake my head slowly. His shoulders drop once more before I turn my back on him and walk into my room, shutting the door behind me so I don't risk overhearing them talking, because I would put money on my name being featured more than once.

Leaving my now empty mug on the side, I walk through to my bathroom with the intention of having a shower before attempting to get some sleep. I know I was supposed to stay awake last night just in case, but it didn't matter what I'd been through and how exhausted I was, at no point did I switch off. With him beside me, I just couldn't relax. It wasn't because I was afraid of him or what he might do—more that I was scared of myself and what I might do. He laid there quite happily in just a pair of boxers, his torso exposed from the waist, his muscles and tanned skin ready for the taking, and fuck if the only thing I could think about was climbing over his body. Those kinds of thoughts should have been the last thing on my mind after the night I'd had, but I couldn't help it. As my frustration grew, so did my doubt about everything he'd told me. My exhausted brain told me that I was imagining things and that he wasn't really that gentle with me, that he didn't whisper the things he did in my ear, that he didn't touch me so delicately and lovingly.

He'd told me that he wasn't going to fall asleep so that he could check on me, but that didn't last very long. It couldn't have been an hour after I pretended to fall asleep that he started snoring lightly. I was tempted to get up and leave then, but I knew he'd freak out in the morning and that kind of drama wasn't worth it. It wasn't until he turned his panicked eyes on me when the sun had risen that I realized I should have done exactly that. The look on his face, the openness, the honesty, the hope, it ripped me wide open and terrified me more than I think I ever have been in my life.

My heart races once again as I think back. I think it was the hope that really did me in. It told me how serious he was about the things he'd said to me about how he really felt, and I panicked.

I have a quick shower. I can't remember if I'm allowed to with my stitches, but there's no way I'm not washing my hair. Ethan attempted it last night, but warm water wasn't much of a match for the dried blood clinging to my hair. I carefully shampoo, making sure I avoid the wound. I immediately feel better knowing that my hair is clean. I have no idea what I'm going to do about my patch that's missing, because I'm certainly not wearing it down to hide it.

Your hair is so beautiful, princess.

His words hit me all of a sudden, and my knees buckle. Thankfully, I manage to catch myself before I end up in a pile on the floor. I tell myself it's a sign that I need some sleep and turn the shower off.

I dry off quickly, my headache that's been throbbing away nicely all morning starting to get the better of me, and I pull on a pair of panties and a tank, ready to dive under the covers and hope sleep will claim me now I'm back in my own bed alone.

I just pull the covers back to get in when a knock sounds out. I know who it is, and it's not just because the girls said they'd leave me to rest. I feel it. The chemistry, the connection, even with the door between us.

Knowing that he's not going to leave until I answer, I walk over to the door and pull it open. His eyes find mine for a few seconds and my breath catches at the emotion swimming in them before they drop and take in my body.

A shudder runs down my spine and my nipples instantly pebble under his scrutiny. He growls, clearly not missing my response to him just standing there.

"D-did you want something?" I hate that my voice wavers, but I can't help the effect he has on me.

"Y-you... uh... left these in the hotel. I thought you might need them." He lifts up the white bag containing my painkillers, and the increasing throb in my head suddenly makes so much sense. It was hours ago I last took some.

"Oh, yeah. Thank you." I take them from him, my fingers brushing lightly against his, causing sparks to shoot up my arm. He must feel it too, because his eyes widen and he takes the smallest step toward me.

He hesitates, unsure what my reaction will be. His hand lifts, but he never closes the space between us, and whatever it is he sees in my eyes must tell him to back off because his hand never touches me.

"Rae," he breathes. I hate that my eyes fill with moisture at the broken tone to his voice. "W-what happened this morning?"

"I came to my senses."

He blows out a breath. "Baby, everything I said to you yesterday was true. You're fucking killing me right now."

I still at his admission, and he uses the opportunity to wrap his hand around the back of my neck and drop his forehead to mine. His eyes stay on mine and I fight to hold his stare. I'm so desperate to close mine so he can't read the truth in them about how I really feel.

"Just give me a chance. Let me show you how it can be."

"I-I can't. You don't want me. You just don't want anyone else to have me."

"Fuck, Rae. I want you so fucking bad. Any way I can have you."

I shake my head against his. "No. No, you don't. I'm sorry." I stand back and briefly look at his defeated stance before I close the door. He has to take a step back for me to fully close it, and he refuses.

"P-please. Leave it open. I need to know you're okay."

I don't have the energy to argue, so I do as he says and silently walk over to my bed and climb in. I know he's still watching me, but I refuse to look his way. If I do, it would mean he's seeing the fact that I'm on the verge of breaking down. He saw me broken last night. That was enough.

I keep my back to him and focus on my breathing, hoping it'll relax me enough to send me to sleep. By some miracle, it works, because everything fades away.

———

When I wake, I'm totally disorientated. Sitting up, my head spins before the incessant banging makes itself known. Everything hits me all at once as I squeeze my eyes shut in the hope of blocking it all out. Sadly, it doesn't work. Looking to my nightstand, I find my tablets where I left them, but beside them is a new glass of water. I try to convince myself that it was Rachel, but I know it's pointless, because it was obviously him making sure I'm okay.

I make use of it to swallow down two tablets before making my way to the bathroom on unsteady legs.

I've no idea what time it is or how long I've been asleep, but it doesn't feel like it's been anywhere near long enough. My stomach grumbles as I sit on the toilet, staring at the wall in a total daze. I haven't eaten anything aside from a bit of fruit in the hotel room yesterday... shit, was that yesterday?

I find my cell the second I get out of the bathroom and discover it's early evening. I slept for longer than I thought.

I put it back in my purse and go to grab something to cover up with when some red fabric folded at the bottom of my bed catches my eye. It's Ethan's Bears jersey, but a different one than the one I stole yesterday, seeing as that's in the laundry.

Reaching out, I lift it and bring it to my nose. Breathing in, I allow my eyes to flicker closed as his scent surrounds me. Something within me settles, and I don't even bother to push it down like I usually would.

Slipping the fabric over my head, I very gently run my fingers through my now dry hair and head for the door.

The house is in silence apart from someone rustling around in the kitchen when I get there.

"Rae, there you are," Rachel's soft voice says when I join her. "How are you feeling?"

"I've been better," I admit honestly for the first time since the incident.

"Have a seat." She pulls a chair out for me and I

immediately fall into it. "Would you like a drink, food..."

"Yes and yes. As long as you don't mind. I'm more than cap—"

"I'd love to." She squeezes my shoulder gently and walks to the coffee machine. "Ethan told me what happened. That must have been terrifying."

"Yeah, it was." *Although not as terrifying as what happened after in that hotel room.* Just at the mention of his name, my heart begins to race. I know I was the one to send him away, but fuck if I couldn't do with being in his arms again like last night. Tears burn my eyes as I think back before I shake my head, feeling like an emotional rollercoaster. *It must be the head trauma that's causing it,* I tell myself, *nothing to do with the man himself.* "Uh... where is he? Um... Ethan?"

"Said he was going for a swim, so probably in the pool. What would you like to eat?"

My stomach rumbles right on cue. "I know it's evening, but any chance of breakfast?" I ask, suddenly wanting her incredible pancakes.

"Sure thing. Pancakes?"

"Please."

I watch her putter around as she effortlessly makes me some food while trying to keep thoughts of Ethan in the pool from my mind.

"Here you go, sweetie."

"Thank you. Do you mind if I take them up to my room?"

"Of course not. Just shout if you need anything, I won't be far away."

"Thank you." My voice cracks as tears well in my eyes once more. What the hell is wrong with me?

Grabbing the comforter from the bed and dragging it out to the balcony with me, I wrap myself up to keep warm and sit in the seat closest to the edge. I know I shouldn't, but I'm a glutton for punishment. Before looking over the edge, I start work on my plate that's overloaded with pancakes, bacon, and syrup. Exactly what I need.

The water splashes below and eventually gets too much, and I shift in my seat so I can watch his body cut through the water. He moves so flawlessly as he swims back and forth. I have no idea how he continues for so long, but I'm not complaining. Watching him is almost therapeutic.

I lose count of how many lengths he does, but eventually he comes to a stop and hops over the little underwater wall that separates the main pool from the jacuzzi, and he rests his head back against the tiles behind him.

He shuts his eyes, but he doesn't look relaxed at all. It's clear to see from here that the muscles in his neck and shoulders are pulled tight and he seems to have a permanent frown on his face.

I continue watching him as the sun descends in the sky as the day I've totally missed comes to an end.

I have no idea if he can sense I'm watching him, but when he eventually drags his eyes open, they lock straight onto mine. I still think that he knew I was here all along. It makes me wonder if he feels the same tingles of awareness that I do when he's watching me.

Lifting his arms to rest them on the edge, I can't help but think he's inviting me to join him. But as much as I'd love to, I sit exactly where I am. Our silent exchange continues for some time as we stay locked in our stare. He's begging me to believe him, and I'm trying to keep my walls up in an attempt to stop him from hurting me, although I know it's pointless. I'm pretty sure he's going to smash them down and force his way in eventually.

When my eyes start to get heavy once again. I give him a weak smile before standing with my comforter around me and head back inside, but it's not before I hear a loud splash behind me.

39

ETHAN

y hand slaps the water in frustration. I'm desperate to go up there and pull her into my arms like I did last night to ensure she's safe, but I know she won't allow it. I understand her wanting to keep me at arm's length. Hell, if she were anyone else, I'd be warning her away from me as well. But she's not anyone else. She's mine.

My heart thuds at that thought. Is she, though? Because she seems to be doing everything in her power to stop that from happening.

Frustrated with myself, I push from the water and head inside.

"Would you like some dinner? I just made Rae pancakes, and there's some batter left."

"No, I'm good. Thank you, though," I say to Rachel as I pass the kitchen. Could I eat? Yeah, I can always eat, but there's something I want more, and I need to see what she's doing.

I've no idea if she's sleeping, but I make sure I'm quiet as I make my way to her bedroom just in case. I can't help smiling when I find her door open, just like I left it earlier so I could check on her. Maybe she is softening to me after all, because not so long ago, if I asked her to do this, she'd have thrown it back in my face.

I push the door wider and poke my head inside. She's facing away as I walk into the room, but I make quick work of rounding her bed so I can see her. I half expect her to look at me and rip me a new one, much like I did every time I came in here to check on her earlier, but to my surprise, she's asleep once again.

It's dark out now, but I close the curtains she left open and flick off the sidelight so it doesn't disturb her. I desperately want to pull the covers back and slide in, but the scent of chlorine on my body stops me. Not for long, though.

After having the quickest shower of my life, I walk straight back into her room and lie down with her. My need to be close and to make sure she's okay is too much to deny. There's a very good chance she'll wake up and freak out, but as I lie there listening to her shallow breathing and being surrounded by her sweet scent, I couldn't care less.

———

She's still out when I stir awake the next morning to head for practice with the guys. I'm not sure what Jake is trying to achieve, but with both him and Coach riding our asses, half the team is going to be dead by Friday. I quickly shut off my cell alarm when it starts blaring, not wanting it to wake her. After everything she's been through, she deserves this time to recharge.

With a gentle kiss to her head, I slip out of her room unnoticed and get ready.

I'm the last one out on to the field, and I get a dirty look from Jake for being late. He soon puts it to one side when Mason asks how Rae is.

"I left her sleeping."

Mason's brow rises. "And you know that how?"

"That's enough, girls. There's plenty of time for gossip later. We've got shit to do," Jake barks, totally focused on the job at hand. He shouts orders for everyone to start warming up, and, like a good little team, everyone hops to it, despite it being the ass crack of Sunday morning and really, we should all still be in bed.

Mason strips his hoodie off and joins me as we start sprints. It's the first time I've seen him join in since his accident.

"Bro, tell me you've been given the all clear to play?"

"Not officially, but I'm not missing it for the fucking world, so I need to get back into shape."

We set off again, and although he covers it well. I still see the pain etched onto his features. I want to tell him that he's pushing too hard and he should still be healing, but I know it's pointless, and I also know that if it were me in his position I'd be doing the same right now, so I can hardly criticize.

We continue until we've got sweat pouring from us and the sun has long risen above the horizon. My muscles ache, not helped by my lack of sleep the last few nights, and my lungs burn as I drag in the air I need.

"All right, ladies. Let's call it a day."

"Thank fuck for that," Mason moans beside me with his hands on his knees. "Are you trying to fucking kill me, Thorn?"

"No, but I want you on that fucking field next Friday. And I know all your asses are going to eat your own fucking body weight in turkey on Thursday, so I'm planning ahead."

A series of groans sound out behind me before Jake suggests we all head for breakfast.

"Aces?" Mason asks with trepidation. "Are they open?"

"As far as I know. Let's go check."

We all head off in various cars before descending on Bill. It is open, but it's quiet, and Bill looks a hell of a lot more stressed than usual.

"Savage?" he calls the second I step into the diner. I nod my chin in greeting and walk over while the guys make themselves at home in our booth.

"How is she? I tried calling, but she's not answering her phone."

"She's okay."

He blows out a shaky breath. "She shouldn't have been alone. I should have been here. I should have—"

"It wasn't your fault. The others should have still been here, but I understand more than most just how stubborn she is, so I get why they left. Stop beating yourself up about it; there's nothing you could have done."

"But she's really okay?"

"Yeah, it'll take more than a knock to the head to take her out."

He chuckles, but he's far from amused. "I bought her a bunch of flowers and some chocolates on the way in this morning. You think you could take them home for her?"

"You should do it. I'm sure she'd love to see you."

"Um..." he says awkwardly.

"I can do it. I'll come and grab them before we leave."

"Thank you. I trust you're looking after your girl."

"I'm trying, Bill. I'm fucking trying." He laughs again, but I can't find it in me to do so. How does everyone already know that she belongs to me? It's about time she got the fucking memo.

40

RAELYNN

tretching out my legs, I roll over and pull my eyes open. I'm shocked to see a huge bunch of flowers on my dresser. It's not the sort of thing I'm used to, and all they do is remind me of what happened. I yawn and stretch out my sore body. I'm not sure I've ever slept quite so hard in my life. My head still hurts, but it's nothing compared to the last time I woke.

I lie there, memories of my dreams fading, feeling embarrassed that I dreamt of him. That he was here. That he crawled into bed with me and pulled my body to his and whispered sweet things in my ear.

Sitting up, I look to the other side of the bed and my body stills. There's an obvious head dent in the pillow, and the covers are a mess.

Holy shit. Was it a dream?

My heart starts to race as I try to distinguish what was dream and what was real, but I've got no clue.

There's once again a fresh glass of water on my nightstand beside my painkillers. Reaching for it all, I swallow two before my being awake makes the pain worse and I curl back into the warmth of my bed, not ready to emerge into the real world yet.

I think back over yesterday and the way Jake laid into Ethan, thinking that he did this to me. I've never had anyone stand up for me like that before, and to his best friend as well. The feelings it drags up unnerve me, but it also makes me wonder if Ethan's friends really have accepted me here. If Amalie and Camila don't just spend time with me because they feel they have to but because they actually want to. Do I actually have friends?

Before I lose my confidence, I climb out of bed and find my purse. My cell is right at the bottom, the battery about to die. Plugging it into the charger beside my bed, I unlock it and find voicemails, missed calls, and messages from Mom, dozens of missed calls from Bill, and a long stream of messages from Cody trying to find out if I'm okay. I feel bad that I've not responded, but I wasn't really in the mood for talking to anyone.

Ignoring them for now, I open up the group chat the girls started that I thought I was just included in to make me feel wanted, and, for the first time, I start a conversation.

> Rae: Are you free? Could do with some company.

My heart thunders in my chest as I wait for a sign that either of them are replying. It only takes a few seconds before a message pops up.

> Amalie: Free as a bird. Jake's out putting the guys through their paces.

> Camila: Yes! What do you want to do?

Seeing as I'm breaking down all kinds of barriers, I reply

with the one thing I never ever thought I would suggest, but with a slight tremble to my hands, I go for it.

> Rae: I need to chill out. Forget all the bullshit. You guys know of a spa that will have us last minute?

Little dots bounce for longer than last time, and the longer the responses take, the more I regret the suggestion.

> Amalie: Hell yes! I've just booked us in. I'll leave the house to pick you both up in 30.

> Camila: Yesssssss!

The smile that breaks across my face is so wide and genuine that it actually makes my cheeks hurt. Could this place that I hated so much when I first arrived actually be my first real home?

I think about Amalie and Camila, and then I force myself to consider the possibility of Ethan and the things he's said to me recently being true. Could this place really be it for me? Could I have a life and a future here?

With an extra spring in my step, I find some clothes and have a very quick shower to fully wake me up before packing a bag and heading downstairs.

The house is in silence, and I love it. Pulling the front door open, I breathe in the scent of the fresh sea morning air, and I sit in the swing seat and wait.

Grabbing my cell, I hit call on Mom's number. Rachel and Ethan have dealt with her so far, so she's probably going out of her mind not speaking to me in person.

"Raelynn, thank goodness," she breathes the second the call connects. "How are you? We've tried to get back, but we haven't been able to get on an earlier flight."

"I'm fine, Mom. It's nothing."

"It is not nothing, honey. Ethan told me everything. He sounded so concerned."

"Well, he doesn't need to be. I'm fine."

Silence fills the line and I begin to dread what she's going to say next. "Um... Eric said..." She trails off, and my frustration gets the better of me.

"What, Mom?"

"Eric said that Ethan mentioned..."

My eyes roll so hard at her avoidance of whatever she has to say that it makes my head hurt.

"What?" I snap.

"Is something going on with the two of you?" My breathing catches and my cheeks heat, knowing that there's no way she'll have missed it. "It's totally fine if it is. You're both adults now and..."

"Mom, stop rambling."

"I'm sorry, I just hate being so far away when something so awful has happened."

"I'm fine," I repeat for what feels like the millionth time. "Ethan's looked after me. I couldn't—"

"Aw," she says. "And to think I thought you hated each other."

"Oh, I do. He's a total asshole."

She laughs. "Honey, if I've learned anything from all my disastrous relationships, it's that if you feel that strongly for someone then they're most probably worth it."

I mull her words over in my mind for a few seconds before a question falls from my lips that I wasn't intending to ask. "So if something were to happen, that would be okay?"

"Oh, honey. You don't need my permission, you know that. If you've found someone who's managed to weasel his way into your heart, then I already know he's worth it." I nod as her words settle. "I know I've not really been around since we moved, but even from a distance, I can tell the change in you. And the fact that you're letting people in after all this time... well." Her voice cracks. "It makes me hope I haven't totally screwed you up with everything I've put you through."

I laugh at her. "We can only hope, eh?" As I say that, Amalie's car pulls into the driveway. "Mom, I've got to go. I'm going to a spa with the girls." The words feel foreign as they leave my mouth, but they also feel right.

Mom squeals on the other end, delighted that I'm doing something so normal. "Have a great time. I want to hear all about it when I get back."

"Will do, Mom."

I hang up and make my way over toward Amalie's car, sliding into the passenger seat when Camila climbs in the back to save me doing so.

"So, not that I'm complaining one bit, but what's this all about?"

"Just really needed to get out and chill out."

"Ethan that annoying?" Camila asks with a laugh.

I'm silent for a few seconds, and it's just enough time for them to jump to conclusions. "Oh my god, something's happened, hasn't it?" Amalie asks excitedly.

"No, no. I mean, yeah, I'm pretty sure he slept in my bed last night to make sure I was okay, but he'd left before I woke."

"And if he hadn't?"

"I don't know," I answer honestly.

I can tell myself all I like that he's playing me and that I need to stay as far away as possible, but having his hot body for the taking beside me, could I have walked away? I really have no idea.

"You so need to go for it with him," Camila encourages.

"Give her a break, Cami. You'll do things at your pace, right Rae?" Amalie asks softly.

"Do you think he really does like me?" I immediately feel

stupid and vulnerable for asking the question, but it's too late now. It's out.

"Yes, Rae. Yes, he really does."

Silence hangs heavy in the car around us as I try to figure out what I'm supposed to do with that piece of information.

Thankfully, Amalie pulls up to a fancy hotel and spa, and I'm able to forget about her words in favor of appreciating the lavish building in front of me.

"Should I have given a budget for this?"

"Don't even think about it. The only thing you need to worry about is what color polish you want on your nails. Leave the rest to us."

I open my mouth to argue, but one look from Amalie stops me. "Okay, okay," I concede.

We're directed straight through to a restaurant where we have brunch, followed by every spa treatment imaginable, most of which I never knew even existed. We spend time sitting around the pool and generally chat about random shit. Thankfully, they steer clear of too much Ethan talk and just allow me to think about that in private, and no one even mentions Friday night, which I'm grateful for. I mean, it's not like I'm going to forget any time soon with the steady throb of my head or my bald patch.

By the time Amalie drops me off later that night, I'm once again exhausted, but in such a good way. I've been waxed, scrubbed, plucked, and painted within an inch of my life and I feel like I'm floating on a cloud after all the soft music and essential oils.

Ethan's car is here, but as I make my way to my room, I don't find any evidence of him. After a quick change of clothes, I get myself under the covers and turn the TV on.

I find some chat show to watch, and no sooner has the sun set outside am I asleep once again.

I have no idea what time it is when the mattress

compresses beside me, signaling that my nighttime minder has arrived. I keep my body still and my breathing slow as he gets himself comfortable. I'm grateful that my back's to him or he'd be able to tell I was awake, I'm sure.

He lies still for a few seconds before blowing out a long breath and turning toward me. His arm comes around my waist, and he slides his front to my back.

The heat of his bare skin against my barely dressed body burns, and everything in me aches to turn over and see what he'd do. But this isn't the time. What Amalie and Camila said might be true. All the words he's said to me in the last few days might be true, but the middle of the night when I'm still in pain isn't the time to figure our shit out.

"Are you awake?" he whispers.

Fuck. I will my breathing not to falter and for my body not to tense. I've no idea if I pull it off or not, but after a few seconds he speaks again and I relax.

"Goodnight, baby. I'm here if you need me."

A lump forms in my throat and tears burn my eyes as he drops a kiss to my bare shoulder and gets comfortable behind me.

What is wrong with you, Rae? Turn around. Turn the fuck around.

But I never do. Instead, I lie there until my exhaustion claims me once again. Make him work for it, they said. Make him prove it. Don't give in just because he's here protecting you like no one else ever has.

———

He's gone again when I wake the next morning. I'd turned my alarm off, knowing that I wasn't going to school this morning. I've got a follow-up with a doctor to check my stitches.

I glance at the clock, and realizing I've still got ages, I

intend on rolling over once again but a piece of paper on my nightstand catches my eye.

I'll pick you up at eleven for your appointment x

My hand trembles as I hold the slip of paper. *He's going to skip school for me?* I don't know why I'm shocked; it's not the first time. He's not exactly a model student. But he needs to be there, not escorting me to a bullshit appointment.

Grabbing my cell, I shoot him a message.

> Rae: It's fine. I'll grab an Uber.

My thumb hovers over the send button before I add some more at the last minute.

> Rae: Thank you, though.

His reply comes almost immediately, and I'm unsure if I'm more shocked by the speed when he should be in class or his words.

> Ethan: For once, do as you're told. I'll pick you up at eleven. Be ready.

Well... fuck.

I fall back on the bed with a groan. I could reply and tell him to go to hell, but I have a suspicion that he'll just turn up here at eleven anyway. If I've already left, then he'll turn up at the appointment, I'd put money on it, so I decide to just take the easy route for once and climb out of bed to shower and dress.

I apply my makeup with extra precision than usual and I

very, very carefully blow dry my hair and pull it back in a loose bun. I tell myself that it's just because I've got the time, but deep down, I know that's not the reason. *He is.*

I allow Rachel to make me breakfast, although the thought of spending time with Ethan awake after everything that's passed between us has my stomach in knots, and the last thing I really want to do is eat.

Ten minutes before eleven, the sound of an engine rumbles through me before his giant truck appears at the end of the driveway.

I stand from the swing and take a step toward him. My temperature soars and goosebumps cover my skin the second his eyes lock on me. Something flutters in my stomach, and I try to convince myself it's not nerves. I don't get nervous.

I walk, on wobbly legs, down to his truck, but before I reach him, he's out and running around to the passenger door to open it for me.

"Whoa, who are you, and what have you done with Ethan Savage?"

He chuckles, but it doesn't meet his eyes. They're deadly serious as he stares down at me.

"I told you. I'm a good guy really."

"So you keep saying. But don't you know that most girls like their boys a little bit bad?"

His eyes drop from mine and run down the length of me. That one look has my heart rate picking up and desire knotting in my lower stomach.

"Is that right?"

I swallow loudly as he closes the space between us. The air is thick with tension as I try to drag some in, but under his intense stare, I'm unable to do anything but feel the crackle of chemistry between us.

Reaching out, he tucks a stray lock of hair that's escaped behind my ear. The second we connect, my entire body flinches with the shock. He continues moving his head toward me. I start to wonder if he's going to throw caution to the wind and be the bad boy I just alluded to and kiss me, but at the last minute, he leans to the side so his lips brush the shell of my ear. A shudder runs up my spine as his breath tickles.

"Lucky for you, I can be bad. *Very* bad. Some might even say I've got a bit of a rep."

My mouth goes dry, stopping any words from coming out.

When he pulls back, a smug smirk pulls at his lips.

"I've had better." It's a total barefaced lie, and I'm pretty sure he knows it. He laughs, and this time it lightens his eyes.

"Then I guess I've got something to prove. Your chariot awaits."

He waits while I climb in—not an easy feat when I'm basically three foot two. I expect him to help me, any excuse to get his hands on me, but to my surprise, he holds back. Maybe he can be a good boy. I refuse to admit it, but I'm kind of disappointed.

Once he's happy I'm settled, he closes the door on me and jogs around to the driver's side.

"I've got to be honest," he says as he turns the car and heads off the property, "I didn't think you'd be here waiting for me."

"I thought I'd keep you on your toes."

"You certainly do that, baby."

His use of my new nickname does things to my insides that I don't need to be thinking about right now.

"How are you feeling?"

"Fine."

"Are you ever anything other than fine?"

"Yeah. Often I'm angry. Mostly at you."

"Fair enough. Are you angry now?"

"No. Just fine."

I stare out the window in an attempt to seem unaffected by him.

"It's not working, you know."

"What's not working?" I turn to him to see him drag his eyes from me and back to the road.

"Looking out the window and attempting to ignore me. I know you can't ignore me. Ignore this."

He gestures between us.

"Oh? And what is *this* exactly?" I copy his previous arm gesture and raise a brow.

"Us. You can fight it all you want, baby. But we both know it's only going to end one way."

He pulls into the hospital parking lot and straight into a vacant space.

"Oh yeah, and how's that exactly?"

He leans over, the scent of him filling my nose, and I damn near moan in delight. "With you admitting how you really feel and with me so deep inside you that you'll never be able to forget me."

My breath catches at his words. It's something the old Ethan would say, but it's laced with something other than hate now, and I'm not really sure how to deal with it.

"You'd be so lucky," I sass, reaching for the handle, but he catches my wrist.

"I really fucking hope I will be." He tugs my arm, and my body moves forward just enough for him to capture my lips. My brain screams fight, but my entire body sags in relief. It's a teasing kiss, just a simple brush of his lips against mine, and when I think he's going to deepen it and give me what I need but won't admit, he's gone and jumping from the car.

"Motherfucker," I mutter to myself, but when he pulls my

door open, the smirk on his face tells me that he knows exactly what he just did.

I take two steps toward the entrance when his fingers tickle against my wrist. My immediate reaction is to pull away, but my curiosity gets the better of me and I leave it to see what he does next.

Not a second later, his fingers tangle with mine and he squeezes. My chin drops. He's holding my fucking hand. My heart begins to race as I fight with myself as to what to do.

He pulls me to a stop, and before I know what's happening, he backs me up against the wall of the reception. He stands staring down at me, amusement shining in his blue eyes.

"Stop over-thinking," he warns. "Just trust me."

A laugh rumbles up. Trust him?

"I told you that I'd prove that all those words I said to you in that hotel room were the truth, and I can't do that if you won't let me." He lifts the hand that's not still gripped onto mine tightly and cups my cheek. "Let me show you how I really feel. What I really want." He presses his body against mine, and I gasp as the unmistakable shape of his hard cock presses into my stomach. He leans down so only I can hear his next words. "Only you do that. No one else in the world could have me hard as we walk into a fucking hospital."

I laugh, because if I don't then I'm afraid I might give the people around us waiting a show.

"W-we're going to be late," I whisper, trying to keep my wits about me.

"We are. Let's go and get your head checked."

Thankfully, the wait to see the doctor isn't all that long. I'm not sure I could have coped with the tension crackling between the two of us if it had been much longer.

He was happy that my wound was healing okay and that

there didn't seem to be any other issues. He cleared me to go back to school—not that his word would stop me from showing up in the morning, but it's nice to know it's actually safe.

"I need to be back at school for practice, but do you want to go for lunch first?" Ethan asks once we're back in his car.

"We need to go to school."

"I didn't have you down as a goodie two shoes."

"I'm not, but I intend on graduating and getting into college, so it kinda needs to be done."

"Oh yeah? What do you want to do?"

"Honestly, anything. All I've wanted for years was just to be in control of my own life. I don't even know where, all I know is that it's going to be my choice and mine alone."

"I understand that."

"I've been dragged to every corner of the country, or so it feels, in Mom's quest to give me the perfect life, or what she deems as perfect, and I've fucking hated it. This is the only place that's ever felt—" I slam my lips shut, knowing that I've just said too much.

"Ever felt like what?"

"Fuck," I mutter, resting my head back and closing my eyes for a beat. "Home, okay? It's the first place that I could actually see myself making a life. It's fucked up, but for some reason, I feel like I might just belong here."

"Why's that fucked up?" he asks, turning to stare at me, but I refuse to look back, knowing that he'll be able to read too much in my eyes.

"Because Mom's barely been here since we moved. It's my gazillionth school in the last decade, and I've had to deal with you."

"Oh come on, I'm not that bad."

"Really?" I ask, now leaning forward to look into his eyes. "You want me to list all the fucked-up things?"

Guilt immediately fills his eyes as he takes a trip down memory lane.

Before I notice his hand move, he takes mine in his and lifts my knuckles to his lips. He places a kiss there but doesn't pull away.

He looks at me through his lashes, and my heart jumps into my chest. "I'm so fucking sorry, Rae. I'll do anything to prove to you that that person back then wasn't me. Name it and I'll do it, just to show you."

"Shut up, Ethan. I don't need you to do something crazy like run through school naked to prove anything."

"Really?" His eyes light up like the idea actually excites him.

"No, don't do that."

"Oh yeah. Why not?" My cheeks heat. "Fuck, I love it when you blush. So come on, tell me why I shouldn't do that. Be brave, Rae. I dare you."

"Y-you s-shouldn't because..." I suck in a breath as I try to come up with a lie that won't expose me too much, but with his eyes boring into mine, begging me to tell the truth, it's exactly what falls from my lips. "I don't want anyone else seeing you naked."

"See, admitting what you really want wasn't that hard, was it?"

"Worse than this gash on my head, I can tell you that for nothing."

He barks out a laugh, and I know there and then that it was worth admitting for that noise alone. I smile and laugh with him.

"So you want to go back to school then?"

"I think we should. We've already missed enough."

"Okay. We'll stop for takeout and head back."

I buckle up while he starts the engine. He drives to a

burger place and orders for us before taking the next turn toward Rosewood High.

"Don't," he warns when I start to open the bag of food that's sitting on my lap.

"Why? Did you buy it for us to look at?"

"No, just... do as you're told."

"Not my specialty."

"Don't I fucking know it," he mutters, pulling into a space and hopping out.

He comes around to my side once again and takes the bag from my lap before taking my hand and helping me jump out.

"Where are we going?" I ask when he refuses to release my hand and walks us around the back of the building.

"Trust me."

"You say that a lot."

"Because you need to."

He walks us toward the football stadium and pushes through one of the side doors. We walk through until we begin climbing the stairs. The place is deserted apart from the two of us. I guess that's what he was going for.

It's not until we're right at the top that he turns, pulls a seat down for me and nods for me to sit. He undoes the bag and hands me my half of the food. We begin eating in silence, but it's not uncomfortable.

"I love it here when it's empty. Things are so crazy on game night that it's nice to come up here and reflect on everything during the day."

"The perfect Ethan Savage with the perfect life has things he needs to reflect on," I quip.

"I'm far from perfect, Rae. Just look how I've treated you. My life was falling apart long before I even realized. If I was paying more attention, or just home more, I might have noticed that things hadn't been right between my parents. I should have seen it coming, and I sure as hell shouldn't have taken it out on you."

"Hindsight is a great thing. Sadly, there's not much we can do about the past."

He tenses beside me. "I'm sorry you had to go through what you did, and I'm sorry I invaded your privacy and found out the way I did."

"It's okay. Well… it's not, but it is what it is. And in a weird way, I'm glad you know."

"Me too."

"No one else knows about it. I've never told anyone."

"No one?" he asks, turning to look at me, but I continue to stare ahead at the empty stands.

"Well, obviously the police officers and social workers, but I've never told anyone in day-to-day life."

"Why?"

"Never had anyone to tell."

"Fucking hell, Rae," he says sadly, shaking his head.

"Don't pity me."

"I'm not. I'm not. I'm just so glad you've got people who care now."

"Have I?" I know I'm pushing my luck by asking, but I need to hear it.

"Yeah. Amalie and Camila love you. Jake cares enough to plow his fist into my face," he says lightheartedly, pointing to his split lip. "And I…" He trails off.

"And you?" It's my turn to turn to him, but he avoids my stare as he considers his words.

"I… I think you're kind of incredible."

"Is that right?"

"You're the strongest person I've ever met, Rae. By a fucking mile. After everything you've been through, you're a fucking warrior."

"It was nothing. People deal with worse."

"Yeah, they do, but you're amazing. That kind of shit would break most people but you're... you're..."

"Amazing?" I add, using the last word he said to describe me.

"Yeah. That and some." He turns to me, his eyes soft, his barriers down. His eyes study mine for a few seconds, his lips parting like he has something to say but is unsure if he should let it out or not. I want to push him, but I find I can't, wanting him to offer whatever it is himself. "And... and I'm falling for you harder than I know what to do with."

My breath catches at the honesty in his tone.

"Ethan, I—"

"No. We're done talking."

"Oh."

His hand slips around the side of my neck, his thumb brushing my cheek gently as he leans in. My brain screams to back away, to protect myself, but my body is all in and I find myself closing the space between us.

41

ETHAN

I brush my lips over hers gently, waiting to see how she responds to me. She was more than up for it when I kissed her in the car earlier, but if I've learned anything about Rae, it's that she's unpredictable at the best of times. My fingers twitch against her neck as I wait to see what she's going to do.

It feels like it takes an eternity, but eventually, her soft lips move against mine and my restraint snaps. Her lips part the second my tongue touches them and hers almost instantly meets mine. I explore her mouth like it's the first time, savoring her taste, allowing it to feed my addiction for this woman beside me.

I shift over in my seat to close the space between us, but already knowing that I'm never going to be able to get close enough with an armrest in the middle.

Dropping my hands to her waist, I lift her from her seat. The remaining food and wrappers that were on her lap fall to the ground as I settle her where she belongs: on my lap.

Her legs just fit on either side of mine, and I groan in relief as her weight presses down on me.

Finding the smooth exposed skin of her back, I slide my hands up, delighting in the fact that she shudders as I do so. My lips curl into a smile as she eagerly continues our kiss.

Her hands thread into my hair and pull, the bite of pain only adding fuel to my already out-of-control fire.

"Rae," I moan into her mouth as they drop to my shoulders and then skim over my pecs and abs. My muscles pull and dance as she runs her light touch over them. "Fuck." Finding the bottom of my shirt, she slips her hands inside. Our skin connects with an explosion of electricity that has my cock threatening to burst through my jeans. Her pussy is right above, and it would be so easy to take her like this for the entire school to see if they were to descend on this place.

That thought is the bucket of cold water I need. This girl is mine; no one else gets to have their eyes on her.

Ripping my lips from hers, I kiss down her neck. "Baby, we need to stop." I hate that the words pass my lips, but this isn't how this is going to go between us. Not now, anyway.

"We really don't," she whispers, throwing her head back to give me better access. My hands slip around to her stomach, and the temptation to push them up to her tits is so fucking strong, but she deserves more than this. She deserves everything and more. Fuck knows if I'm able to deliver it, but I'm gonna give it a fucking good go.

"We do. I want to do this properly. Treat you properly, the way you deserve."

"Didn't stop you before." Her chest is heaving before me, her lips parted to drag in the air she needs. When she looks down, her usually dark eyes are almost black with desire.

"I know," I say, regret filling my tone.

"So make it up to me. I thought you wanted to prove yourself." She tilts her head to the side and her eyebrow quirks in challenge.

"But—"

"Are you man enough, Ethan?" She wiggles in my lap, ensuring I feel every tiny movement. My hands land on her hips, holding her in place, desperate for more of her.

"You fucking know I am."

"So… Prove. It."

The fabric of her fishnets disintegrates beneath my fingers, and in seconds I'm moving her soaked panties aside.

"Fucking hell," I moan as her juices coat my fingers.

"Ethan," she moans in return, throwing her head back once more and thrusting her tits in my face.

Forgetting everything, I push the fabric of her top up and pull the cups of her bra down to give me the access I need.

Pushing my fingers inside her, I lean forward and suck one of her nipples into my mouth.

"Fuck. Fuck."

I suck hard before biting down enough to have her crying out. I pump my fingers inside her, bending them to hit the place she needs before kissing my way toward her other nipple to give it the same treatment.

"Ethan. Shit. Fuck," she moans above me, and my chest swells with everything I feel for the woman. She's so fucking strong. So fucking brave. And needs to be so fucking mine.

I sit back when I sense she's about to fall, because as much as I want her in my mouth, I want to watch her come apart in my hands more.

"Come on, baby. Come for me. Let me see how fucking beautiful you are."

"Oh god."

"Nah, just Ethan Savage, baby."

Her lips curl up as if she's about to laugh, but I graze her G-spot once more and she falls headfirst into her release instead. And it's fucking magical. Her chin drops, her eyes close, and she clenches around me so fucking hard it makes my cock weep to be inside her, to experience just what it'll be like with us connected exactly as we should be.

She falls forward against me as she fights to catch her breath.

"I'm pretty sure that was the hottest thing I've ever seen."

She laughs against me but doesn't say anything for the longest time. When she does speak, I can't help but laugh too.

"I really needed that."

"Glad I could help, baby."

Regretfully, I help her off me and she rights her clothing before falling back down into her own seat. She's too far away, but there's not much I can do about it other than drag her home to bed, but even I know I need to be here for practice. Mason is joining us for the first time to see if he's going to be able to be a part of next week's final.

"So..." Rae starts hesitantly.

"So what?"

"So now what?"

"Well, I think it's safe to say you finished your lunch." I look to where what she had left is now scattered on the ground.

"I meant with us, you idiot."

My heart slams against my chest at her use of the word us. Is there an us? Is she going to allow there to be an us? "I told you. I fully intend to do things right this time. If you'll allow me, that is."

"Hmmm..."

"What's that supposed to mean?"

"It means that I'll consider it." Her lips twitch as she fights her smile.

"You'll consider it?" I ask, arching my brow.

"Yeah. I mean, I have just had quite a significant bump to the head, so there's a very good chance I'm not thinking straight right now."

"I should hope not, after that orgasm."

"Ethan, I'm being serious," she says, swatting my shoulder, but the wide smile on her face tells me otherwise.

"Right. Of course you are."

The school bell rings in the distance, efficiently putting our time to an end. Jake will castrate me if I miss practice, and I'm in too much of a good mood right now to put up with his angry ass.

Reaching over, I wrap my hand around the back of her neck and gently pull her over to me. "This is what happens next. I'll get Amalie or Camila to take you home. Then you can wait for me there. Clothes optional. I fully intend to spend the entire night proving myself to you."

"Oh yeah?" Her cheeks heat at my words, and it's almost enough to blow off practice in favor of her body.

I shake my head, trying to get the dirty thoughts out of my mind before I go and get sweaty with the guys.

"Yeah. By the end of tonight, there's going to be no doubt who you belong to. I guarantee that by morning there will only be one person's name you remember, and I promise you, it won't be yours." Her cheeks only get redder as her tongue sneaks out to lick her bottom lip. "Sound like a plan?"

"Um... I'll consid—"

I slam my lips down on hers before she gets a chance to finish the word.

Pulling back abruptly before I'm in so deep I'm not going to be able to walk away without being inside her, I stand and pull my cell from my pocket.

"Can you take Rae home?" I bark the second Camila picks up. My voice is rough even to my own ears, and she doesn't miss it.

"Of course. Is everything okay?"

Rearranging myself so that Rae has no choice but to know the state she's left me in, I smile down at her. "Yeah, everything's great. We just came back to school after her appointment."

"Oh, she wasn't in my last class."

"No, she was getting a very different kind of lesson."

"Ethan, what are—"

"She'll meet you by your car," I interrupt when Rae looks like she's about to kick me in the balls and steal my cell. I hang up and give her my most innocent face.

"You're a fucking nightmare."

"I'm your fucking nightmare though, baby."

"I haven't decided if I want you yet."

"Oh, ouch."

"Come on, Savage. You've got practice to get to."

"It's just a warm-up really, for what comes later."

I leave her in the parking lot with a sweet kiss that's sure to tide her over until I get home. Camila walks up to us with Amalie hot on her heels, and both of them witness it. As I walk past them back toward the building, I can tell they want to smile, but instead, they both keep their hard eyes on me in warning.

They don't need to say it. If I hurt her, I'll cause myself some physical pain; they don't need to threaten it.

I walk toward the locker rooms with the widest smile on my face. Jake and Mason take one look at me when I join them and slap me on the shoulder.

"We're happy for you, bro. Now, you ready to smash this shit before you can get back to your girl?"

"Fucking right. Let's do this."

42

RAELYNN

"Bloody knew you wouldn't be able to fight him," Amalie says as the three of us climb into Camila's Mini.

I sigh. "I tried. I really did. But man, he knows exactly what to say to make me melt."

"Huh, I never had Ethan down as the romantic type, so I'm assuming you're talking about his filthy mouth."

I bark out a laugh. "Yeah, something like that."

"You want a milkshake?" Camila asks the two of us.

"Yeah. I need to see Bill and Cody, show them I'm still alive."

"Awesome. That'll waste some time until the guys finish and Ethan can eat you for dinner."

My entire body heats with the suggestion. "Jeez, he really has worked his charm on you, eh?" Camila asks, glancing at me squirming in her backseat.

"Do you guys think I'm an idiot for even considering this thing with Ethan?" I hate sounding unsure, but I need to know what they think.

"No, not at all. If you feel that connection, then I say go for it."

I nod, a small smile playing on my lips as I think back over the afternoon with him.

Both Bill and Cody race toward me when the three of us enter the diner. Bill's given me two weeks off fully paid after what I went through. It's not necessary, but I appreciate it and will gladly accept. They throw question after question at me but mostly just repeatedly ask me if I'm okay.

Eventually, they leave the three of us in peace to enjoy our milkshakes, but I don't miss their concerned glances my way. It's not helped by the missing hair exposing my wound. It makes me want to take it down to hide it, but I'm not sure I'm ready to fully embrace it yet, or ever.

"What's going on?" I ask Amalie as she furiously taps at her cell with a wide smile on her face.

"Oh, um..."

"What?" both Camila and I ask simultaneously.

"We just need to wait an hour before delivering Rae back home."

"Why? Has something happened at practice?" Images fill my head of Ethan getting hurt so close to the final game, and I panic.

"No, no everything's fine. Just trust us, yeah?" Amalie winks at Camila as they share a silent best friend conversation over the table and I sigh in frustration.

"Fine, whatever. I want another one of these for it, though."

They both laugh but agree and call Cody back over.

———

It's almost an hour and a half later when we eventually pull up in front of the Savage house. The sun is beginning to set, casting the house in a gorgeous orange hue. Both Jake and Mason are waiting out front, and, after nodding a greeting at me, they climb into the car with their girls.

"Have a great night," Amalie calls out. I look back over my shoulder to find all four of them grinning at me like idiots.

"He's waiting for you," Mason says before Camila revs the engine and they disappear out of the driveway. It's not until I'm alone that my nerves hit.

What the hell am I going to find inside this house?

With a trembling hand, I push the front door open and step inside. There are cases in the hallway, pointing to the fact that Mom and Eric are home. I'm surprised she doesn't come running at me the second I'm in the house, but everything is eerily quiet.

"Hello?" I call out, but really it's not loud enough for anyone to hear me. I find the kitchen and the family room empty when I poke my head inside. Assuming they've gone straight out, I head for the stairs, thinking that it's probably where Ethan is waiting for me. Naked, hopefully. Butterflies take up flight in my stomach at the thought.

My steps quicken as I climb up and race toward my bedroom. My door is ajar when I get there and I push it open eagerly, convinced that he'll be there. Disappointment floods me when I look around and find the room empty, aside from the flowers that I now know came from Bill.

"Where are you?" I mutter, walking farther into the room and dropping my purse to the bed. It's then that a crash comes from outside, followed by a curse in a very familiar voice.

Smiling that I've found him, I walk toward the balcony. The closer I get to the edge, the more my jaw drops as I take in the pool area beneath me.

Twinkling fairy lights are strung up everywhere. There's a little bistro set with candles flickering in the center, and the outside sofa that sits at the edge of the patio overlooking the beach is covered in blankets and pillows. Soft music plays as the scent of the grill floats up to me. Then finally, Ethan appears. He's dressed in a pair of sweats and his usual Bears jersey. I watch him walk to the grill and open the top before he starts poking at the contents. The butterflies that were already fluttering erupt in my belly, and everything below my stomach clenches in anticipation. The memory of his fingers playing me earlier slams into me and spikes my temperature. I can't deny that I need more of that side of Ethan.

I stand and watch him for a few minutes, wanting to take him in while he's not aware he's got company. He looks so relaxed and totally at home. There's nothing pulling the muscles in his shoulders tight, and I'm sure when he finally looks up at me, I won't find any of the shadows haunting his eyes like when we first met. He's like an entirely different person, he's just still wrapped in the same unbelievably hot package.

I don't think I make a noise, so I can only assume that he senses my stare, because after another two seconds of my quiet perusal of his body, his head turns and his eyes find mine. I discover that I was right, because even from this distance all I can see is desire and... love? No, that's crazy. Isn't it?

"There you are," he says softly, staring up at me. "I feel like I should be quoting some sappy line from Shakespeare right now."

"It's okay. I think you may have already maxed out on your romance quota tonight." I glance around at what he's done once more in total awe.

"You like it?" The shyness in his tone has my eyes immediately flying back to his. Surely Ethan Savage isn't unsure of himself right now?

"It's incredible. You did it for me?" I ask, just to be sure this isn't his usual way to welcome home his dad.

"All for you, baby. I told you, I'm going to do it right this time. Give you everything you deserve and more."

I shake my head, tears burning my eyes as I take in the sweet guy before me, the one who's a million miles from the one I first met. Some might think I'm crazy for allowing myself to be swept up by him after what he did to me, how he treated me, but I can't help myself. Our connection was there from the very beginning. I see that now. We both just dealt with it in the wrong way. I understand that he was hurt and lashing out. Did he push boundaries he shouldn't have? Sure. But I get it. And now, I see the genuine regret and need to make things right every time I look at him. And I might have caved earlier than I was expecting, but I still fully intend on making him work for it. I'm not one to make anyone's life easy, and Ethan's going to have to learn that I also like to play dirty from time to time.

"It's amazing. You're amazing."

"Well if that's the case, why the fuck are you still up there while I'm down here?" He holds his arms out as if to say, *come and get me*, and I spin on my heels and run toward him.

"There she is," he says when I emerge into the garden.

I stop in the doorway and just look at him. Really look at him, as if it's our first time. He really is beautiful. His thick hair flops down into his face, his blue eyes stare into mine, and the square cut of his jaw gives him the edgy look that I know he loves to play up. But it's his smile that that gets me moving. Gone is the cocky, arrogant, full-of-himself asshole he shows the rest of the world, and in its place is a small, nervous smile as he waits to see what I'm going to do. That one smile tells me so much. He's nervous that after all this I'm going to turn my back on him, and it's the first time I've ever really appreciated that he needs me just as much as I've realized I need him. It sounds corny as fuck, but as I stand here with him waiting for me, I can't help but feel he's the piece that's been missing from my life. It's not been a place that I needed, or the friends that have eluded me all these years. It's just been him. His sexy smirk, the way he refuses to take my shit or believe me when I'm trying to push him away. The way he smashes through my barriers and climbs over my giant wall. The way he forces me to admit to myself how I really feel. Just the way he is: flaws, broken parts, hurt and all. Just him.

His brows furrow in concern, and it's that move, that final show of weakness for me that has me moving. My legs carry me faster than my brain realizes, and in seconds I'm in his arms with his lips pressing down on mine.

One of his hands slides into my hair while the other comes to rest on my hip and ensures there's no space between us whatsoever.

He kisses me for the longest time. We're both breathless when he finally releases me.

"Whoa, that was some welcome."

"Only the best. Are you hungry?"

"Starved, seeing as someone deposited most of my burger on the ground earlier."

"Let me make up for it."

He walks over to the bistro set and pulls one of the chairs out for me. "Thank you," I mouth, totally blown away by all of this. The self-confessed fuck 'em and chuck 'em seems to be hopping aboard the romance train along with his two best friends.

"I've got meat in every variety you could desire." When he turns to me, I make a show of running my eyes down his body.

"Stop it. Stop it right now," he warns. "I promised you I'd do this properly, but when you look at me like that it..."

"It what, Ethan?" I cross one leg across the other, knowing it'll make my skirt rise up.

"It'll... um..."

"What's wrong? Cat got your tongue?" I stand and close

the distance between us once again. "Where are our parents?" I breathe into his ear.

"G-Gone out."

"So there's no one here to watch what happens next?"

He shakes his head, eyes locked on mine.

"Good." I press a kiss to his chest before dropping to my knees.

"Rae, what are you..." His words trail off as I pull the tie of his sweats.

"What?" I ask innocently, tilting my head to the side and looking up at him. "I thought you only wanted me on my knees."

He tips his head back and barks out a laugh. To anyone else, this wouldn't be funny, but I can't help but join him as we both take a trip down memory lane. Thinking about how he treated me should hurt, but I can accept that it's just a part of our past and what helped us get to this moment.

"So, Ethan. You got me down here at last. What should I do?" I trail my fingertip over the bulge of his growing erection beneath the fabric and delight when a low growl rumbles up his throat at my touch.

"Rae, you don't have—"

"Shhh..." I interrupt, pushing the fabric of his shirt up and pressing kisses along the waistband of his boxers. His muscles bunch with each connection before I run my tongue up the definition of his V.

"Fuck, Rae." His fingers gently hold on to my head, ever cautious of my healing wound. They flex and I smile, knowing just how desperate for more he is right now. I could feel the length of him when I was on top of him earlier; I can only imagine how painful it was for him to walk away and go to practice with balls that blue.

I pull back, wrap my fingers around the fabric of both his

sweats and boxers, and pull. His cock springs free, now totally hard and begging for my touch.

I glance up at him through my lashes. His eyes are locked on me, but they're darker than I've ever seen them, and the muscles in his neck are pulled tight with restraint. It's one seriously impressive sight, and the fact that I hold all the power right now is a serious turn-on. I've never had a man totally at my mercy like this before, and fuck if I don't love it.

His fingers flex again, and I give in. Reaching out, I wrap my hand around his wide length. His entire body shudders at my contact, and the groan that leaves him practically has my panties melting off me.

Leaning forward, I lick the tip of him. His body flinches, and, encouraged by his hand that's still holding my head, I part my lips and take him inside my mouth.

I have no idea what I was expecting, but he's hot, sweet, and silky smooth.

"Fucking hell, baby," he moans, and hearing his enjoyment gives me the confidence I need to continue.

I suck him as far back as I dare before pulling off and starting all over again. His breathing gets erratic above me, and it's not long before his cock gets even harder.

"Rae, I'm gonna come, baby," he warns, giving me time to make a decision, but really, there's not one to make. I'm fully on board with the idea of us now, and I fully intend on giving him everything.

I suck him again, taking him deeper than before, and the second he hits the back of my throat he lets out the most feral moan before his cock twitches violently between my lips and he comes in my mouth.

Sitting back, I wipe my mouth with the back of my hand before risking a look up at him. But the second our eyes connect, I feel stupid for allowing a few nerves to hit me. His eyes are still full of desire, and he's got the laziest smile on his face.

I'm up on my feet in seconds and lifted until I have no choice but to wrap my legs around his still naked waist.

His lips crash down on mine and our tongues duel as our teeth clash.

"So, it was okay?" I ask with a cheeky smile when he releases me.

"Fucking right."

He drops my feet to the ground so he can cover himself up, but his arms soon wrap around my waist once again.

"Good to know. It was my first."

His chin drops. "It was... fuck," he barks. "Could you be any more perfect?"

I laugh. "I'm far from that."

"I don't know. I think you're pretty perfect for me."

I melt at his words, but I don't get the chance to return the sentiment.

"Now, as long as it's not burnt to a crisp, it's time for dinner."

"Sorry," I say with a wince, thinking I've ruined what he's been so lovingly cooking.

I take a step away, but he soon catches my hand and pulls me back into his chest. "Never apologize for that." He kisses my forehead and allows me to take a seat while he plates up.

The food is great and only slightly singed from its few extra minutes in the grill.

"I can't believe you did all this," I say as he pours me a new drink.

"I had some help."

"You're telling me that you didn't make this yourself?" I ask, holding up my glass, gesturing to everything as we make our way over to the sofa.

"No, Rachel helped with the food. The guys helped with the lights and shit."

"Aw, lights and shit, so romantic."

"What you see is what you get, baby."

He takes my drink and places it on the table with his before lying down beside me.

"I'm not sure that's entirely true."

"No?"

"Nope. I'm pretty sure I'm looking at a different Ethan from the one everyone at school sees."

"You might actually be right there."

"Yeah, it seems you do have a heart buried in there somewhere." I place my hand on his chest and he covers it with his own.

"Yeah, and it seems it only beats for you."

I gasp, the honesty in his words taking any I might have to reply with. But instead of waiting for me to say something, he leans over and takes my lips in a sweet kiss. He pulls a blanket over both of us, and his hand leisurely trails around my body beneath, slowly driving me crazy with my need for him.

We make out on that sofa for the longest time with our tongues, lips, and hands exploring every inch of each other's bodies, but at no point do either of us take it further. That is, until Ethan's lips brush the shell of my ear.

"Want to continue this upstairs?"

"Like you wouldn't believe."

He chuckles before untangling us from the blanket and standing with his hand out for me to take. His cock tents his sweats, and my core clenches at knowing what's to come. He's right about one thing: we're going to do this properly this time, and there's going to be no doubt in his mind that I'm fully on board with what's about to happen.

He leads me up to my room before shutting the door behind us. Then he turns to me, his eyes dark and hungry, and a wave of nerves sweeps through me. It's crazy; this isn't our first time, but it's so different. Last time it was just sex, with a truckload of anger and desire. This time, it's so much more. It's the beginning of something. Something that could be epic if neither of us fuck it up somewhere along the way.

Taking a step toward me, he reaches out and grasps the bottom of my shirt. In the blink of an eye he has it off and on the floor. Reaching behind his head, he pulls his jersey from his body and closes the space between us. His arm wraps around my back, and his fingers unhook my bra before pushing the straps from my arms, allowing it to fall to the floor. His bare chest presses against mine, and I can't help the sigh that falls from my lips. Even when we hated each other, there's no denying that together we were electric.

His fingers grip my chin, and he stares down at me, his eyes searching mine for something, although I have no idea what.

"Eth—" I don't get a chance to finish, because his lips find mine and cut off my question.

He walks us back to the bed, only stopping when my legs hit the mattress and prevent us from going any farther.

"You sure about this?" he asks, his lips brushing against mine.

"Yes. Ethan. A hundred times, yes."

He nods, that lazy smirk that I love spreading across his lips once more before he claims mine again. His fingers brush my stomach as they drop to the waistband of my skirt before he pushes it down. He lowers, kissing every bit of skin he can find as he goes, and pulling my nipples into his mouth one after the other until he's kissing down my stomach and pulling my remaining clothing down my legs and off, quickly followed by his.

Once I'm bare, he stands to full height once again before lowering me to the bed. He's so gentle despite the inferno of need I can see in his eyes. He kisses me once again before repeating his previous journey down my body, only this time, when he gets to my center, he parts my legs and drops to his knees. Wrapping his hands around my thighs, he pulls me right to the edge of the bed before lowering his head and licking up the length of my pussy and making me cry out, the sensation overtaking my body. My hips lift from the bed before his large hands wrap around my hips to keep me in place.

"Now it's my turn to have some fun." He flashes me a wicked smile that's full of dirty promises before dropping back down and doing some seriously crazy shit with his tongue that has me begging for more.

His name is a garbled cry on my lips when he eventually tucks two fingers inside me and allows me to fall over the edge. My heart is racing, my skin flushed, and every muscle in my body pulsates as he crawls over and lifts my weightless body up higher on the bed so he can sit between my thighs.

"Good?" he asks, a cocky grin on his face.

"Your ego doesn't need inflating any more than it already is," I mutter.

"Too late for that. Everyone in the area probably knows just how good I am after that." My cheeks heat even more. It even burns down onto my chest. "Fucking love it when you blush."

He settles himself and wraps his hand around his solid length. I take a moment to appreciate the sight of him sitting there, waiting for what's to come, and although he's only just rocked my world, I can already feel the tingles of another from the sight of him alone.

"Shit," he mutters as he teases my clit with the head of his cock before leaning over the bed and pulling a condom from his pocket.

"Sure thing, was I?"

"A guy can only hope."

I'm enthralled as he rips the packet open and quickly rolls it down his shaft. I gasp when he goes back to teasing my sensitive clit that's still swollen from everything his mouth just did to me.

"You need to get on birth control, baby. I refuse to put up with having a barrier between us for too long." My chin drops. I want to chastise him for his alpha caveman act, but I find it hard to when I totally agree. I don't want anything between us either.

"Okay," I whisper before he lowers his cock and pushes inside me just slightly. My muscles tense at the unusual invasion, despite the fact that I'm more than ready after his talented tongue made me all kinds of relaxed.

"Rae?" he asks, all his movements grinding to a halt.

"Yeah?"

Something crackles between us as our eyes hold, our ultimate connection seemingly on hold for a moment.

"Are you sure you want to do—"

"Yes, I said—" I wrap my legs around his waist in the hope of getting him moving. He laughs lightly before placing two fingers over my lips to stop me saying any more.

"Let me finish. Are you sure you want to do this, because once I'm inside you, that's it. You're it for me. End of. Is that what you want?"

I tilt my head to the side and look at him, really look at him. He chews on his bottom lip as he waits for my response, the softer side of him that I love on full display as he openly tells me what he wants. Me.

"Yes. Yes, that's what I want." I barely get the last word out before he surges forward, filling me to the hilt and forcing me to move up the bed.

"Fuck, yes," he groans, dropping forward so he can claim my mouth as well as my body.

My hands run down his back as he starts to move. And as he does so, he kisses me so sweetly, mutters promises that I never thought I'd hear from him, and loves my body in the way he told me he would.

His slow thrusts build me higher and higher until my nails are raking down his back in my desperate need for release. He knows exactly what I need, but he doesn't up the tempo until we're both right on the edge. Then and only then does he pick up the pace until we're both crying out in pleasure as he brings us both to the edge so we can crash over together.

"Fucking hell," he pants, falling down on top of me, his weight pushing me into the mattress in the most delicious way. "I really needed that," he says, mimicking me from earlier in the day and making me laugh.

Rolling over onto his side, he removes the condom then pulls me into his body. "Are you okay? Is your head okay?"

"I'm fine," I say, brushing my fingertips over his rough jaw.

"It's my job to look after you now, so I need to know the truth." He stares at me like he doesn't believe a word of it.

"Okay, so I'm due some more painkillers. But really, I'm okay."

"Okay enough for another round?" he asks, thrusting his once again hard cock against my stomach.

"I'll consider it."

He laughs before a thought seems to hit him out of nowhere. "What now?"

"What do you mean?"

"Do we just walk into school hand in hand tomorrow and announce it to the world?" The thought has my heart rate increasing. I can already picture the horror on all the cheer sluts' faces.

"Um... maybe we should tell our parents first. Give us a little time to get used to it before everyone else has to."

"I couldn't really give a fuck about anyone else's feelings about it. I'm kinda surprised you do."

"Oh, I don't. I'm just not sure I'm ready for the scrutiny I'll get. I'm not exactly who anyone expected you to end up with."

"True," he says with a wince, knowing exactly what I'm talking about. "But if anyone gives you grief, they'll have me to answer to."

"Is that right?" I laugh.

"Yeah, although I'm pretty sure the cheer sluts are more scared of you than they are me."

I can't help but smile. "I should hope so. I'm scary as fuck."

Ethan barks out a laugh as I sit myself up. "Where do you think you're going?"

"I need painkillers."

"I can get them," he offers, moving to get up.

"It's okay. I... uh... need the bathroom too."

I can see he's torn about letting me go, but really, what's he going to do? Pee for me? I drop a quick kiss to his lips before getting out and walking to the bathroom.

"A man could get used to this," he says as he watches me walk naked across the room. "You're so sexy, baby."

I shake my booty a little as I move, lapping up his praise and unable to keep the smile from my lips at how things have turned out.

I do my thing and take my pills before rejoining him. When I step from the bathroom, I find him lying on his front waiting for me. I run my eyes up the length of his body, taking in his toned muscles and bronzed skin.

"Seems I'm not the only one who appreciates the view around here."

"Damn straight. But what I'm more interested in is..." I walk over and drag my fingertip up his leg before I get to his ass, " how you ended up with this on your ass cheek, teddy."

He laughs, the sound making me smile once again.

"Ugh, that. I lost a bet and for it, I had to have whatever Jake and Mason decided permanently stamped on my ass."

"And they chose a teddy bear? Why?"

"We're the Bears." He shrugs. "Although I like to think we're a tad more fearsome than that pansy-ass thing I'm now stuck with."

"It's cute."

"Is it, though?"

Shaking my head at the look on his face, I climb back onto the bed with him. "So, lose a lot of bets, do you?" I ask, thinking back to Shelly's bitchy comment about the reason Ethan went after me the night of the party.

"No, I don't make a habit out of it. I don't want any more stupid shit on me."

"So that night we first slept together, was—"

"Stop. Stop right there," he says, moving over me so I have no choice but to roll onto my back and look up at him. "We have a stupid game we play where we name girls for the night. But it's not a bet. There are no prizes to be won. Just a bit of fun. Yes, I was given your name that night." I open my mouth to say something, but he just continues anyway. "But, that bullshit had nothing to do with us or anything that happened. That only happened because I couldn't stay away from you and you were driving me crazy."

"Crazy, huh? Exactly how crazy?"

"Fucking insane. Allow me to show you." His lips find mine once again and his fingers plunge inside my more-than-willing entrance.

And that's how we spend the remainder of the night. I've no idea what time we eventually fall asleep, and I've no idea what happened to our parents, but quite frankly, I really don't give a shit. All I know is that I fall asleep with a wide smile on my lips and have the most peaceful night's sleep ever with him by my side.

43

ETHAN

When I wake up, I think I'm the happiest I've ever been in my life. I've got my girl tucked into my side sleeping soundly, and we're on the cusp of winning the title we've coveted for as long as we've known how to throw a fucking ball. Despite everything with my parents and all the bullshit that came with that shock announcement, things are good. No, things are fucking incredible.

"Morning."

Her quiet, sleepy voice makes my heart tumble in my chest, but it's nothing compared to when I look down into her wide, dark eyes. They've always amazed me. From the very first moment she appeared in my life, she's totally taken over my world. And right now, it's in a way I never could have imagined. This woman fucking owns me, but I don't think she has any idea. My balls are in her hands. Suddenly, everything I've witnessed with Amalie and Jake and Camila and Mason makes total sense. The lengths they went to, the bullshit they endured. All of it. One hundred percent fucking worth it. Just like everything the two of us have experienced in our short time together. They say everything happens for a reason—well, I guess I should be thanking my parents for their failed marriage because fuck, if it weren't for them, then she wouldn't be in my arms right now, and I already know for a fact that she's the best thing about my life.

"Morning, baby. Are you feeling okay?"

"You know, at some point, you're going to have to stop asking me that."

"Maybe. I'll never stop wanting to know, though."

"I'm fine. I promise."

"No headache?"

"A little, but it's better with every day."

I smile, knowing that she's probably covering up the truth, but I let her believe she's being brave and pretending like what she went through was nothing. I guess, to her, after what she went through at the hands of that monster years ago, it *was* nothing.

"Are you okay? Your entire body just locked up."

"Yeah, just thinking."

"About?"

"How best to start our day."

She squeals as I flip us over and settle between her legs.

"This is a definite benefit to living in the same house," she says as I drop down to kiss her. "Ew, morning breath."

"Don't give a fuck; give me your lips."

By the time we get to school, we're both fully sated and had a very brief conversation with our parents which mostly consisted of Ash making sure that Rae was okay. It seems a little late if you ask me, seeing as it happened Friday night and it's now Tuesday, but hey, what do I know about parenting? They keep saying they couldn't get a flight, but they weren't all that far away. Seems like a great excuse just not to come back. Although, it meant I got Rae all to myself, so I can't really complain.

As Rae requested, once we step foot from my car we act like nothing's changed. I fucking hate it from the second I close the car door and am unable to reach for her. I hate it even more when I glance at her and find her walls built up so high I worry that she might not drop them again. I understand her reasons for wanting to keep this between us for a while, but that doesn't mean I agree. I want to be able to touch her and kiss her whenever the fuck I like, not having to sneak it like I'm her dirty little secret that she's ashamed for others to know. It's a sobering thought, but one I hope is far from the truth. I have to trust her just like I've asked her to do me. She thinks she's doing what's best for us, so I just need to give her the time she needs to get her head around everything, and then I can prove just how serious I am about this.

She walks off ahead of me toward her locker to get her books for her first few classes as I head toward the benches where the football team and cheer squad hang out.

Jake and Mason's eyes are flicking from me to where Rae just disappeared with confused expressions on their faces.

"Jesus, Savage. You fucked up already? I thought you were onto a sure thing with all that romantic shit last night," Jake says, thankfully quiet enough so that the rest of the team don't hear.

My lips twitch up into a smile, one that Mason doesn't miss.

"Wait, look at that smug-as-fuck grin he's trying to fight. He might have fucked it up, but not before he got what he wanted last night. Was stringing up all those motherfucking lights worth it?"

"Fuck you," I say, but I lose the fight with my grin.

"You fucking get your girl, bro?" Jake asks quietly.

"Yeah, I might just have got myself the girl."

"All fucking right. Good one, bro."

"Keep it on the down-low though, yeah?"

"Sure. But why?"

"Rae," I say with a sigh. "She thinks it's for the best if we keep it between us for a while."

"Why?"

I flick my eyes over to the cheer squad.

"Ah, the pack of hyenas that will no doubt be after her blood for taking the legend that is Ethan Savage off the market."

"Something like that," I mutter.

"What? What aren't you telling us?"

"Nothing," I lie.

"Out with it before we beat it out of you."

"Do you..." I hesitate, not wanting to sound like a pussy. "Do you think it's because she's ashamed?"

Both of their jaws drop in shock at my words. I instantly regret letting my fears pass my lips, but once they recover, Mason slaps my shoulder and smiles.

"What are you talking about, bro? Never. She just doesn't want them on her case. I get it, they're like piranhas."

"Just give her some time. She'll come around."

I nod at their enthusiasm and hope that they're right.

Jake starts talking about training this afternoon before we head off for our first classes.

I don't see Rae again all morning, seeing as we're in different classes, so by the time lunch rolls around, I'm damn near desperate. Jake and Mason can sense my separation anxiety and lap it up. After all the shit I've given them about their girls, I know I deserve it, but it doesn't make it any less annoying.

The cheer squad are already at our usual tables, and the second Shelly spots me heading her way, she's up on her feet waiting for me. The noise in the cafeteria is enough to cover my groan.

"Shelly, what do you want?" I snap once I'm close enough she can hear me clearly.

Apparently, she misses the warning in my tone because she steps toward me, and the next thing I know she's running her hand over my chest. My body locks up at her unwanted touch.

"Ethan?" she questions when she notices that I don't react to her like I normally would. It's not like she's expecting me to lean down to kiss her or anything, but I'm not usually so averse to her touch.

"Shelly, I'm not—" Something tells me to look up, and when I do, I immediately lock eyes with a pair of very familiar, very angry dark ones.

She flicks her death glare between the two of us. I'm unsure who she wants to hurt more—me for allowing Shelly to touch me, or Shelly for even attempting to in the first place.

Giving up on trying to explain to Shelly, I push her hand away and step back.

"What the hell, Ethan?"

Ignoring her, I keep my eyes on Rae. She's bristling with anger, but what does she expect when no one knows I'm off the market?

An idea hits me, and before I can talk myself out of it, I'm pushing Zayn out of the way and climbing up on top of our table, kicking a tray of food aside as I garner the attention of more and more students sitting around, eating their lunch.

When I find Rae again, she's taken a couple of steps forward, but her shoulders are still tense, and anger and confusion practically vibrate from her.

Her brows draw together as she watches me, but it's not enough to stop me. I've made a decision and I'm throwing caution to the wind and going balls to the wall. True Ethan

Savage style. I don't do hiding in the shadows; I live my life in the light and don't give two fucks as to what people think. And right now, I need them all knowing exactly who I belong to.

"I've got an announcement to make," I call out over the cafeteria. The volume in the huge room soon begins to reduce as more and more students turn to see what the hell I'm up to. All the while, Rae's eyes get wider and her head starts shaking from side to side. "This is probably going to come as a shock to many of you, but I need everyone to know that that girl over there—yeah, the cute little feisty one." A few laughs sound out, along with complaints and sniggers from the cheer squad. I just about manage not to kick the tray from the table around me onto their laps. "She's taken me off the market. Ethan Savage is off the fucking market and has officially handed his balls over in the hope that she looks after them."

Rae laughs, but she's still mortified at what I'm doing. She continues shaking her head as I jump down from the table and head her way. Ignoring everyone around me and the catcalls, I walk straight up to her, thread one hand into the non-shaved side of her hair, and pull her lips to mine to seal the deal on the announcement I've just made.

Everything around us fades as she parts her lips and accepts my kiss without second thought. Her tongue strokes mine and I lose myself in her taste, her scent, and her touch as she finds the bottom of my shirt and pushes her hands under until she finds the skin on my back.

A groan rumbles up my throat, and I really fucking wish we weren't currently in the middle of a room surrounded by hundreds of students.

I have no idea how much time passes, but eventually someone slaps me on the back and the world starts to make itself known once again.

"I hate to break up this little love fest, but Coach is expecting us for our afternoon session."

I rip my lips from Rae's and pull back a little. Her eyes are dark and full of the same need that I feel.

"I'm sorry," I whisper, knowing that she's going to rip me a new one later for that little stunt I just pulled.

"You're a fucking nightmare."

"Your nightmare, baby."

"Let's go, lover boy." Jake and Mason flank my sides and all but drag me from the cafeteria. I might have been delighted this morning when I woke with Rae in my arms knowing that we didn't have morning practice, but fuck if I want to get changed and embark on an afternoon-long session with Coach instead.

I never thought I'd put anything above football—okay, well maybe partying—but fuck if that little brunette hasn't flipped my priorities on their head.

"So much for keeping it quiet, eh?"

"What? I gave her three hours. How much more time did she need?"

"Rae needs a fucking medal for agreeing to put up with you," Jake mutters as we make our way toward the lockers.

Practice is endless, or so it seems. It's not so bad while I know that Rae is stuck in class, but once school is out and I know she's home alone, hopefully waiting for me, it's fucking torture.

"A little impatient, are we?" Mason laughs when we make our way toward the showers once Coach lets us go.

"Like you're not desperate to get out of here," I mutter in the hope it covers just how impatient I am. "How are the ribs holding up?" I ask when he looks like he's in agony just pulling his shirt over his head.

"I'm not going to lie, they've been better."

"You going to be okay for next week?"

Coach has been taking it easy on him, but I can still see how much of a toll it's taking on him. He's desperate to be part of the final, but the last thing any of us want is him causing himself more damage by pushing too hard.

"Only time will tell."

We make quick work of washing off an afternoon's worth of mud and sweat before heading out for the parking lot. A few of the guys agree to head to Aces, but the three of us have more important things, or girls, to see. I laugh at myself as I take a step toward my car. I've become one of them, one of the guys I've always laughed at when he'd choose spending time with a girl rather than hanging with the guys.

The drive home is fast, even with my growing anticipation for what I'm going to find when I get there. I'm pretty sure she'll still be pissed about what I did earlier, but I couldn't help it. The look on her face when she saw Shelly acting like she had a chance with me, like she owned me... I never want to see it again. Everyone at Rosewood now knows I'm taken, and hopefully it'll keep the vultures away.

Jumping from my car, my muscles scream after the hours of practice Coach put us through, but my need for her is bigger than my need to rest. I grab a bottle of water from the kitchen as I pass before heading up the stairs and hoping she's waiting for me.

Her room is empty, but when I step out onto her balcony, I spot her mom sitting outside around the pool.

"Hey, is Rae home?" I ask, stepping up beside her.

Ash pushes her sunglasses to the top of her head and looks up at me from her magazine.

"No, she's not back yet. Your dad's at the office, too."

I blow out a sigh and take a step to leave.

"Come and sit down. I think it's probably time we got to know each other a little better."

Guilt hits me as her words flow through my ears. I've not exactly been nice to her since I discovered she existed. I guess I owe her this, especially as I'm now dating her daughter. My stomach twists. What the hell are our parents going to think about this?

After a beat, I sit down on the lounger beside her and rest back, staring out over the pool.

"So, you and Rae then?"

"Uh... yeah." I lift my hand to scratch at the back of my neck, already feeling totally out of my depth. It's one thing to meet your girlfriend's mother, but when she already lives in your house, it's only weirder.

"I've got to say, I didn't see that coming. Eric's told me so many wonderful things about you, but I didn't in a million years expect for you to break down Rae's walls. I'm not sure I ever expected anyone to, to be honest."

"Yeah, she's a little... guarded," I say with a wince.

"She's not had it easy. I'm not sure how much you know but—"

"I know everything," I interrupt. I turn toward Ash when I sense her stare burning into me.

"She's... she's told you?"

"Yeah, well. Kind of," I admit, thinking of the morning I found her diaries. "What's important is that I know."

Ash nods. "My daughter's complicated and beautiful. She doesn't let anyone get close, so the fact that she's allowed you in tells me all I need to know. I would tell you to look after her, but I know I don't need to. Rae is more than capable of looking after herself, she doesn't need me warning you. She's been stubbornly independent from the day she was born. It's frustrating as hell, but I can't imagine her any other way."

I laugh, thinking just how true that is from just the short time I've known her.

"I should head inside. Your dad's due back any moment. Would you like another?" Ash asks, nodding to my now empty bottle of water.

"I'm fine, thank you."

She nods and pushes from the lounger before collecting up her things and walking into the house.

Resting back, I run our short conversation through my mind, assuming that was her way of telling me she was fine with us being a couple. I drop my head back and close my eyes, enjoying the peace and the sound of trickling water from the pool.

I must drift off, because the next thing I know, there's a shadow looming over me.

"Well, that was fucking embarrassing." Rae falls down on the lounger her mother vacated however long ago and turns to me.

"Sorry," I say, but it's anything but sincere.

"Really?" She laughs. "You didn't seem all that sorry when you molested me in front of the entire school."

"You didn't seem all that bothered either."

"I was just glad to see that hussy's hands off of what's mine."

"What's yours, eh?" Getting up from my lounger, I lift her and settle us so she's lying on top of me, stomach to stomach.

"Yep. I don't take too kindly to cheer sluts touching my property."

"I'm not an object for you to own."

"No? So I can't do whatever I want to you?" She trails her fingertip around the neck of my shirt and my skin prickles.

"Oh, you can most definitely do that." She leans forward and presses her lips to the underside of my jaw. "I should probably warn you though that your mom's inside and possibly watching us."

"I know. I spoke to her. She'll be busy making herself look pretty for your dad. They're going out for a meal, which means." Another kiss. "We've got." Kiss. "The house." Kiss. "To." Kiss. "Ourselves." Kiss. "Whatever shall we do?"

I run my hands down her back until I can squeeze her ass,

pressing her hard into me so she has no choice but to feel exactly what she does to me. "Hmmm... I've got a few ideas. What time are they going out?"

"In about an hour."

"Perfect. How do you fancy a dip in the pool? I've wanted to fuck you in there since I first saw you emerge in your wet, see-through clothes."

"Now that sounds like a perfect way to spend the evening."

44

RAELYNN

nock, knock, knock. "Rae, Ethan, you guys awake yet?" Mom calls hesitantly through my bedroom door. I have no idea if she knows for sure that Ethan's in here with me or if it's her way of finding out. I don't really care either way, mind you. Ethan seems to have moved himself in, and I'm not arguing about being able to fall asleep in his arms each night and wake each morning the same way.

"No, we're really not," I call back groggily, wishing she'd leave and allow us a few more hours of peace, but I already know it's not going to happen. She laid out all her Thanksgiving plans when I got back from hanging out with Amalie and Camila Tuesday night. That may have been over twenty-four hours ago, but I'm still unsure I'm at all prepared for it.

"Well, get your asses out of bed. We've got plans, kiddos."

"Please tell me she's fucking joking," Ethan says, pulling me tighter into his body. "There are things I need way more right now than to spend some one-on-one time with my dad." His erection presses against me and heat floods my core.

"You've got ten minutes to be dressed and downstairs. No excuses."

Ethan groans again, and I can't help but laugh. "It's only a few hours, and then we can spend the evening together."

"But I want to be together now," he sulks.

Flipping over in his arms, we lie with our noses touching, our eyes locked on each other's. "Just a couple of hours, then we can have our first Thanksgiving together."

"First of many?" he asks optimistically.

"I hope so." A little zing of excitement races through me at what the future could hold for us. "But right now, we need to go and be good kids for our parents so they don't suddenly start complaining about what we're up to under your dad's roof."

"He's not really in any position to complain, seeing as we know exactly what he's been up to."

"Maybe not, but this is still his house."

He groans. "You know, I prefer it when you're a rule breaker."

"Even bad girls need to toe the line every now and then. Now," I say with a kiss to his nose, "we need to get moving."

"But—"

"No buts, Savage."

I jump from the bed and pull the sheets with me, leaving him totally bare behind me. Glancing over my shoulder, I run my eyes over every solid inch of him. My muscles clench to jump on top of him, but I know I can't, so instead, I continue walking toward the bathroom.

He's still in exactly the same place when I emerge and does everything he can to tempt me back into bed.

"You know delayed gratification is a thing, right?"

"I'm too impatient for that. Especially when it comes to you."

"It'll be so worth it later. Now get dressed before your dad drags you out of the house buck naked." I throw his clothes at him in the hope it gets him moving.

Thankfully he does, but when we get downstairs, both our parents are waiting not so patiently for us.

"Finally," Eric mutters. "We don't want to know what took you both so long."

"Don't look at me. I've been ready for ages. It was your son who refused to get out of bed."

The four of us head for Eric's car so he can take us out for breakfast before we separate. Mom and I go home to help Rachel with the Thanksgiving preparations. Mom tried to tell her that we didn't need her, but she insisted. I have no idea what her story is, but I can't help but think that the Savages are her family of sorts.

Once everything's sorted and in the oven, we make ourselves a pitcher of margaritas, which is something of a tradition for our Thanksgiving celebrations, and Mom drags me up to her and Eric's bedroom.

"This really isn't necessary."

"Oh, come on. Don't you want to look the part for Ethan?"

"Ethan's more than happy with how I look now. Bald patch and all," I say, pointing to the side of my head.

"I'm sure he is, honey. But how about we surprise him? Show him what you've really got."

"He's aware," I say and then instantly regret it. Heat hits my cheeks as what I've just admitted to her hits me full force.

"Rae, you're an adult, so I'm not going to give you *that* speech, but I will say this..." I groan, wondering what the hell is going to follow. "I am way too young to be a grandmother, so please, I beg you, be safe."

"I'm not intending on being a parent anytime soon, don't worry." I don't tell her that I've already made an appointment to get myself on birth control as Ethan suggested. A girl's got to have some secrets. It's bad enough that Mom and Eric are going to be a front row seat to our relationship. Well, when they're here, that is. What happens after high school is still up for discussion. I might be crazy even considering a future together. College is still a long way off, but we need to at least get our ducks in a row, and I need to take a serious look at where I want to go and what I want to study.

By the time Mom has finished with me, my makeup is light and perfect, and my hair is hanging around my shoulders, the ends styled in loose curls. I stare at myself in the mirror, wondering who the hell the girl is looking back. I'm not sure I've ever seen myself looking like this. At least I've got my usual clothes on to remind me of who I really am.

"I've got a present for you." The second the words pass her lips, my stomach drops. It only gets worse when she pulls out a Macy's bag from her closet.

"Mom, you really didn't need—"

"Oh shush. I wanted to treat you. I hope you like it."

Knowing that Mom has spent most of my teenage years trying to make me a girly girl, hence the Thanksgiving makeover, I dread to think what I'm about to pull out. Probably some frilly, flowery cocktail dress. Something I wouldn't be seen in in a million years, yet something I already know I'm going to wear just to make her happy. There's only ever been one person I'd put my own feelings aside for, and that's her. She might have made my life harder than it's needed to be over the years, but I know deep down she's only ever done it in an attempt to better our lives. She's not always gone the right way about it, but she's tried, I'll give her that.

Sucking in a large breath, I open the bag and pull out the fabric, praying I'm not going to hate it.

Much to my surprise, the material that emerges is a deep purple, exactly the color I'd choose for myself, and as of yet, no frills.

When I finally hold the dress up, I can't believe my eyes.

It's a tight-fitting, body con style with a huge feature zipper running down the length of the back. It's got thin spaghetti straps and a really quite low V at the front, which I'm sure Ethan is going to love.

"It's stunning. I love it," I say honestly, totally relieved that she's not about to dress me up like a doll.

"I knew you would the moment I saw it."

"Thank you so much."

"You're welcome, honey. Now go and slip it on. The boys will be back soon."

With a kiss to her cheek, I leave her to get dressed and head to my room with my new dress in hand.

Already knowing there's no chance of wearing a bra under it, I ignore that drawer and instead open the one full of the fancy Victoria's Secret panties I bought with Ethan's credit card. I search through until I find the tiniest pair I bought and then make quick work of changing.

I stand in front of my full-length mirror, wondering who's staring back at me. The shadows I'm so used to seeing in my eyes are gone, my glossy dark hair shines around my shoulders, and my skin looks fresh—not only with Mom's makeover, but with the hint of a tan I've managed in my time here, despite it practically being winter. I've never spent so much time outside, and it shows.

The new dress shows off my curves to perfection until I get down to my boots. I laugh at myself. They're probably not what Mom had in mind to complete this look, but I still need to have a bit of myself in this outfit.

With a nod of my head, I turn and walk out of my room, butterflies beginning to dance in my stomach as I think about Ethan's reaction to this new and, dare I say it, improved version of myself.

"Honey, that looks incredible." Her nose wrinkles when

she sees my feet. "Really?" she asks with a laugh but thankfully doesn't bother arguing.

I shrug, walking over to help her finish setting up the table with Rachel.

"You're staying to eat with us, right?" Mom asks her.

"Oh no, I couldn't."

"Do you have anywhere else to eat?" Mom persists.

"Well, no. But—"

"No buts. You're as much a part of this family, if not more so, than we are. Set yourself a seat."

Rachel nods, her cheeks a little rosy and her eyes glassy.

The front door slams, and my heart jumps into my throat.

Clenching my fists at my side, I listen as their footsteps get louder before they both appear in the doorway. Eric immediately walks over to Mom, but whatever happens past that, I've no idea, because all my attention is solely on Ethan.

With his eyes wide, he slowly runs them over every inch of me. I squirm under his attention. Not knowing what he's thinking unnerves me, but it only lasts so long because his eyes find mine once again and I can read every single thought in his head, and every single one is filthy and should not be thought about with our parents only feet away.

I swallow nervously when he takes a step forward. Time stands still as I watch him, but then he's right there in front of me, my face framed by his hands. I have no choice but to step back until I gently hit the wall behind me.

"Rae," he breathes, his eyes dancing all over my face, down my hair and to my chest for a beat. "Fuck." His eyes find mine once again, and they bounce between them as he fights with the words he wants to say. "Fuck it. Rae... I think I'm falling in love with you." I gasp at the raw honesty in his words. "You turned my world upside down, but it turns out it was in the best way fucking possible. I was nothing before you, and I already know that I never want to go back to being him. You've made me, Rae. You've made me the man I am, and I'll forever be grateful you saw through all the bullshit and gave me a chance." He doesn't give me the opportunity to respond, because his lips find mine and he kisses me much too deeply and passionately for our parents to witness.

"All right, son, put her down. You're even embarrassing the turkey," Eric says lightly.

Both of us pull back with wide smiles on our faces, hunger shining in our eyes.

"I mean it," he whispers.

"I know. I feel the same." The wide smile that stretches across his face is everything. It's so beautiful and honest that it totally makes all of the bullshit we've both endured worth it. "Now, let's go and celebrate our first of many Thanksgivings."

EPILOGUE

Ethan

The rest of Thanksgiving was beyond perfect. We enjoyed our dinner together like the dysfunctional family that we were. We watched the game, Rae and Ash pretending to understand what Dad and I were shouting about as things got tense toward the end, before Dad and Ash disappeared from the family room to enjoy the rest of their evening together and leaving Rae and me alone at last.

I wasn't really up for spending the morning with Dad. We'd only seen each other in passing since the day he dropped the bombshell that was Ash and Rae on me. It's safe to say that life has changed a bit since then, and I have a bit of a different view on life and relationships.

Dad was hesitant to say anything about our current living situation, but he soon realized that things between Rae and I were serious and he relaxed. After breakfast at a diner, we walked down the beach to get a few things off our chests.

It was exactly what we needed. We cleared the air. Dad told me, much like Mom did, that things weren't as black and white as I first thought when it came to the end of their relationship and the beginning of his with Ash. He was more than relieved that I'd let go of my anger and he was very intrigued to discover how much Rae had to do with that. He gave us his blessing, and although I didn't really feel like I needed it, I did feel better about everything for having heard it from his lips.

"This is the start of a new chapter for both of us, son," he said. "The end of your football season. The beginning of a new relationship. The future is yours for the taking."

Those are the words that run around my head as I sit in the locker room of the stadium that's hosting tonight's playoff final while Jake paces back and forth in front of me, a ball of nerves, fire and anticipation.

"Pack it in," I bark at him. The atmosphere in the room is heavy as we all try to get our heads in the game before we walk out onto that field together for the final time.

My fists clench in my lap as I try to get myself together. I don't get nervous. I blow out a breath, willing my stomach to settle and for my hands to stop trembling. This is the biggest night of all our lives. Some of our futures depend on this—college scouts are going to be watching this game. The entire fucking town is watching this game. The. Pressure. Is. On.

Fuck. I need Rae.

Her method of distraction earlier worked at the time, but right now, the feeling of her lips sliding down my cock is long forgotten as I watch Jake continue to pace.

"Seriously, bro. You're not helping."

"I don't give a fuck if I'm helping you. It's helping me. Fuck." He shakes his arms out at his sides and jumps up and down a few times as Coach walks over.

"All right, ladies. Get in here," he calls and everyone comes running. Every single face shows the enormity of tonight. Most look nervous. Some look downright terrified. "This is it, boys. This is what you've worked all your life for. You will forever remember this night. Now, let's make sure it's for the right fucking reasons, shall we?"

There are a few mutters of agreement, everyone too lost in their own heads, going through plays and focusing.

"I didn't fucking hear you, ladies. Are we going to fucking do this?"

"Yes, Coach."

"Come on, we can do better than that. We're the fucking Rosewood Bears," Jake bellows, coming to a stop beside Coach. "Now, are we going to do this?"

The eruption of noise from the team makes me wince as our nerves begin to give way to our excitement. This win is so close. Jake's dream. The only thing he wanted for so many years is almost in touching distance.

"Let's fucking do this." The floor vibrates beneath us as the team falls into line behind Jake, Mason, and me. I look to my left and find a wide smile splitting Mason's face. I couldn't be happier that he's experiencing this with us.

Jake, who's just in front of us, is totally focused. I doubt he even hears the Billie Eilish song that's booming through the sound system of the stadium or the roar of the crowd that only gets louder as we emerge onto the field.

I look to the stands where I know my girl is. I find her almost immediately, and everything inside me that was unsettled inside that locker room immediately relaxes. Her hair is much like it was the night of Thanksgiving. It's been that way since I expressed how much I liked it. I didn't tell her that to make her change—she could shave it all and I wouldn't give a fuck because it's her I want, the incredible person who's on the inside. The outside is just an added bonus. Her makeup is back to her usual style, dark and edgy. She looks hot as fuck up there, standing like a human barrier between both my mom and dad. I wasn't expecting Mom to turn up to this, despite how much I wanted her here, but she surprised me last night by calling and telling me she was in a car outside the house. I'm pretty sure she was more excited to meet Rae at last than she was to attend this game, not that she'd ever admit that. It means the world to me that she was able to put aside her issues with Dad and be here for this.

Rae's eyes find mine and an encouraging smile spreads across her face before she blows me a kiss that I catch in my hand like the whipped motherfucker that I am. I would be worried that the guys witness it, but when I look their way, I find them locked in their girls' stares as well as they soak up every bit of their optimism that we're going to smash the Rebels and claim our rightful place as state champions.

The cheerleaders do their thing ahead of us, dragging up as much excitement as possible from our Rosewood crowd. We've had a big game or two in the past, but we've never had this many people travel to watch us play. It's a sobering feeling, knowing that they all came here for us.

———

The roars of excitement continue to ring out around us when Jake suddenly stops his progress out to the middle of the field.

"Motherfucker." I barely hear his voice over the crowd, but when I follow his gaze, I soon find what he's talking about—or I should say who.

A smile twitches at my lips. It's such a great sight to see her back where she belongs.

As if she can feel our attention, she turns. Her light blue eyes find Jake's before she drags them away toward Mason. She smiles weakly, an apology of sorts before she finds me. A more genuine smile pulls at her lips, a thank you for my support, before she looks over my shoulder. Someone holds her attention, and I can't help but turn to see who it is, but almost all the guys are staring in her direction, looking shocked to see her leading her squad once more.

"What the fuck is she doing back? Tonight is not the night for her bullshit," Jake snaps when he turns to us.

"Just ignore her, bro. Tonight isn't about her. Don't give her the satisfaction. She's clearly making a statement by showing her face," Mason says, anger filling his eyes as he glances back at her.

"That's enough. Let's just focus on this win, yeah?"

"Everyone in," Jake barks, making the guys huddle around. All hands reach into the center of our circle. The stadium might be a hive of activity around us, but in this huddle, only we exist. "Champions on three. One. Two. Three."

"CHAMPIONS."

Rae

I watch as the guys huddle on our side of the field. Excitement knots my stomach. I still know fuck all about football, and I'm not sure I'll leave this place with any more knowledge other than if our Bears have managed to pull it off or not.

I tell myself to keep my eyes on them, but I can't help them from wandering back over to the cheer squad and the girl I've never seen before. There's no doubt she belongs, but I can't miss the angry looks that are constantly being flicked her way.

Leaning forward, I tap Amalie on the shoulder. It takes a few seconds, but she eventually pulls her eyes from Jake to look back at me.

"Who's that?" I nod toward the girl, but Amalie doesn't need to look.

"That? That's Chelsea. Bitch extraordinaire."

My lips form an O, but I don't say any more and Amalie turns back as the guys get ready to start the game.

"Oh my god, I'm so nervous," Ethan's mom, Kelly, whispers in my ear. "I love watching him play almost as much as I hate it."

"This is my first game," I admit.

"Watching them do what they love, watching them win, it's the best feeling in the world, but when one of them goes down, it's like time stops. It doesn't matter if it's Ethan or one of the others, my heart stops every damn time."

I look back to the field as her words settle in my mind. I hadn't even thought about the possibility of him being hurt. That certainly doesn't help settle my nerves any.

The whistle blows, and everyone jumps into action. Kelly reaches out and grabs my hand, hers trembling violently, making me resist from pulling away like I'm desperate to. The crowd around us starts shouting and screaming even louder, and I can't help but wince as I try to figure out when I should be cheering and when I should be worried.

I keep my eyes on number eighty-nine the entire game. They manage to take the lead early on and maintain it for almost the whole game, but fifteen minutes before we're all celebrating, the Rebels manage to score.

The tension around us becomes so thick you could cut it with a knife as the Rebel crowd at the other side of the stadium start cheering and shouting. They're reigning champions, I know that much, and they're expecting to leave here with their reputation intact.

The shouts get louder, the chants get more aggressive, and Kelly's grip only gets tighter. In front of us, Amalie and Camila shout and scream, their own hands locked together as they pray for a chance to take back the win.

I'm not sure I've ever felt so sick as the clock starts to count down toward the final whistle, calling time on the Bears' chances, but then all of a sudden, we take possession of the ball. One of our guys runs at full speed down the field, making everyone who wasn't already on their feet rise from their seats.

Come on. Come on, I chant silently in my head as I struggle to keep my eye on the ball. I glance up at the clock. One minute. One fucking minute. *Come on.* I want to scream, shout, do anything, but as the tension reaches breaking point all I can do is stand and watch, and pray.

Then the almightiest roar, the volume of which I don't think I've ever experienced before, erupts around me. I lift my eyes from where they were locked on Ethan to see the rest of the team running at Jake before he disappears under the pile of red. The final whistle blows and the stadium vibrates with excitement and energy. A delighted cry rumbles up my throat, my cheeks aching with the size of my smile. I have no choice but to turn to Kelly when she pulls me to her. She has tears rolling down her cheeks, her smile almost as wide as mine.

"They did it," she murmurs, wrapping her arms around my shoulders. No sooner has she released me does my own mom pull me into her while Eric hollers next to her.

The excitement is palpable and still vibrating around us once we're able to start making our way out of the stadium. Tonight's party is at Shane's, but before we go there, we're all out for a celebratory family meal, awkwardly with both my mom and Kelly. I'm just hoping that the joy from tonight will be enough for there not to be any tension between them all. They're all there for Ethan, so hopefully they'll remember that.

There's already a massive crowd surrounding the door the guys are going to come out of. Front and center unsurprisingly are Amalie and Camila, along with the entire cheer squad ready to congratulate their team, probably on their knees at the first chance they get.

I run my eyes over them as they bounce in excitement for the guys to appear and notice that Chelsea is standing off to the side, the rest of the squad with their back to her. I've been told some of the history there, but it seems she has bigger issues than she was possibly expecting by turning up tonight of all nights. I guess she wanted to be a part of the fame alongside everyone else.

The door cracks open, and a new round of screams sound out before almost all the team emerges with the biggest smiles on their faces. They eagerly get pulled this way and that as everyone congratulates them. I look to Amalie and Camila when none of our guys appear, and I see a flash of concern pass between them, but it doesn't last long because not even a second later, Jake appears with his two main men on either side of him. Amalie and Camila take off running and immediately jump into their boys' arms while Ethan scans the crowd, a frown forming. I step forward, the connection that's always pulling me to him stronger than ever after the night he's just had. It's that moment that he finds me in the crowd just a little behind the cheerleaders. He pushes them aside when they try to get a piece of him. He's not interested. He's got one destination in mind, and none of them feature.

"Hey, champ," I say, a wide smile spreading across my face.

"Fuck yeah," he barks, his elation oozing from him.

He lunges for me and I squeal as he picks me up and spins me around while laughing in delight.

Everyone around us vanishes. It's just me and him celebrating the epic performance he pulled off tonight. He brings us to a stop, but he doesn't let me down. Instead, he pulls me tighter to him.

"That win was good, but winning you was better." His lips

crash down on mine, and I put everything I have into my kiss in an attempt to show him just how I feel, although I fear I'll never be able to communicate the intensity properly.

He pulls back, both of us fighting to catch our breath, and stares into my eyes.

"Rae, I—"

I shake my head, stopping him from saying any more. "I love you, Ethan."

"I fucking love you too."

We're dragged from our intimate moment when Jake, Mason, Amalie, and Camila surround us.

"We fucking did it," Jake screams, and the three of them embrace while we stand there and watch, each of us with tears filling our eyes at watching our guys celebrate the win they've been working toward for years.

A flash of red catches my eye, and when I look up, one of the team is pulling Chelsea away from the crowd and into the shadows. I elbow Amalie, who glances at me before following my stare. She just rolls her eyes and turns back to our group.

"You better get your asses to Shane's the second you're done with your family shit," Jake says to Ethan.

"Too fucking right." Ethan says his brief goodbyes before pulling me into his arms. "You ready for this, baby?"

"A meal with our parents? No, probably not."

"No. That'll be a piece of piss. I meant this. Us, our future. You ready for that?"

"Too fucking right. Bring it on, baby. Bring. It. On." With his arm wrapped around my waist, we make our way out to the parking lot to embark on our new lives together with wide smiles on our faces.

Are you ready to properly meet the Queen Bitch?
FIERCE is NOW LIVE!

FIERCE SNEAK PEEK
CHAPTER ONE

Chelsea

I stare out the window at the building I've spent the past eight weeks of my life inside and as much as I hate the place, I can't help but crave being back inside. It's safe in there. People understand me. They don't look at me like I don't belong, like I'm a piece of shit on their shoe after all the mistakes I've made.

My hands tremble in my lap as the gray brick walls disappear in the distance as my driver heads toward my home.

Home. It's a funny word. It's meant to be a place where you feel safe, loved, protected. You're meant to feel like you belong.

I've never felt any of those things. Even before I was old enough to know things around me weren't right, I knew. Even now being somewhere where those feelings should come easily, they don't. My past is too ingrained. The fear too real after all these years.

I blow out a breath as anticipation races through me for

what I'll find waiting for me. My parents have visited me weekly after they shipped me off to "have a breather" as they put it. They made it sound like they were doing me a favor, but after the drama I've brought down on them, I'm pretty sure the breather was more for them than me.

Derek and Honey are the perfect parents on paper. I guess that's why they signed up to foster broken kids all those years ago. Shame this broken teenager doesn't fit into their perfect life.

I've done everything I can to become a person people would want to spend time with, to want to be friends with. But I still end up as the outcast. Okay granted, most of that is my fault. I've spent the past eight weeks reflecting on all my mistakes, on my weaknesses. The counselors seem to think I've turned a corner and am strong enough to show my face in a place where everyone hates me. I, on the other hand, am not so sure.

I think back over what my senior year at Rosewood High has been like so far. I've lost the guy I've wanted for as long as I can remember to a freaking supermodel. I drugged said supermodel in my attempt at him noticing me once again like he did that one night in the summer. When that didn't work, I moved on to his best friend in the hope it would make him jealous. Wrong. All that resulted in was my parents sending me away for my breather.

Everyone hates me and I'm about to go walking back into that school like nothing happened. It has disaster written all over it. But what else am I supposed to do?

I refuse to cower down. I'm stronger than that.

I'm Chelsea fucking Fierce.

. . .

My parents must have been at the window waiting for my arrival. They wanted to come and get me themselves, but I refused, knowing that I'd need this time to try to adjust.

The smiles on their faces are wide, but I'm not stupid, they're just as worried about this as I am, if not more so.

They've done everything for me. I couldn't ask for better parents really, but their traditional views on things make my rule-breaking all the worse in their eyes. Just coming home drunk is a major sin, let alone some of the other things I've forced them to deal with.

Sucking in a huge lungful of air, I push the door open and step out.

"Chelsea, it's so good to have you home," Mom sings, rushing toward me with her arms out wide.

She engulfs me in her hug and for the first time since I watched that building disappear, a lump crawls up my throat and tears burn my eyes.

I was safe there. No one wanted to hurt me. No one wanted to make me an outcast for my mistakes like I'm sure this entire town does.

I'm not naïve enough to think what happened that final night stayed inside the walls of the Savage's house. I'm sure everyone knows what a disappointment I am, just how screwed up I am.

"Everything's going to be okay," she whispers in my ear, sounding a little emotional herself. She hands me off to my dad who gives me a much briefer one-armed hug. He's not really the touchy-feely type like Mom, so even this gesture is a lot for him.

"We've got a surprise for you inside."

I have a fleeting thought that they might have got some friends to come and meet me, but I push it away instantly. I lost my squad the moment I dropped that pill into Amalie's drink, let alone Mason's. It was stupid. I was desperate. I just wanted someone to want me.

I shake my head. My excuses mean shit. My behavior was inexcusable, which is why none of my squad will be here. They'll have turned their backs on me as fast as I ran from Ethan's house that night.

I might have spent my entire Rosewood High career trying to be the cheer squad captain, needing the title, the accolade to make me feel like I belong, but I'm not stupid enough to think that the rest of the girls weren't doing something similar.

Yes, we had each other's backs. We played the part of being best friends. But the reality was that we were all as fake as each other. None of them will have missed me. I don't need to look any farther than my cell phone to know that's the case. The only person who's bothered to reach out is Ethan. Guilt fills me that I mostly ignored his attempts to check that I was okay, but I wasn't in the right frame of mind to talk to anyone from Rosewood. I'm still not, but I seem to have little choice about it now.

I follow my parents up the steps onto the porch and into the house. They both look excited about whatever is inside for me. I, however, don't feel any of it. Dread is what fills my belly.

The downstairs appears empty—I was right about the squad then—so I expect them to turn toward the stairs. But when we don't do that, I'm thoroughly confused.

Dad steps out of the open back door, and Mom and I follow. I glance around, but everything is as I remember. That is until Dad opens the door to the pool house, it's then I see that things have changed.

So they've decorated the pool house. Am I really supposed to get excited about this?

"Um... I don't understand." My irritation levels are beginning to rise. All I want to do is fall onto my bed and forget that I'm back here. I really don't need to give my opinion on the shade of cream Mom chose for the walls.

"It's for you," Dad says, gesturing to the space beyond.

"You decorated it for me. Why?"

Mom takes my hand and leads me to the new couch in the center of the living area. With both my hands in hers, she blows out a breath.

"This is a fresh start, Chelsea. For all of us. We know we've been hard on you, had unrealistic expectations. We love you, but we also know that we've been a little overbearing in our need to protect you. We neglected to notice that you're a young woman now who's going to be embarking on her life without parents very soon. And as much as we hate that our time together is coming to an end, we know that we need to accept it. You're no longer our little bug, but a beautiful young woman who has the world at her feet.

"So this is for you. We've moved all of your stuff from your room. You've got your own front door key." Dad pulls it from his pocket and hands it over. "There's food and drinks in the fridge along with everything else you might need."

"I... um... I don't understand." I can't deny that this sounds freaking incredible, but I was expecting to come home and find myself locked in my bedroom and only allowed to attend school for classes for the foreseeable future.

"This is for you. We want you to be able to have your space to do as you wish. You're eighteen now, Chelsea," he says, reminding me that I was forced to celebrate my biggest birthday in that place. "We think taking control of your life will help you. We—"

"We'll only be in the house, and it's still your home, we're not kicking you out or anything," Mom adds, clearly not as on board with this plan as Dad.

"Of course. You're our daughter. We love you, but we came

to the conclusion while you were away that we're smothering you. So we did this."

I look around, now seeing a few of my ornaments and picture frames that I didn't notice when I first entered.

A genuine smile creeps onto my face. It's an alien feeling as every one I've given for almost as long as I can remember has been fake.

All but that one night, a little voice chirps, but I shoot it down. I don't think about that night. Nothing good can come of what happened that night.

"Are you serious?"

"We are. We know things have been strained, but we hope that by giving you space you'll be able to continue with everything you've been working on without us breathing down your neck."

For the second time in less than fifteen minutes, tears burn my eyes. I'm not used to these overpowering emotions. I much prefer being the hard as nails girl everyone is scared of, not the weak emotional one I've turned into.

"T-thank you," I choke out.

"We'll leave you to get settled. We're both home all day if you need anything. I'll give you a shout when lunch is ready."

They both get up to leave, but Mom turns back before she gets to the door and pulls me into another hug.

"We're so proud of you, sweetie."

"Thanks, Mom."

"Are you going to the game tonight?"

I blow out a breath. Tonight is the final state championship game. Other than the cheer finals, it's the one day I've been looking forward to more than any other. I knew our boys could do it—or more so that Jake could do it—there was never any doubt in my mind, and I'd love nothing more than to watch them lift that trophy.

"I'm not sure."

"Your uniform is washed and pressed in your closet. It's time to restart your life again."

I nod against her, and she releases me to explore my new home.

I spin on the spot, a smile creeping onto my face, and excitement bubbling in my belly. I've basically got my own apartment; this couldn't be any more perfect. Well, actually that's not true, a lot of things could be a lot fucking better right now, but at least I've got some privacy while I try to figure my shit out.

I look around before walking toward the bedroom. They've painted it a deep purple, my favorite color. I run my hand over the comforter and push down on the luxury memory foam mattress. I think I'm going to like that.

Poking my head into the bathroom, I find the purple theme continues and that I've got a brand-new suite and what looks like a waterfall shower.

Maybe this homecoming isn't going to be so bad.

ACKNOWLEDGMENTS

Ethan, Ethan, Ethan... where do I start. I knew this was going to be a rough ride but hell, I didn't quite expect this. But I guess, Savage by name, Savage by nature.

This book consumed me. I was totally addicted right from the get go. I loved Rae's fire as much as I loved their mutual hate for each other. I found myself typing so fast during their intense interactions, I just couldn't get enough. Ethan needed a strong woman to bring him to his knees and I hope you agree that Rae was the right woman for the job.

This book is by far the longest I've written. But it just wouldn't stop. Rae and Ethan just kept talking so I kept writing. I really hope their story engulfed you as much as I has me.

I need to say a huge thank you to Michelle who one once again alpha read this as I typed. She put up with my typos without complaining too much.

My betas, Deanna, Nicole, Lindsay, Susanne and Tracy for dropping everything and diving into this bad boy. I'm so glad you all fell for Ethan like I did. He might seem tough but really, he's just a huge teddy bear... he's got the evidence to prove it!

Sam, I keep saying it but I've no idea how I ever survived without you. You make everything so much easier and give me time to continue with these crazy characters.

Ellie, at My Brother's Editor, thank you so much for working your magic on Savage, and Evelyn, at Pinpoint Editing, for the finishing touches with proofreading.

To you for following this crazy journey with me and these guys. I wouldn't be able to do it all without your support. So, THANK YOU!

Originally, Savage was going to be the end but there is no way I can walk away from this group yet. Rosewood High has a lot more to give and I'm so excited for what I have coming your way... are you ready to really get to know the Queen Bitch? Chelsea is back and man, has she brought a secret with her. Keep your eyes peeled because it's coming this summer!

Until next time,

Tracy xo

ABOUT THE AUTHOR

Tracy Lorraine is a *USA Today* and *Wall Street Journal* bestselling new adult and contemporary romance author. Tracy has recently turned thirty and lives in a cute Cotswold village in England with her husband, baby girl and lovable but slightly crazy dog. Having always been a bookaholic with her head stuck in her Kindle, Tracy decided to try her hand at a story idea she dreamt up and hasn't looked back since.

Be the first to find out about new releases and offers. Sign up to my newsletter <u>here</u>.

If you want to know what I'm up to and see teasers and snippets of what I'm working on, then you need to be in my Facebook group. Join <u>Tracy's Angels</u> here.

Keep up to date with Tracy's books at
www.tracylorraine.com

ALSO BY TRACY LORRAINE

Buy your next paperback personalised by me!

www.tracylorraine.com

The Rosewood High Series

Thorn #1

Paine #2

Savage #3

Fierce #4

Hunter #5

Faze (#6 Prequel)

Fury #6

Legend #7